SHADES OF AURA
TOTERRUM TRILOGY

BOOK 1
THE WALLS OF TOTERRUM

BOOK 2
THE CALAMITIES OF TOTERRUM

BOOK 3
THE HOPES OF TOTERRUM

SHADES OF AURA

THE CALAMITIES OF TORTERRUM

BENJAMIN KAMPHUIS

BENGAR PUBLISHING

Copyright © 2025 by Benjamin Kamphuis

All rights reserved.

No portion of this book may be reproduced in any form without written permission from the publisher or author, except as permitted by U.S. copyright law.

Contents

Dedication	VII
Map of Biome	VIII
1. Better Off Alone	1
2. Zela	11
3. The Blackstone Mountains	17
4. The Cortex	28
5. The Soothsayer	32
6. The Surprisants	46
7. Healing	61
8. My Dream	65
9. Preparations	78
10. The Siege of Labyrintha	94
11. Loss	108
12. The Cottage	124
13. Light Within Darkness	140
14. New Horizons	155
15. The Riddle	168
16. The City of Gold	185
17. King Resin's Time	201
18. Family	220
19. The Red Stone	236

20.	Firesuns	249
21.	Growth	265
22.	The Dead Forest	283
23.	Devoted	299
24.	The Crown	316
25.	Golden Flames	330
Epilogue		348
Glossary: The Auras		352
Glossary: Hierarchies		355
Glossary: Beasts of Biome		358

This book is dedicated to anyone who has ever been betrayed. It will be hard, but you can trust again. Good people still exist. You just have to find them.

To William and Amelia - Never lose your imagination and sense of wonder. When Calamity comes, do not back down. Fight for what you believe in.

BIOME

LABYRINTHA

BLACKSTONE MOUNTAINS

CORAL FOREST

GREAT PLAIN

RITHBAR

TOTERRUM

RITHBAR RIVER

FOGLANDS

FLAUNTE

DEAD FOREST

ROLLING HILLS

1

BETTER OFF ALONE

A sharp, deafening screech echoed along the cliff's edge. Ricochet arched his light blue back and growled at the Kanterfluff, snapping its massive, sharp beak in my direction. Made of tough navy skin, the center of the Kanterfluff's body was covered in purple, fluffy fur that now flared out in wispy rays. A long neck and legs made its walking pattern normally awkward and haphazard. The beast widened its two large eyes and clicked its purple beak.

"Easy now," I said to the beast. "We aren't here to hurt you." We stumbled on the beast's nest while walking outside the city. Little navy heads peeked out the pile of little rocks behind the massive Kanterfluff.

The Kanterfluff snapped its beak again. Its Aura swirled in bright reds and lashed at our Auras. Ricochet's purple spots shined bright green and yellow, ready to blind the beast. My partner beast leaped forward and expelled blinding light. I shielded my eyes just as he began. As fast as the flash appeared, it faded. Ricochet barked at me as I moved my hands from my eyes and witnessed the stunned Kanterfluff scratching its eyes with one of its two large legs. Ricochet and I ran off, leaving the beast with its nest.

Once far enough away from the wild beast, I rested my hands on my knees and heaved for air. "Thanks, buddy. You're always here for me."

I leaned forward and scratched Ricochet's ear. He licked my hand and looked up at me, neon green eyes piercing through me. A tightness clenched my chest and pulled the air from my lungs. I looked away, unable to hold eye contact, but able to breathe again. I couldn't hold eye contact with anyone, let alone the one living thing that knew me better than any other living creature. Love was all he offered, and I couldn't handle it. He whimpered before walking off toward his little pond on the outskirts of the city.

Whenever Ricochet left me, I dreaded the human interaction I would have to have once I reentered the city. Whenever he was around, I avoided letting his wise presence pull at my disgruntled emotions. But when he left, my adrenaline faded, and loneliness found me once again. Holding my breath, I stepped into the city and immediately entered a crowd of Mentalists.

Little iridescent bubbles floated around each person I passed. So much could be said about someone based on their Aura. The slower bubbles near the back of the head meant the person was hiding something about themselves that no one else knew. The faster rainbows near the eyes meant that person desired something someone had. Bubbles near the mouth showed a person was pretending they were something they weren't. All these things I learned since arriving in Labyrintha, the Mentalist capital, furthering my claim to be a Mentalist. All these things I learned on my own.

Of the five Auras, I wasn't able to Manipulate the Perception Aura. Luck, Empathy, and Vigor were out of the question. So, Mentality it had to be.

This clarity about who I was resulted from the Event. The three months since arriving in Labyrintha allowed for three emotions to fester within—guilt, anger, and numbness. Three months of expected Mentality training. Three months of nothing happening. Only Brysen met with me from the Cerebrals, Labyrintha's governing body. As leaders of the city, the Cerebrals decided whether to approve my training in the Mentality Aura. But each postponed request for training led to more time sitting and waiting. My mind remained in a constant haze filled with pointless thoughts since my parents' death during the Event.

Correction: my fake parents' death.

"Find the truth about your real parents." These were the last words I heard from the woman I believed to be my mother before Gamma killed her. They echoed in my head like they did since she died. Her life faded right before me. And then the Surprisants swooped in and saved us.

My brain rattled as I forced the nightmarish memory back, trying to forget everything I could about her and her lies. A high-pitched ring became louder as I pushed the words back, a sharp pain following deep inside the portion of my head just above my ears. I pushed my hands hard on the sides of my head until the ringing died down and the pain subsided, her words no longer lingering.

I looked around and found Mentalists staring at and judging me like I judged their Auras. However, they didn't judge me as much as they judged Naso. He even cut his bluish-tinted hair into a short, clean cut, like the Labyrintha's sterileness. His attempts to blend in with the culture fell on blind eyes. The city carried a general disdain for non-Manipulators. How they knew Naso couldn't Manipulate angered me. By either gossiping or reading his mind through the Mentality Aura, they judged him, making me miss the city of Flaunte's life, energy, and inclusiveness even more. All until my presence within Flaunte brought death and war to the city.

I ducked my head and ran toward the edge of the city. Once away from their string and judgmental gaze, I looked up to the surrounding Black Stone Mountain. Not a Mountain…a wall. I traveled so far and found myself trapped within another walled city. Vigorists loomed outside the wall, not inside, torturing me. I didn't hate the Blackstone Mountain like I hated Toterrum's wall. The Mountain kept us safe, at least according to Brysen.

Not having any other choice, I wandered back into the city, away from the busy streets. Windows covered the buildings instead of walls, leaving everything exposed except for bathrooms and bedrooms. Through unsolicited observation, every interior mimicked the city—clean and crisp. The city even smelled of staleness: wet rock and dewy air.

Just like the windowed buildings, each Mentalist left all the details of their life revealed to everyone else, including their flaws and sins. Everyone held the other accountable for the open-door lifestyle. For each interaction I had, each person hid nothing. Yet, a sense of falsity hid within their words and actions. It was as if they were all a part of the same charade. It was as if they were hiding something. Debilitating uneasiness about their falseness weighed me down.

Two-legged Kanterfluffs, the non-aggressive kind, wandered the streets. The Mentalists rode them when they saved us during the ambush. Some of the Mentalists kept and rode them when dire situations arose. The attack outside the Mountain qualified as a dire situation. The Mentalists saved us from the Vigorist ambush riding the beasts.

The only buildings not made of windows were the Cortexes—the religious buildings—and the Cerebellum—the Capitol Building. All that time ago, Aurora said Labyrintha was filled with religious buildings. She was right. Labyrintha was littered with Cortexes. Nearly everyone attended the weekly services and involved themselves with the communities within. Aurora, Naso, and Herita would go to the weekly services, but I would stay home. The less interaction with people I had, the lower the likelihood I would hurt anyone else.

What was the point in interacting with others anyway?

I rounded the corner away from a Cortex imposing its presence on me, stopped just in front of a meadow, and found green eyes staring back at me.

"Cerebrum Brysen wants us to meet him at the training grounds," Aurora said. Her body cringed at my presence. Without a chance to respond, she turned away and walked off, just like every other interaction we had. Aurora taught me so much about Aura and rescued me outside of Toterrum. Now, I treated her like a stranger.

I didn't even deign to respond to her. Our relationship would never be the same after what I had said to her when she only tried to check on me.

"Yaron, your parents were killed," Aurora had said. "You can't pretend like it didn't happen."

And how did I respond? "Stop pretending like you know what I'm going through. You need to get over your obsession with me."

Any brightness her eyes held toward me evaporated right at that moment. Any interaction we had since mimicked her short words and quick retreat from me. Three months later and nothing changed.

"A bright morning," a person said from behind. I turned to find one of the religious leaders stepping out of yet another Cortex I hadn't noticed. Wearing a simple blue robe, the warm-eyed leader dipped their head toward me. "Though darkness comes and takes us all, the True Light shines and keep us forever. Knowing only works if you listen."

"Yeah." I nodded and walked off.

The words sparked glimpses of blind hope, but before they took root, I pushed them back down with everything else. What was the point? The religious leaders relentlessly harassed me in hopes I would attend the weekly services. Though I attended the original services dedicated to the dead a few months ago, I avoided them ever since. I only went to them out of respect, not for my own comfort. Herita, Aurora's aunt, promised me they would help me heal. I said no and she left it at that.

The city seemed to speed by me without notice as I walked up to the open training grounds at the same time Aurora did. She kept her distance from me and I kept my distance from her. Naso often stood by Aurora rather than me. I didn't blame him. At least she talked to him.

Cerebrum Brysen smiled at my presence, which made me look away. I had trouble looking at him since his husband sacrificed his life to help save me during the Event. Brysen never acted like it was my fault, but I couldn't help but feel it.

"Welcome our new members, Aurora of Flaunte, Naso of Toterrum, and Yaron of Toterrum," Brysen announced. A thin, curled, gray mustache moved side to side above his narrow mouth. Just like his perfectly defined mustache, his hair was cut and tied back into a perfectly neat bun.

The Surprisants lightly bowed as they said, "Knowing only works if you listen." They wore gray leather outlined with blue leather. Each had a tan cloak on with the hood down. A blue staff sat in their right hands, capped with a white stone. They called the staffs Facts since they would hit people across the head with them. The past me would've found the notion funny. The real, new me found it pointless, just like everything else. Though, the idea of hitting many people back in Toterrum across the head with Facts amused me.

"I, and some of you, have seen these three specimens battle during the Battle of the Blackstones," Brysen said. I was unaware they gave the ambush a name. "They have some abilities that will help us grow. Our friend Yaron may be a Mentalist himself. We should help him when he starts learning our ways."

"Are you teaching me the ways of Mentality?" I asked, growing impatient with being taught nothing about the Mentality Aura since my arrival.

"This is not my decision to make, but combat may reveal our great Aura by chance," he replied. "Not by the Luck Aura, of course." He cleared his throat. "Do I have a volunteer to spar with Yaron? I would like to see what he can do."

A woman with the bluest hair I'd ever seen rose. Golden skin and dark eyes gave a curious intensity to her demeanor. "I have seen what he can do and would like to teach him how to listen," she said with a stern look.

The other Surprisants started whispering. Had she meant to offend me? I wanted to wrap my arms around my chest and protect myself from their judgmental stares. Instead, I straightened my posture and remained steady.

"Words are empty," I replied. The normal fear I held was gone. Numbness replaced it as I watched her Aura swirl.

She bowed to me, and I bowed back. A strong push on my Aura followed right after the bow. My mind raced around, but my body didn't move. The world around me closed in like a tunnel, and my mind went foggy. I didn't recognize where I was. I scanned the people before me. Who were they? Why was another woman facing me?

A shadow caught my attention. I moved toward it and remembered the space around me. The woman facing me was my adversary. She pushed at my Aura. Yet, my Aura barely moved, still within the darkness that surrounded it. It felt as if she was searching for something. I mimicked her movement and found something. As I did, I said, "You want revenge."

She faltered but then charged at me, swinging her staff back and forth while I tried to dodge. I kept pushing on her Aura, even though the resistance was stronger. She hit me across the head, and I fell. "You will not defeat me with your small tricks," she said.

I rose from the ground and shook my head before pushing back at her Aura. She roared in protest and rushed me again. A piece of her Aura shimmered brighter than the rest, so I touched it. "You want to avenge those who died." The world became a little blurry as silhouettes fought one other. One of the silhouettes that looked like her knocked a bright red silhouette to the ground and smashed his head. "You want to kill."

She stopped in her tracks and looked around as the other Surprisants aggressively whispered.

"Vengeful murder is not our way," Brysen said to her with a disappointed look. He then turned to me. "How did you do that?"

"Do what?" I asked.

"Read her mind?" Brysen asked.

"I just saw what her Aura showed me," I replied.

"Amazing," Brysen replied. "The speed you performed this Manipulation has only been matched by the Soothsayer. Even then, she has never found something so deep and personal. Normally, they are just small glimpses."

Every Surprisant gazed at me. Brysen called on others to combat me. No matter what blows I took, I revealed secrets about them. One was in love with his best friend, even though the other had no idea. Another enjoyed stealing from the baker even though he could afford the goods. Each time, Brysen's amazement grew at my ability to repeat strong Manipulations. "You are one of the best Mentalists I have ever met," he said. "The Cerebrals must meet with you soon. That will be enough today." He quickly started toward the Cerebellum.

Aurora approached me wearing a Labyrintha blue shirt, her eyes glowing a brighter green than normal. For a moment, I expected a joke and for things to be normal. "You can't go around and reveal all these people's secrets," she lectured me, my ignorant dream fading. "Have you no respect for anyone? You've done enough already."

I clenched my fist and rotated them for a moment. Her Aura gravitated toward me as she walked away. My Aura radiated bright red hues. One more movement of her Aura, and she would pay. Ricochet's Aura distantly brushed against mine, my Aura returning to a stale white. Aurora found me callous and unaffected by my actions. Had she forgotten who I was?

Before I could stop myself, I pushed at her Aura again, and it reminded me of something I knew about her. I said, "You know the world you want of diversity and harmony isn't achievable." She had hit me deeply, and I wanted to hit her back. "You will only end up with disappointment just like everyone else."

She took one last firm step, turned back with fists clenched and eyes fiery, and yelled, "Stay out of my head, my Aura, and my life." Loud footsteps thundered as she stormed off.

The Surprisants who watched our public debacle finally turned their attention away as I shot glares at each of them. The training grounds became silent as everyone left.

"You didn't have to say that to her," Naso said. His presence surprised me.

"You don't always have to share your mind," I replied. "Your mom is still alive, but if you keep running your mouth, she may end up dead."

"Seriously?" Naso replied. "You are so…" He grunted without any further words, very unlike him, and fled the scene just like everyone else.

My ears buzzed within the lonely situation I longed for and achieved. I didn't need either of them. Brysen witnessed my greatness and growing power with my Aura. Detaching myself from the trivialities our world pushed at us proved to be the right decision. This new awareness I had with my Manipulating was limitless. I could only climb and become more powerful. My emotions and my empathy only stood in the way.

A familiar Aura brushed against mine like wind upon my hair. Ricochet sensed my loneliness and pulled at me. So, I followed his lead and made my way back outside Labyrintha's city limits and toward his pond. Large trees with white bark and bright blue leaves surrounded the dark green pond and my light blue partner beast, green dots dimly glowing as he napped. Labyrintha lacked the rich biodiversity Flaunte had. Maybe because of the colder temperature or maybe because of the surrounding mountain, the space had less to explore.

"Hello, my friend," I said as I lowered myself on a grassy patch near him. He perked up, wagged his tail, and moved to curl up next to me. I stroked his coarse hair, the smell of damp plants and dirt wafting from his dirty state. Glancing over at the space he moved from, a letter sat on the ground, another letter from Felicity, my girlfriend back in Toterrum. Memories of her black, curly hair, bright brown eyes, and lips lined in shiny lip gloss gave me some relief from my constant dissatisfaction with life. Though the letters caused me trouble with my fake mother and her betrayal, Felicity proved herself loyal to me. She and Ricochet were the only consistent things left in my life. I opened the letter to read it.

Yaron,

I still haven't been able to find your parents. I keep looking and am running out of ideas. Keep me posted if your mother is in contact with you. I hope they are okay.
Asher just got back from another mission. He was gone for two weeks this time. He is starting to look much more muscular. I keep trying to talk to him, but he ignores me and hangs out with Samson. Their group isn't the same anymore. It has been just him and Asher. They keep to themselves.
A group tried to escape the city using one of the mines. They were captured and displayed for public punishment. Our group was ready to attack in case things escalated, but luckily their main punishment was being downgraded to janitorial. Instead, we are short on another escape route.
People are losing faith in what we are doing. We had gained so much momentum and I have no idea what we should do now. Anything you know would really be appreciated. We need a spark.

Love,
Felicity

I had yet to tell her about my parents' death. Unsure of why I didn't tell her about my continuing lack of vulnerability was unfair. But then again, what was the point?

My mother's glossed-over eyes and shaky voice haunted me. She had rolled the chair, helped free me, told me to find the truth about my real parents, and then was killed. A foreign shiver tickled my throat. The numbing sensation pushing at my eyelids begged for tears to be released, but I held them back. My head throbbed from the suppressed emotions trying to escape me.

I blinked, and the numbness returned. Maybe writing her about their death became necessary.

Felicity,

I have to tell you something I should have told you a long time ago.

Three months ago, we were ambushed. Toterrum sent a group who captured Naso and me. They found out where we were from a letter I sent to my mother. They punished my father until she told them where we were heading. They killed my dad and took my mother with them.

Toterrum's leader is the orange haired man you saw before. His name is Gamma. During the capture, he asked me questions and revealed he had my mother. She did something to help Naso and me escape, but in doing so was killed. Right before she was killed, she told me she is not my biological mother.

I don't know anything further, but I do know she betrayed me, she lied to me, and now she is dead.

Maybe trying to figure out more about Gamma might help you get more information.

Love,
Yaron

I folded the letter, and off it went. My head vibrated as I processed the words I just wrote. The letter was the first time I voiced what happened. I thought about what happened to my fake parents. A pulsing rhythm resounded in my head. My head ached from all the blood making its way up. Tears tried to force their way out. My head throbbed even more aggressively, and it hurt worse. I pushed back the vibrations even harder, and my head pounded harder, like a war drum arriving to tear me down. A splitting headache forced me to rest my head on the grass, trying to keep any semblance of my calm and control.

I kept breathing in and out. In and out. Ricochet licked me. He closed his eyes, and his green spots glowed brighter. The pond turned into the beaches of Flaunte. The salty air surrounded me. My breathing calmed.

"Thank you, Ricochet," I said as I petted his head. "I miss that place, too. Things were so much simpler back then."

Reality hit me. As much as I missed Flaunte, I didn't belong there. I wasn't a Perceptionist. Did I belong in Labyrintha? Though Brysen's praise made me think I did, something was off. Doubt found me again until it dissolved within my numbness.

At least I had Ricochet.

2

ZELA

On my way back to the city, the female Surprisant I fought earlier approached me and said, "Cerebrum Brysen has obtained the Cerebral's attention, and they wish to see you. Please follow me." Her blue hair contradicted the scowl she gave me, still upset with me after announcing her private life.

As I followed her, an unfamiliar curiosity pushed at me, something I hadn't felt since the incident. "What's your name?" I asked.

Without turning to look at me, she replied, "My name is Zela."

"I'm sorry if I overstepped earlier," I said, my numb state of mind rustling. A curiosity at her overall demeanor pulled at me. Why was I shifting my emotions? Something interesting about her nonchalant attitude and stern expression made my numbness excited, which seemed counterintuitive.

"I'm a Surprisant," she said. "I need to learn in order to get stronger."

I understood that. Everything I did was to learn my Aura and become stronger. Everyone else tried to smile at me and act like everything was normal. Her scowl was the first normal interaction I'd had in a while.

"If it matters, I want revenge as well," I said. "They killed my parents."

My confession earned a small glance from her. "I'm sorry about that," she replied. "However, I can't let trivial things impact my abilities."

Finally, a Mentalist spoke about their Aura.

"Why?" I asked.

"In order to see the Mentality Aura in detail, you must keep a clear mind," she answered. "Holding onto our world too much can derail an objective. My parents were killed as well." Her face softened for a moment, but then she lightly shook her head, the scowl returning. "Don't mistake this for bonding. I'm only telling you since you will eventually find it in my Aura."

The one thing I understood about the Mentality Aura was the search involved with it. Zela confirmed my suspicion.

"I'm sorry about your parents," I said.

Zela pressed her lips together and stared at the ground before glancing back up at me. "I was young when it happened," she said as she pushed her hair back with her gloved hand. As she did this, something reflected off her wrist, something large and metal shimmered.

"What's on your wrist?" I asked.

She looked down, her face reflecting off the small bit poking out near her glove. She took off her glove to reveal a hand made of metal, metallic fingers wiggling in the air.

"When my parents were killed, I lost my hand," she said.

"How is it moving?"

"Mentalists can't Manipulate their own minds but can Manipulate their own body's network," she replied. "In a way, at least. Our engineers created a hand that is fused to my network, and I'm able to move my hand."

"A network? What do you mean, a network?"

"A whole bunch of small wires, though they aren't actually wires, that run through all our bodies." She fluttered her fingers, drawing wires in the air. "It's the best way to think of them. They allow our minds to communicate with the rest of the body. The mind is the most important thing in us. It keeps the body moving and alive. The body is nothing without the mind." She smiled but looked down at her hand, forehead crinkling.

Her Aura went gray like mine. She was uneasy like me, which, for the first time since arriving in Labyrintha, made me feel normal.

We arrived at the Cerebellum, its large blue doors intimidating me. An engraving on the door showed a large oval in the center with curvy lines coming off it. The lines crossed over and curled around one another, like what I imagined the network Zela spoke about looked like. A silvery metal exterior with sharp, straight edges gave the Capitol Building a very simple, geometric look to it. I imagined if I touched its edges, the building would lacerate me. Even the metallic scent of the building sat stark on my nose. I oddly envied the building's straight forward, plain demeanor. If my life only mimicked it.

Before we entered, I said, "Thank you for talking to me. This may sound weird, but something about you makes me feel better considering my current situation."

"Okay, I guess, but this still isn't bonding," she coldly replied. "Head straight through these doors, and you will find them on the third floor. Always greet the Soothsayer first."

"But who is the Soothsayer?" I asked, but the door shut in my face before she heard my question.

I turned away from the door and faced a large room. The same metal from the exterior extended into the interior walls. Various inspiring quotes were painted across the walls, such as *The mind is the key to the soul,* and *When you seek truth, be prepared for the aftermath.*

A spiral staircase rose from the middle of the entrance and spiraled up through an open area with wings coming off to the second floor before ending at the third floor. I made my way up, passing the second floor, which had large glass panels with many people working on various projects. On the top floor was a large library with a metal table in the center. Ten people surrounded the table, with an older woman seated at the end. She had gray hair and wore a light blue suit. Brysen sat on one of the side seats as I walked up.

Fixating on the old woman, I said, "Soothsayer, I'm pleased to finally meet you."

The old lady just nodded with a small smirk. I took a seat in one of the chairs.

A younger girl with short, brown hair turned to me and said, "How has your stay been so far?" Her dark blue eyes, almost brown, stood out due to her similarly colored eyebrows.

I kept my attention on the Soothsayer as I answered, "It has been very pleasant. Brysen has been very welcoming while we waited."

"Cerebrum Brysen," the younger girl corrected me. "Were you unhappy with the wait?"

"I just expected to be taught much quicker," I replied, still facing the Soothsayer and her wrinkled face. "Flaunte moved me into training upon arrival."

"Flaunte is more of a show. Labyrintha observes before we act," the young girl replied.

"Observes?" I asked.

"We have been observing your habits and have honestly been disappointed," the girl said. "You are fortunate Cerebrum Brysen saw something worth pursuing."

I turned to the girl and said, "I didn't catch your name. You seem to talk a lot for the group."

"I am the Soothsayer," she flatly replied.

My cheeks warmed after realizing my error. How could I be so stupid?

"You are the Soothsayer?" I slowly asked. I turned back to the older lady. "She isn't?"

"She is Cerebrum Grace," the real Soothsayer replied. "She oversees Patience, hence her lack of words."

"The right time is worth waiting for," Cerebrum Grace replied. "Especially when it makes a fool of an arrogant human."

Dull whispers echoed between the Cerebrums. Another wave of tightness squeezed at my lungs. Part of me wanted to run out of the room and hide at the pond with Ricochet. However, I needed this meeting.

I wasn't starting out strong, but I could recover. The Flaunte council accepted me more than this group did, even with Ruth, the Perceptionist saboteur who nearly had me captured back in Toterrum. I just needed to find some charisma.

"I'm so sorry for my assumptions," I said.

"Knowing only works if you listen," the Soothsayer said. "I would introduce you to our Cerebrums, but this information is not worth telling you. Cerebrum Brysen. Please stand and combat Yaron so we may see these abilities you speak of."

Brysen stood up as I stood up. We faced one another, and he pushed into my Aura without hesitation. Zela's words about clearing your mind to make a good Manipulation hit me at the right time. I leaned into the constant numbness hovering around me and then pushed back at him. He tried to search my numb Aura, which gave me time to find what I needed. A blurred image of Brysen hugging and kissing another man came up.

"You want someone to love again," I said. "You feel weak without them."

Brysen lowered his arms, and his face softened. I went too far. So much for charisma.

The Cerebrums started mumbling to each other. Brysen sat down, blankly staring ahead. The echoes made my ears burn.

"I know," he said.

The group echoed, "I know," while others said, "I do not."

The Soothsayer let out a deep sigh and stood as she said, "Per the Cerebrums' vote, you will be trained further. Your Cerebrums will be Cerebrum Brysen, Cerebrum Grace, Cerebrum Alex, and myself. You will only be allowed time with Cerebrum Grace and Cerebrum Alex once you are approved by me. Cerebrum Brysen may continue training. Knowing only works if we listen." The Soothsayer stood and walked away.

That was quick.

The rest of them left the table one by one and headed toward the staircase. The Soothsayer walked in the opposite direction toward the library.

I ran after her. "Soothsayer, when will we start?"

"Tomorrow morning," she replied and kept walking.

"What will we be doing?" I asked.

She turned to me, her shorter stature somehow looking down on me. "This decision is against my better judgment and what I know about you. The darkness that looms over you troubles me. The Mentality Aura is not drawn to such darkness. Only the Light will show the way. Plan on attending the weekly services of your choosing. This is not an option but a demand. Good day."

As I watched her walk away, the blatant disrespect she bestowed upon me brought back the war drums and their rhythmic beat within my veins. If I were still in Flaunte, they would've respected me. I missed Flaunte's inclusivity.

"Congratulations," Brysen said, stepping next to me.

"It doesn't feel like it," I said, watching the Soothsayer walk through a door, slamming it behind her.

"You will grow on her," he replied. "Give it time."

"I'm sorry about—"

"Do not worry about it," he cut me off. "You did exactly what you needed to. It impressed many of the Cerebrums."

"I thought the decision wouldn't work that way," I said. "I thought the leader of Labyrintha would make the final decision."

"Facts are presented, and decisions are made," he said. "We value various perspectives to properly decipher facts. Once a decision is voted on, everyone must accept it."

"That seems frustrating," I said.

"Oh, it is," he replied with a laugh. "But we eventually have to overcome our frustration. Emotions hinder Mentality."

My dislike of Labyrintha began to fade. I agreed, but my emotions were in the way. I needed to embrace my desire for Mentality. Maybe it would stop the constant vibrating in my head. Mentality may free me internally.

"I appreciate your efforts to get me here," I said. "It means a lot."

"It is my pleasure, Yaron of Toterrum," he said with a bow and a swift departure.

Though a lot of the day remained, I realized I had no one to spend it with. Loneliness transformed into growing sadness, which I pushed down. If I was going to make room for Mentality, I needed to rid myself of all other emotions.

That was the solution. I needed more numbness to keep the other emotions away. Instead, Ricochet's Aura brushed against my Aura again. No matter how hard I tried, I couldn't keep his presence away.

3

THE BLACKSTONE MOUNTAINS

The morning sun shone between the cracks that peaked through the towers of bookshelves. The eerie quietness within the library made me shiver. The smell of musky vanilla and sweet dirt enveloped the room in the commanding smell of old books. The Soothsayer sat at the other end of the table, her brown hair bobbing as she aggressively wrote in a notebook.

"Sit," she said as I walked up, not looking up from her task. Her voice echoed throughout the library, causing another shiver to erupt across my numb skin. After sitting across from her at the table, she asked, "What is Mentality?" She still didn't look up at me.

The vague question caught me off guard. "Mentality involves information about yourself or others."

"Is the information learned limited to only being about people?" she asked, her head still bobbing from the writing. I was impressed by how she wrote in a notebook while listening and asking me questions.

"No," I replied. "It's about, well, everything."

She placed her pen down and looked up at me, dark blue eyes, almost brown, analyzing me. "How much do you know?" she asked.

"Not a lot." I gulped, intimidated by her dark glare.

"How do you learn about new things?"

"By experiencing them."

She crossed her arms and leaned back. "Do you learn from others?"

"Yes."

"How?"

Her rapid questions worried me. I swallowed, pushing away any emotion that wasn't numbness.

"By watching them, listening to them, and—"

"Listening." She cut me off, leaning forward and resting her elbows on the table. "That is the key." She pointed at the air as if pinpointing her emphasis. "To learn more from our world, we need to first figure out how to listen to ourselves. As I said yesterday, there is darkness in your Aura. It is clouded, and I do not think you even know how to hear it."

Without warning, anger bubbled in my chest, something numbness had no control over. I knew who I was and what I thought. In fact, clarity overwhelmed me since my fake mother's death. Trust proved to be just folly and an ignorant endeavor. I would be strong and protect myself.

"I hear myself," I snapped back. "I'm a Mentalist who has found strength in adversity and wishes to grow more. My emotions are what's in the way."

The Soothsayer stared at me. She then closed her eyes as a very strong push on my Aura made my head throb. No matter how hard I tried to resist, her overwhelming power flooded my Aura. She opened her eyes and said, "You lie to yourself."

"I get you're very powerful as a Mentalist, but you don't know me." Sitting up straight, I looked down on her. "I think the real problem is you're worried that I might be more powerful than you."

Unphased by my claim, she blinked, took in a deep breath of the old book smell, and tilted her head, her neck cracking slightly.

"Do you know what the Soothsayer is?" she asked.

The answers seemed obvious, but the way she asked made me unsure. I hesitated but locked in my answer.

"The leader of Labyrintha."

"No," she replied. "I am not the leader. Our community is represented by the ten Cerebrums. Each provides strengths where others do not. We balance each out and lead in unison." A little smile curled up her cheeks before she stiffened her face. "But I digress from my purpose. The Soothsayer has been around since the Great Light blessed us with our Manipulations. One takes the Soothsayer title and all we have learned during our lifespan and passes it to the next Soothsayer. One may call us the most knowledgeable person in the world."

"So, you know everything?" I shrugged and sat back, crossing my arms.

She grunted, my nonchalant attitude getting the best of her, but inhaled more of the old book air and steadied her voice. "No one knows everything, but we know a lot. We are still only human."

I grew tired of talking about the Soothsayer's greatness. If she knew all of history, she would know why Vigor did all that they did. She had to have the answers on how to defeat Vigor. Empathy handled them and disappeared. Did she know more about Empathy?

"Tell me what happened with Empathy and Vigor when the war started," I demanded, ready to push for more answers.

She grunted again and shook her head. "What does this have to do with our conversation?"

"You say you know everything, and I'm here to learn my Aura and defeat Vigor," I said.

"Your intentions are muddy." She paused. "You must understand even though the knowledge about the situation may or may not be in my possession it does not mean it needs to be shared with everyone. The Great Light decides when important information is to be provided. Your darkness and intentions are far separated from the Light. Nearly everyone living is separated from the Light, preventing important information from being shared."

"This war could be over with the information you have, and you won't share it?" I scoffed and rolled my eyes. "Talk about darkness."

Though her face remained stern, her eyes vibrated. "I understand the issues you are dealing with are delicate, but you will not grow further if you hold tightly to them."

"I'm holding onto nothing." I slammed my hands on the table, the top book on her pile of books falling off, the smacking noise the cover made against the surface echoing throughout the room. "I feel stronger than I ever have. Speaking of listening, will you be teaching me anything, or is this just a counseling session?"

A fiery intensity sparked between us, our Auras clashing into one another like fists during a fight, yet our bodies didn't move. I moved my hand forward as she raised hers faster. I looked at my hands, wondering what I was doing with them.

"Do not test me," she said.

I remembered what I was doing. I tried to Manipulate her Aura again. She cowered before me and shrunk back. A dark abyss surrounded me as I closed in on her. All of her fell under my control. Her weakness danced in between my fingers.

Suddenly, the darkness disappeared, and the world appeared upside down. I fell forward off a chair that I hung upside down from. She smirked at my muddled body on the floor across the room from where I started.

"What happened?" I asked. I pulled myself up by using her table as a prop. My hands clenched the table so hard that my fingertips went numb.

"You learned what the Mentality Aura can do." As she breathed out, a delicate whistle came from the escaping air. "Now, I have already stated my purpose. Take it or leave it."

"Then I'm done for today." After hoisting myself up to my feet, I lifted my hands off the table I accosted with my firm grip and gave her an arrogant grin and head dip. "Good day, Soothsayer." I turned to walk away.

Halfway to my exit, she said, "One more thing." She paused, but I kept walking. "I want to help you, but you need to understand talking about your darkness will help, even when you think it will not."

I paused in the doorway, almost turning back around, but grunted and exited the building. The audacity she had to act like she not only knew me so well but that I needed to be fixed irked me. I wanted to scream, but I worried I might break one of the delicate windows covering the surrounding buildings. Instead, I marched forward. Naso loved to talk crap about people, but I remembered what I said to him. Aurora liked to listen, but she hated me. Around my first turn, Zela's blue hair caught my eye.

"Hey," I said to her as she looked over.

"Hello," she replied. "What were you doing in the Cerebellum?"

"The Soothsayer is requiring me to train with her before the other Cerebrums can see me other than Cerebrum Brysen," I answered. "Which reminds me. You forgot to mention the Soothsayer was the younger girl when I met with them yesterday. I called Cerebrum Grace the Soothsayer in front of the group while belittling the real Soothsayer. I looked like an idiot."

Zela started to laugh. "That is embarrassing," she said. "Are you passing her tests?"

"I think I'm failing miserably." I rolled my head, cracking my neck.

"Good thing you're good at Aura combat." She waved her hands in the air, mimicking combat moves before nodding her head forward. "Walk with me to Surprisant training."

"Whatever you say, captain." I gave a goofy salute, and we began walking. For the first time in a while, someone else's presence didn't irritate me. "So, what does an important person like yourself do in her spare time?"

"I would not call myself an important person." She scoffed. "But as a normal person I like to hike the surrounding mountains. It keeps me in shape, and the view is great. You should join me next time. After training today."

"I would love to." An unfamiliar excitement climbed up my chest.

"Are you going to the service?" she asked. "I haven't seen you at them. Do you go to one of the other locations? I thought you would be with the group you came with."

Any excitement I had dissipated. Why did everyone in Labyrintha care so much about the Cortexes?

"I haven't gone." I focused on my steps. "The Soothsayer is demanding I go while I work through her program." I paused as Zela gave me a side-eye. "The whole religious thing is odd to me."

"There is actually quite a bit to learn from the services," she said. "They helped me cope with my parents' deaths and many other issues that have come along."

Zela joined the list of people trying to fix me. Why couldn't anyone just let me be?

"The whole thing sounds…"

"Fake?"

She took the words right out of my mouth, leaving me silent and dumbfounded. Zela surprised me again, more like me than I'd ever imagined. I nodded in response.

"There are a lot of things that cannot be explained in our world," she said. "That's why I tend to go. The mystery and all. The Great Light is believed to give and sustain all of it. Sometimes answers are not always needed."

I found myself staring at Zela, trying to find some indication of a joke or something to rebut what she just said. Her face remained soft, looking ahead of our walk.

"It's funny how the Mentalists are the remaining followers of the Cortexes," I said. "For knowing so much, Mentalists admit how much isn't known."

"Knowing only works if you listen." A little smile curled up her cheek as she said it, giving me another side-eye glance.

After walking several blocks, we arrived at the training grounds. Naso and Aurora were already there. I went to stand next to them, but Aurora moved to another area.

"Hey," I said to Naso as he nodded back without eye contact.

"She looks mad," Zela said. "What did you do?"

My interaction with Zela pulled out a different kind of guilt I hadn't felt in a while. They didn't deserve the way I treated them.

"I said some things I shouldn't have said," I replied before turning to Naso. "I'm sorry."

"I get you're going through a lot, but just watch what you say to your friends," Naso replied. "You tend to turn into an ass." He grinned. "As for me, you're going to have to do a lot worse before I disappear." He punched me hard in my arm.

"Same goes for you." I winced from the strike but just rubbed my arm in response, a rare happiness warming my chest.

"Surprisants," Brysen announced from up front, the Surprisants turning their attention toward him. "Today, we will be practicing stun attacks to use against an opponent. Zela, please come up here for a demonstration."

Zela rose and marched to the front, a confident sway to her stride. Just as she faced Brysen, he charged at her. He swirled his arms in one rapid swoop before drastically slowing down his swing. Zela looked around as if admiring the trees. She forgot she was fighting him. Brysen took his staff and swung it at her feet, Zela falling to the ground with a hard thud. She instantly jumped to her feet from her back and swirled her hands as Brysen swung his staff in a circle, knocking himself on the head. Zela punched his gut, knocked the staff in the air, and caught it as it swung in rapid circles in the air.

"Whoa," Naso said, leaning forward.

"Very good, Zela," Brysen said, the slightest sound of pain in his voice. "Everyone, pair up and practice some of the movements you just witnessed."

I turned to Naso, ready to ask him, but he cocked his head and crossed his arms. "I'm going to work with Aurora today." He walked over to her area.

All the other Surprisants paired up as I spun around, looking for someone to even notice me. Cold sweat dripped down my back as a familiar sense of insignificance encapsulated me. I was alone. Numbness rushed across my body to protect any self-worth I still held.

"Need a partner?" Zela asked me from behind me.

I turned to face her, cold loneliness lifting from my body. "Yes," I replied. She noticed the solidarity I longed for but also my desire to be wanted. "I will go easier on you today." An uncanny grin curled up my cheeks, no matter how hard I tried to keep it at bay.

"Your Mentality Manipulations may be strong, but your combat will not match mine," she replied, an unwavering, confident stance facing me.

We sparred for a couple hours, and I loved every minute of it. Just as Zela said, my actual combat abilities proved subpar to her own. My Mentality Manipulations were able to stun her, but my ability to capitalize on it produced nothing. Zela rebounded so quickly from anything that came at her. Yet, she remained a good teacher. After each mistake I made, she would teach me the better movement to use. By the end of training, I at least hit her after a Manipulation.

After training, I searched the Surprisants for Naso and Aurora to invite them on the hike, but they were already gone.

"Ready for the hike?" Zela asked.

"Yes." I sighed but pushed past missing my friends. Ricochet's Aura swirled around my own Aura, warming me.

"Be sure to keep up." Zela grinned and ran off. I attempted to keep up. The run was my first in months. Buildings zipped by as I followed her blue streak. My reflection shined from the countless windows we passed.

As we approached the mountain, fewer buildings could be seen before we were at an open field that defined the city's edge. Wet rock overtook all other smells, the strongest the scent had been. Whistling grass blew in the wind, creating a tranquil melody. We trekked across the field, grass brushing against my leg, interrupting the symphony, until we arrived at a zigzag path climbing straight up the mountain. My neck ached as I surveyed the monstrosity surrounding Labyrintha, a far greater barrier than the wall of Toterrum.

"You didn't tell me it was this steep." I gulped down all the fear lining my throat.

"I figured you had eyes." She looked over at me, face tense. "You do have eyes, right?"

My neck cracked as I faced her. "Yes, it's just—"

"I'm joking." She laughed, looking up. "I'm so used to walking it." And just like that, she marched up the path, me scurrying behind.

The first few minutes, I was doing fine. Then, my lungs became heavy. Air became difficult to breathe in.

"Well, this is fun." I took in a deep breath.

"Toterrum lungs are much weaker than I expected." She laughed. "The mines didn't help much, did they?"

"Toterrum. Weak." I took one more deep breath, let out a weakened laugh, and kept moving. "Deeper in the ground versus high up in the sky are different. Plus, I didn't hike them that much." Asking me questions seemed silly when she could just access information as a Mentalist. "How come you don't just search my Aura for personal details?"

"It is not the way of our kind," she responded. "Plus, nearly all Mentalists can only move information. For example, I can move memories, facts, and other information away so you forget, or I can add things I know to impact decision-making. We can analyze and take facts from people for ourselves, but personal information is much foggier and unclear. This is why everyone is amazed at what you can do. This is a high-level Manipulation that you somehow mastered on your first try. You've even impressed me."

A newfound gusto puffed up my lungs following her compliment. Though happy I impressed Zela, the Soothsayer was not anywhere near being impressed with me.

"The Soothsayer can access personal information, but can others?" I asked.

"Yes, but in different ways."

"How so?"

"Well," she started, "some specialize in physical pain. These Mentalists look through your network and find where a pain's source comes from. They can sometimes rework the network to alleviate the pain or at least find the information for a doctor to heal with other methods. Others can do this same thing but with sickness. If someone has an abnormality happening with their physical body, the network can find what is causing this and possibly determine further sickness such as cancer, autoimmune disorders, and heart issues."

"How does physical health impact the Mentality Aura?"

"Anything that impacts or impairs the body impacts or impairs the Mentality Aura," she replied. "You can learn a lot by listening to yourself."

She sounded like the Soothsayer. "Yeah, I guess."

We stopped talking for a while as we began a steeper climb. Maybe about a third to half of the way up, we came to a tunnel that I followed her through. Little blue stones illuminated a small cave, just like when we entered the maze of the city for the first time.

Just as we exited the cave onto a narrow ledge, the straight drop down made my heart leap. I jumped back and held onto the cave wall before the most overwhelming view I'd ever seen made my body tremble. I focused on the smell of wet rock to calm my heartbeat. While closing my eyes, the whistling wind hit such a high note my skin tingled. When my heart was calm, I opened my eyes. To the right, the peninsula and beach we had traveled along with Era curled toward the sea below. Straight down to the left were the large black stones where we were ambushed. Many trees had fallen over. We were high up, but if you squinted, you could see small Waldabears wandering the forest.

My eyes traveled up the mountain's edge, up and up, until a thick fog covered the top of the mountain. A sudden chill wrapped around me as if the fog reached down and grabbed me. Zela stood next to me, right on the edge of the cliff, looking up.

"We are only about a quarter up the mountain," she said.

"That's it?" I cracked as she shrugged. "Have you ever been to the top?"

"Yes." She patted my shoulder, making me grip tighter on the cave walls. "The path disappears, and only small ledges remain. You need a group you are tied to. This is to prevent falling and other things."

"Other things?" I looked over to her as she shrugged. "I bet the view is amazing."

"Of clouds, primarily. Don't get me wrong, it's still amazing, but mostly of the sky. Look that way, and if you look really closely, you can see the ruins of Rithbar."

I squinted and pretended like I saw the ruins, but only black dots made up my view. The country's vastness pulled at me in a new way. I had traveled so far. I had seen so much. If that was Rithbar, I remembered my first encounter with a Waldabear and fighting it with Aurora and Naso.

"Naso and Aurora would have loved this view," I said.

"Speaking of those two, what's going on with them? You arrived in Labyrintha together. I assumed you were close with them."

Then, I remembered how they treated me and shut me out. But I had done so much. I didn't deserve it, no matter if I said some things I shouldn't have.

"People change." I huffed. "But I think they envy my power in Mentality."

"Very modest." Zela sneered and let out one big, irritated breath. "I don't think that's the truth."

"I have no idea what else it could be." I turned away from the horizon. "I'm the one that lost important people in my life. Not them. They don't understand what's going on with me."

A foreign grip tightened around my throat and crept up across my face. My cheeks warmed as the desire to cry became unbearable. Zela's face softened in response, so I swallowed deep, pushing the tightness away and allowing numbness to seep back in. Zela shifted her stance, one hand on her hip and the other up in the air, rotating.

"Have you tried to explain it?" she asked.

"No." I picked at my nails. "I shouldn't have to. They should get it. Knowing only works if you listen. Right?"

"But you need to speak about something to allow for the option of knowing." Her hand twirled more aggressively. "I held a lot in when my parents died. I thought the same way you did, but I eventually had to talk about it if I wanted to grow. If you keep pushing people away, you will never heal."

Her parents were dead, just like mine. Maybe she did understand me more than I thought. Then again, her parents were probably her real parents. Not liars like mine were.

Zela's Aura floated around her, like the little stones in the cave but able to move. The rainbow iridescence most other people's Aura had didn't mimic her own. Darker shades covered her Aura. It even moved cautiously, like mine did.

"But did you really heal?" I asked. "Your Aura is dark like mine."

She looked over her head at her Aura, brows furrowed. "I don't see my Aura as dark." She paused, pondering something. "I have tried since you said it before, but I see my normal Aura. Maybe you just see the Aura clearer than I do because of your abilities."

I continued watching her Aura and the mortality it knew too well. "That must be it. Do you really think you healed?"

"Yes and no. No one fully heals, but we still heal some. There are times when I remember my hurt, and I cry. At the same time, our scars give us more character. New avenues open within our network to allow more new growth. We only need to recognize it and grow from it."

How was she reading me like a book? Maybe she did extract personal information from my Aura without knowing she was.

I carried my insightful conversation with Zela back down the mountain and to my new home. Just like all the other buildings in Labyrintha, it was made of glass. Aurora and Naso sat at the dining room table playing a card game. I stood outside the house, just watching them. Aurora pushed her hair behind her ear and rolled her eyes at something Naso said. Naso shuffled the cards while his face animated from something he was telling her. Had my life become something where I watched my friends have fun from afar? Then, Aurora smiled, a rare thing she displayed when talking to Naso. Her cheeks curled up as she covered her mouth from an uncharacteristic laugh escaping her strong composure around Naso's ridiculous jokes. Whatever he said was actually funny. I wondered what it was.

Suddenly, Aurora turned to face me, her smile vanishing. I dipped my head and walked to the door as she stood from the table and walked to her room, door slamming behind her. The glass walls vibrated with the slightest hum before fading away.

"Where did you go?" Naso asked, shuffling the cards.

"I went on a hike with Zela," I said. "I was going to invite you both, but you were gone before I could after combat practice."

"Aurora wanted to head back," Naso replied.

Herita walked out of the kitchen, holding a glass of tea. "Oh, you're back. I have food that I kept warm for you in the kitchen." She narrowed her gaze, a strong, minty aroma wafting in the air. "You seem different."

My cheeks flushed. "I had a good conversation with Zela."

"Did you want to talk about it?" Herita sipped her tea, eyes fixated on me. I held her gaze and shook my head. "Okay." She shrugged and finished off her cup. "We are heading to do some shopping after the service if you want to meet us after. We can come back to the house."

"I think I'm going to come to the service," I said.

Naso rapidly shook his head. "Really?"

"The Soothsayer is requiring I go," I said.

"Did you meet with her?" Herita asked.

I realized I never told either of them I had. "Yes," I said. "She's requiring I get through her before I do any further testing or training. She's allowing me to continue combat training with Cerebrum Brysen." I thought about what else I wanted to tell her. Then, it hit me. "Also, I totally thought Cerebrum Grace was the Soothsayer when I met them all. This younger girl kept talking and interrupting my questions to Cerebrum Grace. I, like a fool, ignored the younger girl and eventually asked why she was talking so much. Only then did I find out the younger girl was the Soothsayer."

"You did not!" Herita said with a gasp.

"Oh, I did," I replied.

Herita started laughing. Naso asked, "Is that a big deal?"

"Yes," Herita said. "Yes, it is. The Soothsayer is the all-knowing being of Mentalists. From the beginning, all the information learned from the prior Soothsayer is passed to the next. Yaron pretty much offended the smartest person in the world."

"You idiot." Naso grinned before joining in with Herita's laughter.

This was my first interaction since arriving in Labyrintha that was like what our group used to be. I wished Aurora would come out and join us. I pictured her devious smile and meadow green eyes, something I hadn't seen in too long. Yet, she chose to run. Zela provided some great insight, but I wondered if Aurora and I would ever be the same.

4

THE CORTEX

The next morning, the walk to the service was brisk. Aurora wouldn't look at or even acknowledge me, so I tried not to look at her. On certain mornings, the large white flowers lining the mountain walls would let off a silvery dust. Foggy glitter filled the sky as its sweet aroma filled my nose, sweeter than in past days. Did it mean a good day lay before me?

The Cortex stood tall, with various stone beasts covering the exterior. These beasts seemed to be climbing the walls when, in reality, they didn't move. As we approached the front door, their stone eyes seemed to follow me, filling me with a sense of uneasiness. Little whispers I couldn't understand surrounded me as if they were talking about me, yet no one else was affected by the sound. I covered my ears as my head started to vibrate. I stopped walking, letting the others go ahead of me, eyes fixated on the stone beasts. They were doing this to me. I knew they were.

I shook my head as the whispers suddenly stopped. The stone beasts weren't moving. Nothing was happening.

"Are you coming?" Herita asked, holding open the large wooden doors.

I nodded and grabbed the cold metal handle from her. After closer inspection, the doors were etched with the sun peeking through clouds. The lower section of the doors were carved people looking up at the sun while covering their faces with their hands. Swinging the door open, the smell of rock and wood swept across me. The inside of the building had wooden benches, all facing toward the front. A light shined from a skylight window high up in the ceiling. People slowly entered and sat down quietly. Some closed their eyes while others held whispered conversations with each other.

Among the attendees were the Soothsayer and Zela. The curved wooden beams lining the outside walls traveled up to the ceiling until meeting at the center skylight. The light brown wood contrasted with the dark gray stone that supported the walls and ceiling. Very tall and narrow colored windows covered the walls. The sun illuminated them with beautiful blues, reds, greens, yellows, and many other colors in geometric shapes, reminding me of the Capitol building in Rithbar. The sun's beams prismed through the dusty air, creating a multicolored light show. Unlike the outside of the building, with the stone beasts amplifying my worry, the inside was peaceful. This was a feeling I didn't trust.

I had every right not to trust my surroundings. Where had it brought me before? Ruth Char was supposed to be my mentor, but she chose power and tried to capture me. My fake parents lied to me my entire life and gave my location away. I almost died because of them, and they died because of their choices. Why was I even in the building?

Just before I could run out of the service, echoing footsteps became louder as the crowd quieted. A woman with bright hair and olive skin stepped to the center wearing a light blue robe accented with white dots.

She announced, "Welcome back to our place of peace. I am Servant Kham for those new faces I see. Today, we listen to the Great Light about our pain. Some of us have physical pain. Some emotional pain. Some caused by a disease. Others by betrayal. All this pain breaks us from our Aura and makes us imbalanced. Whether you can Manipulate, or you cannot, the Aura is something we all feel and can all tap into through our different abilities. Let us meditate."

Everyone sat there silently. Although meant to be a time of serenity, the silence made me uncomfortable to the point I almost giggled. I thought about the leader's words to divert my inevitable breaking. The word *betrayal* stood out to me. The idea impacted me. I felt betrayed. Betrayal did hurt me. Therefore, I needed to be careful trusting others. If I kept myself distant, I could avoid future pain. Familiar numbness settled my desire to giggle.

"Let us slowly let ourselves back into this space," Servant Kham said. Her voice was gentle yet firm. "We may feel that caution will keep us from future pain. Maybe we stop doing the activity or work that hurts our body. Maybe we avoid addressing the loss of someone or what someone said to us. Maybe we act like a disease is not there and keep it to ourselves. Maybe we have stopped trusting others to avoid the possibility of future betrayals. What a life of disconnect. What a boring life. The Great Light wants us to connect and live. Let us lift our voices in song."

Everyone pulled out a book from underneath the bench as great pipes started playing music near the back walls. Everyone seemed to know how to sing the song based on the pages I looked at. I understood the words, but the other writing above made no sense to me. I tried singing the words, "Oh Great Light, open our minds to hear you and to be mended," but I sang it out of tune and out of rhythm. Naso and Aurora started to giggle before Herita hushed them. I looked over at Aurora, and her smile shifted back into a frown as she looked forward.

Servant Kham followed the song with a speech on connecting to our network and listening to the Great Light. She ended it by saying that once it is completed, our Aura will be free to flow again. There were more words in between, but I wasn't listening.

"I want everyone to stand," Servant Kham said and we all did. "Let us all close our eyes and say what has happened to us out loud. If you are not ready to do so, find time to listen to the Great Light later this week. Allow the Light to come in and give you courage to tell your loved ones or those who did you wrong what your problems are."

People started saying things out loud. Some said a disease out loud. Others mentioned their physical pain, such as a bad knee or back pain. Others mentioned people who died and how they miss them. I heard Naso say, "My emotional pain from my mother's sickness."

Aurora said, "My emotional pain from words said by someone I care about."

My brain rattled like it was being shaken in a metal pan. I wanted to say something, but my mind kept convincing me otherwise. What if someone heard me? What if people found me weak? What if this information allowed someone from Toterrum to find me?

I closed my eyes tightly, pushed past my doubt and worry, and said, "I have been betrayed and lied to by someone I used to love my whole life." It came out a little louder than I wanted. I let out a deep sigh, and my chest tightened. I said it out loud. The words said out loud carried so much more weight than thinking them. Herita grabbed my hand. I squeezed back.

"Good," Servant Kham said as everyone opened their eyes. "Now, let these problems be lifted to the Great Light and pray that our hearts stay open to the Light's healing power. We all need Mentality. We all need the ability to Perceive. We all need Luck. We all need Empathy. And we all need Vigor. Enjoy your day, children of the Light."

The building quietly emptied. Were all the Auras necessary? Even Vigor? How could they think that?

As we exited, the Soothsayer walked up to me. "I am glad you came," she said. "I will see you tomorrow morning." She abruptly departed.

The service did affect me, but how?

Aurora walked up. "I'm unhappy with what you said to me."

I gaped at her. She was talking to me. My heart fluttered at her unwavering attention.

"I'm so sorry," I replied. "I'm not ready to talk about everything, but my brain went fuzzy, and those words just flowed out. I didn't mean them."

"But you said them." Her cheeks and eyebrows scrunched toward her eyes. She reached toward me in the slightest way before retracting. "I think, deep down, you actually believe them. That's my problem."

The moment when I spoke the words was long gone. I couldn't take back what I said, but had I meant what I said? Maybe she was right. She deserved an apology.

"Whether I did or I didn't, I'm really sorry for saying it." I half-smiled.

"I don't think I'm ready to forgive you." She crossed her arms and raised her chin. "But I guess I'll stop ignoring you so much."

An intense heat flushed across my cheeks and warmed the rest of my body.

"That's more than I could ask for," I replied with a full smile.

"Did you really offend the Soothsayer like that?" Aurora asked.

"So, you were listening last night," I replied. She shrugged. "I totally did," I responded, "and looked like the biggest idiot."

Her body shook within a chuckle. "I wish I would've been there."

Then, she laughed. Like a symphony to my ears, she laughed. Her nose scrunched and she held her hand over her mouth to hide the noise. Judgmental glares from passing Mentalists didn't make her waver. I joined her laughter. My numb mind slowly cracked at each laugh.

My first time going to the service, and a good thing happened. Maybe my disdain for Labyrintha wasn't warranted.

5

THE SOOTHSAYER

A new smell reached me when I entered the library—flowers. Not just any flowers but those from Flaunte. My mind returned to the ocean breeze, crashing waves, and coarse sand in between my toes. Then, roaring Waldabears, fighting Officers, and the life fading from the Officer's eyes I killed tainted the memories.

I fixated on the incense burning next to the standing Soothsayer that carefully watched me walk in. "Tell me, what did you take from the service yesterday?"

The closer I came to her, the stronger the floral smell was, coming from the incense. Did she have that specific incense burning to invoke my memories of Flaunte? She certainly dove into things quickly.

"We're getting right into this," I said, her gaze unfaltering. "I guess I'm recognizing and wanting to address issues in my life?"

"And what are those?"

She was right about the service, but it didn't give her the right to hold an inquisition. But was it worth fighting about? Maybe I needed to trust her process.

"I was betrayed by my mother," I cracked out, glaring at the Soothsayer. "I told her where I was, and she gave this information to Toterrum." I took a deep gulp. "This caused us to be attacked and for many people to be...murdered." The words just danced off my numb tongue. Then, my chest fired up as I thought about my mother's betrayal. "I'm angry at her." I stared intently into the Soothsayer's eyes.

She breathed out of her nose, little whistles escaping. Then, she sat down. "As much as a battle does have death, murder is not the correct term for her sins. Murder is with intent. Those in a battle do not pick their victims; they are forced to commit a killing for survival. Beyond this, did your mother choose to provide your whereabouts?"

What was happening? The room became hotter and the air thinner.

"My father was being tortured, and they promised to stop torturing him if given the information," I replied.

Her face remained firm. "She did it to protect him."

"They killed him anyway!" I yelled. "She should have known the information wasn't going to save him!"

"We do desperate things when those we love are threatened." The Soothsayer just stared at me, unblinking.

I slammed my hands on the desk, books shaking making the incense smoke create waves in the air. "I was threatened!" I took an uneasy breath. "I needed to be protected as well."

A deafening silence loomed between us, the incense smoke still trying to force Flaunte memories upon me.

"Tell me about your parents' history," the Soothsayer said.

I slowly blinked, trying to figure out what game she was playing, but I would prevail over her.

"She worked as a forager." I cleared my throat. "And he worked in janitorial. They were quiet and followed the rules."

"What about your birth?"

Was she reading my mind? How did she know what to ask? I grew more and more irritated.

"Why does that matter?" I jeered.

She sighed. "I am irritating you." She paused. "I lean into the Mentality Aura and follow its guidance."

She was reading my mind.

"I never asked about my birth," I said. "They aren't my actual parents." I paused for a while as my words pierced me more than I expected them to. "She told me right before she died."

For the first time since entering her library, her face softened. "That had to be very difficult for you." Her Aura brushed against my own. If she had been reading my mind, I would've felt my Aura be tampered with. Right? Then why was I feeling hers for the first time?

"It was at the time, but I have moved past it," I said.

She pressed her lips together and arched her eyebrows up so high I swore they would fly off her face. "Big news like that does not briefly pass through us. It takes a heavy toll."

First, all the questions. Then, she tried to console me? What was her problem?

"I said I'm over it," I sharply replied.

"Understood." She raised both hands as if yielding, another wave of incense smoke washing over me. "So, you do not know much about their history?"

The audacity she had.

"I don't," I admitted.

Just as I answered her, a deep, hard pit formed in my gut. The pounding in my head returned. I didn't know who they were or how they found me, and the reality of not knowing worried me. My legs shook so I finally took a seat, anger no longer in control. Numbness washed over me like it always had since the Event. The sensation that first wave of numbness carried with it relieved all my worries. Existential relief, like cold water poured over your head on a hot day.

Then, clarity came in the form of mistrust. Why had I just told her all that? I locked in on her.

"Did you manipulate my Aura?"

"Yes." Her calculated, emotionless stare provided nothing more. "Sometimes the Mentality Aura is necessary to provide clarity."

Fire ignited in my gut and burned up to my thoughts. How dare she violate me like that.

"You have no right." I glowered.

"I have heard you have been Manipulating the Surprisants with ease." She cocked her head, the first real movement she displayed since I arrived.

"Yes, and?"

"What is the difference with you Manipulating and me doing the same? We are Manipulators, after all."

A primal grunt forced its way out of my chest, relieving the fire. I found myself admiring her tenacity. "Fair."

Whether out of mutual respect or mutual irritation, a necessary silence fell in between us. She pressed at my numb countenance, yet she appeared just as numb as I was. I respected that.

"If you allow me," her words flickered my wandering mind back to reality, "I can access your network and find memories from when you were young. These memories could shed some light on their history."

"Why is that necessary?" My voice teetered between carelessness and curiosity. Numbness would do whatever it could to keep me docile.

"It may help understand why she did what she did." She leaned forward, elbows resting on the desk. "Do you really think she did not care for you?"

"Of course not," I said so quickly I surprised even myself. "She died trying to protect me." My hurt from her betrayal had just in turn been betrayed by my instinct to defend her.

"Their history may give you answers to the questions burning within."

Anger returned. "What gives you the right to this information?" I asked as I pushed her Aura away from mine. "And stop trying to Manipulate me!"

She glared at me. "You think you are stronger than I am?"

"I have abilities that the other Mentalists cannot comprehend."

Whatever contest she had with me, I would best her. I believed it. I had control over my emotions.

"Fine." A guttural sigh blew at the papers on her desk. "Stand and duel with me." She stood up and stepped into an open area of the room.

Words were one thing but dueling with the Soothsayer, the strongest Mentalist in Labyrintha, would be a bigger feat than the Surprisants I bested. Puffing my chest out, I mustered all the courage I could find.

I stumbled over my chair as I stood to face her. This had to have been her end goal the entire time. She wanted to learn my weaknesses and then defeat me to stop the whispers of others. Little did she know I was much stronger than she could ever anticipate.

"Good," I said. "Are you ready for me?"

"Please, begin," she calmly said.

I quickly grabbed her Aura and pushed it to her eyes. A young girl stood before her with her back facing me. The younger girl said to the Soothsayer, "When can we be normal?'

The Soothsayer looked at the girl for a moment before looking up at me. She quickly swirled her right hand and sliced toward me. I looked up at the ceiling for no reason and started to run in circles. I became so dizzy but didn't stop running. I eventually fell over from being so dizzy as I heard footsteps come toward me. The person took their foot and planted it on my side as if I were a small hill they were claiming.

"I claim victory," the Soothsayer said before moving her hands slightly, and the room looked familiar to me again. She helped me up.

"I..." I began to say but had no words. Just as she made me confess my secrets, she made me lose my mind. Instead of anger, I desired her power. She could teach me. I needed her.

"You have much to learn," she interrupted my silent response. "Tell me, what does Aura look like to you?"

Her question surprised me. "The Perceptionists asked me the same question, and they determined I wasn't a Perceptionist because of it."

She stared, unblinking. "What does it look like?"

My response worried me. "Like little bubbles flowing around, reflecting every color." I watched her Aura dance in response. "Does that sound…right to you?"

"Unlike Perception, Mentality looks different to every Manipulator." She looked above my head at my Aura. "It is the beauty of it."

"What does it look like to you?"

Her eyes fixed on me again. "Beauty is to the one who sees it."

"That isn't an answer." I raised my eyebrows.

"It is not." She dipped her head slightly. "Now, would you like me to help you?"

"Yes," I said, finally believing the power she held. "What do I do?"

"Lay on this couch and close your eyes," she said to me. "Relax and breathe in and out. I am going to lightly touch your head, and you will feel pressure in your mind. The pressure is normal, and I cannot have you lose focus on your breathing."

I positioned my back on the couch, and she touched the side of my head. I quickly felt my Aura jabbed. The pressure was more like a punch. I stopped breathing for a second but remembered to concentrate on my breathing. Suddenly, a clouded world appeared. I could look around and hear it, but I could not feel it. I recognized where we were. We were in Toterrum. There was a small child playing in a room. I quickly recognized my home back in Toterrum. The wooden cabinets and wooden walls blended into one another. The child fell over and hit their head on a chair. The child started crying as two people ran in and helped the child up. They were my parents. That child was me.

My mother picked me up and said, "Shh, it will be okay. You're going to have a lot of pain in this city, but you need to be strong. You have so much inside you, and we will do all we can to protect you."

I settled down. She put me back on the ground with my toys. They headed to the other room. "You're a good mother," my father said.

"Should we have really brought him to Toterrum?" she asked.

"We had an opportunity we had to take," he said. "His parents would have done the same."

"I know," she replied. "I just feel like we are responsible for something we never thought we would have to be. I love him, but this role wasn't what we planned."

"Their death wasn't something any of us planned either, but we made a promise, and we will keep it," he said.

The world faded as I opened my eyes. I was back in the library.

"They aren't from Toterrum?" I asked.

"It appears they are not," the Soothsayer said.

"Why did they bring me into that wretched city?"

"I am not sure, but it seems like they chose to."

"They are bigger monsters than I thought." Had they even loved me?

"We will just have to figure out whether they are good or bad monsters," she stated. "Do not make up your mind so quickly. We only saw a couple minutes of their history. If we judged everyone for only a couple minutes, we would make so many mistakes on people's character."

My mind buzzed from her wisdom. I had a lot to learn, and she would be my teacher. I just had to follow her lead.

"Then let's keep looking," I said as I put my head back down.

"I think that is enough for today," she said. "Remember, I am still human, and this type of Manipulation drains me. Especially when the subject is resistant."

"Sorry. I'll be better next time."

"I know you will." She picked up a book from her desk and handed it to me. "In the meantime, I want you to read this book. It reviews the geography of Biome. You may as well start gathering more knowledge as we go on."

"Thank you," I said, my head still shaking from all the thoughts I had about my fake parents.

"Knowing only works if we listen," she said as she smiled. "And as much as your mind makes you think it needs to keep everything in, doing this will cause more damage than healing."

She knew about the shaking in my head. That was no surprise since she had just entered my mind. I stepped outside and instantly Ricochet's Aura tickled mine. He beckoned me to the pond. I leaned back into his and made my way.

The thing I appreciated about Labyrintha's streets was how quiet it was. I ran into few people, which allowed me to leave the city quickly, make my way to the small forest, and find the pond where Ricochet greeted me with nudges and licks. He always made me feel welcomed.

I spent my afternoon by the pond reading the book the Soothsayer gave me. The book kept me distracted from my tired thoughts. Ricochet and I played fetch in between chapters. Each time he jumped to catch the ball, I swore I saw the ball as a faded dot within my own sight. Ricochet's Aura lit up as I noticed this in bright yellow streaks racing to my own Aura. The approach made me stumble before it faded away. He ran over to lick my face.

"Sorry, buddy." I scratched his ear, trying to push his fishy, hot breath away from my face. "I don't know what that was." He gave a look of indifference and another lick before his ears perked, Aura flooded to his sides, and he ran after something he heard in the forest.

After repositioning myself into another lounged position, I breathed in the scents of the mossy pond and flipped open the book. I already knew some of the information found in the book. Toterrum sat in the mines, Flaunte near the mouth of the Rithbar River, and Labyrintha was within the Black Stone Mountains. The south, where Luck was supposed to be, was smudged. There were hills around the smudge that read "The Rolling Hills." The Coral Forest was north of Toterrum, with the Great Plains in between. Rithbar had another river running North to South. It was called the Biome River. Straight North of Rithbar, where the Biome River ended, was the Tundra. It had white specks on it like the Black Stone Mountains, but more. The specks indicated snow, and it looked like it had a lot.

One interesting note during my quick review was about the history of the wall. Constructed during Toterrum's beginning, portions of the wall had been knocked down during small battles, by unruly citizens, and through natural disasters. But the history of its breakage stopped around the fall of Rithbar. My teachings with Allen Sand reviewed many attempts to break the wall. I heard rumors within Toterrum of people trying to break the wall. But no one succeeded. In fact, the wall may not have been damaged since Toterrum claimed dominion over Biome. Why was that? I remembered its eerie presence when standing next to it. It always omitted such unsettling energy.

Then, I came to another section about the Rolling Hills.

The Rolling Hills landscape consists of large, grassy hills with rounded edges. Unlike the jagged edges of the Black Stone Mountains left by abrupt shifts in the ground, the Rolling Hills have been slowly eroded over time. This gives them a smooth surface where grass grows in abundance. Whenever it rains, the hills direct the water to various pockets. These pockets form small lakes. It is said the water from these lakes bless anyone who drinks it with good luck. The bottoms of the lakes also are a source of gold. But the lakes are very deep, making it very difficult to mine the gold. During a sunny day, the lakes glow golden.

The water sounded like water I desperately needed to drink. With so much bad luck, I could use some good luck. This also made sense as to why the Luck Manipulators had their capital in the area. Along with luck, I could also use some gold. The Tundra description caught my attention as well.

The Tundra is covered in snow most of the year. Only during the summer months are the color-changing stones covering the ground revealed. These stones are unique to this area. In the sun, they glow red. When cold, they glow blue. Many other colors are seen, but the sources of the changing color are still unknown. A large, inactive volcano sits in the middle where few people have been. The travel is difficult and only recommended during the summer. Even then, the terrain shifts without snow, keeping the rocks together, and the color-changing rocks release a lot of heat it absorbs from the sun.

"I bet you could run right across those rocks, Ricochet," I said as I rubbed his head. He yawned in response. "I knew it, a piece of cake." I took a little nap with him by the water.

***

When I woke up, I realized I had slept much longer than I wanted to and was late to combat training. I ran to the training grounds where people were paired up.

"Nice of you to join us, Yaron," Brysen said to me.

"I'm so sorry," I replied as best I could in between heavy breathing as I bowed.

"Today, I taught on pushing into someone's Aura and being able to tell when they will attack," Brysen said. "When this is sensed, you should throw something at the person's head to ruin their concentration. This allows you to rush in for a closer attack."

"What do you throw?" I asked.

"Whatever you find around you," Brysen replied. "It could be sand, a rock, sticks, water, or really anything. Our bodies reply to stimuli around us. When you throw something at the face, the body has reflexes that will overpower concentration. Try it on me. Do not throw too early, wait until you sense my Aura moving on yours to attack."

I stood across from him. He went in for a physical attack, so I threw sand at him. He brushed it away with his hands as he closed in and knocked me over. "Ouch," I said as I hit the ground.

"Remember, it is the Aura you want to watch, not the physical movement," he said. "The physical movement is not deterred as much. It is all about where the concentration lies."

We tried again, and he charged at me. I dodged and pushed away from him. Then, his Aura began to vibrate, and I threw the sand. He hit it away as I closed in and knocked his feet out from under him. "Very good," he said as I helped him up.

We practiced this for the next hour before we practiced general combat again. Aurora and Naso trained with other Surprisants. Naso struggled at the beginning but seemed to get it by the end. As I watched him, he carefully analyzed each foe and threw sand just as they moved their hands. Of course, he didn't need to be a Manipulator to figure out the opportune time.

Brysen brought everyone back together and announced, "I have been very pleased with everyone's progress. We normally have a lot more training before I induct you as a Surprisant, but the pressure on Labyrintha is growing, and we need you ready to fight if the threat comes along. Therefore, we will be climbing to the top of the Black Stone Mountains for your ceremonial induction. We will take a break tomorrow and meet earlier the next morning to make the hike. Knowing only works if you listen." He bowed.

Zela ran up to me and said, "This is exciting! Remember when I said I have only been to the top once? This was what it was for. You get to climb to the top!"

I was nervous and excited at the same time as I looked upward. The black stones disappeared in a thick, white cloud. I couldn't even see the top. "Are you going up again?" I asked.

"Yes!" she said. "Of course I am. No hang-out tonight. I have a date."

"Oh!" I said. "With who?"

"You do not know her, but she…works in the library," Zela responded.

An odd jealousy burrowed down my throat and clenched my chest.

"Her?" I asked without meaning to out loud.

"Yes, she is my fiancé," she responded with a raised eyebrow. "What did you think? I was into you?"

Whatever momentary jealousy revealed itself disappeared into a meaningless memory.

"No." I blushed. "I just thought you weren't into dating."

She responded as if knowing my thoughts, "I'm sorry your ego was harmed. You know people can just be friends with each other?"

Without a doubt, I knew Zela was a friend. It made me laugh to think of her in any other way.

"I know," I said. "My head is just all over the place lately."

"It's okay," she said. "I know I'm attractive, and you cannot keep your eyes off me." She batted her eyes. We both laughed. She zoomed away in excitement.

I walked over to Naso and Aurora. "I didn't know we were joining the Surprisants."

"Neither did I," Aurora responded. "But it's better than sitting around. We should be helping."

"Maybe I'll get to use these new Snowberries Herita found while hiking," Naso said as he held them up. "If you drop them down a snow hill, they will start grabbing onto everything around as they roll. They eventually turn into a ball made of snow and other stuff, reaching the size of a house. I think bowling some Vigorists sounds fun."

"That climb looks...fun," I said.

"Fun is not the word I would use," Aurora said, looking up with me.

"It'll be a piece of cake," Naso said while putting an arm around each of us.

"Pretty sure you're afraid of heights," I said.

"This was before I became a Surprisant," he said as he started kicking and punching the air.

"So scary." Aurora chuckled as I joined in before she narrowed her eyes on me.

"What?" I asked.

She smiled. "Nothing."

***

The next day, I entered the library and didn't see the Soothsayer.

"Hello," I said with no response.

She must've been late. So, I started reading book titles from the nearby bookshelf. One book caught my eye, titled *Navigating the Rolling Hills*. I opened it up and flipped through the pages. I read a page I landed on.

Follow the path of the water to each part.

Bring the correct item to start.

Here is where you will find the game.

Winning it will give you reward and fame.
Keep moving forward or fall behind.
Only then will you seek what you want to find.

A picture of green hills with golden water in between was painted below the poem. The flow of the hills seemed to make a progression to larger lakes. I quickly turned to the next page, but it was ripped out. From then on, the book covered various uses for the Rolling Hill's grass.

"That book holds a lot of mystery," someone said from behind.

I fumbled at the book and dropped it to the floor. The firm smack it made echoed.

"I see why a future Surprisant is named the way they are," the Soothsayer continued. "So jumpy."

"I'm sorry if I was looking at something I shouldn't have been," I said as I picked the book up and put it back.

"This is a library," she said. "All of these books are available to anyone who wants to look. Knowledge is not limited. It is available to those who seek it."

"So, you can tell me what the missing page says?" I asked.

"Me telling you what is available to you is not any sign of effort to seek it," she replied.

"So that's a no," I said as she smiled.

"Should we start looking at your past again?" she asked.

"Yes," I said as I lay down. She touched the side of my head. The same feeling rushed through me as she touched my Aura, and the world changed around me.

Two toddlers playing with blocks sat on a familiar floor. Two females' voices echoed from the kitchen. I moved toward the voices until I saw Mrs. Crimson talking to my mom. My mother was crying. I realized the other child with me was Asher.

"I just can't keep living in this city," my mother said. "There's no freedom, and everything I do is wrong and corrected by people I hate."

"This is the difficult part of being an informant," Mrs. Crimson said. "We are giving up our freedoms so we can hopefully create a safer world for our kids. I question everything I do every day. My husband's life is in danger every time he gets more information to pass on."

"It's only a matter of time before something happens," my mother said. "If my husband dies, I will have nothing else to live for. This will all be for nothing."

"You have Yaron to live for," Mrs. Crimson said as she reached and held my mother's hands. "Just like I have Asher to live for."

"But Asher is your child," my mother said. "Yaron was given to us to protect."

Mrs. Crimson cocked her head. "Yaron isn't your son?" she whispered.

My mother's eyes enlarged. "I shouldn't have said that." She paused. "We knew his parents, and we made a promise that we would keep Yaron safe," she whispered back. "We were already chosen to be informants and couldn't back away from this, even with our new companion." My mother leaned in to whisper more, but I couldn't hear it. I tried to get closer, but still nothing.

"You are his mother now," Mrs. Crimson said as she held my mother's face. "Listen to me. You must be strong. Any sign of weakness, they will know. Don't tell anyone else about Yaron's origin."

My mother wept as their images faded away, yet the room stayed the same. I moved back to the living room, where the toddlers no longer played. Instead, my mother was sleeping on the couch while holding me. A loud knock on the door made my heart jump. She woke up and put me on the couch as I let out small cries but appeared to remain somewhat asleep. The window was foggy, and I couldn't tell if it was night or day. I noticed the blocks Asher and I played with earlier, still laid out across the floor. I think it was the same day.

My mother opened the door as a hooded figure stepped in and shut it quietly behind, while waving their hand around. Mrs. Crimson was revealed beneath the dark hood. She held Asher underneath her cloak. Mrs. Crimson put Asher down on a chair and started sobbing as my mother hugged her.

"What happened?" my mother asked.

"He's dead," Mrs. Crimson said. "He was killed."

"Who's dead?" my mother asked.

Mrs. Crimson's swollen face just stared at my mother's. My mother covered her mouth with her hand. It was Mr. Crimson. It was the day he died.

"What happened?" my mother asked.

"Another Officer working with him found him sneaking information and confronted him," Mrs. Crimson began, holding back whimpers. "There was fighting. I had to use everything I could to keep anyone from seeing it. The other Officer took him down. I took all my Aura and threw it at the Officer, and his mind broke. Everything else is a blur." A held-back screech squeezed out of Mrs. Crimson, like she was trying to keep her sobs hidden.

"Did anyone see you?" my mother asked.

"No one did," Mrs. Crimson replied. "I have to tell my sister. She needs to know."

"Your sister?" my mother asked. "Does she live here?"

"No," Mrs. Crimson said as she shuffled through her bag. "She's my contact, and I can write to her using this." She started writing, but tears dripped onto the sheet as she wiped them away with her sleeve. She was using the communication method I learned and still used from Flaunte. "I can't do this."

"I'll do it," my mother said as she took the pen. "What's her name?"

"Herita," Mrs. Crimson said as she sat down and stared at Asher. "Please tell her we are safe and the package was delivered. Can you please tell her that you are watching over me? I don't want her to attack the city."

My mother picked up the pen as toddler me sat up and rubbed his eyes. My mother put her other arm around the younger me to scratch my back as she wrote. It made me angry watching her hold the pen and paper that I used to reveal my location when she betrayed me. Yet, she still comforted the younger me.

Herita,

Douglas has been killed. Asher and I are safe. The package was delivered.

We are going to stay. I have a friend who is helping look after me. If for some reason you ever come across her adopted son, please protect him. His name is Yaron Meek. He is a good friend of Asher.

With a deep heart,

She handed the letter over to Mrs. Crimson, who signed her name and folded the letter. She opened the window and let the letter go. "Thank you," Mrs. Crimson said as they all faded away. I was back in the library and sat straight up.

"Herita knew who I was." I cracked out. My heart weighed on me so much I leaned forward. "Mrs. Crimson knew my mother was not my mother." Rage built up within me.

"This is curious," the Soothsayer said. "Cora did not read the letter when she signed it."

"Why does that matter?" I asked.

"Herita does not know this was a fraudulent request," she said.

I wished the Soothsayer would stop analyzing things so much. All I wanted to feel was anger at Herita's betrayal.

"So, are you saying Herita shouldn't have taken me in?" I asked.

"Yaron, Herita had no obligation to you either way. Herita is a good person."

I thought my fake parents were good people. I thought Ruth was a good person. Where did that get me?

"She's a liar," I coldly replied.

"You are being irrational." The Soothsayer shook her head. "You must face your trust issues that are continuing to break you down. This is causing anxiety that is blocking your network."

I didn't care. At all cost, I would protect myself.

"Are we done for today?" I asked with a blank stare, the same emptiness curling up within myself.

"Yes," she said. "Please be wise with your words."

"I will," I said as I stormed out the door.

I had no idea what to do. My breathing hastened. My chest tightened. I had to speak with Herita. I searched the city but couldn't find her. My head vibrated so hard my head pulsed with deep pain.

Just before I collapsed to the ground to contain my raging headache, Herita stepped out of a building near me. Serendipity at its finest.

Without hesitation, I walked straight up to her and said, "You're a liar." My finger jabbed into her chest.

"What's wrong?" Herita flatly asked. Her eyes drooped with dark gray bags underneath them. "Are you mad about me seeing a doctor?"

"No," I replied suddenly realizing that was where she just came out of. "You knew my name. You knew that my mother wasn't my mother."

Herita stared at me and rubbed her forehead. She seemed to know what I was talking about. "Yaron, I did," she admitted. "I knew way before we met. But I'm tired and can't deal with this today."

"You can't just avoid me! I deserve the truth!"

She threw her hands up as an illusion of a crowd came through, and she disappeared.

I looked around and couldn't find her. "Herita!" I screamed with no response. I slammed my back against the wall, dug my fingers into my hair, and looked up as I screamed at the sky.

Herita had been lying the entire time I had known her. How could I have been so foolish? I took a deep breath and allowed numbness to wash over me. Clarity returned. If she kept me at a distance, I would do the same. I would focus on the Mentality Aura and becoming a stronger Surprisant.

6

THE SURPRISANTS

Early morning fog still covered the city, like it did every morning. The morning sun wouldn't peak over the mountain for hours, yet my energy level was the highest it had been in too long. Despite how angry I was with Herita, I wouldn't let her deter me from bettering myself. I needed to focus. We would ascend the Black Stone Mountains that day.

I stayed up later than I wanted, waiting for Herita to arrive back at the house, but she never showed up. So many secrets continued to threaten me. And Herita, of all people? Why did people keep lying to me? I was sick of it, but dwelling in my frustration with her would do nothing for my hike, so I focused on the day ahead. Aurora and Naso walked into the kitchen and we all quietly made our way to the training grounds. I wanted to confront Aurora about what I had learned but decided to hold it in. It was not the time, but it crawled around in my head, wanting to break free.

Before I knew it, we arrived at the training grounds. We each looked up at the Black Stone Mountains. They suddenly appeared much larger than before.

"This will be a piece of cake." Naso scoffed. Aurora snickered.

Just as the last of the future Surprisants arrived, Brysen welcomed the group. "Good morning, my friends. In these bags are coats for anyone who does not have one." He looked at us. "As we get closer to the top, it will get much colder than it is down here. Much, much colder. The other bag has harnesses and ropes we will need for the steeper parts. You do not need to put those on now, but please make sure you have one. Most of you have hiked the trails that will bring us to the steep cliffs. This will be much more difficult. The mountains are known to provide insight where it is needed. You will find the steep cliffs will push your mind even harder. Surrender to the push. Let it wash over and take you over. A Surprisant must allow this in order to hit peak enlightenment. If you do not surrender, the mountain will push harder. Be prepared for this."

Brysen turned and walked toward the mountain as we all followed. Each person grabbed a Fact from the pile of battle sticks to help balance during the hike. The rod was much lighter than I expected, and its round head made of a denser part of the wood. Each time I lifted my Fact, the heavier head would fall just a little bit forward.

As the terrain steepened, the sticks bobbed more. Aurora's stick knocked against mine, which irritated me more than it should. Her curious expression lifted toward the mountain, reminding me of Herita, and that Herita lied to me. Why I felt the need to argue with Aurora about it was beyond me, but I closed my eyes a took a deep breath.

"Is something wrong?" Aurora asked.

I opened my eyes to find her soft meadow eyes and shoulders dipped down. Part of me wanted to collapse into her arms, but I needed to find strength.

"Nothing to do with you," I snapped back. I had to keep it contained.

Her shoulders stiffened. "Okay?" She furrowed her brow. "It sounds like it does."

And she was right, but I found myself continuing to push her away. I tried to let any numbness I could muster in as my anger bubbled. My throat became itchier the harder I kept it down. Then, it just popped out. "Did your aunt know about me prior to my arrival to Flaunte?" I asked so fast I barely had time to breathe. Though I failed at my task, the relief washing over me made me feel less guilty.

She chuckled and shook her head but stopped after witnessing my stern expression. "What are you talking about?"

"Just answer the question." I glared at her.

"How would she know about someone from Toterrum without going there herself?" Her posture stiffened even more. She threw her hand in the air. "It sounds like you are insinuating that she did."

I tried to keep it in. I wanted to keep it in, but I needed to let it out. Once I mentioned the truth, Aurora would fold.

"She's full of lies and found out about me from a letter your mother sent to her several years ago." Only after I said it did I remember she probably had no idea what I was talking about, but I wanted to let it all out against Herita, and Aurora was the closest I could get.

"What?" Aurora rolled her eyes. "One, you sound crazy. Two, how would you learn something like this?" She went pale. "Have you been communicating with my mother? Are you revealing more secrets again?"

"No!" I threw my hands in the air. "A session with the Soothsayer revealed it." I swallowed hard. "And what's that supposed to mean?"

"It sounds like you knew about it then." She turned her attention forward. "Otherwise, how would the Soothsayer find it in your mind?"

"You don't understand how our system works." Did I? "Your aunt is a liar."

She let out an irritated laugh and hit her Fact against mine. "So, now my aunt is someone else who you trusted and now betrayed you? Is that what this is?"

"If the shoe fits." I hit her Fact with mine.

"You have got to be kidding me!" Aurora yelled.

"Quiet down," Naso whispered. "You're making a scene."

Aurora gave Naso a brief glance before turning to me. In a loud whisper, she said, "My aunt has taken you in. She has clothed you, fed you, taught you, vouched for you, protected you, traveled with you, and so many other things. Do you really think she is an evil person you can't trust?" She jabbed the heavy end of her Fact into my chest.

"My mother did all of these same things for me and look what she did to me." I stepped forward, glaring into Aurora's meadow eyes.

For a moment, Aurora's eyes softened. "Yaron, I empathize with what you are dealing with and what she did, but Herita has done nothing to harm you." She stepped toward me, a new intense shade of green brightening her irises. "She's honest, trustworthy, and cares deeply for you. If you have a problem with her, bring it up to her. I'm sure she has a reason if it's true."

"I brought it up last night when I saw her downtown, and she refused to talk about it." My words were losing their edge. "She used a Perception and disappeared. I haven't seen her since."

"That's strange..." Aurora started before the group stopped hiking.

"Now that we are at the cliffs..." Brysen coughed after announcing, shifting awkwardly and staring at Aurora and me. "You will want to put on your harness and attach the two carabiner ropes to the front loop. There is a carabiner on each side of the rope. Make sure the carabiner is attached to the front loop for each rope. The other carabiner will be attached to the metal cords running zig-zag up the cliff. Make sure you fasten the carabiner each time you move the clip. Both carabiners should be attached before you move to another. For those of you who have not used a harness before, the veterans will walk around and assist you."

As I held the harnesses up, I didn't understand how it worked. Even after observing the others put them on, my comprehension of what was up and what was down made no sense. It became worse when I tried to put it on, getting tangled in a mess. I tried turning the harness around, but it still didn't look right. I threw it to the ground in frustration, Aurora making a noise at me.

"Need some help?" Zela asked as she walked up. "You know they go on your legs?"

"Yes," I flatly said, though the storm raging inside me that wanted to let loose.

Zela crossed her arms and popped her hip out. "Okay…" She calmly showed me which holes to step through as she somehow tightened them afterward. After she was done, she pulled on the front loop straight up, lifting me into the air by my hips as the center portion hiked up my groin area.

"Ouch!" I yelled.

"Ouch means it's on good."

Zela smacked my back, hard, forcing me to waddle forward, unsure of how to walk in the harness. After Naso got help with his, he moved forward, legs not bending, looking more uncomfortable than me. Aurora put hers on with ease. Zela then showed Naso and me how to work the carabiners. One by one, each person started to clip onto the wires and climbed across the ledge. Aurora went first followed by Naso, trembling so hard the wire shook.

"I thought this was a piece of cake?" I asked.

"Shut up. Shut up. Shut up." Each of his steps moved slower than the last.

Naso let nearly everyone pass us, except for me and Zela right behind me. I tried my best to keep some distance between Naso and me so as not to put too much pressure on him.

"Your friend is slow," Zela whispered from behind.

"I know," I replied.

"I can hear you and imagine I'm glaring at you…but I'm not going to turn my head around." Naso tried to sound arrogant but the shakiness in his voice sharply contradicted any attempt he made.

For every gap we moved along the wires, there was a large landing separating us from the next portion with a little less of a steep hike. Then, we were back to the wires. We did this about five times. The mountain began to level off as we came to a very snowy portion. Frigid air cut across my cheeks even after putting on the thicker coat. Billowing snow traversed just above the ground at the wind's command, making it difficult to see.

"Stay close together as we hike through this portion," Brysen yelled through the wind. "Here is where the mountain will test your mind."

Brysen said the mountain would test our minds, but what did he mean by that?

We hiked through the thick snow. I could only see Aurora in front of me and Zela behind. Though Naso stayed close to me during the steep portions, he could care less once on terrain he felt comfortable hiking. Aurora moved slower than I expected, the high altitude slowing her breathing. The wind howled a tune of disheartening melancholy. We hiked for maybe ten minutes, but it felt like hours. Aurora stopped and turned to us.

"I can't see Naso in front of me," she yelled while shielding her face from the bitter wind.

I tried stepping forward and didn't see him either. Zela did the same, and nothing.

"Stay here," Zela said closely to our faces. "Hold onto this end of the rope while I hike a little bit ahead to look for the group. I don't know the top of the mountain well enough to lead us." She walked away, disappearing in an instant.

"Way to go!" I yelled at Aurora.

"He was right in front of me!" she yelled back. "It's not my fault!"

My mind throbbed. A storm swirled inside me like the storm whipping around me. My Aura started to bounce on my brain at the beat of the war drum that constantly haunted me and my every decision and thought.

Bang. Bang. Bang.

I couldn't contain it. Harsh words started pouring out of my mouth. "You're *just* like your aunt. Untrustworthy."

Aurora pushed at me and roared, "You're the one who keeps causing problems for everyone else!" She pushed me again. "As much as you blame your mom, you're the one who told her where we were. You're the reason we were ambushed."

"If I cause everyone else so many problems, why do you keep staying around me?" I stepped into her next shove.

"That's a good question!" She shoved harder, knocking me to my butt. "I don't know why I bother." She started walking away.

"Stop that!" I yelled. "We're supposed to stay together!"

She faced me. "Then act like we should stay together!"

"You don't understand what I'm going through!" I stood up.

"You're so self-absorbed!"

"Better to be self-absorbed than so unaware of the lies that surround you." I stepped toward her.

"What are you talking about?" She threw her hands in the air. "What did the Soothsayer show you? What in your past could cause you to think so many things?"

I bit my lip, trying to hold the next part in. "The day your father died," I flatly said, watching her expression shift. "My fake mother was the person your mother confided in. She had her write the letter to Herita explaining what had happened. She had her write that my mother was keeping her safe and that if she ever came across her adopted son, Yaron Meek, to please take care of him." I licked my freezing lips, causing them to freeze together for a moment before pulling them apart. "Herita received this letter and had my name way before I came to Flaunte."

"You were there when my father died?" Aurora asked, shaking. She sat down in the snow.

"I was," I replied. "But I was so young."

"Were you even planning to tell me this, or were you too fixated on how this impacted you?" Small icicles rolled down her cheeks.

My Aura bounced more aggressively, pounding on my head. Bang. Bang. BANG.

"I'M NOT OKAY!" I yelled as I fell to my knees. "All of these people I trust are failing me. Everything I knew was a lie. Toterrum. My parents. Ruth. Herita. I have nothing to hold onto anymore. Nothing makes sense."

My brain rattled from exhaustion and effort to keep warm. A sharp pain pierced the area where my brain met my neck. I could fall into the snow and never rise. Would that be so bad? It would stop the pain in my head. As my cheeks numbed, I craved more numbness to keep my racing thoughts at bay.

After a brief pause, Aurora walked over, knelt, and hugged me. I put my head on her chest, her warmth rushing over me. "You aren't the only one who feels like their parents abandoned them," she said. "Mine literally gave me up. I know it was to keep me safe, but they kept Asher."

A soft silence surrounded us, only accented by the whistling wind. The melancholy it once had was eclipsed by Aurora's steady breaths. Then, a little beast popped its head out of the snow. Large, blue eyes stared at me within a round, fluffy white fur-covered body.

"We are apparently the unwanted kids," I joked. Her laughter made my head vibrate. The odd sensation made me join her laughter.

"I don't trust anyone either," she said. "Just like I told you in Flaunte, my friends turned on me when I was young. They were people I trusted, and they betrayed me. I am never good enough."

"Are you kidding?" I asked. "You're one of the most beautiful, talented, strong women I know. I just realized something." A deep shade of maroon flushed her cheeks, a stark juxtaposition to the white snow billowing around us. My chest warmed. "You're one of the few people I trust."

"Then why have you been pushing me away?" Her meadow green eyes vibrated. "And you have to stop saying things like this. You have Felicity."

I did have Felicity. "You're right. I'm sorry. You and Naso are my best friends. I haven't been a good friend lately."

I noticed another beast popped its head out next to the other. It was the oddest thing, as little toothy grins peeked out of their fluffy bodies.

"Thank you." She stared above my head. "I've missed you. But your Aura...it hasn't been the same. It's like you've been a different person."

I *was* a different person.

"I don't know," I replied. "I think I'm afraid I'll lose you someday. I have to have my heart ready for that."

Aurora stared at me before pushing my shoulder. "That's stupid. You won't ever lose me. I trust you. More than my own mom. You make me feel better about who I am."

My Aura finally stopped bouncing around my head and gravitated through my body at a speed it hadn't in quite some time. It went over to Aurora's Aura without me prompting it and rubbed against hers. A warm sensation rushed across my body. My head still pounded as I thought about Herita and my dead parents, but having Aurora to talk to was just...right. Three more beasts popped out around us. Aurora finally noticed them.

"Looks like we have company," Aurora said, smiling at the beasts.

"I think they are sensing our distress," I said. "Little beacons of hope." I patted the ground near one of the beasts as its little body shivered in delight. "Can I tell you something?"

"Of course," she replied.

"I think I have something wrong going on in my head," I admitted. "You're right. My Aura has been off. There has always been this weird pounding in my head, but it's been worse since coming to Labyrintha. I feel disconnected. More than I ever have before."

"That I understand," she said. "I think this is why we get each other so well." She smiled. "Thank you for telling me this."

"Thank you for listening," I replied. "It feels good to say it out loud."

"My aunt has been sneaking around more than she ever has," she said out of nowhere. "I have been anxious around her. Something is going on with her, and part of me questioned her trustworthiness when you confronted me. I think that is partly why I was so defensive."

I suddenly remembered Herita coming out of a doctor's office when I confronted her. "When I accosted Herita in the city, she was coming out of a doctor's office and looked distraught."

"She what?" Aurora cocked her head.

The rope tightened and pulled at us. Without hesitation, we stood and followed the rope, the little beasts burrowing back into the snow. The blowing snow worsened, but we kept pushing forward. Before I knew it, we left the snow and walked into a brilliantly clear sky. We were on top of the mountain, and everyone else was looking around. Behind me, a wall of snow whistled its song of melancholy. The pounding in my head lessened.

Brysen stood next to Zela, who held the rope, and said, "I see. The mountain was not satisfied with you. I am glad you overcame what needed to be overcome."

"The mountain?" I asked.

"I was serious when I said the mountain will push on you," he responded. "If it finds an area that you are not confronting, it will force it out of you until you do."

I realized I had something big to admit while in there. "I felt pushed," I said.

"Me too," Aurora added.

"Hopefully, you got some answers," Zela said as she smiled at us. "It wanted just the two of you."

"Gather around!" Brysen yelled. "Please, take your Facts out and hold it in front of you." Brysen held out his Facts, grasping it with two hands and holding it parallel to the ground. "You have all overcome physical and mental training. Welcome to the highest point in Biome. Mentality has washed over each of you and made you stronger, wiser, and more confident. Being inducted into the Surprisant Rank is a lifelong offering. When called upon, you are making a pledge to protect, build up, and push Mentality onto any foe that stands before you. Knowing only works if you listen."

"Knowing only works if you listen," we as a group echoed.

"Please, soak in this accomplishment and be proud of who you were, who you are, and who you will become," Brysen said.

Just as Zela said, the entire horizon was covered in clouds. The way the sun shined on them made them look like giant, warm mountains slowly moving across time and space. My heart thudded so loudly in my chest; its rhythmic beat made me want to dance. Rather than dance, I found myself taking in the view with Aurora on my left and Naso on my right. I reached out around each of their shoulders and pulled them in.

"I'm sorry for the way I've been," I said. "I'm pledging to you both right here and right now that I'll deal with my issues. Just hold me accountable. No more keeping things a secret. You're my best friends, and I love you both."

Aurora kissed me on the cheek, and I blushed. The touch reminded me of when Aurora kissed me during the Festival in Flaunte. She had shown her affection for me, and I shut her down. The rosiness in her cheeks made me think she thought about that previous interaction like I was. I glanced over at her before Naso smashed his lips against my other cheek, smothering his lips against me. An unwelcome, necessary distraction from the heat left on my other cheek that Aurora kissed. All of it was for the best.

"Aw, thanks. I love you, too." He pushed his face against mine as I tried to push him off. He glanced at Aurora. "And just to keep the whole secret thing off the table, Aurora and I have been practicing something new."

"New?" I asked.

"I've been noticing more and more how Aura interacts with people and beasts," Aurora said. "I know Perceptionists are known for gaining partner beasts, but I think anyone may be capable of it."

"Anyone?" I asked, unintentionally glancing at Naso.

"Hey!" He rolled his eyes. "Yes, anyone. I've been trying to connect with beasts."

I thought about Ricochet and how important he was to me. Could Naso do the same?

"And?" I eagerly asked.

He sighed. "And nothing so far."

"But we're making progress," Aurora added with bright eyes and a large smile.

I wondered at the idea of Manipulators and non-Manipulators obtaining partner beasts. Aurora's affinity for beasts and their interaction with Aura went unmatched. I believed she'd figure something out.

***

The journey back down the mountain seemed effortless compared to the way up. At least it was through the thick snow. Whatever caused my Aura to pound against my head did nothing to me the second time through. The descent, on the other hand, terrified me. Staring down every step you took meant you couldn't ignore just how far one could fall if a step slipped or was misplaced. Naso had the hardest time of everyone. We had to blindfold him during the steepest portion. He wouldn't move if we hadn't.

"Hey, you three," Zela said to us as everyone split up at the bottom of the mountain. "We are having a small party at my house to celebrate. You should all come."

"I really have something I need to take care of," Aurora said.

"I'm sure it can wait until later." Zela patted Aurora's back. "You just accomplished something amazing and deserve to celebrate it."

"Can we please?" Naso pouted his lips and widened his eyes like a puppy. "I've never been to a house party. Unless the public punishment of my father five years ago in our own home counts."

He grinned. We all stared at him quietly.

"Oh, come one," he said. "I was joking!"

"I guess I do not understand Toterrum humor," Zela awkwardly replied.

"Neither do I, and I grew up there," I added.

"Oh, whatever," Naso said. "I still really want to go."

We looked at Aurora. I knew she really wanted to talk to Herita, but I think we deserved to have fun.

"Okay, fine," Aurora agreed.

"Great!" Zela said. "Follow me."

We followed Zela through the city. She lived in the far northern section. The houses started to run up cliffs along a zig-zag street that climbed up as the cliffs became steeper. Zela's gray stone house lined in a crisscross pattern with gray wood stood two stories high. Fewer windows covered the walls compared to the buildings in the rest of the city. The inside was covered in gray floors, gray walls, and gray furniture with pops of blue here and there. Other non-Surprisant citizens already filled half the space.

"I want you all to meet my fiancé, Lilah," Zela said.

A taller girl with fair skin and dark hair stepped up next to Zela. Blue sparkles lined just her eyelids.

"It is very nice to meet you, especially you, Yaron," Lilah said. "Zela has said so many great things about you."

"It's great to meet you," I said. Zela really didn't talk about Lilah much, but apparently, Zela talked about me. "Zela is quickly becoming a very good friend of mine."

Naso scrunched his face, just like he did when we learned about Lady Sandra from Flaunte and her relationship with women. In Toterrum, same-sex relationships were forbidden, so the idea was still new to us.

"Naso, say hello," I said.

Naso looked over at me and then said, "It's great to meet you as well. I'm sorry for my blank look. We are still getting used to the cultures in other cities. Not that your culture is different, we just aren't used to people like you. I don't mean people like you, I mean..."

"Naso," Zela interrupted, "calm down. We know Toterrum does not allow same-sex relationships. Therefore, we are happy we do not live there."

Naso let out a sigh of relief. "I'm really just adapting." He scratched the back of his head.

"And that is okay," Lilah said. "As long as others are open to diversity, we are patient with their learning. We are blessed by the Great Light to live in Labyrintha. This city welcomes all who are transparent, like our buildings. Knowing only works if you listen."

"I like you, Lilah," I said. "You are very comforting."

"You are too kind," she responded. "I do not deserve any praise. I still have listening I need to do to improve."

"Lilah sells herself short," Zela said. "She is the Cerebrum of Diplomacy. She was picked for her brilliance and inclusivity. She also—"

Lilah interrupted her, "That is plenty of praise for one day." She kissed Zela on the cheek.

I suddenly recognized her from the initial meeting I had with the Cerebrums. "You were at my first meeting with the Soothsayer," I said.

"I was," Lilah said with a smile. "I know we did not get a chance to meet, but I did not want to assume you remembered me."

My face suddenly dropped. "You were there for my misidentification of the Soothsayer."

"I was, and it was most embarrassing," she responded as she giggled. We all laughed. "Zela speaks highly of your Mentality Manipulations. I hope I get a chance to see them soon. We will have to wait on the Soothsayer for that."

"I'm making progress." I shrugged.

"Good." She smiled with her eyes shut and head turned to the side.

"Let me grab you all drinks," Zela said as she scooped a blue drink into glass cups. She handed a cup to each of us.

Little pops and sizzles came from the concoction as a berry-forward scent galvanized my thirst. The drink went down sweet with a warm feeling at the end. It really made me relax.

"What is this?" I asked.

"Mind Freer," Lilah responded.

"It's delicious," Naso said.

"Do not drink it too quickly, though," Zela said. "Your mind will become too free." They laughed. "We should get some music going!"

We began dancing. Everyone seemed to know the words to the songs, but we at least could move the beat and have a good time. The next few hours went by quickly as we all had a great time. The more Mind Freer we drank, the looser our limbs flailed around.

Moments came when I feared an Officer would appear and break up the party and punish all involved. Those moments faded. Moments came when I remembered dancing in Flaunte and all the freedom we had there. I held tightly to those moments. Maybe the past and present could coexist. At a party, that certainly seemed possible.

Aurora finally was ready to leave. We could have stayed longer, but she wanted us to walk her back.

"That was fun!" Naso exclaimed. "We need to go to parties more often."

"Hopefully, they become a normal thing once Toterrum doesn't suppress its citizens," I replied.

"Amen to that," Naso said as he ran ahead, still dancing. The Mind Freer seemed to still be keeping him free.

Aurora was quiet. "What did you want to bring up to Herita?" I asked.

"I'm not sure," she replied. "I want to ask her about the doctor she's seeing."

"Are you nervous?" I asked.

"I think I am."

We walked in silence for the remainder of our trek back. Once we arrived, Herita sat by a light, reading. As we entered, Herita said, "Hello. Where were you all?"

"At a house party!" Naso said. "I like house parties."

"I assume this means you are all Surprisants now?" she asked.

"We are," I said begrudgingly.

"Aunt Herita," Aurora said. "Can I talk to you?"

"Certainly," she said as she put her book down and glared over at me.

"In private," Aurora said, looking back at us. "Maybe outside?"

"Wherever you find it best," Herita said as she rose. They made their way outside and started walking down the street.

"How mad are you at Herita?" Naso asked.

"I'm pretty mad," I replied. "I feel betrayed."

"There are a lot of bad people out there," he said. "Toterrum was covered in them. We both know what those people are like. Herita is not a bad person."

It was a brief statement, but he was right. As much as I was mad at her for not telling me, she was not a bad person. She really had done so much for us. Or maybe the Mind Freer still kept me looser than I should be.

"It's still hard," I said.

"You'll get over it," Naso said. "There are worse things that have happened to you, and you have gotten over them."

"My mom is making the whole situation much more difficult," I said.

"She made things much more complicated," he added.

"Yes, she did," I said. "She was still a good mom. As much as I am mad at what she did, I don't think she had a lot of options with their situation."

"She was a great mom." Naso put his arm around me. "She has helped my family so much."

"She also helped the Crimsons as well," I added.

"She did?" he asked.

I stepped in front of him and outside of his grasp. "My mom supported Mrs. Crimson when Mr. Crimson was killed. She has done so much."

"Herita has become another mother to me," Naso admitted. "I have really missed spending my whole day with her like I did in Flaunte."

"She has become a mother to me as well," I concurred. I never thought about it that way until Naso said it.

"Well, I'm tired and need to write my mother," Naso said. "Today was fun." He touched my shoulder and made his way to bed.

"Today was fun," I said as he closed the door. I made my way to my room and saw a letter from Felicity. As tired as I was, I read it right away.

Dearest Yaron,

My heart is so heavy for your loss. Your parents were such kind people, and I cannot imagine what you are going through. You had no obligation to tell me sooner. I'm glad you now have. I wish I could see you and hug you.
I have no words for her reveal. Being lied to this whole time cannot be mixing well with her murder. One thing I want to say, whether you want to hear it or not, is she loved you. She protected you and must have had her reasons for what she did. This in no way warrants a large lie like this, but possibly softens it some.
There is a younger, red headed guy in the council meetings. I have not heard his name yet and when I asked my father, he was unsure who it was, but I think he may be lying to me. He does not speak much but listens and writes down a lot. The higher Officers fear him. This may be Gamma. I will keep you posted.
If you are not ready, I understand, but please tell me how you are. I hope I am still a person you can talk to about anything.

Love,
Felicity

Her last statement stood out to me. I think Felicity had become someone I didn't confide in as much as I used to. Whether that was supposed to be a slam or just an observation, I needed to tell her more about myself.

Felicity,

I'm struggling. I was in a deeply troubled state for a few months but have recently started moving beyond it. I have good friends that surround me and push me. I'm also talking to someone who knows more than most. I'm learning a lot about myself and my past.
I became good at combat. I think I could hurt some Officers. Hopefully, I can come to Toterrum and help with the coups.
How are you doing? It seems like we talk less and less about each other lately.

It's all business.

Love,
Yaron

    I stuck the letter by the window, and it floated away. I rested my head on a pillow and closed my eyes.

* * *

I was quickly awakened by a slamming door. Aurora's door opened, slammed, and then the front door slammed followed by Herita saying, "Aurora, please talk to me more. I'm so sorry."

    Silence followed, so I slowly opened my door to Naso popping his head out of his door. Herita sat in a chair, crying.

    "Are you okay?" Naso asked her.

    Herita looked up and said, "You both should come out here so we can talk."

7

HEALING

The Luvalas sparkled outside the window. The beast's tiny body illuminated like little stars. About the size of my pinkie nail, the Luvala's large, round eyes glowed a dim yellow, a little beacon drawing in bugs until the beast opened its little, smirking mouth to show a sharp row of teeth, perfect for eating the lured prey. Though interestingly vicious in their feeding habits, the beast only looked like pretty stars greeting the nighttime like an old friend.

After we sat down, Naso asked, "What's going on?"

Herita took a deep breath, batting away the tears. "I had to talk about something I *wasn't* ready to talk about. Thank you for that, Yaron."

"Excuse me?" A fire ignited in my gut and forced me to lean forward. "You're mad at me for telling her something? Maybe that's *your* problem. You're supposed to tell people you love things that are important."

"You have no right to tell me what I should and shouldn't tell people," Herita replied. "You also can't accuse me of something that you neither know nor understand. I get you're mad at me for not telling you that your mother wasn't your real mother based on a letter I received years ago that I honestly forgot about." She rubbed her eyes with her fingertips. "Even if I remembered the letter, in what world was that my thing to tell you? I remembered pieces, but prior to her death, I didn't want to intrude on a conversation she had the right to have with you. Sometimes we are entitled to have conversations in our own time when talking to someone who is more important to us than life itself. You were out of line. I was respecting the situation I was thrown into."

Tears pooled and trickled down her cheeks before she turned her head to take a deep breath. Just the ticking of a clock nearby echoed in our glassed cage. She was right, but a wall started growing in my heart and my mind. War drums pounded at the beat of each brick being laid one by one. Stubbornness prevented me from admitting my fault.

"I'm sorry," Herita said. "I shouldn't be accusing you of things like this. I have a lot on my mind."

I should have apologized. I should have said something, but I just sat there. Then, something new distracted me. Her arms shook in a way I never noticed before. Her face looked paler in the nighttime light. I turned away from her to relieve the growing pressure in my head and noticed Naso narrowing in on her, curious at something about her.

"I know Yaron isn't saying this, but I know he's sorry for what he did," Naso said. "Do you want to tell us what's going on?" He reached out and held her hand to steady her shaking.

Herita whimpered from the touch. "Yes, I do," she pushed out. "Believe it or not, you two have become like sons to me. I'm trying to help with your grieving process as much as possible, but this whole situation is rough. I love you both so much."

I glanced up at her to witness tears trickle down her pale cheeks. The Luvala's ambient light reflected off each cascading tear. The war drums banging in my head dissipated, and a new, slow beat pulsed and slowed my heart rate. I didn't know why. I just knew that she was so important to me.

"I love you too," I said more to comfort her than anything else.

"So do I," Naso added.

Herita's face scrunched, suppressing another cry, and she took a steady, deep breath. "I've been having some weird physical sensations since arriving." She paused. "At first, I thought it was from the battle and shrugged it off. The pain continued around my hip area, so I went to one of the doctors. They checked my body's network and determined I had an abnormality that they further tested. They eventually determined I have..." Her chest vibrated as a firm, shaky breath streamed out from her. "I have cancer." She gazed intensely at both of us, her eyes glossed over and a forced half smile on her face as if to curb the tension surrounding us. "It's in my liver, and they have been treating it."

My mouth dropped open. I had no idea how to react, so I sat there silently. Just as when we first entered Labyrintha, my thoughts began to float above my numb body. It was the same feeling I had after my mother's death. I didn't know what to feel, so the numbness embraced me like a close friend.

"Are they curing it?" Naso asked, drawing my attention back to the room.

"They were very optimistic with the treatment and saw the area shrinking," she said. "When I went in the other day, they told me it had grown back. I had just found that out when I ran into you, Yaron."

I stared at her. She glanced back at me then alternated looking at Naso and me. "Are you going to beat this?" I asked, trying my best to keep my composure.

"I don't know," Herita said. "I truly don't know."

Just like that, tears dripped down my cheeks in frigid streams. Naso sniffled next to me. The death of people I loved threatened me again. It was starting to become a force that would not leave me alone. The threat crawled across my skin and festered into my chest. The constant war drums echoed in my head, beat by beat.

"I can't lose you," I said, slamming my hands on the table at the exact moment of a drumbeat. "I have lost too much already. It isn't fair."

"I'm doing everything I can," she said as she sat up straight, trying to look strong. "I have seen every doctor here, and they are some of the best doctors in Biome. They are trying innovative treatment regimens they are hoping will work better. I start those tomorrow."

Naso stood up, smiled, and said, "Good. They'll beat it. You'll beat it. You're strong. I have seen a disease in action and know how strong you are. My mother has stayed strong, and I honestly think you are stronger than her. We will be with you every step of the way."

Aurora slamming the door when coming back into the house flashed through my head. She had to be heartbroken. "Is Aurora okay?" I asked.

Herita cocked her head and let a soft smile curl up her cheeks. "Thank you for caring about her. She's mad that I didn't tell her and sad about the situation. I know you all are greatly affected by this, and I wanted to tell you, but I was scared. I fear what will happen to me. I also worried about how to tell you about this. I was a coward."

"You are no coward," I said. "You're someone who took us in, kept us healthy, protected us during a battle, taught us so much, and is traveling with us to make sure we are protected and cared for. You're far from a coward."

She reached out and squeezed my hand. "That means a lot."

"We're here for you like you're here for us," Naso said.

A flurry of deep hugs was exchanged.

"Should I go check on Aurora?" I asked.

"No," she replied. "Give her some time. We should all get to bed. Today was a long day."

"Goodnight, Herita," Naso said as I nodded.

"Goodnight, my two favorite men," she replied.

Just as Naso shut his door, I stepped back out to Herita. "Herita?" I asked.

"Yes?" She tilted her head.

"How do I know I can trust you?"

Herita paused, pursing her lips. "You don't." She blinked. "The tough thing about trust is you never really know someone's true intentions. You just have to hope what they tell you is the truth."

"That's a hard thing to do when…" I didn't finish my thought, but Herita picked up on my intention.

"Ah, yes. When someone you've trusted your whole life breaks your trust, it's hard to trust again." She stepped forward and placed a hand on my shoulder. "I can't tell you to trust other people again, but I can promise that your trust in what I'm saying is true. I wouldn't be so vulnerable with you if it weren't." She lowered her hand. "Now, get some rest."

I went into my room and fell into my bed, thinking about all I just learned. Did I trust Herita? I did. Without a doubt. I had to. The real focus my life needed to involve my worry about Aurora.

8

My Dream

I arrived late for my meeting with the Soothsayer the next day. Aurora never came out of her room, and I waited too long to check on her, so I was now late. The mirror in the living room kept me distracted, as something seemed different about myself. I couldn't figure out what. Before I knew it, the clock chimed, which was when I was supposed to be with the Soothsayer.

"I'm so sorry I'm late," I said while heavily breathing.

"No worries," the Soothsayer replied. "You had a long day yesterday. Congratulations on joining the Surprisants."

"Thank you," I replied. "The mountain certainly did a number on me."

"It does that." She stared at me for a moment. She seemed surprised by something. "Tell me more."

"As the mountain pushed at me, my Aura hit harder against my brain. Then, these little white beasts began to appear as Aurora and I finally talked. Openly and honestly talked. More of the beasts appeared as the Aura's pounding ceased."

The Soothsayer lowered her chin, an uncomfortable look on her face. "Little white beasts? The Snobbler?"

"Are they covered in white fur with large, blue eyes?" I asked.

"Yes." She still didn't smile, which is what I expected when talking about the adorable beasts. "They were surrounding you?"

"Maybe about ten of them." I paused. A tremble began in my legs and moved up to my arms. "Why? Is that a bad thing?"

The Soothsayer leaned back into her chair. "The Snobblers live up in the snowstorm and scavenge for victims of the storm. They have a curious digestive system where they absorb all parts of a person, their stomach then grinds up the bones, and they expel a white power that mixes into the snow."

My skin began to itch as I folded my arms over one another. "What?" I exclaimed, thinking about the little toothy smiles the beasts showed me. It wasn't a smile.

"I am afraid they were not appearing because of your breakthrough but saw you as their next meal."

My mouth hung open, unsure of what to say.

The Soothsayer grinned. "It is good you had the breakthrough and did not let the storm break you. I am afraid you would be dust by now."

I shook my head. "Thanks for the encouragement. What little…demons." The chills across my body tickled my skin once more before dissipating.

"Far from. The powder they create gets pushed down into the snow. As more snow piles atop it, the pressure forces the powder into rocks, which turn into boulders, which turn into more parts of the mountain." She beamed. "The Snobbler, in a way, helps build the Black Stone Mountains."

"That's twisted." I scrunched my face in disgust.

"It is nature."

"Whatever you say." I took a deep breath, trying to shake the image of the little, fluffy beast gnawing on me.

"What did you find out? After you passed the Snobblers."

Grateful for the new topic, I dove right into talking about myself. "I'm constantly worried about people I can trust. I'm paranoid with everyone. I feel like people are always talking about me or scheming against me." My arm itched as I spoke more. "I think I always carried this fear inside of me, but recent events have made it very evident. I have lashed out at people I love." My chest tightened. "I've lost control of my emotions." A solitary, slow, deep breath steadied my shaking body.

She stared at me and then smiled. "Good. Very good. You are beginning to listen to yourself and, in return, are applying Mentality to your situation. Your true situation. Knowing only works if we listen. Let me share some knowledge with you. Your network is hindered by anxiety. We all have anxiety that creeps into our lives and messes up our connection to Mentality. Some have circumstances or genetics that make them more prone to anxiety. When left untreated or ignored, anxiety will completely take over your network and control you. I have seen this in you from the beginning, but I knew it would not be addressed until you discovered it yourself. Did you feel anything abnormal happen to you after the events with your mother?"

Every word she said described me exactly. After all this time, I finally had a word for my condition—*anxiety*.

"Yes, I did." I blinked rapidly. "I felt like I left my body and saw it from above while detached from any feelings associated with it. It's continued over the last few months, especially when my emotions go awry. It helps me numb any toxic reactions. It has become so…natural."

"Dissociation," she said as soon as I was done. "That is what this out-of-body experience is. Anxiety takes over, but our body tries to fight it. Sometimes, our minds become exhausted from its draining impacts, so the mind flees. Doing this can hurt you." She pressed her lips together. "Did you have these experiences when you were younger?"

I thought about it and remembered when I became angry or stressed, and I would go into a daydream state and detach from my body. "Yes, I have. But I'm only just realizing it."

"You have never addressed your anxiety, and your body is used to this method," she said. "This may be the biggest thing to happen to you, and your body went into a much larger and much deeper escape, which explains why you have said and done things you are not proud of."

I remembered what happened with Herita the night before. I realized Herita having cancer was another big thing to happen to me. So important that my body did what I thought felt right. Instead, I had no control over my emotions and reactions to life's events. Oddly enough, thinking about it made my head pound, my legs shake, and my chest tighten. Just like that, my mind tried to escape again. Before it went further, I started talking again.

"What do I do about it?" I asked. "If my body is used to it, won't it just keep happening? Because it honestly keeps happening."

"There will certainly be times it will happen, but I know of some tools that may help address it," she said. "Now that you are recognizing you have anxiety and notice what it feels like, be ready to attack it back. Think of the people that love you. People that you trust. Tell yourself, I am loved. I have people I trust. I have good in my life, and I know that these things are good."

I laughed. "It can't be that simple."

"You will be surprised what simple words can do," she said. "But you also have to believe in them yourself. Words can be powerful when there is truth behind them."

I sighed. "I'll try, I guess."

"You also can use these tools to combat things you are expecting to happen," she said. "Let us say something bad is coming up, and you are worried about it. Tell yourself good things to boost your positivity. This will help weaken the blows that will come. They will still come, and they will still hurt, but they can at least be weakened some. Practicing gratitude can change your attitude."

Practicing gratitude would be difficult with all the bad things happening in my life. Herita stood at the front of the line. I hadn't really processed her news yet. What if the illness got worse? What if the doctors couldn't find a cure?

"Something is troubling you," the Soothsayer said. "I can see it in your eyes."

I fixated on her. "It's nothing big."

She smirked. "Labyrintha has transparent walls and transparent hearts. My obligation to the city makes me aware of the happenings within. I may already know what troubles you."

"Are you reading my thoughts?"

She shook her head. "I am not as intrusive as you think."

Though I knew how powerful she was, I believed her. "It has to do with someone important to me and their health."

Without hesitation, she said, "Herita has the best doctors in Biome working on her cancer."

"Of course, you knew." I leaned my head back and groaned. "I was so mad at her, and now I'm worried. I don't know what to do."

"Herita is a dear friend of mine," she said. "She has not only helped our city in countless ways, but she also listens to me." The Soothsayer chuckled, a twinkle in her eye I had not yet seen. "Many people often forget I am human as well. It is taxing to know so much, and many find it very intimidating. Herita does not. Nor does her wonderful niece Aurora."

"You don't know that much." As soon as I joked, I became nervous. Then, the Soothsayer laughed, and it extinguished my worry. In between the twinkle in her eye and her small frame bouncing up and down, she reminded me of a child.

"You treat me the same way they do, and I appreciate that." She nodded.

"I'm glad." I debated leaning further into the new vulnerability between us. "I actually thought you hated me."

A stern grin curled up her cheeks. "Frustration is often misinterpreted as hatred. I truly try not to hate anyone. Everyone has the right to redemption and growth. The Great Light can shine anywhere, including dark places."

"Darkness like my anxiety?"

"Exactly." She paused. "Shall we take another dip into your past?"

"Yes, please." I nearly ran over to the couch. Each revelation brought me closer to the truth about myself. I would do everything I could to find out more, and the Soothsayer gave me the opportunity to.

After the uncomfortable transition to the past's realm, we were in my bedroom. Rain pounded hard on my window, and flashes of lightning lit up the room in terrifying shadows. The wind whistled behind the shaking windowpane. An eight- or nine-year-old me sat straight up in my bed and screamed, "Mommy!"

After only a few seconds, my mother came charging through the door. "Honey, what's wrong?"

"I had my dream again." Little me leaned into her chest.

She sat on the bed and hugged me close. "Shh, it will all be okay," she said as she lightly rocked back and forth. "I know your dream is scary, but your mother is much stronger than any red star."

"Why does it keep happening?" the younger me asked her.

"My mother always told me our dreams are warning us of things to come," she said. "My father said they are random images with no meaning. I think they are important things in our imagination. They keep us alive and paint the world in new colors. As much as it scares you, it has a purpose of some kind."

Younger me yawned while my mother hummed a song and placed my head on the pillow. She left the room but left the door cracked open allowing the hallway light to shine in. With the help of the Soothsayer, I was able to follow my mother out of the room, leaving younger me behind. A conversation began between my father and mother.

"Did he have the dream again?" my father asked.

"Yes," she said. "I'm glad it's the dream and not something worse. Every day I fear we make a wrong move and are discovered. They will take him away and find out who he is."

"We are lucky to still be safe," he said. "Someday, we will leave this place and never look back. We just need to gather the necessary information to take them down."

The world faded, and I was back in the library. I sat straight up, curiosity begging for more information. "Why did you stop?"

"What dream are they referring to?" the Soothsayer asked.

"It's a dream I have all the time," I responded. "It has little importance."

The Soothsayer shifted in her seat, arms crossed. "Then it should not be bothersome to tell me about your dream."

"Fine," I replied. "It always starts with me lying in the ocean looking up at the sky. The ocean is dark and still. Most of the time, the sky is riddled with stars, and sometimes the moon is there as well. I lay there for a while before one star starts to glow brighter. It continues to grow and shine brighter. It eventually starts turning red and transforms into a fist. The fist comes rushing toward me until it hits me, submerging me underwater. Sometimes, I see a person behind the fist. Sometimes, I have a person behind me when I'm submerged."

She took a deep, calming breath before her face softened. "What do you think it means?"

I had never been asked this. My dream haunted me so much that I just accepted it as normal. What if it did have a meaning? What if my ignorance of its importance was part of my problem?

"Well, the fist has something to do with the Vigor Aura, I think. Part of me thinks it's a warning for my future. I assume the big thing that hits me in the dream has already happened, but the dream still occurs. Though, without the fist." I paused, pondering. "Anyway, they killed my parents. But I feel like something worse is coming and will push me under." My heart quickened. A new idea flooded my mind. "I feel like the person behind the fist is a betrayer or betrayal, and the person underwater is going to help me."

An odd shiver erupted in my chest.

"What of the ocean?" she asked.

"I don't know." I shrugged, still fixated on the shiver. "Maybe it's my anxiety? I only just now thought of this."

"You are listening to the Mentality Aura." She smirked. "Your parents knew a lot. We need to figure out what that was."

"I agree," I said. I thought about my parents, this time without any war drums or headaches. I looked at the Soothsayer as a question popped into my head. "If you don't mind me asking, what were your parents like?"

Her eyes widened, and her face scrunched. "Oh. Well, from what I can remember, they were very kind people. My mother was a Cerebrum and my father a Surprisant. They did so much good for this city and so much good for me." She shifted in her seat again. "I miss them."

"What happened to them?" I asked.

"They were killed while traveling between Labyrintha and Flaunte," she responded. "They were carrying important information when they were ambushed. I was very young when it happened and was left orphaned. I was a prime candidate as the next Soothsayer."

"I'm sorry to hear that." I reached my hand forward for a second to touch her arm but recoiled. Was she becoming a friend? "What made you a good candidate?"

"I had little that tied me to our fickle world." Her eyes shifted down, fixated on the ground. "The Soothsayer is not only entrusted with the Mentality of the generations, but also entrusted with superior wisdom. Mentality can tell you so much about our world and ourselves, but wisdom is knowing what is right and what is wrong when faced with situations. It is hard to be the one people look to for wisdom. Many things are not clearly black and white."

"Do you ever get to have fun?" I asked.

"I have a couple of hobbies I enjoy," she responded. "I like reading and painting."

"Reading? You mean gathering more Mentality?" I asked.

"I like reading fantasies." Her cheeks blossomed in rosy colors. "I like things that are not real and where I can escape into another world."

"Another world where you aren't the Soothsayer?" I asked.

She smiled. "What about you? What is fun to you?"

"Want to meet a Riddledog?"

Her mouth hung open. "I have heard of your partner beast." She grinned. "I would like to meet your beast more than ever."

"Come with me." I stood.

We made our way out of the building and toward the pond where Ricochet was. He jumped up in excitement but quickly growled at the Soothsayer.

"Easy," I said to Ricochet. "She's a friend. Let him approach your Aura."

She looked at me and relaxed. Ricochet reached out, and the Soothsayer giggled. His Aura shifted into a tight spiral and moved toward her Aura. Launching into the air like a winged beast, his Aura sprung off hers. Ricochet suddenly flipped backward in the air. He barked, spun in a circle, and looked over to me. His Aura radiated layers and layers of rainbow glory.

"What just happened?" I asked.

"He was so courteous to me, I shared some Mentality on how to do a backflip," she nonchalantly said.

"You can do that?" I asked.

"I can give you Mentality you do not have. What you do with it is entirely up to you and your abilities." She furrowed her brow, staring at me. "I thought you were a professional Mentalist?"

"At combat." I coughed, to which she laughed.

"I have a question for you," I said. "Do you always block other Mentality Manipulations with your own Mentality Manipulations?"

She hummed before answering. "At times, but I often try to avoid this and conserve energy."

"So, there's another way?"

She nodded. "Yes. It is a bit complicated, but anyone is capable of it." Her head snapped back, and she pressed her lips together, eyes wide. "I should not have told you that."

"Yet, you did…" I leaned my head forward, beckoning for more.

Opening and closing her mouth repeatedly, she conceded. "Fine. With total concentration on something mundane around you, your Mentality Aura stays fixed on where it is. If the Aura cannot be moved, the Manipulation cannot happen."

"Fixed?"

She searched the area and pointed at a rock. "There. Focus on that rock if you feel your Aura shift. A Mentality Manipulation always starts with a buzzing in your mind. Once you feel that, focus on the rock." She held her hands out and swirled them. "Ready?"

I gaped. "Now?"

Without hesitation, she pushed her hands forward. Just as she said, a buzzing noise vibrated my brain. Instead of watching her, I found the rock and analyzed it. The rock was smooth on one side and broken into jagged edges on the other. I wondered if the rock had been broken or had been worn that way by the elements. While the rock occupied my attention, the buzzing noise still sounded in my mind. With one quick flick of my wrist, I moved the Soothsayer's Aura to her eyes. The image of an older woman appeared next to her and whispered in her ear before fading as fast as it appeared.

"Do not do that." The Soothsayer kept her head toward me, but her eyes searched to the side where the older woman stood.

"Sorry, I thought…" I didn't know what I thought.

She sighed and grinned. "Well, you did it. Great job."

My chest warmed from her compliment. Not wanting to speak about it further, we played fetch with Ricochet. I even had Ricochet show off some of his Perception abilities.

"I have to tell you," she began, "you taught me something new today."

"What's that?"

"I have neither read nor heard of someone interacting with a Riddledog like this," she said. "You could be quite the Beastalogist. I have heard about you humanely releasing weaponized Waldabears back to their natural state. You are very talented with beasts."

"Thank you." A burst of air filled me and made my heart buzz. "They are the living things that make the most sense to me. I wish humans were easier to understand."

"You and me both," she scoffed. "There are so many frustrating people. I wish they were all like Ricochet." She scratched his ears.

"Do you like beasts?"

She hummed. "I do. I find them fascinating."

"You should talk to Aurora. She's trying to teach Naso how to gain a partner beast."

The Soothsayer straightened her posture. "She is?" She scratched Ricochet's ear. "I might just have to see if she has figured out anything. To have a partner beast sounds so…nice."

I appreciated Ricochet always being there for me. The Soothsayer appeared so lonely, but with Ricochet, she seemed peaceful.

"It has to be tough leading Labyrintha," I said.

She turned her head and looked at me with an odd smile. "Thank you for this. People do not let me relax in Labyrintha. There are always problems people want fixed, battles to manage, or crises to avert." She shook her head. "But I am not the leader. Petra is."

"Who is Petra?" I asked.

"She was at the original Cerebrum meeting," she responded. "She is a quiet leader who spends most of her time listening. More of a recent development in our city. Sometimes when a bunch of Mentalists are in a room, decisions are not made quickly. With looming war, a point person for quick decisions was necessary. Thus, Petra."

I was very surprised and confused. "It's curious you don't have her stand out more. Everyone knows Lady Sandra is the leader in Flaunte."

"Even though Petra is the designated leader, the Cerebrums are equally responsible for the city," she said. "This is why decisions take so long, such as your training decision. We cannot all be as decisive as Ricochet." Ricochet wagged his tail and rolled onto his back.

"This pond was originally Ricochet's favorite place to go since it reminds him of home." I looked around at the green water and hanging branches. A cool breeze swept across, carrying the smell of the mountain's wet rock. "It has recently become my favorite place to escape to as I try to figure out more about who I am. He does have it right for keeping things simple."

"This place may be the best place to figure it out." She closed her eyes and took a deep breath of the same breeze invigorating me.

A white bird circled from above as it slowly descended upon us. A glittery trail followed behind its long tail. It was Pearl. She landed on the Soothsayer's shoulder and dropped a letter to her, sealed with Flaunte's yellow crest. The Soothsayer quickly opened it.

"What happened?" I asked.

The Soothsayer placed a hand on her forehead and rubbed. "Flaunte captured some patrolling Vigorists and found out a siege is planned on Labyrintha in two days." Shaky eyes locked in with mine. "They are planning to scale the Black Stone Mountains."

My heart dropped as the peace the pond gave me evaporated. "What do we do?"

"Rely on the Surprisants to defend." She paused as the reminder of my Surprisant title hit me. She wrote something on the letter and rolled it up before giving it back to Pearl. "Pearl. Please go find the Cerebrums and deliver this message." Pearl cooed and took flight. "We need to head back to the Capitol Building. Please join me for the meeting. Your knowledge from the Flaunte battle may prove useful."

Anxiety from remembering what happened in Flaunte slammed against my mind like a war drum. War found me again. No matter how hard I tried to stay away, it lingered like a Darkened Elderkaw hunting a Silverback Riverok. We rushed through the city to the Cerebellum, and up to the library. The Cerebrums quickly filled the room, one by one.

As soon as the last one arrived, the Soothsayer said, "As you all have read, we are due for a siege within two days. The Black Stone Mountains are to be scaled, so we must activate the traps along them. Cerebrum Callum, please ready your engineers to make sure they are functioning. Please begin this now."

An older man rose. "Right away, Soothsayer." He departed.

Cerebrum Lilah stood and nodded. "Thank you for your swift communication, Soothsayer. The traps will do most of the work for us. As for the rest, Cerebrum Brysen will have the Surprisants ready to attack from the tunnels. I am sorry you just made an ascent and have to do it again."

"For Labyrintha, I will do anything." Brysen bowed his head.

"The mountain will do its own work as well," the Soothsayer said.

"That is great insight," Cerebrum Lilah said. "After you attack from the outer mountain, move to the inner for any who breach. Do not give away our hidden tunnels. We do not want them to find easier ways in."

"We will surprise and disappear," Brysen said.

"Very good," Cerebrum Lilah said. "If any other Cerebrums come up with other ideas, please let me know. Our city has yet to be breached, and it will not happen on my watch. Knowing only works if you listen."

I recalled our battle with the Vigorists in Flaunte. They were able to enter the city because of the crystals Ruth activated. I wondered...

Just as everyone shifted their chairs back, I said, "I might have something." I cleared my throat as the Cerebrums shifted their gaze to me. A few even glared at me. The Soothsayer caught my attention and nodded, a new courage finding me. "When we were attacked in Flaunte, crystals from Toterrum were filled with the Perception Aura by Ruth and then activated to break the island's hidden wall." I paused. "I worry the Vigorists may somehow do this with the mountains, but I also wonder if we can use this mechanism to our own advantage."

The group grew silent, eyes moving from one to the other. "That idea seems farfetched," an older Cerebrum said. "And certainly not our way."

The older Cerebrum wouldn't even acknowledge me as he spoke. I fixated on his Aura moving around his head, just as smug as he spoke. One movement and I could reveal something about him. The Aura gravitated around the back of his head.

"Forgive me, but my mind slips from when you were ever involved with the Surprisants," Brysen said to the other Cerebrum, removing my fixation on the older Cerebrum's Aura. "In fact, have you ever fought for our city?"

The older Cerebrum's face reddened before Lilah cut off their heated discussion. "I think Yaron has a point worth considering. We will have Cerebrum Callum look into this. We do not have many crystals, and I fear we do not have time to gather more, but we could see what we can do. Thank you, Yaron." She nodded in my direction. "And if any other ideas come up, bring them to me right away. The Cerebrums that are not otherwise occupied will meet again in thirty minutes to discuss other diplomatic actions. In the meantime, those who must prepare for battle get things together."

"Listen we will, Petra," the rest of them said in unison.

Were they talking about Lilah?

As everyone left the room, I ran over to Lilah. "Why did they call you Petra?"

"Hello, Yaron." She smiled. "Cerebrum Petra is my formal name, but my close friends call me Lilah."

"Are you the leader of Labyrintha?" I asked.

"Zela really does not tell you much," she said. "Yes, I am."

"Why didn't you say anything at the party?"

"Titles really muddle people's interactions with me," she replied. "I wanted to get to know the natural you rather than the forced you."

I slowly moved my head back and forth. "I'm...I'm very surprised."

"Surprisants are not the only ones with tricks." She winked. "I must be going now. I am sure we will see each other later."

As she left, I fell into a chair and let out a deep breath. The Soothsayer sat next to me.

"What's next?" I asked.

"We wait and pray to the Light," she said. "Please accompany me to the service tomorrow. You help keep my stress levels down, and I need it more than ever."

I nearly hurt my neck as I turned to face her. "I am?" I gulped. "Okay. I'd love to do that."

As I walked toward the door, I passed a mirror and glanced at my reflection. I stopped as something caught my eye. The unclear thing I noticed earlier about myself became clear. Something was different about me. I walked closer to the mirror and stared at a face that seemed slightly unfamiliar. My eyes had changed.

"You noticed too," the Soothsayer said from across the room. "I have been told eyes sometimes change as we change. Gray looks good on you."

I stared at my previously blue eyes turned as gray as a cloudy day. The smallest blue tint still outlined the edges and near my pupil, but my eyes were not the brighter blue they were before. I was changing.

***

Back at the house, Aurora sat on the front porch staring at the sky. I paused to collect myself before entering a difficult conversation with her. I had no idea what to do, but I needed to be a good friend.

"Hey," I said to her.

"Hey," she said with little emotion. I sat down next to her.

"Are you okay?"

A long, deep breath made her lips vibrate to a little hum. "I feel betrayed."

I echoed her deep breath. "I know." I watched her green meadow eyes fill with tears that reflected the sky.

"I'm not okay." Her voice cracked.

"I know." I placed my hand on her shoulder.

"I'm not ready to talk about it."

"I know." I patted her.

"Thanks." She placed her opposite hand on my hand as a tingly sensation swept across me.

"I'm here when you want to talk." My cheeks warmed as I tried to think of anything to get her hand off mine. "On another note," I coughed, "we are going to be attacked in a couple days by Vigorists."

"What?" she exclaimed as she sat up and pushed my hand off hers.

I found the right topic.

"They're planning an ascent on the Black Stone Mountains and come at us from above," I said. "Lady Sandra sent a message to the Soothsayer. They think it will be a surprise, but the Surprisants will beat them to it."

"Good," she said. "This sounds bad, but I need a distraction."

"War can do that." The idea of a distraction wasn't a bad idea to me, either. "I think Cerebrum Brysen will call us all in soon to begin preparations."

As if on cue, Zela came running up.

"We are doing emergency training now," she said. "There's an—"

"An attack," I interrupted. "I know. We'll grab Naso and come now."

9

Preparations

On the way to the training grounds, I asked Zela, "Lilah, Petra, whatever is the leader of Labyrintha?"

"Yeah..." Zela raised her eyebrows with a guilty grin. "I thought you recognized her from the Cerebrum meeting..."

"No one told me she was the leader," I said. "I thought the Soothsayer was."

Zela shrugged, not seeming to care about this conversation. She was right. We had much larger things to worry about.

We were the last to arrive at the group of uneasy Surprisants. Averted eyes, restless bodies, and quiet conversations occupied the warriors.

Cerebrum Brysen nodded as we approached, scanned the group with a regal demeanor, and said, "For those of you who are unaware, Toterrum plans a siege against Labyrintha. Your duty calls, and we must protect the city. Today, you will learn why we are called Surprisants." He stood erect and proud. "Many we face may be better at combat, especially those that Manipulate Vigor. You never know if someone is strong until you are fighting, and at that point, it could be too late. Therefore, we rely on Mentality. Know your terrain. Know your enemy. Be patient and listen to your surroundings to gain the upper hand. When the time is right, you strike and surprise your foe. The Vigorists are planning to summit the Black Stone Mountains since our maze cannot be cracked." He paused. "My friends, we will not let that happen. What about our surroundings can we use against them?"

Cerebrum Brysen's confident stance spread confidence across the citizens. Eyes shifted from staring at the ground; feet fixed their stance firmly on the ground, and brightness lit faces.

"The clouds and snow seem to cause confusion," Naso said while elbowing both Aurora and me.

"That is right, Surprisant Naso," Cerebrum Brysen responded. "Many of the Officers do not carry the mental strength to make it through the haze. What else?"

"We can use the tunnels while they are climbing," Zela said.

"We strike while they climb," Cerebrum Brysen added. "It is important we remain hidden so they do not breach the tunnels. The other advantage is that the tunnels can be used for a quick reentry to the city if any Vigorists successfully summit our mountain. The insides of the tunnels are where we will have to rely on our combat strength and other tricks. Staying hidden will no longer be an option. Anything else?"

"We have the Light on our side," one of the female Surprisants said. Many in the group let out a calming hum.

"We do." Cerebrum Brysen lifted his face to stare at the sky, a beaming smile shining in the sunlight. "The Light will protect us, and it has blessed the mountain with its own advantages. It is not made to climb." He returned his gaze to the group. "We also have traps built along the cliff. The engineers are activating them as I speak. It is important to pay attention to where you step if you need to climb. Whenever you see a White Grande Lily, avoid this area. The flowers are native to the mountain, but we placed our traps below these flowers. Not all of them are, but it is best to play it safe. Here is what the lily looks like." He pointed to a white flower with five large petals on a nearby rock. The pure white petals radiated from a long, silvery stamen reaching out the middle. The flower looked larger than my head. A soft glow seemed to come from the flower's center.

"For the remainder of the time," Brysen continued, "please pair up and practice your combat skills. We will meet here again tomorrow after the service. I want you all to get acquainted with the tunnels and what we expect. More than anything, pray to the Great Light."

For the first time in a long time, Aurora paired up with me. She didn't speak much and attacked me very aggressively, but the interaction reminded me of all the time we spent at the Flaunte Arena under Ruth's guidance. I began blocking her advances, but she came at me so hard. I swept her feet from under her, which only irritated her more and caused her to parry faster.

"Take it easy," I said.

"They won't take it easy on you," she replied.

"I understand that, but you're going to burn up all your energy." I blocked a punch.

"I will go and train on my own then!" she yelled as she stormed away.

And just like that, my fond memories of training with her drifted from my grasp.

"What did you do to her?" Naso asked.

"Nothing," I said. "I think she's upset about the Herita situation."

"Maybe you should go and check on her?" Naso cocked his head. "I don't know girls all that well, but my father always went after my mother when she was angry like this."

I shrugged. "I think she needs some time to herself."

"She needs to clear her mind for the siege," Zela said. "We do not want her to make an error that jeopardizes the team. You can finish training with Naso and me."

After I tried to shift my training to them, Aurora's distant expression distracted me. Zela struck me one time, knocking me to my back. Zela helped me up, sighed, and nodded her head to the side toward where Aurora went.

"I'm going to check on Aurora," I said. "You're right about having her mind clear."

I didn't know why, but I veered for Ricochet's pond. Ricochet ran up to me with a concerned look on his face. Aurora stood on the other side of the pond, punching the air. I patted his head as he walked over to Aurora with me. She was sweating practicing some combat moves with various Perceptions. She gave me a curt glare and refocused on her tree adversary.

"Why did you follow me?" she snapped.

"This is where Ricochet and I hang out a lot," I said. "I think I should ask you why you followed me."

"I needed to clear my mind." She kicked the tree, pieces of bark falling to the ground.

"This is a good spot to do that," I said. "I found this place helpful while I dealt with my mom and other things. Plus, Ricochet likes it here."

"It's because it reminds him of Flaunte." She stopped her assault and breathed heavily.

"I know." I paused. "Is that why you like it here?"

"It is a place away from irritating people, yet here you are." She put her hands over her head as her chest heaved up and down.

"Zela is concerned your head will not be clear for the siege."

"That is what I am trying to do, clear my mind." She performed a Perception Manipulation where the sky burst into dark purple fireworks. I jumped back a little. "You're still here, though. I won't get anything done."

"May I train with you if I don't talk?" I asked.

"You speak one time, and you're done."

I nodded and joined her on top of the stone she stood on. I pushed my Aura onto hers as she pushed back. She caused various Perceptions while I revealed truths about her desires. The ocean appeared. She would turn it into a storm. I caused the clouds to turn into buildings as people of different skin colors, physical attributes, and personalities flooded the streets in harmony. She made the buildings collapse around me as I fell over. Saying nothing as I rose, I regained my composure, and we continued practicing. We did this until the sunset.

"I'm tired," she finally said.

"Okay." I rested my hands on my knees, searching for air to breathe. Before we left, I bid farewell to Ricochet. "I will see you tomorrow, buddy. We are going to have an adventure tomorrow." I gently scratched the area in between his eyes.

"Thank you for respecting my process," Aurora said as we entered the city.

"I understand you."

She reached out and held my hand. The touch surprised me at first, but I kept a firm grasp as we walked. Should I have pulled away? Felicity crossed my mind for a moment. I was unsure. All I knew was her calloused hand felt good in mine and Felicity faded from my thoughts.

We said nothing the rest of the way, including back at the house, where she went straight to bed. Herita sat at the kitchen table drinking tea. She smiled at Aurora as she walked in, but Aurora didn't even look at her.

Herita sighed, turning her attention to me. After a soundless interaction, I did what Aurora did and went straight to bed.

***

The next morning, I left the house before everyone else was up. The silence across the city held an eerie calm. One wouldn't know the city was about to be at war; another war I brought to a city that didn't deserve it. Any guilt I held needed to disappear, so I focused on the silence and tried to soak in my numbness. Hopefully, the city's somber state would bring silent serendipity. The morning fog danced across the street as I walked up to the Soothsayer sitting on the steps of the Cerebellum.

"Good morning, Yaron." Her warm smile made me wonder if I only dreamed we would be at war.

"Good morning," I replied. "May I ask you something?"

"Of course."

"Why is Toterrum trying so hard to capture Naso and me?" My restless mind needed an answer, and who better to ask?

She stood and crossed her arms. After analyzing me like she often did, she replied with another question. "Why do you think?"

"Because we escaped the city and deserve punishment?" My response didn't sound right to me. "My confusion is, do they do this to others who escape?"

"Labyrintha and Flaunte are rarely attacked, but there have been many attempts over the years." She stood from the step. "Toterrum still wants their dominion to be known. Sometimes, an attack sends a firm reminder. We do not take many who seek asylum, but as you know, Flaunte does. I cannot say there have been attacks due to certain refugees." She hesitated. "What does your friend Felicity think?"

I was taken aback. I had not mentioned her name before. "How do you know who that is?"

She raised an eyebrow. "I respect others' minds as much as I can, but I often happen upon information I did not intend to find. Her name is riddled across your mind. Almost as much as Aurora's."

Heat colored my cheeks. Aurora's name was in my mind more?

"Felicity hasn't said anything about why they are trying to capture us," I replied.

"What does she say the city says about you?" she reframed the question.

"There have been rebellions in the city along with graffiti stating 'If Yaron and Naso are free, so we should be.'"

"Do you think the Officers are happy about this?"

"No." Her leading questions, as they often did, brought light to my situation. "They want order back in the city and capturing us will show the citizens any escape attempts aren't worth it. They will eventually find and capture them."

"We need to make sure that does not happen," she said.

"I still find it odd to put this much effort into capturing us." I looked up the mountain until the clouds overtook the view. "It seems like we are missing an important bit of information to understand what they are trying to do."

"I agree." The Soothsayer looked up at the mountain with me. "I am trying to figure that out as well."

My terror of Toterrum returned, eclipsing the numbness I tried to embrace. My limbs trembled, and sweat pooled down my back. No matter how hard I tried to forget about

Toterrum, the city haunted my every thought. I hadn't felt the fear in a while. It needed to go away.

I remembered the illusion Aurora caused when we were floating down the river toward Flaunte. The taller buildings and walls filled with so many people I knew. That was the last time I "saw" Toterrum. I remembered the white-haired lady who resembled Sagiterra, the last leader of Rithbar I read about in that book I found in the ruined city. The Soothsayer watched my every movement as I remembered it all.

"What?" I asked.

"Your network is clouded." She swirled her hand in the direction of my head. "What is wrong?"

The Soothsayer's keenness to my mental state surprised me. "I remembered my fear of Toterrum." A chill swept up my back.

"You remember your fear of the Officers," she corrected. "The city has done no wrong to you. It is the people who lead it. Most people who make up the city are not Officers."

Was she right?

"Another thing troubles me." I thought of Sagiterra. "Have you heard of the Supreme Leader?"

"I am the Soothsayer. Of course, I have." She raised an eyebrow.

"Of course you have." I pressed my lips together. "What do you know about this person?"

"That is interesting that you ask this," she said. "It is an area that has troubled me for a while now. I know they were the elected leader of Biome picked by the representatives of each segment."

"So, they were a Manipulator?" I asked.

"Yes," she replied. "Their purpose was to step in and make decisions when a unanimous one was not achieved. From there, the history is blurry. It is as if someone intentionally scrambled the history."

The fog across the ground began to rise as if moving in response. All the warmth left my cheeks. The Soothsayer's face went pale.

"What about the last leader, Sagiterra, before Rithbar fell?" I asked.

She leaned her head far to one side. "You know of Sagiterra?" She blinked. "This surprises me. I have tried for a long time to find out more about her. Very little is written, and very little is known." She crossed her arms. "How do you know about her? Allen Sand told me he had nothing about her."

"I found a book while in Rithbar and stumbled upon a page about her," I said. "It was a book called *Governing Done Right*, and I found it in an office. I believe it used to be a Mentalist office."

A loud, slow breath whistled through her nose. "Very curious. And you have this book?"

"I gave it to Allen," I said. "I didn't know I would end up in Labyrintha. I should have asked for it back."

The Soothsayer stood in silence, staring blankly ahead before shaking her head. "No worries." She smiled. "I can have Allen transcribe some of it and send the text over to me."

"If it's okay that I ask, I would appreciate whatever you find out about her, please let me know," I said. "Something keeps drawing me to her."

"I will relay any knowledge I find back to you." She bowed her head. "Knowing only works if we listen."

We walked up to the Cortex and entered. We were the first people to arrive. I hadn't noticed before, but an earthy smell of dirt and rock mixed with freshly chopped wood surrounded me. I closed my eyes and took a deep breath, letting the scent flow throughout my body. Daylight began to shine through the opening in the ceiling, which didn't make sense for how early in the day we were.

"Why do you get here so early?" I asked.

"To pray." Her voice echoed as she slowly looked around the room. "The quiet gives my soul rest. It allows me to clear my mind so I can listen with great focus. The Great Light speaks differently each time."

"How do you know the Great Light is there? I have yet to see it."

She smiled. "Neither have I."

I nearly snapped my neck to face her. "How do you know it's real then?"

"I do not know." She took in a deep breath. "I believe." She stepped forward, footsteps echoing. "There are so many different things in our fickle world to know. Even when you think you know something, it changes. You learn more about it, and the knowledge you thought you once had gets replaced. Knowledge is constantly evolving and changing." An ethereal sigh escaped her. "It is exhausting. Faith is something different. It is believing in something you cannot see but gives you peace with all that happens. For how much I know, I seem to understand things less. The Great Light gives me the wisdom I often lack when discerning facts."

So many pointless words danced through me. Was what she was saying valid?

"How come the Great Light allows people like the Officers to do so much harm? It seems odd to believe in something that allows so much hurt."

"I do not know." Her shoulders arched so high into a shrug that I was worried she would fall over. "I do know that everything happens for a reason, and sometimes the reason is not clear until much later on."

"Flaunte believes the land gave them their ability to Manipulate Perception," I said. "Labyrintha believes the Great Light showed them how to Manipulate Mentality. They both can't be right."

The Soothsayer raised a finger in the air. "Ah, so you know this, or you think this?"

I sat quietly for a moment to think. "No," I eventually replied. "It just seems inconsistent."

"The world is inconsistent," she said. "Why trouble your life for an answer that solves nothing?"

"I think it can solve a lot." Her vague responses were irritating me. "Beasts are constantly evolving and becoming better. There must be a moment where these gifts were found, given, or whatever explanation that fits, causing a divide to occur. These differences, which are all from the same beasts, somehow became the most important thing in the world. If we knew the correct answer to where these gifts came from, wouldn't this help unify the division?"

"Many of the Soothsayers before me dedicated their lives to figuring this out," she said. "Do you know what they found?"

"No. That's why I'm asking."

"They found many different answers and possibilities." She wiggled her fingers at her sides. "Not just one."

"Another inconsistent answer," I grumbled.

"Maybe...or does having so many different answers seem to be a consistent response?" Her eyes lit up as she walked around on her toes. "Maybe you are just saying varying answers are inconsistent when you are the only one that is inconsistent."

My head was spinning. Part of me thought she was doing a Mentality Manipulation, while in reality, she was just talking circles around me. "I'm going to figure it out." The conversation needed to end before my head exploded.

"Good," she said. "Now let us rest our minds in the tranquility of the Light."

I rubbed my temples as I sat down. "I will quiet myself per your request."

Within her mandated silence, I noticed the architectural details I missed the last time I was at the religious building. The light wooden beams still traveled up the walls and to the skylight, but the stone pillars I hadn't noticed the first time stood out to me. As you followed the black stone pillars up, there were engravings with smooth indentations that were painted white. Right on the edge of the indentations was a light blue color. I didn't notice the blue before. The rest of the pillars shined in a natural, polished black stone. At the top of the pillars stretched large arches connecting the side of the pillars to the ceiling. The same white and light blue painted on the pillars ran along the curve. The pitch-black ceiling allowed the skylight to be the focus of the room. The light shined into all the dark areas. Light radiated from the shiny stone along the ceiling. Light literally took over the darkness.

Along the sides of the building, the painted glass windows caused a little rainbow light show to dance along the pews and ceiling. Each was long and narrow with various shapes. I thought a story was being told from one to another, but I didn't understand it. I had a strong urge to close my eyes after looking at the architecture; the serenity the Soothsayer spoke of finally finding me.

Suddenly, I entered my dream. Was I asleep? I opened my eyes and was back in the religious building. I tried closing my eyes again. As soon as I calmed myself, my dream returned. I decided to keep my eyes shut.

Just as before, I lay in the ocean. The sky sparkled with stars above. The moon was full, and the sky as clear as glass. The same star began to glow and transitioned into the fist. A person pushed the star from behind as it quickly approached. I wanted to open my eyes, but I let it come at me. It came closer and closer. Suddenly, a bright light shined on the horizon. Overcome by the new feature of my dream, my attention turned toward it. It looked like the sun. I looked back at the fist as it disintegrated in the light. The person behind the fist remained, falling as the light shined. For the first time ever, I could see the person as clear as day.

It was me.

I opened my eyes and gasped for air. People began filling the pews around us, staring at my panicked state. The Soothsayer touched my back and whispered, "Are you okay?"

"Yes." I slowed my breathing. "I had a weird daydream."

She kept her voice quiet. "Tell me about it."

"Well, it was the same dream I used to have all the time, but I was much more aware." My skin tingled like the water still surrounded me. "This time, a bright light shined on the horizon and overtook the fist. The person behind the red fist was revealed in the light." I gulped. "It was me."

The Soothsayer sat back, resting her arm on the back of the pew, and leaned closer to me. "The Great Light has spoken." Her voice was so faint. "You listened, and it replied."

"It did?" I asked. "But there were no words."

"Communication comes in many forms." She smiled up toward the light in the ceiling. "This is good. This is very good. How do you feel?"

"I think I feel good." For some reason, I patted my shoulders to feel for something different. "Am I my own problem? Is that what that means?"

"Partly." She leaned back forward. "But your dream has many layers to it. This is a great start."

The service music began playing as the leader rose and greeted everyone. As she started to speak, I glanced over at Herita and Naso sitting by each other. Aurora was nowhere to be seen. Naso looked over at me as I mouthed, "Where is Aurora?"

He shrugged and looked like he mouthed back, "She didn't want to come."

A deep concern sparked within me, but I remembered she gave me space when I didn't want to come to the service. She deserved to move at her own speed. Everyone stood to sing as I rose late to join the singing. The words hit me differently. The odd peace I found washed away something that continued to haunt my every step—my anxiety.

"The Light is good," the leader said. "The Light is very good. We are freed of all our anxiety, depression, anger, hatred, and fear. We are protected. Even when darkness stands on our doorstep, we trust the Light will prevail. Look up to the Light." She paused for a while as everyone looked up to the skylight. Everyone gazing up captivated me. My attention lifted to the Light. The light seemed to glow brighter than normal as my face warmed. "Great Light, you are welcome here. Invade our land and our hearts. Overcome those who persecute us. Let them see Your Light."

Another song broke out. The people sang, "Open our minds to Your presence. Let us join in with Your joy." Everyone continued to repeat these same words. Some raised their hands in the air. I sang the words with everyone. A connection to all around me sent an electric pulse through my bones, a feeling I had never experienced before. The feeling was very different from how I felt in Toterrum—disconnected.

The rest of the time, people spoke out loud about their fears and anxieties. The passion in the surrounding voices brought tears to many and hope to others. The upcoming siege was a very real and very relevant fear. Yet, the same serenity that found me washed over everyone.

After what felt like minutes but was closer to an hour, the leader said, "Enter into today and into tomorrow with a clear mind. Rely on the Light. We will be protected."

"Come to the library with me," the Soothsayer said immediately after the leader ended the service. "I think we need to do another session."

"Okay," I said, a bit surprised at the sudden request. "But I'm supposed to go to the tunnels. I don't think I can."

"Cerebrum Brysen," she said as he passed by. "I know the Surpriants are traveling up to the tunnels this afternoon. Can I steal Yaron for some important training this afternoon?"

Zela stood next to him. "Yaron traveled up there with me the other day," Zela said. "He is acquainted with the area."

"Okay," Brysen responded. "Make sure you go over the plan with either Aurora or Naso later."

"I will." I nodded.

"Let us be on our way," the Soothsayer said. I followed her to the library and rested my head on the couch as she entered my mind and memories.

Giant crystals surrounded me. I was back at the mines. Naso, Asher, Robyn, and I were taking turns throwing rocks as far as we could. Robyn looked so foreign to me, more like a silhouette. Since my good friend disappeared, so much had changed. Asher's warm smile seemed so distant. For being familiar, they felt like strangers to me. We looked younger. It must have been five or so years before.

"What do you think it's like outside the city?" Robyn asked.

"I imagine fields of sun and freedom," Naso said. "Nothing like this dark place. No Officers, no rules, and no punishments." A purple bruise shined on Naso's right cheek as he rubbed it. It must have been prior to his mother's sickness when he caused more trouble and didn't care what the Officers did to him.

"I think there are other cities out there," younger me replied. "Different types of people with more freedom."

"I bet there are beasts of every kind running around," Robyn said. "Everyone takes care of each other and the world is in harmony. What about you, Asher?"

"I think it's all the same," Asher said.

"What do you mean?" younger me asked.

"Do you really think if there are other people out there that they are all totally free?" He picked up a rock and threw it.

"Probably," I replied. "Maybe. I don't know."

"Someone's always in charge." Asher scowled.

"That's what your mom said to me last night," Naso said with a big grin. Asher threw a small rock at him and Naso dodged it. "Hey, watch it!"

"I'm just saying," Asher continued, "I don't want to dream about something that isn't there."

An awkward silence surrounded our group.

"I heard there were people with powerful abilities out there," Robyn said.

"Powerful abilities?" I asked.

"Yeah," she continued. "There are some that can control minds and make you see things. My mom says the Officers are protecting us from them. She said it while laughing, though."

"It sounds like a joke," I said. "If I had a power like that, I would make Officer Grant run into a wall."

"I would make him kick himself in his crotch," Naso said, laughing as he mimicked Officer's Grant face.

"Be careful," Asher said. "You never know who could be around."

"Lighten up," Naso said. "We're still young and don't have much to live for here. Let us dream and joke around."

The mines faded as my Toterrum home appeared. A younger me, around the same age as the last memory, turned to face the front door and the loud knocks coming from it. Asher appeared behind the door before quickly stepping inside and shutting the door behind.

"Naso's mom is sick," he said. "She has the disease."

"What?" younger me exclaimed. "She was perfectly okay yesterday."

My mother rose from the couch and asked, "Did anyone in the family do anything bad yesterday?"

"We were at the mines playing with some rocks," I said.

"Why?" Asher asked.

"Nothing," my mother said, the worried expression on her face morphing into a smile. "That's very sad news. We will bring some bread to them."

The world started to spin, and I was back on the couch. I sat up as the Soothsayer asked me, "Who is Robyn?"

"She was a good friend of mine who was captured one day by the Officers," I responded. "She and her family disappeared. We were told they were executed."

"I am sorry," the Soothsayer said. "Losing a friend had to be hard."

"It was," I said. "I forgot that Naso used to be like that."

"He appears to act the same as he does now." She furrowed her brow.

"He was until his mother had the disease," I said. "After that, he was very careful and followed the rules. He was rarely punished."

"Did you ever find out what they did to get this disease?"

"No." I thought about the interaction more.

"Was it Naso's fault?"

"No." The question made me think a little harder. "At least I don't think so. It's strange that his whole attitude changed right after she was found sick."

"Why do you think your dream decided to appear at the service?" The abrupt change in topic caught me off guard. The Soothsayer always had an abrupt agenda.

"I have no idea. I think it was to tell me I'm the root of my problems."

"That may be part of it." She pressed her lips together before popping them. "But I think the Light was warning you."

"Warning me?"

"As a Mentalist, I have been gifted with many things," she said. "One, which is foggier, is interpreting dreams and the future. Dreams are often warnings of the future, and your dream became vivid to me during the service. Therefore, I pulled you in. I let your mind guide me today, and it brought me to this memory."

"That's strange." My head pounded like a drum. "What do you think it means?"

She paused, watching me. "I think someone close to you will betray you."

"Betray me?" My voice cracked. "Naso is here with me. Robyn is dead. Asher is held captive in Toterrum. Is Asher going to betray me?"

Growing up, I trusted Asher more than anyone else in the world. Naso and I always clashed. Asher was always there for me. What if the person I trusted most betrayed me? I didn't even know Asher anymore. He had to have changed. I had changed. Naso, on the other hand, became one of my biggest confidants. I trusted him.

"The interpretations only go so far." Another pause. "I do not have a clear answer."

"I need to talk to Naso." I stood and paced.

"I will see you in the morning before the siege."

War looming closer, I found myself running to the house. I needed to find the truth among all the lies. Naso sat on the couch with Herita.

"Can I talk to you?" I asked Naso.

"Sure." He shrugged, not standing.

"Outside?"

"Okay?" He stood to follow me outside. "What's up?"

I looked my friend over. He traveled so far with me, and we fought in two battles together. "This is going to sound strange, but are you talking to the Officers?"

He laughed, but I looked at him seriously. "Seriously?" he asked.

"Yeah." I tried to keep eye contact with my confused friend, but it only made my head hurt.

"No." He laughed. "Why in Biome would I talk to them? I've only spoken to my mother."

"Okay." I took a deep breath.

"Can I ask why you would think this?"

"I don't think it." I aggressively shook my head. "My session with the Soothsayer revealed my recurring dream is a warning of an upcoming betrayal."

"And you think it's me?" He pointed his thumb to his chest.

"No." My gut twisted. "But I think it's Asher."

"Asher would never..." He squinted as if trying to figure out something about me.

"I don't think we know him anymore."

"There was a letter on your bed," he said. "Maybe Felicity can help look into him?"

I nodded in agreement and made my way to my room. I ripped the letter open.

Yaron,

I'm good. Thank you for asking. I've never felt more alive. I see so much hope for Toterrum with movement happening. I know that's business, but to me it's now personal.
I forgot to tell you the other day, but Asher is living with Samson and Officer Grant. I think he has been living there for a while. I asked him about it, and he said he is. Samson and he do everything together even when they aren't away for the new training.

Also, I briefly heard talk of two planned sieges of some kind. They didn't say where or how big, but I wanted to give you the heads up. Please be safe and smart.

With much love,
Felicity

Asher was going to betray me. The words sank in like sickness. He was friends with my enemy. Two sieges? I obviously knew where one would happen, but what about the other?

Felicity,

Please find out as much about Asher as you can. I think he may be doing something bad. I don't know what, but he's on my radar and should be on yours.
There's a siege coming to where I am. We luckily found out about it a couple of days ago. They are supposed to attack tomorrow, but we are ready. Please try to find out where the other one will happen.

Love,
Yaron

I folded the letter and let it go. I quickly ran out of the room, and Herita rose. "What's going on?" she asked.

"There's another siege happening somewhere else," I said. "I need to tell the Soothsayer."

"I will take care of it," she said. "I need to write Lady Sandra anyway." It was like she knew what I was thinking. I was worried about Flaunte as well.

"Okay," I replied. "Thank you."

She grabbed a cloak and exited. As soon as she left, Aurora stepped out of her room. "Yaron?" she asked.

"Yes?" I replied.

"Can you lie down with me for a little while?" she asked with a few tears coming down her face.

"Of course," I replied as my adrenaline pulsed.

"Please, don't ask me anything," she said. "I just want you near me."

When I needed space after my parents' death, she gave it to me, even though I harshly pushed her away. Aurora needed space but wanted me nearby. I wondered if I would've healed sooner if I asked for affection rather than distance.

I crawled on her bed and held her. She quietly wept. Her pain fit into my stress like a glove. The way we complemented one another baffled me. My mind raced, but her presence made me relax. No one else mattered except for her.

10

THE SIEGE OF LABYRINTHA

The morning sky blushed in an array of pinks and yellows. Ricochet walked next to me, his Aura dim but vibrating. He sensed the discomfort in me and the others surrounding him. So many people walked the streets in somber silence. The calm before the storm. I tried my best to give reassuring nods or small smiles, but the restlessness brewing within my stomach urged me to just lay in bed, holding Aurora.

"Today's a big day." I scratched Ricochet's ear. "A big day."

He nuzzled into my hand and licked my fingertips. His body trembled. Unlike before, my Aura moved toward his and wrapped around it, comforting my nervous beast. Bright green eyes glanced up begging for the same thing I wanted to do—to just curl up and sleep away the day. But we couldn't.

"Though we'll be apart, I'll be with you, and you'll be with me. Watch over the lower areas in case any Mentalists need your help."

He almost nodded before sprinting off. Our Auras remained close to one another, yet his Aura became foggier the further he went. Visions of cuddling with him crossed my mind. They made me think about holding Aurora the night before.

My heart pounded as I recalled her sweet scent and soft skin. My cheeks turned the same color as the sky, an intense warmth filling every inch. Yet, a sour guilt formed a pit in my stomach. All these feelings about Aurora swarming me were the same feelings I had with Felicity. Had I betrayed her? No, I was just being a good friend to Aurora. She needed me. Felicity would've understood.

The Cerebellum caught my eye as blue twinkled from the morning sky and reflected off the windows. The song *The Light Will Overtake the Dark* from the service played over and over in my head. An odd trust kept me steady. Was it the Light? Was I just finally confident with my abilities?

The Soothsayer stepped out of the Cerebellum, wearing dark blue pants and a long-sleeved, woolly shirt. "A pleasant day," she said. "Now if it only were not overshadowed by war."

"Herita spoke to you last night?" I asked.

"She did," she said. "I am glad you obtained this information. We only hope it makes it in time. Hopefully, the notice is for nothing."

"I hope so." I scratched the back of my arm. "Where will you be today?"

She pulled at her sleeve, glancing up at me. "I am coming with you."

"You're going up there?" My eyes gravitated upward toward the caves.

"Correct me if I am wrong, but I wiped the floor with you when combating with Manipulations." She raised her eyebrows up and down, a new positivity I hadn't seen in her before.

"Of course, how could I forget?" I laughed. "You have lifetimes of Mentality on your side. I'm glad you'll be there to protect me."

"We should head to the training grounds. Cerebrum Brysen has a last-second plan that should make this victory swift."

Just as we started walking, I shivered, thinking about fighting. Why it took so long to hit me didn't make sense. "Are you nervous at all?" I asked.

"I am human," she said. "I am terrified. But I trust the Light will protect us, and the mountain will not be breached."

All the simple words the Soothsayer used to ss irritated me when we first met. My mindset shifted since, leaning into the responses and searching for the wisdom she shared.

"I'm thankful for our friendship," I said. "You've helped me escape the dark part of my soul."

She placed a hand on my shoulder. "I am thankful for it as well." Her hand fell from me as quickly as it came. "But can we not act like today is the day we die?"

"Fair." I nodded.

"As for the darkness, it will never fully disappear. It is a part of you."

***

We arrived at the training grounds, Aurora's warm smile finding me from across the Surprisants. Without even realizing, I gravitated over to her and her meadow eyes. Little sparks of yellow green flickered in her eyes before fading. She grabbed my hand as soon as I walked up and squeezed it before retracting.

"Hello, Soothsayer," Aurora said. "Are you checking on the Surprisants before?"

"Actually, I will be joining the Surprisants," the Soothsayer replied. "The library gets boring." She stared at Aurora for a second. "Your network..."

"I know." Aurora adjusted her tied-back hair as if adjusting her Aura. "Life is...life right now."

"It is a good thing you are strong." The Soothsayer held Aurora's cheeks in her hands.

Naso walked up. "I see we're doing some good old cheek grabbing before battle. I'm ready for you, Soothsayer." He leaned forward with a devilish grin. The Soothsayer turned to Naso before lightly patting his right cheek a couple of times. "Hey, now." He rubbed his reddened cheeks, and uncomfortable laughter filled our group.

"Surprisants and Soothsayer," Brysen began, "today is the day we defend our great city. We have the mountain with us, we have the Great Light, and we have Mentality. On top of those things, I created this." He held up a metal object with some type of loose fabric hanging off it. "Our engineers were able to generate twenty for us to use. Though we will not all wield one, this device can be loaded with Exploseeds and shot at Vigorists climbing the walls. Once hit, they should be stunned and possibly fall from the cliffs."

"Exploseeds?" Naso asked.

"Exploseeds are found within the Sediflowers," Brysen responded. "They line the inside of the mountain. White Grande Lilies on the outside and Sediflowers found inside. The Exploseeds are harmless in small amounts. When put into these little capsules and flung at high speeds, they release a small explosion." He loaded his device and launched it at a target across the yard. The projectile hit the target as it fell over, smoke all around.

"Why don't the Exploseeds damage the city when they fall off the cliffs?" Naso asked.

"Great question, even though we are not doing biology right now," Brysen said. "They cause a small poof, allowing them to embed into the cliffs and grow. Many even get caught in the updraft during the windy season and climb the mountain. They are fascinating," he replied. "This is why, when lumped together, they feed off one another in massive explosions after to blast rocks...or Officers...off of ledges."

"Brilliant," Naso exclaimed. He looked around. "No one else is excited about this?"

"I appreciate the enthusiasm, Naso," Brysen said. "The Officers will be climbing the southern and eastern portions of the mountain. We have ten tunnels. This means two of these weapons for each tunnel."

The Soothsayer stepped forward. "Lastly, our engineers were able to utilize some of the Toterrum crystals we had per Yaron's suggestion." She pulled out a bag from a backpack. After opening the bag, little blue crystals with silvery metal shimmered. Pulling out one of the crystals, she revealed a necklace with one crystal pendant hanging near the center. "The crystal has been loaded with some Mentality Aura and should provide a temporary, close quarters Manipulation. The surrounding people will have a slight lapse of judgment, giving you an opportunity to attack or run away." She began walking around, handing out the crystal necklaces to each Surprisant.

"Thank you, Soothsayer," Brysen said. "Now, let us climb and split you up."

I fumbled with the necklace as I put it around my neck. The cool metal tickled the back of my neck. After our gradual ascent, Brysen dropped off the first group at the farthest northeast tunnel and split the Surprisants up. As we continued, Naso, Aurora, Zela, the Soothsayer, and I were placed in the same tunnel near the southeast side of the mountain.

"I call the seed spitter!" Naso exclaimed.

"You are lucky there are two," Zela said as she took the other. "I think we have the best tunnel."

Aurora moved away from the group to the other end of the tunnel. The others continued joking, trying to avoid thinking about the impending battle. Aurora sat on the edge of the end of the tunnel, feet dangling off the ledge. I sat down next to her, looking over the forest below and the shifting trees. I knew that whatever made the trees move was coming for the mountain and us.

"Are you nervous about today?" I asked.

"Not at all." She straightened her posture and crossed her arms. "I'm ready to fight."

I watched her confident stare as she looked down at the Vigorists, almost baiting them to come for her. "I had the strangest experience at the service yesterday," I said.

"You wasted your time going to that?"

"You were the one that told me they are helpful." I leaned closer to her.

"A Light that protects us but allows good people to become sick." She scoffed. "Seems like something we surely can trust." Sarcasm split the air as it hit me.

I chose to ignore her uncharacteristic negative attitude. "Well, anyway, my dream began as I closed my eyes before the service."

"You fell asleep?"

"That's the crazy part, I was awake," I said. "A bright light shined at the fist and made it disappear. It then revealed me behind the fist."

"That is strange." She shrugged, unimpressed.

"I know!" I tried my best to keep her engaged. "Then, the Soothsayer took me to another session, and it was revealed that someone close to me would betray me. It was like the Light was trying to tell me this."

"Maybe." She glared down below, unaffected by my revelation. "You know how I can make you see, hear, smell, and feel things that aren't really there? How do you know that you're not being filled with false information?"

"You think the Soothsayer is Manipulating me?" I glanced back at the Soothsayer, laughing at one of Naso's jokes.

"No." She flicked a ting pebble off the ledge. "Not at all. I'm saying I think our minds can mess with our Aura and make us see things that aren't there and think things that aren't there. Our mind uses Aura to make us feel better about our stressful lives. Our minds sometimes trick us to calm us."

I tried to ignore the validity of her statements.

"When did you become the mistress of darkness?" I lightly shoved her arm. "Do you sit and stare at the wall each morning to liven yourself up?"

"Funny." She sighed. "I'm just saying, our world is complicated, just like our minds."

"I think everything doesn't need an explanation."

"She got to you, huh?" Aurora looked back at the Soothsayer. "She provided her insight?"

"Maybe." I shrugged. "But I think it has a lot of truth. It can get tiring explaining everything. Hoping and having faith in something with greater power isn't a bad idea."

"That's what the island is to Flaunte." She flicked another small stone. "Nature protects and provides things that don't always have an explanation. I think we all pick something to comfort our troubled minds."

Why was it that everyone who shared their insight on life made sense but didn't cross over with other peoples' thoughts?

"Agree to disagree?" I asked.

"That works with me." Aurora's teeth sparkled in a real smile, meadow green eyes lighting up the dark parts of the tunnel.

"What made you switch from liking the service to not?" I asked again.

She rolled her eyes, her smile fading. "I like the comfort of the community, not really the teachings." She flicked another pebble. "Right now, I feel like everyone is looking at me and talking about my aunt. I know they probably aren't, but it feels like it. I'm avoiding big groups as much as possible until I calm down."

Right then, her body tensed up. I reached over to place my hand on her back but stopped, hovering just above it. I slowly lowered my hand back down, trying to avoid any further intimacy.

"I understand completely," I said. She reached over to hold my hand. Unlike before, Felicity filled my mind, and I didn't push the thoughts away. Instead, I pulled my hand away from Aurora. "I don't want this to turn into something it isn't."

The yellow striations sparked within the green of her eyes. "Why now? Because you're thinking about Felicity?"

"Yes, because of Felicity." I swallowed hard, watching the color in her eyes intensify. "I shouldn't have led you on like that."

Sharp eyes pierced me. "Naso told me she dated you in secret for quite some time out of embarrassment." Sharp words spewed from her soft lips. "I don't intend to be cruel. I'm just wondering if you think it's weird that she started being outward about your relationship only after it brought attention to her."

What was happening?

"What do you mean?" I asked.

"I'm tired of pretending like the way she treats you is okay. It seems like you put much more into your relationship than she does." She sighed. "It doesn't sound like she appreciates you."

Was she right? It didn't matter. She had no right to say what she was saying.

"You don't understand what we have." I scooted away from her. "I really would prefer not to talk about this anymore."

"Fine."

An icy chill filled the void between us.

I looked down at the side of the cliff. A dense fog formed below, blocking any view of the ground. I looked up as little white dots slowly fell from above and then more and more dots followed. The clouds swirled from the top of the mountains as they came down the cliff, the snow from the mountaintop preparing for something.

Zela walked up behind me. "Looks like it will be snowy today."

"Does it normally snow this far down?" I asked.

"It is pretty common for the snow clouds to descend some," she replied. There was a loud boom as the mountain shook, little pebbles falling off the cave walls. "What was that?"

Naso and the Soothsayer ran over as we all looked down at the side of the cliff. From the dense fog, a large gray beast emerged. It had long arms and long legs covered in thick, bushy gray hair. Two large, round ears topped its large head as piercing red eyes visible from all the way up the mountain fixated upward. The beast slammed its large fists into the side of the mountain. Another boom and another shake vibrated up the mountain. After a deep roar, four other beasts emerged from the fog. My heart jolted, and Ricochet's Aura met mine instantly. A cloudy image of Labyrintha sat in the corner of my eye. I rubbed it away.

"What are those?" Naso exclaimed.

"Tundrillas," the Soothsayer said. "But how did they get here?"

Atop each beast, I squinted to see a person riding on the back of the Tundrillas. "I think the Vigorists weaponized them like the Waldabears," I replied.

"This is a shame," the Soothsayer said. "They are typically very docile unless provoked."

"They look pretty angry to me," Naso said.

"Everyone, stay calm," Zela replied. "We will get through this. The Great Light and Mentality are on our side. The White Grande Lily traps will help as well."

The beasts bolted up the mountain, clouds of dust whipping around. One of them came up to a patch of White Grande Lilies. Just before the beast stepped on the flowers, it stopped and sniffed. One deep roar and it climbed around the lily.

"It doesn't look like the traps will help," Naso snarked.

"Aurora, can you Manipulate the Tundrilla's Aura from here?" the Soothsayer asked.

"I'll try." Aurora cracked her neck and concentrated below. The leading beast charged forward, closer and closer. "I can see it."

"Help the beast find a lily," the Soothsayer said.

Aurora moved her hands as the lily disappeared. The beast charged forward right where the lily was, and a large boom and cloud of smoke surrounded it. Just below the cloud, the beast fell. The lilies from the explosion fell to the ground, dancing in the breeze.

"Nice!" Naso exclaimed.

"Do not get too excited," the Soothsayer said.

The smoke cleared as the Vigorist riding the beast whipped something out that attached to the cliff as he and the beast swung back to the mountain. The Officer moved his hands and held the Tundrilla as the beast latched back onto the rocks.

"Damn that Vigor Aura!" Zela said.

"Aurora, keep doing this to the others," the Soothsayer said. "Naso and Zela start shooting at the Officers. Yaron, be ready. You and I will need to Manipulate."

"Get ready to shoot the one on the far right," Aurora said.

She twirled her arms and made the lily disappear. Naso and Zela shot at the Officer riding the Tundrilla. The projectile exploded near the Officer's head as the Tundrilla stepped on the spot. Another larger explosion and the beasts and Officers fell into the fog, White Grande Lillies swayed in the air with the snow.

"Nice work!" Zela said.

Other booms happened on both sides of us. It sounded like the other Surprisants had the same issues.

"Aim for the leader again," Aurora said.

She made the lily disappear. Naso and Zela were about to shoot, but we all heard a loud "*Kaw*!" Out of the fog, ten white-winged beasts rose. Just behind them, one multicolored winged beast appeared. The Tundrilla hit the hidden trap and began to fall, but the Officer, who wasn't stunned, attached to the mountain and swung them back to climb again.

"Elderkaws?" I asked.

"Ten Tundra Elderkaws and one Coral Elderkaw," the Soothsayer corrected. "Ridden by Officers."

The Tundra Elderkaws flew up the cliff at a much faster pace than the Tundrillas. However, none of them moved as fast as the Coral Elderkaw. The bright colors zoomed by everything else.

"They cannot breach the mountain," the Soothsayer said as she closed her eyes and slowly moved her hands from one side to the other.

Another cloudy image formed in my eye, showing Labyrinthians running around and hauling items up to the other caves lining the mountain. I blinked, and the image was gone. Ricochet's Aura buzzed against mine.

A Tundra Elderkaw zigzagged before it ran into other Elderkaws. Three began to fall.

The Soothsayer shifted her focus to the next. A Tundra Elderkaw flew straight into the cliff, causing a landslide. The falling rocks just missed two of the Tundrillas, dancing around in acrobatic flips.

A Tundrilla hit one of the White Grande Lily traps. Boom. Another landslide. More and more lilies floated in the sky. The boulders hit the Officers and beasts as they fell into the fog. Part of the landslide caused a boulder to hit the entrance of our cave. We jumped back, but it ripped off the covering that kept the cave hidden.

The Soothsayer fell to the ground but caught herself. She balanced on one knee, panting for air. She looked at me. "Don't just sit there!"

The Coral Elderkaw locked in on us. The beast hurled itself at us, its Aura zigzagging around. I couldn't pin it down.

The Officer's Aura, on the other hand, moved slower. I moved his Aura as a very beautiful woman appeared in front of him, leaning on the Elderkaw's head. He tried to look around her, but an inopportune infatuation drew his attention.

He released the Coral Elderkaw's Aura. The beast stopped and flew in a different direction. Out of my range, I let go of the Officer's Aura, and the woman disappeared. I tried my trick again, but he moved my Aura first as my arms went limp.

Aurora turned her attention to the beast and made the snow turn into a thick snowstorm, concentrating on the Coral Elderkaw. Naso and Zela shot the projectiles straight into the storm. After a few explosions, the Officer fell into the fog, disappearing. Aurora let the snowstorm subside, and the Coral Elderkaw flew to a small ledge and perched.

"Thank you," I replied as my Vigor Aura returned.

The Soothsayer attacked Elderkaws to the left. The Elderkaws on the right dove straight for our cave. The remaining Tundrillas charged from below. The Soothsayer caused two of the Elderkaws to fly full speed, zooming past the cave and straight into the Tundrillas.

The Tundra Elderkaw's Aura was much easier to pin, so I moved it to a large, white tree with no leaves that appeared on the side of the cliff. Two of the other Elderkaws' attention turned to the tree as their red eyes faded to light blue.

"Naso!" I yelled. "Shoot the Officers!"

The Officers attempted to weaponize the beasts again, but Naso struck two of them in the head. The two Tundra Elderkaws flailed from the explosions as the Officers fell down into the fog. The last Officer regained control of the Tundra Elderkaw he rode.

A cloudy image appeared again in my eye. This time, I saw another cave with other Mentalists shooting through a hole. A Tundrilla burst into the space and knocked a Surprisant against the wall before a bright flash of light filled the image before it faded. I let my Aura reach out and feel Ricochet's still pulsing Aura.

I blinked, and the image disappeared. My focus returned to the Tundra Elderkaw. Zela and Aurora focused on the Tundrillas. Aurora stood very close to the edge. Suddenly, a bright streak of color came straight at Aurora.

"Watch out!" I yelled.

She jumped back as the Coral Elderkaw missed her and flew to another stone to perch.

Aurora nodded to me as she rose to focus on the Tundrillas again. The Coral Elderkaw swooped at her, and she jumped to avoid it.

Four Tundra Elderkaws remained. The Officers turned their attention away from us and began to fly up the cliff. The Soothsayer tried to Manipulate again, but she needed to recharge. We failed as the beasts made the ascent.

"Hopefully, the mountain will impede them," the Soothsayer said.

A loud boom came from below as we ran over to the edge to see what was happening. The remaining Tundrillas and their Officers fell into the fog. No other beasts or Officers remained.

"Great work, everyone," the Soothsayer said. "But we need to head back to the city and search for the beasts that made it through."

Everyone ran to the other end of the cave, but Aurora stood there for a second, looking down.

I turned away from the others. "What are you doing?" I asked.

"I'm just—"

Time moved slowly. A streak of color hurled at her. The Coral Elderkaw struck her side. She lost her balance and fell off the edge.

"Aurora!" I yelled as I ran to the edge. She was holding onto a rock. On my stomach, I reached for her hand. "Don't let go!" I reached, and I reached. I almost had her. "I'll get you!" My eardrums pounded from my heartbeat. I looked to the side as the Coral Elderkaw flapped its colorful wings and hurled its body at her again.

I blinked away from the beast and fixated on Aurora's meadow eyes.

"Watch over Herita," Aurora cracked out.

"NO!" I yelled as the Coral Elderkaw struck her side, crashing both their bodies into the cliff.

I blinked.

The beast fell unconscious from the impact.

Aurora began to fall.

I blinked.

Her meadow eyes didn't move from mine.

Her body flailed in slow motion, her hair untied, wild in the wind.

I blinked.

White Grande Lilies danced around her airborne body.

Aurora and the Coral Elderkaw disappeared into the viridescent fog.

My world went quiet. White Grande Lilies danced in the air and into the fog, flashes of yellow light flickering from below.

Aurora was gone. A sharp pain twisted my gut. Bile coated my mouth, but I swallowed it down.

"No." I kept reaching, hoping I was hallucinating. Maybe it was a Perception. Maybe she was only tricking me. "No, no, no." It was a bad joke, but I'd forgive her. "Come back." My throat was so dry.

Ricochet's Aura pushed at mine, but I ignored it. It tried to warm me, but a frigid chill kept me still.

Naso ran over and pulled at me. I fought him. "Stop it." I kept reaching for the fog and the lilies. "Let go! Aurora!" My body went limp as Naso finally pulled me up, wrapping his arms around my trembling body.

Naso patted my back. "Where's Aurora?"

Reality punched me in the gut. I gasped for air. "She…" I couldn't breathe. "She's…she's gone," I screamed.

"What happened?" the Soothsayer asked.

"The Coral Elderkaw," I said, finally finding air. "It hit her. She fell." I fixated on the Soothsayer, Naso, still holding me upright. "She's gone." I wept.

Naso lowered me to the ground, still supporting me as we sat. "It's okay," he said, holding back his own cries. I leaned into my friend's embrace. "Shh. I'm here." His voice cracked.

A furry body slammed into the side of me. I worried it was a Tundrilla but looked down at Ricochet. How he got there was beyond me, but I knew he sensed my pain.

Zela knelt next to me, placing a hand on my shoulder. "I hate to keep us moving." She paused. "But we still have the Officers to deal with." She waited until I looked up at her. "Aurora would want us to keep moving."

A rush of adrenaline rushed across me. Zela was right. I stood up and wiped my nose, icy tears falling down my face. Ricochet's Aura swirled around mine, a new wave of energy rushing over me.

I cleared my throat. "They're going to pay for what they did." I marched to the cave's other end. Throbbing war drums overcame the wrenching grip on my heart. My anxiety, on the other hand, overtakes me.

The Soothsayer stepped up next to me, keeping my pace. She said nothing as she grabbed my hand. Naso ran up to the other side and grabbed my other hand. Zela came behind me and patted my back.

"For Aurora," Naso said. The group hummed in response.

We exited the cave and looked up. There were no signs of the Elderkaws, but the Officers climbed down the cliff. Not climbed, stampeded. The cloudy image reappeared closer to the Officers at their side. Ricochet hopped from rock to rock next to the impending enemies.

"What happened to the Elderkaws?" Naso asked.

"I imagine they drained their energy to make it through the snow cloud," the Soothsayer said. "Their Vigor Aura moves with them."

"There are more Officers coming down from other areas." Zela pointed north.

"I can handle these. Help the others," I said. "Ricochet will help you."

"You cannot do this alone," Zela said.

"I will help," the Soothsayer said.

"Okay," Zela replied. "Naso, come with me."

"Time to light them up," Naso replied while holding his launcher upright. "Be careful," he said to us. They ran off.

The war drums in my mind sounded like a battle cry. The pounding in my head and the ache in my chest enveloped me. The Officers' Aura moved in rapid circles as they closed in on us. The Aura I could see barely moved, like the Vigor Aura was interfering.

"Their Mentality Aura is off," the Soothsayer said.

"I see that," I replied.

Ricochet landed next to me, growling. He let out a flash, but one of the Officers struck him down before he could do anything else. The cloudy image vanished.

All my pain for Aurora made my head throb. I could barely move with the headache, so I did what I did best—I dissociated. Watching myself, the numb me clenched my hands into fists and punched forward. I had no idea why I moved like that, but the motion felt natural. It was as if a burst of air swept through one of their Aura clusters. One Officer stumbled as he crashed into a pile of rocks. He rose and charged at full speed again. I punched toward the other Officer. He fell but got back up. They seemed to move slower each time I punched the air. So, I rapidly punched forward as their Aura continued to slow down.

"Look behind!" the Soothsayer exclaimed.

Ten more Officers charged down the cliff. I remembered the crystal necklace. After tapping the crystal, two of the charging Officers stumbled, forgetting how to walk. I used this opportunity to repeat the punches. All of them fell in front of me. They fell just like Aurora did. While continuing to punch, I wailed as tears flooded down my cheeks like the many Officers flooding down the cliffs in other areas. Surprisants fell as the Officers overwhelmed them. Their Aura flickered as it dimmed. I focused on the Officers before me. Rage swirled in my mind and Aura. Their Aura beckoned me. I grabbed it as the glass I had shattered in the past revealed itself. With one simple slice, I had the power to end them.

"Don't do it," the Soothsayer said. "I know what you're thinking."

"I have them," I replied. "It's because of them that Aurora's gone."

"If you do this, you'll become just like them."

"He's too weak," one of the Officers on the ground said. "He was born weak, and he'll die weak."

I ripped the Officer's Aura up to his face as he wailed. "I would watch your words," I said. "I'm the one in power right now."

"The Light will shine in the darkness," the Soothsayer said. "Do not let the darkness overcome you. You are strong, Yaron. You have come so far, and Mentality is on your side."

"Why have Mentality when you can have Vigor?" another Officer I held said.

"Quiet." The Soothsayer moved her hands as the Officer lost the ability to speak.

"How many have died because of their hands?" I asked.

"Many," the Soothsayer replied, "but the Light will judge them. You are not their judge."

"But I'm Aurora's revenge." I raised my hands while holding their Aura all at once, ready to slam it down.

A force halted my body, but the familiarity of a Vigor Manipulation was absent. My mind pushed against a wall, blocking my movement. A Mentality Manipulation pushed against me. I easily fixed on the Vigorist before me, moved past the Manipulation, and forced my hands forward.

"No more." The Soothsayer touched the sides of my head.

The surrounding mountain faded as a small girl surrounded by unconscious people sprawled across the ground. What an odd view. It made me giggle. I closed my eyes.

Meadow colored eyes haunted me before they disappeared within a dense fog.

11

Loss

My frail body lay atop the frigid ocean. An abnormal, sunny sky blinded me, yet I couldn't move my arms to shield my eyes. A wave of darkness began at the horizon and covered the sky like a blanket. Little flickers of light, like little holes in fabric, let bits of the sunlight escape. Each shimmered at its own pace until one dot shined brighter. They weren't dots, they were stars. The lovely dot transformed into a terrifying fist, hurling at my once careless body. Right before it hit me, a girl jumped in front with her back facing the fist.

"Goodbye, Yaron," the girl said as the star collided with her. Aurora's face disintegrated in cloudlike patches, like fog.

"Aurora!" I yelled, nearly catapulting myself off my bed. My body convulsed for air, an overwhelmingly minty scent filling each breath.

Was it all a dream?

A faint song from outside my window started out soft but grew in intensity. The words covered me in beautiful agony.

> *Wash over our pain.*
> *Give us hope again.*
> *Heal us someday.*
> *Wash over our pain.*

What did the words mean, and why were they being sung?

Standing from the bed, a sharp pain throbbed from the front of my head. Ricochet stood from the ground and pushed his nose into my hand. His Aura didn't touch mine, but it hovered close. His eyes drooped, and he let out soft whimpers.

"Was it just a dream?" I asked Ricochet.

His Aura caressed mine. Why was he in my room? He never left his space.

I took a moment to let the pain in my head subside before stepping out into the living room, Ricochet following close. Beams of sunlight rushed through the window, the sun just peeking over the mountain. Herita sat at the table drinking tea, watching various people walk by while singing. Her attention turned in my direction before she quickly averted her eyes, tears glistening as she whimpered.

It was real. Aurora was gone. All the air left my lungs. I stopped moving and put my hands on my knees. Ricochet pushed his Aura on mine and soothed the knot in my chest. I breathed deeply and stood back up. My eyes ached from the tears I held back.

Dreading interacting with Herita, I walked over and sat across from her.

"Herita..." I began as my throat dried. I swallowed hard. "I'm so..." Losing all control of my speech, I let the tears loose.

Without any words, Herita rose from her chair, wrapped her arms around me, and in unison, our bodies shivered in sobs. "Wash over our pain," filled the void in between each tear. Our Auras twirled together. Ricochet's Aura covered ours.

My chest tightened, and my throat dried. I needed to scream and hold my breath at the same time. My body didn't know what it wanted.

"I tried to grab her," I pleaded. I pulled away, looking in her eyes as I gestured my intended actions. "She was right there." I whimpered. "She was hanging on...I was so close...it's all my fault."

The White Grande Lillies covered every bit of my thoughts. Their careless movement juxtaposed the rapid, harsh way Aurora fell. I should've just jumped off and followed her down. It wouldn't hurt more than I hurt right then.

Herita placed a hand on each of my cheeks and lifted my face. "Listen to me," she said. "This is *not* your fault. Don't *ever* think that. You're one of mine, and you loved and protected her." She paused. "My little minnow."

I lost it, collapsing back into her arms. Herita was all I had left of Aurora. The sweet scent of flowers covered me. The softness of her shirt brushed against my irritated cheeks.

"No sign of her?" Naso asked as he walked through the front door. He paused and took in our interaction.

"No." Herita wiped her eyes. "They tried again not too long ago, but the Vigorists' camps were still there."

"Who are they looking for?" I asked. They both gave me soft looks. "Why are they even looking? That fall was so far and so high. There's no way she—"

"Yaron," Naso interrupted me. "There's always hope."

"I don't see the purpose," I said. Talking about Aurora made my head throb. "What happened with the rest of the battle? The Soothsayer knocked me out."

Naso sighed, sounding almost satisfied with my topic shift. "We were able to apprehend most of the Officers. One made it to Lilah, or Petra, or whatever her real title is. They almost struck her, but Herita handled the attempt."

"It was nothing." Herita shrugged.

"Also, something strange happened," Naso said.

"What?" I asked.

"The Soothsayer said after you knocked out the Officers, which she was unable to explain how you did. Two Tundra Elderkaws were spotted flying from the summit out of the snow cloud after the victory," he said. "It was almost as if you knocked the Vigor Aura back to their hosts."

A flurry of questions swarmed my mind, but I lost all ability to form them into words. I punched Vigor Aura back to its host?

"Really?" Herita asked.

"According to the Soothsayer, Yaron performed very impressive Manipulations," Naso said.

Herita's gaze drifted over to me. "Yaron of Toterrum." She nodded before her eyes enlarged, and a frown formed. "Before I forget, there was another attack." She paused. "It was Flaunte." She placed a hand on my forearm. "Lady Sandra was assassinated."

"What?" I exclaimed, ripping my body from the chair and slamming my fist on the table. "No!"

Would anything good happen to me anymore? I wanted to run to my bed and forget my world.

"I know." Herita patted my hand, my heart slowing. "They were ready, but the Officers weaponized the Rithbarian Riveroks." Herita exchanged a painful stare with me. "They spent all their time on the shore, but a small team made it into the Capitol Building and killed Lady Sandra. It is said that Pearl screeched so loud after Lady Sandra's death that it caused her to go into a craze, ripping apart the Officers." Herita sighed. "Pearl then curled around Lady Sandra, extended her wings, and ended her own life, covering Lady Sandra in a pure white, winged shell."

Everywhere I went, people died. Herita told me not to blame myself, yet I couldn't help it. If I never came to Flaunte, Lady Sandra and all those citizens would be alive. If I stayed away from Labyrintha, their city wouldn't have been attacked. If I never met Aurora...

"Why are good people dying?" I cried. "What's the point of trying to be and do good?"

As we settled into silence, we were surrounded by singing. Though peaceful to me before, the song irritated me.

"I don't have the answer to this," Herita said. "But we need to move forward. Lady Sandra's death will be for nothing. Aurora's..." She couldn't finish, a wave of sobs stripping all control she had.

Naso wrapped an arm around her. "Yaron, the Soothsayer wanted you to come to the library once you woke up."

"Okay." I would go anywhere to get away from the pain filling our Aurora-less home.

As soon as I walked out of the house, the singing intensified. Echoing wails bounced from mountain to mountain. I was wrong. Leaving the house only made me think of her more. At each house I passed, someone sang out the window, "Wash over our pain." I covered my ears and sped up my pace.

I stopped just outside the library after I noticed Ricochet following. "Stay here, buddy." I knelt and pushed my head against his.

He panted his hot, fishy breath that made me clench my nose. We saw things together during the battle. His eyes widened as I thought about it. He pushed at my Aura. He was worried about it.

"Do you not want me to talk to anyone about it?" I asked, unsure of why that question came to my mind. He raised a paw into my hand. The rough callouses of his paw bed scrapped against my palm. "Okay. I won't."

We parted ways, and I entered the building. In the library, the singing grew faint. Somehow softer, the music hit me even harder, like a faint memory begging to be remembered. I bent forward, hands on my knees, and gasped for air. I didn't want to remember. I wanted to forget.

The Soothsayer sat in a chair, staring out the window. "Yaron," she said with a faint smile. Gray semicircles drooped from her eyes. Red streaks lined her eyeballs.

"You look exhausted," I said.

"I am," she replied. "I am troubled by so many things." She rubbed her face with both hands. A potent scent of incense wafted through the air and reminded me of Flaunte. "I am sorry for knocking you out."

The incense made me want to vomit. No matter where I went, I thought about Aurora and her haunting meadow eyes.

"I'm glad you did." I glared at the incense. "You kept me from making another mistake."

On top of all the dread circling me, thinking about the Officer I killed back in Flaunte seemed pointless. Hurting the other Officers became necessary. All life would lead to death.

"I did not know you made this mistake in the past," she said. "You kept it hidden. Naso told me about the—"

"I think the grief from my mother overtook that feeling," I cut her off, my stomach wretched. "I haven't thought about the murder I committed in quite some time."

"We may want to address this today," she said, narrowing her eyes. "Is the incense bothering you?"

"It smells like Flaunte."

She walked over and snuffed the incense, smoke filling the space and intensifying the smell for a moment. "But if you really want to prevent the desire to kill in the future, you need to find the root of your rage to better understand it."

As long as we didn't talk about Aurora, I would do anything the Soothsayer said.

"I agree." I imagined she would be accessing my past again. "How are we able to hear others talk when in my past? Specifically, those not in a direct conversation with past me? Aurora…" There I went, talking about her again. I gulped. "Aurora questioned this."

Her eyes drooped from the look of pity she gave me. "The mind holds many interactions surrounding you when you have a memory. You may not be able to remember it yourself, but I can access the subconscious portion and amplify it. This allows us to access areas you were around, but not fully aware of the conversations happening. Why do you ask?"

She seemed blindsided by my request but not by my intent. After all that happened with Aurora and all the interactions I longed to have with her but denied because of Felicity, I questioned my relationship with my girlfriend. Aurora had said she didn't think Felicity even liked me unless it was for her benefit. I owed it to Aurora to ask, and I owed it to myself.

"I want you to access some periphery conversations with Felicity," I said. "Specifically, within the last couple of years."

The Soothsayer shifted. "Are you sure this is wise? Learning things from the past can damage us more than it can help. I caution you with this decision."

"I don't care." I huffed. "Aurora said something to me before she was gone, and I need to figure it out."

Reluctantly, the Soothsayer nodded. "As you wish. For Aurora." She gestured to the couch. "Please, lay down." After I lay down, she touched the sides of my head. "Let me look around for a second. Ah, there we go."

The world went blurry, and we were in a nearly empty Toterrum classroom before class started. Naso, Asher, and I were talking. The conversation moved from us to Felicity and her friends on the other side of the room. Past me looked up at Felicity and smiled before she looked away.

"Are you still seeing him?" one of the girls asked.

"Yes," Felicity said. "I can't help it. He's obsessed with me." She pressed her lips together and twirled her hair. "Plus, I like the attention."

"He isn't good for your image," the other girl said.

"I know," Felicity said. "He's going to have a rough life. I want to give him something good before it gets worse."

"Brutal!" the other girl said as they all giggled.

"I'm planning to end it soon." Felicity glanced over.

The class filled, and I suddenly realized we had entered the same day Felicity called me a stalker. It was right before I left. All the embarrassment returned like a wave crashing against my heart. Asher and Naso told me I shouldn't ignore what she said. One of her last interactions with me when she treated me like that. The room went blurry, and the library returned.

Felicity used me. She wanted my company when it was convenient for her. She wanted my desire when she only let me have glimpses of her. How could I've been so stupid? My head tilted at unstable thoughts and true disdain for someone I thought I loved.

"She was right." I regretted not listening to Aurora. I regretted not holding her more. I wasted so much time on the wrong person.

"People can change," the Soothsayer almost whispered.

"That wasn't even that long ago," I said. "Naso and Asher were right. All she cares about is her own appearance."

"But she's leading many into a revolution," the Soothsayer said. "It sounds to me like you changed her."

Why was the Soothsayer defending something she didn't know?

"Because I'm just a stepping stone for her own goals," I said. "She used me then, and she's using me now."

The Soothsayer raised both hands, palms forward. "Emotions are high right now. I just don't want you to make a rash decision."

"Thank you for watching out for me." I stood. "I trust you and appreciate your insight. I'll give it some thought," I lied. I had already made up my mind. I would tell Felicity my true thoughts. It was what she deserved.

"Very wise." She drummed her fingers across the desk, pondering something further.

To deter any suspicion, I cleared my throat. "So, you wanted to address my murderous soul?" I cocked my head and forced a creepy smile.

She let out one solid laugh and shook her head. "I will need a lantern for how dark it will be."

I welcomed the banter.

"You make jokes now?" I asked.

"I spent too much time with Naso yesterday analyzing the...city." Her smile diminished.

I slapped my hands on my chest and repositioned myself on the couch. "Let's get this going. Is this the same kind of thing from before?"

She nodded, placed her hands on the side of my head, and the world went blurry. Shining crystals surrounded me in intricate patterns. An echoing laugh vaulted from one side of the room to the next, the silhouette of a hand running across the crystals. The room lit up, and the Flaunte Arena's walls closed in.

Ruth Char held Naso captured as Aurora and I confronted her. The reminder of Ruth's betrayal of Flaunte and me still sat fresh in my thoughts. Aurora's meadow green eyes surveyed Ruth while her hands twirled, stimulating various Manipulations. I shifted my attention from her and the ache she caused in my chest.

The Officer stepped out, dark green eyes narrowing in on me, so familiar yet so distant. The exchange of motives and words coursed between us, but I tuned it all out. The Officer's body flew back and plopped in the water terrain.

Past me beelined straight at the fallen Officer.

"You attack us," past me said. "You persecute us. You hurt people who trust you. You are bad people, and I can't take any more of it."

My hand grabbed the air and threw his Aura to the ground, body limp. The Arena flickered away as I stared up at the library ceiling, unmoving.

"I'm sorry you saw that." My chest rose and fell as I released a deep breath.

"What were you angry about?" the Soothsayer asked.

"He was an Officer that attacked us," I replied. "Naso was in trouble. They're bad people."

"Hm. The Officers seem to always be bad people in your mind. Did you want them dead in the past?"

I blinked, turning my attention to her soft gaze. "I never wanted them to die." I bit my lower lip. "But I wanted *him* to suffer."

The words came out harshly, but they felt so good to say. My eyes drifted back to the ceiling, unable to look at the Soothsayer's judgmental stare.

"Our Manipulations can often mimic our true intentions." Her voice was so soft.

My brain went foggy. A swift numbness encapsulated me. Why did I feel so good thinking about the Officer's death? Why was it that I didn't hesitate to strike down the Officers when they breached the Mountain?

"I'm still learning what to do with it." My tone was flat, another lie. I knew what I was doing. "I wasn't even practicing the right Aura."

"What you did appears to be something you knew how to do."

I moved my gaze to hers, trying to keep my body still. My legs shook as trembling regret cascaded across me. The numbness tried to put it away, but the Soothsayer closed her eyes, touched my shoulder, and let out a deep breath. Whether by choice or by Manipulation, I mimicked her breathing. Every part of me caved in after that.

"I was afraid!" My eyes moistened. My tired legs tried to support my heavy body. I lost all recollection of how my body was supposed to function. I just wanted to fall over and let the ground consume me. "Okay? Is that what you wanted?"

"What were you afraid of?" She gripped my shoulder tight, an intense stare looking down on me. Little sparks ignited in her deep, dark eyes.

"Losing someone I cared about." I cracked out. "The Officers had done so much bad to Naso and his family." I sniffled. "I didn't want anymore to happen to him."

"Did you think you could protect him?"

"I don't know."

She shook me. "You did!"

For the first time since meeting the Soothsayer, I feared her.

"Yes," I admitted. "I thought I could protect him!" I ripped myself from her grasp and sat up, elbows on my knees and face in my hands. "I...I used this Manipulation in Toterrum to help us escape the first time." I turned to face her again. "I trusted myself to do *whatever* I needed to do."

Her demeanor shifted, eyes softening again and glare dissipating.

"What were those Manipulations you did yesterday?"

"I don't know." I crossed my arms, trying to contain my pounding heart. "It was new."

"What were you feeling when you instinctively did it?"

"Mad. Sad." I gulped. "*Furious.*" A fire ignited within my chest again. "They attacked the city. I lost Aurora. They continue to hurt innocent beasts." I looked up, remembering the new way I saw their Aura. "Something about their Aura told me what I needed to do." I punched the air. "The movement directed me to firmly strike it."

She nodded. "What did you expect their Aura to do?"

Any doubt about my abilities no longer had a grip on me.

"I expected it to leave." I paused. "I *knew* it'd leave. To follow my command and leave someone that was going to hurt others."

She stared at me, perplexed. "I have no words for what I saw you do yesterday." She pressed her lips together. "It is something that feels familiar to me, yet I feel like I have never witnessed it before. You are a good friend who felt like they failed. Your fear of letting others down drives your hatred. The more you feed your hatred, the more your heart will desire darker ill toward others. We are all afraid, but you cannot let the fear overtake you."

As silence fell between us, the echoing voices from outside repeated the same song. My head throbbed with each word. The song no longer held peace.

"What now?" I asked.

"We will take a break from our sessions."

I jolted my head in her direction after her unexpected revelation. "But I...I like spending time with you."

"We will still be friends." The Soothsayer walked over to stand in front of me, taking my hands into her own. "I just think we both need a break from all of this." She pulled me up. "There is a cottage in the northern part of the mountains through a cave. I would love for you, Naso, and Herita to join me."

The agonizing song from outside made my decision easy.

"I think that sounds perfect."

"Go and let them know so we can depart this evening." She released my hands, patted my shoulder, and walked over to her desk.

"Thank you, Soothsayer." I walked toward the door.

"One last thing," she said. "I found out a little more about Supreme Leader Sagiterra."

I stopped and turned back so fast I nearly tripped. "You did?"

"It is not that exciting." She shrugged. "I found out every document about her is missing."

"Oh…" The brief disappointment I held evaporated as the singing made my head pulse again.

"This means something wrong happened to her." The Soothsayer dipped her head. "Something about her has been covered up, and I am not sure what that is. It makes me wonder why she and her situation stands out to you."

My headache faded as my mind raced with questions. Who was Sagiterra, and why did I keep trying to find out more about her? Was the Great Light guiding me toward her? What happened to her?

"What do we do about it?" I asked.

"Search for more knowledge, of course. Let the Mentality Aura guide us."

"Of course," I said. "Thank you for finding what you could. I'll go gather the others."

I paused after one step, realizing "others" no longer meant Aurora. She was gone.

"Oh, and I miss her too." The Soothsayer took the words right out of my mouth. "I miss her a lot."

***

I wanted to go see Ricochet before I went back to the house. At the pond, he greeted me, and we played fetch. The mundane task was everything I needed. Though he seemed tired from the battle, his eyes were vibrant and body without injury. But he moved sluggishly.

Recognizing my partner beast's exhaustion, I sat by a tree with him. He rested his head on my lap. The green tint of the pond reminded me of the lagoon in Flaunte. My thoughts returned to Aurora and all the time we spent together. The moment I met her. Her meadow green eyes judged anyone and everyone she encountered. The way the little yellow striations sparked within the grassy color when she grew excited. Her eyes were gone, and mine had changed. Ricochet licked my hand. His Aura brightened against mine. All at once, his touch, both physically and via Aura, released the gates holding back terrible tears now flooding my broken heart. I grieved over all those beautiful, distant memories.

Leaving the pond, the mountain drew my attention upward, the clearest day I had seen since arriving in Labyrintha. Squinting, the snowy mountain peaks reflected the bright sun. Then, black smoke appeared over the snowy tops. Once back into the city, not thinking much of the odd plumes, I ran into Brysen.

"Yaron, I am glad I ran into you," Brysen said.

"It is good to see you as well." I forced a halfhearted smile.

"We have learned some new information based on recent events." His gaze drifted to the mountaintops.

"Does it have to do with the smoke?"

"It does." He looked back down. "We had one of our Surprisants report the smoke is coming from beyond the mountain." He reached out and held my shoulder. "The bodies are being burned by the Vigorists."

I held no hope for finding her, but if even a glimmer remained, it burned away like the bodies. Aurora was dead, part of her traveling high into the sky with the smoke.

I took a deep breath. "Thank you for telling me."

"It is my duty." Brysen nodded and released my shoulder.

The smoke floated into the white clouds. Then, the fog reappeared, and the mountaintops vanished. Had the mountain intended for me to witness the smoke? Witness Aurora flying away?

Naso and Herita sat at the table eating lunch when I arrived back.

"The Soothsayer invited us to her cottage north of the mountain," I said. "She said we'll leave this evening."

"Wonderful," Herita said. "The place is beautiful."

"You've been there before?" I asked.

"With the prior Soothsayer," she replied. "She was a very good friend of mine. This is why the current Soothsayer and I are so close. She has memories of our interactions together." Heavy bags weighed down Herita's eyes. She rubbed them, noticing my stare. "We have to go to the market." She stood. "There are some ingredients I want to purchase before we leave. Care to join me?"

"Sure." Naso shrugged.

"I'm going to stay back," I said. "There are some things I want to take care of."

Back in my room, I found a letter from Felicity on my bed. I wanted nothing to do with her and her lies. After a few minutes of staring at her gut-wrenching handwriting, I opened it.

Yaron,

I hope the attack against you didn't do too much damage. I did find out the second attack was on another city of some importance. The Flaunte Island, if that sounds familiar to you. They're planning to assassinate each leader. Asher left with a group of Officers for one of the attacks. A week ago, he was loading and sorting equipment for the Officers. I'll let you know when he returns. I hope he isn't hurt. He looked scared.
I really hope you're okay. I would be devastated if something bad happened to you. I can't lose you.

Love,
Felicity

Devastated? Can't lose you? Her arrogance was appalling. Asher went to battle? I put my head on my pillow and took a deep breath. It was time to speak my mind. Tell her how horrible she was. The Soothsayer warned me not to be rash. I wouldn't be rash. I knew exactly what to say. I sat back up and carefully wrote each letter as the words came to me.

Felicity,

I'm alive. There was an attack, and it caused some damage I don't want to discuss.
Certain information was brought to my attention. I have a few questions to ask you:
1. Were you planning to end things with me before everything that happened in Toterrum?
2. Did you decide against this since dating me brought you higher social status?
3. Is love just a word to you?

Sincerely,

Yaron

I folded the letter and let it fly out the window before I could think it over. A soft breeze carried the scent of wet rock. The singing continued, forcing me to sit and rub my temples. I needed to leave the house and get away from the noise. Felicity mentioned that Asher left Toterrum. Had he attacked Labyrintha? I needed to check the prisoners. I needed someone to take me to the jail cells.

I found Zela at the training grounds, punching at the air. The singing echoed between each grunt she made.

"I need your help with something," I said.

Her intensity faded as she charged to me and embraced me for a hug. "I should have given this to you in the cave." Her salty sweat drenched each area she touched, leaving an unpleasant scent.

"It was better you didn't. I think it would have stripped me of my concentration."

She pulled away from me. "Then you wouldn't have become a warrior." She patted my chest, leaving another wet mark. "Everyone is talking about what you did."

I nodded, numb to the praise. "Where are the prisoners held?"

"In the catacombs." Her eyebrows wriggled downward. "It is the safest area to keep Manipulators. There are certain rocks down there that suppress Aura."

"Can I see the prisoners?" I asked.

"Are you sure?" She cocked her head. "You were pretty hot-headed the last time you saw a Vigorist."

"I have to." I straightened my back.

She placed a hand on her hip, looking me up and down. "Fine. The music is getting to me anyway."

She led me to the western end of the city. A black gated entrance guarded a staircase going straight into the ground. From the dark hole, the same blue lights that lit the maze when we first entered Labyrintha illuminated the stairway. Two Surprisants guarded the gate.

"Zela and Yaron," one of the Surprisants said. "It's good to see you."

Zela smiled and nodded. "May we enter?"

"Knowing only works if you listen," the other Surprisant said, opening the gate. Echoing creaks overtook the city's ceremonious singing.

Descending through a long, winding path, my motivation to keep moving dwindled. Glowing, light blue stones lined the walls.

"I have to tell you something," I said.

"What?" Zela ran her hand along the wall.

"I found out that the attack on Labyrintha had one goal—assassinate Lilah," I said. "We're lucky she was kept safe."

"I feared that," Zela said. "We were lucky Herita was watching Lilah. That old lady packs quite the punch."

"I'm thankful she didn't meet the same fate as Lady Sandra," I said. "Lady Sandra was a strong and kind woman."

Zela patted my back. "As was Aurora."

We arrived at a block of cells. The bars lining each cell glowed a faint, light blue like the rocks. I brushed my hand against one, cool metal running across my fingers. Twenty Surprisants paced up and down the rows of cells. The stench of stale body odor and lifeless rocks overwhelmed me. It was a terrible smell.

Studying each cell as I walked by, I didn't find Asher appeared in any of them. As my hope diminished, anxiety filled the void. What if I found someone I knew? Some of the Officers yelled harsh words. Others glared quietly from against the wall.

"You're the one who didn't have the strength to finish us," one Officer said.

"You're weak," another said.

"You'll pay for this spineless little boy," another said.

I quickened my pace, flashbacks of Toterrum punishments riddling my mind. One cell remained. Rounding the corner, a familiar face caught my attention. It wasn't Asher. Great Instructor Wiley, my old teacher, leaned against the wall.

"*You*," Wiley said with a scowl. "I know *you*."

"Great Instructor Wiley," I said, using his full title. He didn't deserve that respect. "How's your stay?"

"You *weak* child." He spat at my feet. Zela took a step forward, but I blocked her. "The Strong will prevail."

An evil grin curled up my cheeks. The fear I once had facing my old teacher no longer existed. "I should thank you." I chuckled. "Your punishments made me into quite the warrior. Enough to defeat your weak army."

"I heard they killed your mother and father." He stepped forward as I grabbed Zela's Facts and knocked him on the head. He only laughed. I hit him again and threw her Fact back to her.

I gripped the cellblock bars in each hand, leaning in as close as I could to him. "Hear me. I *will* invade Toterrum. I *will* liberate the innocent. You'll hold no place of honor or power. You'll be *weak*."

After staring him down, I grabbed Zela's Facts again and struck him one more time. Though my energy weakened each time I moved, I remembered how he made me feel so weak back in Toterrum. A new strength overtook the blue stone's effects. He hit me all the time. It felt good to return the favor. That felt so good. I had power. True freedom brought me unimaginable power and I relished in the stance I held over such an insignificant man. Giving him no further attention, I marched away.

Zela rushed up to my side. "Whoa. Is that why you wanted to come down here?"

"Nope." I failed my original mission, but the consolation wasn't too bad. "But it certainly was a bonus. Thanks for bringing me down here."

"That is what friends are for," she said.

We exited the catacombs, and my energy returned as soon as I passed the gate. "How do the Surprisants deal with the energy depletion?" I asked, heaving for air.

"Many rotations and constant eating and drinking," she said. "It keeps energy high." She patted my back. "Did you want to have dinner with Lilah and me tonight?"

"I would love to, but the Soothsayer invited us to her cottage," I said. "She thought it would be a good escape for us."

Zela aggressively nodded. "I'm glad you're getting a breather. This has been a tough couple of days, and I know how important Aurora was to you."

"Raincheck for after my return?" I asked.

"Absolutely," she replied as we parted.

***

Naso and Herita arrived back from the market after I took an afternoon nap. The catacombs and sleep were the only places I could escape the singing. Finally it was time to meet the Soothsayer at the Cerebellum.

"Hello, my friends," the Soothsayer said. "Let us make our short journey."

Ricochet brushed along my leg, surprising me with his appearance. I hadn't seen him leave the pond much, but his company was much appreciated.

Once we departed the northern part of the city, a small forest took over the land. The trees stood very green but lacked leaves. Little spines covered the branches that held a type of scaly fruit. Crisp, moist air reminded me of how freshly cut vegetables smelled after Herita finished preparing a meal. Long blades of sporadic grass tickled my legs.

"See those there," Herita said to Naso. "Those are Conitrees, and their fruit are Scaliplums. They have a rough exterior, allowing them to be protected from small animals. Only the Grufflings can eat through the tough skin. They want these beasts to eat them since the Grufflings can climb the cliffs and disperse the seeds. Thus, you see the Conitrees covering the edges of the cliff."

"Any other uses for the Scaliplums?" Naso asked.

"The fruit can be thrown and hit someone as if a rock did," Herita responded. "Plus, you can eat the fruit after you hit your foe."

"Brilliant!" Naso exclaimed as they laughed.

Up the winding path, we approached a small cave. A gray beast with a large head covered in shaggy fur grunted as we passed it. Short, thick legs helped the beast waddle along the cliff's edge as if walking on flat ground.

"Why haven't I seen a Gruffling on the other parts of the cliffs?" I asked.

"They are not fond of people," the Soothsayer said. "The northern edge of the Black Stone Mountains is less populated, so they are more common here."

"Fewer people sounds great," I said.

Through the cave, lined with small plants growing in and among the stone walls, dark blue waves took over the horizon. A salty breeze reminding me of Flaunte wafted in the air. The ocean crashed against the rocks below as I found a staircase leading down to a small house. A roof and siding the same color as the mountain stood in geometric shapes, different from the surrounding rocks. We walked down the stairs and entered the cottage. The crashing waves echoed from outside, drowning out all other sounds.

"Welcome to the Soothsayer cottage," the Soothsayer proclaimed. "I hope we can all clear our minds and heal our hearts. To Aurora!"

"To Aurora!" the others yelled.

"To Aurora," I whispered.

12

THE COTTAGE

Sunlight warmed my face as the salty ocean breeze blew through the window. I pictured Flaunte's black beach, so many different people walking the streets, and food stands on every corner. Intracod cakes sizzled as they cooked, and their salty, sweet scent lured me in like the fish itself.

Naso swam over waves as Herita tended to plants that weren't even hers on the edge of the beach. Aurora sunbathed and laughed at something I said, flashing her meadow green eyes in my direction.

I opened my eyes—no black sand, no Intracod cakes, and no Aurora. Instead, I overlooked a dark sea far, far below me. The distant waves below produced a much saltier smell and cooler breeze than Flaunte ever had. Rocks replaced the black sand, and the waves hit with a mighty force compared to the gentle waves that rocked my relaxed body in Flaunte.

Naso let out a low snore before turning to his side from the bed across from me. The wind rustled something on the end of my bed that wasn't there before. Felicity's handwriting once gave me joy, but today worried me, especially for how quickly she wrote back. I stared at the letter, willing myself to pick it up.

She could say nothing. Was I overanalyzing the situation? Should I have ever asked her those questions in the first place? She could have just been saying those terrible things about me to impress her friends. She could also be admitting she meant them. What if Aurora was right, and our whole relationship was a ruse?

Before anxiety made my head explode, I ran away from the letter, leaving it on my bed. Shutting the door behind me, I leaned back and tapped my head a few times on the door, trying to make my stupid headache go away.

"Good morning," Herita said.

I jumped, watching Herita take a loud sip of tea. "Good morning. That was the best sleep I've had in a while."

"You don't seem rested..." Herita raised one eyebrow.

"It is said the cottage clears the mind," the Soothsayer said, walking out of another room. "It was built long ago and has survived many storms." She placed a hand on the wooden wall and closed her eyes. "Past Soothsayers have thought the Great Light spends its time here and protects the cottage." She moved away from the wall. "While here, the Great Light keeps our Mentality Aura at a minimum. Everyone becomes more equal." She sat next to Herita as Herita poured her a glass of tea. "You can see why this place is appealing to someone like me. As much as I appreciate the abundance of Mentality bestowed, it is nice to feel normal."

"And we like having you around," I said. Suddenly, a long-necked beast popped its head out of the water before diving back down. "Was that a Riverok?"

"You both missed a group of Riveroks swim by," Herita said. "It was amazing." Herita's eyes avoided my own as a glossy film formed over them.

I thought of Era. Could Aurora's Riverok partner beast be nearby? Could she sense what happened?

"I wonder if Era senses the loss," I said.

"I'm sure she knows." Herita used her pointer finger to briskly flick the tears away. "I really miss her." She took a deep breath and another sip of tea. "I know I've already said that, but I really didn't realize how much I actually missed her until I sat quietly watching the Riveroks this morning riding over the ocean. It reminded me of all the times we sat on the Flaunte beach and watched the sunrise. Mornings were something we both appreciated. Even when she was young, she would tell me about her dreams to be the leader of Flaunte and make everyone feel included. No matter what they looked like or where they were from. Even the Vigorists." She scowled. "It could've been since her father was a Vigorist, but I truly think it was because of her pure heart. She was always so brave."

"She came and saved us," Naso said as he opened the door. "All by herself to a city that tortured Biome. She's truly the bravest person I've ever met. She changed my life for the better."

"I love all of these beautiful memories of Aurora," the Soothsayer interrupted. "I was hoping to hold a memorial for her tonight. I thought this would be best with her closest friends and family. How does this sound to you all?"

Naso and I turned to Herita. In all reality, she knew Aurora best and deserved to make the decision.

"That sounds perfect," Herita said. "These are the people I would want with me. Well, I would love for Cora and Asher to be here."

Mrs. Crimson left Aurora to Herita, and Asher never knew Aurora. I knew Aurora and she would prefer it'd be just us.

"You raised her," I said. "As much as I love Mrs. Crimson and Asher, they weren't a part of her life. Asher has never even met her." I pressed my lips together, observing Herita's warm expression. "*You* are her mother."

Herita's face went tense. "I appreciate that." She stood and flicked her eyes again with her pointer fingers. "If you all don't mind, I'm going to lie down. I'm already emotionally exhausted and have to prepare my mind for tonight."

"Please, rest," the Soothsayer said.

After Herita left, Naso walked toward the front door. "I'm going to explore more of the northern mountain plant life." A singular tear rushed down his cheek before he disappeared.

"It looks like it is just you and me." I dipped my head toward the Soothsayer.

"I would not have it any other way," she said. "May I ask you something?"

"Absolutely."

"This is not a session, but can you explain your mother's Manipulations during your capture?"

I lost my balance a little, surprised at the topic change. Her probing questions should've stopped surprising me.

"Well," I started, "she made her chair fall, and it broke the bindings that held her. The chair moved perfectly to break it. She continued to dodge the Officers' Manipulations that attacked her. She even caused their Manipulations to hit other Officers."

She placed a hand on her chin and fervently nodded. "I never asked you this, but what kind of Manipulations did you think they were?"

"Mentality." I believed in my response, but the way she asked made me think otherwise. "She made them forget who they were attacking and where they were aiming."

The Soothsayer patted the chair next to her. "What about the chair?"

"What do you mean?"

She tipped the chair back and let go as it thudded on the ground. "How did the chair move perfectly? A normal chair would be a difficult thing to follow as it fell."

"It landed on her bindings and broke them. She just knew what would happen."

"Did she Manipulate it that way?" The Soothsayer lifted the chair back onto its legs.

"No...it was lucky." As soon as I said the word and watched the Soothsayer nod, I realized the real answer. "Lucky...was she a Luckist?"

The Soothsayer raised her finger, pointing at the ceiling. "Yes!" She stood up. "She made an inopportune moment lean in her favor by breaking her bindings. She made Manipulations move in a different direction. She fits the mold."

I leaned on the couch, supporting myself with one arm. Was my mother a Luckist?

"Did you know this the whole time?" I asked.

"I had a hunch, but it only became clear once I saw you combat the Officers yesterday," she said.

Suddenly, my mind returned to the Flaunte Council room when they told me I wasn't a Perceptionist. I swallowed, hard. "What do you mean?"

"You moved the Vigor Aura right out of the Officers," she said. "This is not typical of Mentalists. To be frank, I never thought you were a Mentalist. Your ability to know certain facts about others really impressed the rest, but I know you did nothing beyond this. It was all very...well, lucky."

My head became light as I tried to blink away the dizziness swarming around me. Did I waste more time?

"You think I'm a Luckist?" I asked.

"Only time will tell," she said. "Well, and an actual Luckist would be helpful to help determine this. I only know results. I do not know the intricacy of their Aura."

The Soothsayer smiled and continued to nod, impressed by herself. Her attitude annoyed me. Why did she treat me like a puzzle to be solved?

"Why did you train me? How long did you know?" I asked.

"*How long did I know?*" she mocked. Then, an avalanche of words tumbled out like she could finally release a secret she had held for months. "Knowing is my strong suit. I listened. I observed. You showed no sign of the Mentality Aura, even as soon as you entered our city. But the Great Light pushed me to teach you. It pushed me for a long time. At first, I ignored it. But it was persistent. I finally folded to its will. You and I were meant to cross paths. I was meant to guide you without telling you what you needed to figure out. I thought my role was to be your mentor, but so much more came from our relationship."

"What?" I sat on the couch, overwhelmed by how fast she spoke.

She sat next to me, leaning close. "You have taught me to listen to myself. It is a difficult and heavy burden to be the Soothsayer, and I have been completely consumed by it. You let me start to be me. I have not been this happy in so long. The Great Light had a plan, and I think we both moved through the plan properly." She leaned back and let out a deep breath, smiling at the ceiling.

As much as I was glad to see her finally relax, her confession irked me.

"You earned this with a casualty." I shook my head. "I love our relationship, but part of me thinks that if you would've told us earlier, Aurora would still be alive because we would've left."

The Soothsayer leaned back forward. "Yaron, I do not think—"

"I'm not blaming you," I interrupted, realizing my misplaced anger held no power over me. "I've learned quite a bit from you and the Mentality Aura, even though it never really followed my Manipulations." My head pounded, but her smile relieved my stress. "You helped fix this." I pointed at my head. "Well, at least some of it."

"Yaron, I—" she began.

"I've always had this void from my anxiety. Aurora filled this void, and now..." My forehead ached as I held back tears. "Now, I feel lost. One week, I'm a normal human. The next, I'm a Perceptionist. Then I'm a Mentalist. Now, I'm a Luckist." I sighed. "The one constant thing since my freedom from Toterrum has been Aurora."

Somber silence surrounded us.

"And Naso," she added. "He actually has been around longer."

After all that had happened, I realized I didn't give Naso the credit he deserved. He stood by me through every battle, in every city, and with Aurora's death. Yet, Aurora had a different relationship with me. One beyond friendship.

"I love Naso, but we have a different relationship," I said. "Aurora was so much more. Aurora was..." I couldn't find the word.

"Read the letter from Felicity," the Soothsayer said. "I think this will help describe Aurora to you. Especially with the memorial tonight, you will want the right words."

I needed someone to tell me to read her letter. Dwelling on Aurora all the time only gave me great pain. Maybe reading the letter from Felicity would make me more present with the people who loved me. I eyed Naso from across the deck.

"I'll read it, but can you teach Naso about blocking a Mentality Manipulation? Like you did with me?"

She furrowed her brow before relaxing her face. "Of course, I will."

I marched into my room, grabbed the letter, and closed my eyes. Before I allowed any further apprehension to stop me, I ripped it open.

Yaron,

I don't know the right words to say…but I want to be sincere. And remember that I love you.

I was going to end things with you before that day. I was a different person. I know not a lot of time has passed, but I've changed. Really. You changed me.

It's true, I stayed with you after you became, well, famous. You gave a new power to me that I didn't expect. As time went on and you told me what the Officers could do, my definition of power shifted. I formed a new group dedicated to stopping what the Officers did to us. What you showed me they did to us. My relationship with you made me a leader. I liked the attention.

When you first said you loved me in that letter, I didn't know how to respond. The first time that I wrote that I loved you back was to appease you. I'm so sorry. But then I actually fell in love with you. I realized that you made others see me as special, but you always saw me as special. I'll never be appreciated like the way you appreciate me.

Time went on, and I fell more in love with you. I received your last letter, and my heart sank. Eventually all the bad things we do will catch up with us. I knew that. I was angry but realized I was only angry with myself. I focused more on wanting to know who helped you realize this but realized none of it mattered. I acted the way I did.

Please forgive me. I'm so sorry that my actions made you feel any less worthy. You're so much stronger than I am. You not only made me feel important and become a leader, but you also opened my eyes to the injustice our city faces.

With real love,
Felicity

Near the "Please forgive me" was a smeared watermark, making the words a little blurry. A tear for my terror. Aurora was right. Naso and Asher were right. She was using me. As much as I believed she had changed, her actions still hurt. Before I knew it, I was writing. Since the Soothsayer's aid in accessing the nightmares of Felicity's true actions, all the words I wanted to say stood ready.

Felicity,

I'm glad you got everything you wanted. I love so much about you, but as you said, time as passed and we have changed.
My heart hurts, but I won't hold this against you. Our personal relationship is over. To be honest, I've loved someone else for quite some time. Sadly, that's gone.
I still view you as a close friend. I think my love for you transformed into more of a friendship quite some time ago.
I think we'll still benefit from each other's correspondences in the future. It's our duty. I hope this change in our relationship doesn't impede our interactions. What we tell each other is very important for the future of our land.
I really hope you get to see the Coral Forest someday. I really do. Its beauty still reminds me of the days I thought we had a real relationship.

With sincerity,
Yaron

I sat and stared at the wall for a few moments. The words came so easily, yet coldness gripped my heart. I remembered Felicity flirting with me at school. I remembered her pulling me aside the first time and asking me to meet her in the back alley. The cloudy, smoggy sky hovered over me as I snuck out, risking a punishment to see her. I didn't know why I wanted to see her so badly, but I followed my heart. She stood below a streetlight and looked up at me with a mischievous smile that made me melt. She told me her feelings and kissed me.

My world stood still in that moment.

I remembered sneaking around at school to see each other every moment we could. In a closet. In one of the hallway nooks. No one knew about us, and I was okay with that. She smiled at me and kissed me.

My world stood still in that moment.

The day they captured Robyn shattered my life. Felicity held my hand for a moment in the crowd as Robyn was taken. Felicity came to my home and hugged me. She made everything seem like it would be okay. She kissed me.

My world stood still in that moment.

All such important moments in my life froze in sweet memories gone sour. Still pictures I could replay over and over again lost all beauty and joy. Felicity made me feel wanted and loved. She made Toterrum more bearable. I still wanted to hold onto the tainted memories and moments I had with her.

The coldness gripping my heart melted away. Tears escaped my eyes as the melted coldness found a way out of my exhausted body. The fact our relationship was over wasn't the problem. The true problem reared its ugly head: I missed Aurora so much. I saw the dense fog flashing dim yellow lights as the White Grande Lilies floated around and opened a lifeless mouth and consumed green meadow eyes. My world stood still in that moment.

I wanted to run to Aurora and tell her how I truly felt. Any Felicity-based guilt no longer stood in the way, but it was too late. The still, rotted pictures in my head of Felicity didn't have the same effect. They were frozen, lifeless moments filled with irrelevancy. My world shifted. My world moved again.

I folded the letter and let it go. The Soothsayer was right. The words finally came to me.

After several hours of driftless solidarity, we came together on the cottage's deck overlooking the sea. The Soothsayer walked up as a pile of White Grande Lillies rustled on the ground near her feet. As much as I wanted to flee from the flower's presence and all they represented, I dipped my head and continued my trek to the deck.

As the group faced the Soothsayer, she handed each of us a Grande White Lily. "As each of us says our memory of Aurora, let the flower fall to the sea," the Soothsayer said. "A beautiful living thing returns to its most beloved destination. The perfect analogy of Aurora's life returning to the ocean she loves."

"Beautiful," Herita said, caressing her flower's petals. "I would love if you would start, Soothsayer."

The Soothsayer lifted her White Grande Lily as a glowing light floated in the air. The light faded before pulsing again, revealing the little wings and body of a Luvala. The beast twirled around the Soothsayer's head before resting on her shoulder.

"Fascinating." The Soothsayer's face lit up and faded at the beast's command.

Their Auras pushed back and forth against one another before intertwining. A burst of colors pulsed within the exchange, just like I did with Ricochet's Aura.

"Did you...?" I trailed off, lost in wonder.

The Soothsayer blinked her attention up from the beast to me. A radiant smile curled up her cheeks. "Yes, I did."

"Did what?" Naso asked as he looked back and forth between our silent exchange. "Are you kidding? You have a partner beast?"

"Aurora taught me her findings, and I have had some interesting exchanges with this beast the last few days." The Soothsayer paused. "I did not realize she followed me here." She tilted her head forward as the Luvala nuzzled up to her in bright pulses.

"I do all this work, and you get the partner beast?" Naso flung his arms in the air.

"I am sorry," the Soothsayer said. "I did not mean for it to happen."

"It's okay." Naso sighed. "It's not like it's anything big or cool."

The Luvala zipped off the Soothsayer's shoulder and zipped in circles in front of Naso's face. Naso's head followed the beast before he raised his hand and smacked himself across the face.

"What was that?" Naso exclaimed.

The Soothsayer tilted her head while observing the Luvala return to her and zip around before resting back on the Soothsayer's shoulder. "I am afraid you offended Iri," she said. "She wanted to let you know that you should not judge a book by its cover."

"*She* did that?" Naso chuckled. "Fair point, little beast."

"How wonderful," Herita said. "But now can we get back to this...event?" Though Herita forced a smile, the darkness covering her expression contradicted it.

"Of course," the Soothsayer said. "It would be my pleasure." She took a step toward the deck's edge, positioning herself to face us while looking over at the ocean. "Aurora met me just as I became the Soothsayer. I had very few friends—no one paid much attention to me before—and then everyone wanted to know me. Aurora befriended me in a way not for my attention but because of her nature. She saw something in me that I did not see in myself. I did the same for her." She paused, looking down at the large flower. "Perceptionists are supposed to change how others see the world around them, but she always saw the world around in the purest way. I hope I get to know other genuine hearts like Aurora's in the future." She stretched her hand out with the flower over the edge of the deck, holding tightly to the petals as the wind tried to carry the flower away. "May the Great Light carry you over into the sea and beyond. May you find the inclusive world that you always dreamed about." A glistening gem fell from the Soothsayer's cheek before bouncing on the petal. Iri brightened and caused the petals to glow in iridescent brilliance. The Soothsayer let the lily fall into the ocean.

Aurora's body appeared next to the falling flower, body flailing next to the bright Coral Elderkaw.

"If it's okay with everyone, I'd like to go next," Naso said, stepping up to the Soothsayer as she touched his shoulder and stepped to the side. Naso observed his flower before looking out at the ocean. "One of the first interactions Aurora and I had was when she giggled at me after hitting my head with a branch." Herita and I chuckled at the thought. "I know I'm a comic relief for everyone, and not many people take me seriously, but Aurora did." His voice quivered as he continued. "In between her sarcastic remarks and amusement at my stupidity, she never treated me like I wasn't important." Naso faced me, forehead tense and the flower shaking in his hands. "I feel like Yaron gets all the attention since he is the Manipulator, and I'm not, but Aurora treated us the same. The same respect and the same importance in battle." He stood up straight, steadied his voice, and looked back at the ocean. "She's the friend I felt I always had even though I didn't know her long. I'm beyond blessed to have known her greatness. She's my sister..." His voice cracked. "...and I love her." Iri brightened the lily as Naso quickly let the flower go and then wiped his nose. "I hope you have someone as funny as me wherever you are."

Aurora's body dropped toward the ocean, next to the flower. Her hair whipped in the wind even though her body moved so slowly, allowing me to witness every detail again. Meadow eyes pierced me, forcing my body forward. I nearly dropped the flower over the edge before catching it and pulling it close. I steadied my heart and closed my eyes.

"Aurora..."

A strong wave shook my body. My lungs tightened, and my throat dried. A multitude of bitter tears forced their way from my eyes. I couldn't force words out. My thoughts ripped away from my body, hovering over the tragedy before me. Then, Herita stepped forward and ran her hand across my back. The sensation drew my mind back, bringing my attention back to the present.

After a steady breath, words poured from my mouth in an endless waterfall. "Aurora changed my life forever. She taught me about Aura. She taught me about Manipulating. She wanted to help me figure out who I was and what I could Manipulate as much as I did. She cared about me so much. You never realize how important someone is to you and how much you really wanted to tell them how important they are until they're gone." I gripped the flower tightly, wanting to rip it in half. Wanting to make the memories reality again. But destroying such a delicate thing wouldn't bring her back. "I love you, Aurora." I clenched my jaw, my body convulsing. "I love you so much." Every truth I wanted to speak, wanted to show finally found freedom. "I've loved you since the moment I met you. I was so *stupid* to think others could even come close to how important you are to me. You *were* to me." I pushed my face into the delicate petals, the sweet aroma of death from the White Grande Lily overwhelming my senses. "I want you back. I want you back in my life so I can tell you how much I *need* you." I pulled my face away from the ruffled flower. "Don't *ever* forget me. I'll follow you someday. We will be together."

Any of the tears I couldn't control finally dried up. I did my best to straighten the folded petals. The petals lit up and stretched back into their original shape. I peeked over my shoulder at Iri's brightness fading. I held the White Grande Lily out, hovering over the edge. Even after willing my fingers to let go, I couldn't. I didn't want to let go. So, I slammed my arms down on the banister of the deck, a sharp pain traveling up my arm. The flower escaped my grasp. It fell in slow motion down into the waves.

Aurora's innocent face stared back at me, the flower dancing next to her. The face faded, leaving only the white petals, the wind, and the ocean.

I wept, pulling away from Herita and finding my own space to sink into my grief.

Herita gave me a teary nod before taking a finger and flicking away the tears flooding her eyes. "Thank you all so much for these words." Herita steadied her voice. "I remember the moment Cora told me I would be raising Aurora." She caressed the flower. "I was terrified. I never picked a life as a mother, yet the responsibility was thrown at me. I remember the moment Cora handed her over to me, and I stared at her beautiful face. Her eyes remained the same plant-like green her whole life." She let out an exasperated sigh. "How could something so small be trusted to someone as weak as me?"

Herita lost control and sobbed over the flower. Iri glowed and caused each of Herita's tears to glow just like her. Naso positioned himself next to her and gripped her arm. "We're here for you," he said.

Herita nodded and steadied her shivering body. "I grew from that moment on. I became stronger. I became wiser. I became everything I was meant to be because of Aurora. She pushed me to grow in new ways every moment I was around her. She challenged me to change for the good. She was stubborn." She chuckled. "*So* stubborn. Many times, when we fought, she would tell me that I wasn't her real mother. Her real mother would treat her better." She brought the flower to her chest. "It broke my heart every time she said it." Eyes closed and arms crossed, she swayed herself back and forth. "She was right. But every time, she apologized and said even if I wasn't her real mother, I was the only mother she knew and that she loved me. She had such a forgiving heart, which taught me to develop a forgiving heart."

Herita gestured for me to come by her. "Are you sure?" I asked.

"Get over here," she said before wrapping her right arm as best as she could around Naso and me, her other hand holding tightly to the flower. "When she ran off to save the two of you, I had never been more afraid ever in my life. But I remembered how strong she was. I mean, I raised her. I knew she would be okay. When she came back to Flaunte, I hugged her and whispered in her ear, 'I love you, Aurora. I didn't doubt for one second you wouldn't return. Whoever you brought back is going to change our lives in astounding ways.' And wow, did that become true." She smiled at each of us.

"I'm still a fool," Naso joked.

Herita touched her head to Naso's. "She added two more children into my life. I view you both as my family. I love you both so much and know the Great Light was working on all of this from the beginning." She focused on the Soothsayer. "I admit, I'm mad at the Light for taking her away. I'm furious."

The Soothsayer nodded. "As am I."

Herita released Naso and me, turning to the ocean. "Aurora, please hug your father. He loved you." Soft whimpers filled the space in between each word. "I *never* thought you would leave this world before me. Especially with the little time I have left. I will see you soon. Very soon, my little minnow."

Iri glowed brighter than she did with the other flowers. The lily glowed as bright as the moon on a clear night. In one loud wail, Herita released the White Grande Lily as it whipped through the sky before finally falling toward the sea. Aurora's green eyes shined so brightly right in front of me. Then, they faded into the fog, just like the day she left me.

Amid Herita's loud wails and the rest of our accompanying cries, the Soothsayer said, "Great Light, we thank you for the life that is Aurora of Flaunte. Daughter of Cora, Douglas, and Herita. Sister of Asher. Friend of Yaron, Naso, and me. She was a light to our world. Please let her light continue into the beyond and within each of our hearts."

I lost track of time. Harsh sobs transitioned into soft whimpers. Eventually, somber silence covered us like a blanket. Not a blanket of peace but a brief sense of safety from our agonizing grief. The Soothsayer started a fire as the sun sat. Pinks, deep purples, and light blues painted across the horizon in chaotic simplicity. No one spoke, but I kept thinking about Herita saying that she didn't have much time left. Was she sicker than I thought?

"Herita," Naso broke the delicate silence. "I don't mean to be rude, but what did you mean by 'not much time left'?"

Herita stretched her neck and leaned forward, blinking her eyes with compassion. "The Health Mentalists have run out of options for me." She pressed her lips together and bobbed her head for a moment, eyes glossing over. "They said the cancer spread, and I may have one month, six months, or maybe up to a year to live."

Every part of my life collided with the others. Nothing made sense. My sense of reality drifted as I just wanted to roll over and die.

"You're joking?" Naso eyed her but Herita's expression didn't shift. "No. You can't. We need you."

"I was going to tell you later," she said. "Truth is, I've known for a few days, but everything just came crashing in on itself." For how torn up Naso and I were, Herita held a calm demeanor.

Through my numb thoughts and trembling chest, I asked, "Why is nothing good happening?"

"Believe me, I wish I could change this outcome, but my bed has been made, and I'm preparing to curl up in it." Herita shrugged and leaned back.

"There is another option," the Soothsayer said.

"There is?" Naso asked, looking back and forth between the Soothsayer and Herita. "Tell us! We'll make it happen no matter what."

"Your Mentalists are out of ideas." Herita furrowed her brow. "Please, don't give us false hope."

"Luck," the Soothsayer said, nodding. "Luck can change the outcome."

"That's your idea? Luck?" Naso asked. "Just hope it works out?"

"The Luck Aura," I clarified after I realized what the Soothsayer was trying to say.

"What?" he asked.

"I have recently told Yaron about his adoptive mother's heritage along with his lack of Mentality Manipulation abilities, and I think Luck is his next option," the Soothsayer casually said.

Herita leaned forward, cocking her head. "What?"

"Did I miss something?" Naso added.

"The next place Yaron should go is to Hallow, the Capital of Luck," the Soothsayer said. "Not only will they train him in Luck, but there have been many miracles accomplished by the Luckists. It is worth a shot."

Herita and Naso exchanged glances, a perplexed silence falling between them.

"Yaron isn't a Mentalist?" Naso asked.

"He is not," the Soothsayer said, sounding a little impatient. As smart as she was, she sometimes forgot that her words moved faster than people could comprehend. "The Manipulations he displayed during the siege are not Mentality Manipulations. This only solidified what I have known."

"Hold on a second," Naso said. "This whole time, you knew he wasn't a Mentalist, yet you trained him?"

"I actually guided him, I never trained him," the Soothsayer replied. "Cerebrum Brysen was the only one who did any training. That was more combat than Mentality Aura training."

Naso stared at her before laughing. Not just laughing but rolling onto his back, holding his gut. "Are you kidding me?"

"Why did you waste your time then?" Herita asked. "I know Mentalists don't like to waste their time on things that don't benefit them."

"You know us too well." The Soothsayer held up her hands. "The Great Light guided me to work with Yaron. Most Mentalists follow their own desires. I truly listen to the Light."

Naso continued to laugh. "This makes absolutely no sense!"

Herita shoved Naso. "You're also a genuinely good person, Soothsayer," Herita added.

"Thank you," the Soothsayer responded, staring at Naso. "Returning to our original topic, Hallow is a wise destination for further treatment."

Naso took a deep breath, regaining his composure. "I thought their capital disappeared?"

"No one has been in contact with them in decades," Herita added.

The Soothsayer sat there with a concentrated gaze before a devious grin curled up her cheeks. "I may know a way to get there." She nodded her head.

"Please, enlighten us," Herita said.

"I will once we return to Labyrintha," the Soothsayer responded. "Please relax for our remaining time here. Also, please do not mention this to anyone upon our return. I need to address the Cerebrums prior to you telling anyone."

"How can a Luckist do more than a Mentalist?" I questioned as I paced. "I thought you specialized in the body's network."

"We do, but our ability to heal is based entirely on techniques or treatments we know and can use." The Soothsayer held her hands out and moved them around as she spoke. "The Luckists can trigger healing of the unexplained. As you can imagine, Mentalists and Luckists are opposites. We lean on facts and plans. They lean on opportunity and happenstance. When the two interact, they argue more than anyone else in Biome. I have not witnessed this firsthand, but the history passed on to me from previous Soothsayers account for these debacles."

"We've been pretty lucky," Naso responded while looking at me. "You've done things that no one can explain as we've escaped tricky situations." He looked up and moved his lips to the right.

"Let's hope my Aura can finally be explained." I pointed at my chest. "More than anything, I really hope we can heal you, Herita."

"Only the Great Light will make that decision." Herita looked up to the sky and closed her eyes.

"Do not say that to a Luckist," the Soothsayer said. "They are not religious in any way. Unless things have changed, but they would not allow for the Great Light."

"I need to rest my head," Naso said as he rubbed his temple. "This morning has been an emotional rollercoaster; this evening was uplifting and sad, and now there is another upcoming journey. Can we stop for the day?"

"We should all meditate." The Soothsayer brought her hands together. "I will guide us all."

"Not what I had in mind, but I have no energy to argue." Naso sat and crossed his legs, eyes already shut.

I sat across from Herita, watching her. A spark returned to her eyes as hope gave her another fighting chance. Leaving Labyrintha made sense. Every time I looked at the Black

Stone Mountains, I saw Aurora falling into the fog. Leaving the constant reminder of her could mean a fresh start.

13

Light Within Darkness

"We have accomplished a victory, which is rare in these times," Lilah announced to the Cerebrums, Herita, Naso, Zela, and me. "I am proud of our city."

Applause echoed around the Cerebellum room, so different from the serene cottage by the ocean. Two days later, I wasn't ready for harsh reality.

Lilah continued, "The part I do not look forward to is reviewing the damage done. As we look at the damage done in battel, we will review our recovery options. Cerebrum Brysen, how many casualties were there?"

Brysen glanced at our group and gave an uncomfortable smile. "Great Cerebrum Petra, there were twenty-five casualties." He cleared his throat. "A much smaller number than I expected, though still a monumental loss. Great lives who did more than we could ever ask perished. The good news with this situation is that many more lives could have been lost. I am beyond satisfied with what the Surprisants accomplished, and we honor those who gave their lives to obtain this victory."

I squeezed Herita's hand, my sweaty palms slipping along hers. I tried to pull away, but she held on tight.

"This is enlightening news," Lilah responded. "I am sure your stress level is high with replacing these Surprisants. It seems like you already did this a few moments ago."

"We will find more," Brysen said as he bowed his head.

"The White Grande Lily traps did their part," Lilah continued. "We will need to replace the ones lost. They are important to our defenses."

"They will all be replaced," another Cerebrum rose to say before sitting down.

"Excellent," Lilah responded. "We will also continue to protect our friends from Flaunte and Toterrum."

The Soothsayer stood. "I speak for my friends that the gesture is appreciated. However, Labyrintha will no longer house them."

A steady mumble echoed around. Concerned glances and firm glares directed toward us. Zela mouthed, *What?*

"But Yaron still has training to accomplish with the other Cerebrums," Lilah said. "The timing also seems inappropriate with the Officers sitting right outside our mountain."

"Training that is unnecessary for one who cannot Manipulate Mentality," the Soothsayer said. "Based on Yaron's Manipulations from the siege, I can confidently say Yaron is not a Mentalist."

The mumbling erupted into loud exclamations.

"But he bested many of the Surprisants," Zela interrupted. "His Mentality Manipulations are like none we have ever seen." She put her hands on her hips and cocked her head.

"Because they were not Mentality Manipulations," the Soothsayer said. "We have all been mistaken."

Her deception surprised me. It must have been easier to lie than explain the wasted time. Based on my basic knowledge of Mentalists, they despised wasted time.

Lilah let out a deep sigh. "Where is the next destination, then? He is not a Perceptionist. He is not a Mentalist. Which of the two lost cities should they go to next? Or do they return to Toterrum? The options seem to be limited."

"Hallow." The city's name echoed across the room as the Soothsayer said it. "Hallow is the next destination."

The discussions amongst the Cerebrums morphed into shouting and screaming. My muscles tightened as sharp eyes snapped between the Soothsayer and me. The blatant irritation covering the group made it difficult to distinguish who it was directed at.

The Soothsayer warned me before the meeting that hatred of Hallow was embedded deep in Labyrintha's history. Ever since Hallow abandoned Perception and Mentality during the siege of Rithbar, Labyrintha has never trusted them. The Soothsayer also told me that their lifestyles, religious beliefs, and overall way they each Manipulated Auras differently added to the divide.

"Quiet down!" Lilah yelled, waiting for the Cerebrums to settle. She rubbed the bridge of her nose before fixating on the Soothsayer. "Are you telling me you *know* the location of Hallow?"

Every head in the room snapped over to the Soothsayer in a harmonious rhythm.

A new paleness flooded the Soothsayer's cheeks. "You are correct," the Soothsayer calmly replied.

Accusations, harsh words, and slamming fists took over nearly every Cerebrum.

"Enough!" Lilah yelled, slamming her own fists on the table. She joined in with the directed glares at the Soothsayer. "How long have you known?"

"Three lifetimes," the Soothsayer whispered, averting her gaze. "This information was discovered three Soothsayers ago." An audible gulp escaped her before she held eye contact with Lilah. "The information was sworn to be protected from Soothsayer to Soothsayer until an opportune moment arose. This is that moment." Her head turned to me. "I believe Yaron is a Luckist."

As if on cue, every Cerebrum moved their sharp glares from the Soothsayer to me. The only Cerebrum to not look in my direction was Brysen. Why had the Soothsayer turned all the attention to me?

"Did I do something wrong?" I asked.

The Soothsayer walked around the table, pointing at each Cerebrum as she passed. "How *dare* you assume the worst of Yaron. He saved our city. He fought by your side. Our history with Luckists does not mean we are to hate the first one we met in many decades."

The attention moved away from me. I leaned over to Herita and whispered, "Did I miss something?"

She leaned back. "Mentalists hate Luckists. Luckists have a history of hating Mentalists." She shrugged.

"The Soothsayer is right," Lilah said. "We should not let our history dictate our future."

The group reverted back to calm discussion instead of chaotic screaming. A few Cerebrums stood up and walked out of the meeting, glaring at me as they passed. Naso stood up and smacked his hands on the table. I tried to pull him down, but he didn't budge. Attention all turned to him.

"Friends." Naso meticulously eyed each Cerebrum. "You are all my friends. I have learned so much from you. I fought with you." He pointed at his chest, a small thump following from the impact. "I can't Manipulate." He pointed at me. "My friend Yaron has fought harder than anyone I know. He risked his life for your city." He lowered his hand and focused on Herita. "We lost our dear friend Aurora for this city." He held out his hands, gesturing to the group. "Was it all for you to act like children?" He raised his right index finger. "I'm ashamed. The war with Toterrum was lost a long time ago because we didn't team up together."

"Because the Luckists abandoned us!" one of the Cerebrums yelled.

Naso crossed his arms and nodded toward the Cerebrum. "A good friend told me not to judge another's decision until you know why they made it." He looked over to the Soothsayer. "We need to reach past our pride. Very far past our pride if there is any hope for the future."

The Cerebrums' discussion faded into mumbling. Naso screeched his chair back and sat down, arms crossed.

"Thank you, Naso," Lilah said, watching him. "He is right. Our city has lost too much to act like children. Yaron and company, we will support your journey in any way we can."

The mumbling quieted. An eerie, foreign silence fell over the group.

"This brings up one last thing," the Soothsayer added. "I am traveling with them."

"What?" Lilah snapped, standing.

The silence ripped cleanly out of the air as the shouting and screeching returned like glass shattering in a quiet kitchen. Sharp and abrasive. My shock at her announcement made me want to scream. What was she thinking? She was the most valuable Mentalist in Labyrintha.

The Soothsayer patiently waited for the yelling to stop. Each Cerebrum realized she wasn't going to say anything else until they gave her the opportunity to do so.

"The Great Light continues to guide me on a path with this group," the Soothsayer said. "I will not ignore it. Nor do I need approval from the Cerebrums."

"We cannot have you leave," Lilah said. "We need you here."

"The Soothsayers have a history of leaving Labyrintha," the Soothsayer said. "My job is to bring wisdom to all leaders of Biome." She moved her hands in an outward circle. "I intend to fulfill this."

Lilah watched her before shaking her head and laughing at the situation. "You are a troublemaker today, Soothsayer. Everyone, please leave the Soothsayer and me alone. Knowing only works if we listen."

Everyone stood up and departed. I exchanged glances with the smiling Soothsayer. Zela ran up next to me as we walked out.

"What in the Great Light was that?" Zela asked.

"I had no idea she was coming with us," I replied as she squinted. "Honestly, I didn't!"

"Whatever you say." She pushed my shoulder. "You are not a Mentalist? What other enlightening things happened at the cottage?"

"Enlightening." I laughed. "Plenty of things. But we're planning on leaving tomorrow. Can we have dinner tonight?"

As much as I was ready to leave Labyrintha, my friendship with Zela became something I deeply cherished. I wished she could come with me.

"Absolutely," Zela responded. "I will make sure Lilah calms down for it." She patted my back.

One of the Cerebrums that departed early bumped into me and pushed his hands forward, shoving me to the ground. Scrapping my forearms, I pushed up, glaring up at the Cerebrum. Zela bumped her chest into the Cerebrum, ready to fight, but Brysen ran up to push Zela to the side.

"Cerebrum Nicolai," Brysen said to the older, bald man. "Are we going to have a problem on this nice day?"

"He is Luckist scum," Cerebrum Nicolai said as he spat on my shoes, residual droplets spraying my arms. "He has caused our city to be attacked. He only brings shame."

"Go home, Cerebrum." Brysen got really close to the Cerebrum, emphasizing the height difference between the two and staring down at the now cowering Cerebrum. "I would not want my Facts to hit you across your dense skull." He slammed the staff into the ground.

Cerebrum Nicolai narrowed a stare on Brysen before shuffling back. He held his pointer finger up at me, trembling. "I will be on my way, Cerebrum Brysen." He threw his hand down and stormed off.

Brysen turned back to me and helped me up. "I am sorry you are dealing with this," Brysen said. "Our ways are old and stubborn."

"It's no problem." I lied, rubbing my scrapped arms.

"Zela," Brysen said as he turned, "do not lash out against citizens like that. I understand you care for your friend, but your duty is to the city."

Zela kept her firm posture and nodded with a scowl. "Yes, Cerebrum Brysen." She walked off.

"She is a spitfire." Brysen sighed. He turned and bowed. "Anyway, it has been an honor to serve with you, Yaron. Good luck on your new venture."

Brysen had done so much for me. He risked his life, and ultimately his husband's life, to save me when the Vigorists ambushed us outside the Blackstone Mountains. He showed me kindness and knowledge when I secluded myself from everyone. He accepted me and trained me as a Surprisant. I respected, adored, and considered Brysen a true friend.

Overwhelmed by all the memories, I stepped forward and embraced him in a hug. A sweet, nutty scent came from his hair. He hesitated but embraced me back gently.

"Thank you for believing in me when others didn't," I said. A tear escaped and ran down my cheek.

"I know a good person when I see one." He pulled back and held my shoulders. "And remember, death may steal those we love, but we must live on and spread their legacy."

A thin sheen of moisture covering his eyes reflected the sky above. The Officers took his husband all that time ago, just like they took my mother. Just like they took Aurora. A somber understanding fell between us that only death could cause. That wonderful man turned and disappeared around the corner.

I waited for the Soothsayer to finish her meeting with Lilah, worried about what was being said. A pack of rodent beasts scurried past, hairless ears flapping behind them. Though I lived in Labyrintha for a good amount of time, I had missed so many attributes about the city. Now that I was leaving, I took my time taking the city in.

So many little beasts moved across the ground, jumped from roof to roof, or flew around the sky. They lacked the bright colors and features found in Flaunte, instead taking more muted tones allowing them to hide in the city. Water droplets trickled off buildings, echoing as they hit the ground. Labyrintha held such pristine silence most of the time.

The glass walls of the buildings allowed me to see the interior of homes. The people inside pretended like they didn't notice me staring. After a while, they looked at me, throwing their hands in the air. I shifted my gaze away, my heart pounding from being caught.

"I see you are doing some light stalking today," Lilah said.

I jumped, completely unaware she had left the Cerebellum. My heart smashed against my sternum, trying to run away from the harmless encounter. Clenching my hand to my chest, I said, "You scared me."

"Zela taught me a thing or two about being a Surprisant." She winked. "Are you waiting on the Soothsayer?"

I nodded. "I'm just concerned about my friends and their conversation."

"You have had quite the impact on our city." Lilah spun, hands extended before stopping and fixating on me. "Most importantly, you have had a positive impact on the two most important people in my life."

"They're two of my favorite people." I grinned.

"I am going to talk to Zela, but I think we may hold our wedding tonight," she said. "I know we want the Soothsayer and you to be present. Who knows if and when we will all be in the same city again."

I blinked, surprised at my importance to them. As much as I enjoyed seeing new places, I adored the people I had met in both Flaunte and Labyrintha. Leaving Flaunte, my close friends came with me. Though the Soothsayer planned on leaving, leaving Zela behind struck me.

"I would be honored to be part of your day," I said.

"I better get going then," she said. "There is a lot to put together for a last-minute wedding. I will see you later today. Plan on the lagoon unless you hear otherwise."

"Good luck," I replied.

Knowing the Soothsayer was finished, I rushed inside to the library. The Soothsayer piled books upon books in a large bag next to her. She carefully pulled a book out of the pile before shaking her head and putting the book back. Without turning to face me, she asked, "Do you know how hard it is to limit the number of books you travel with?"

"Don't you have them all memorized anyway?" I joked.

She held her pointer finger in the air. "You are right." She pulled five books from the pile. "I will bring the important ones with maps and pictures." She stopped and leaned her elbows on the table, and pushed her face into her hands. She groaned and stretched back into a standing position. "I must confess, I am a bit frazzled. The excitement to go on an adventure is blurring my mind."

The Flaunte incense finally hit me as I approached. Rather than think too much about Aurora, I tried to think about the first time I entered Flaunte and all the wonderful things it held. Labyrintha took a while, but its features gave me wonder. Would Hallow have the same effect?

"Did you intend to go with us this whole time?" I asked.

"I did not." She shook her head. "I decided right before I spoke." She rubbed her hands on her face again, stretching her cheeks down and making her eyes take a funny shape. "Impulsivity is not like me. I looked over at you, Naso, and Herita and saw a light glowing over your heads." She gestured to the space above my head. "I felt as if the Light was telling me to go with you." She clenched the air as if grabbing the Light she pictured from before. "My life has changed for the better since knowing you, and I did not think our time together was ready to end."

The shadows on her face danced as her lips curled upward. The genuine happiness found within her smile contrasted with the cold, lonely person I first met when entering Labyrintha. She had changed. So had I.

"I'm glad you're coming." My normally tense body relaxed. "There's still so much more I need to learn about myself, and a Mentalist would be a great addition to the team."

"Petra does worry about our departure from the maze," she said. "There are still a good number of Vigorists surrounding the area. They are planning to create a diversion and have a small team of Surprisants escorting us out of the area. I am glad she thought of this. It will be a tricky departure."

I crossed my arms, my body tensing. Leaving Labyrintha would be difficult. What if we didn't get out? What if we were caught? My mind tried to drift from my body and dissociate from the new stimuli, but I shook my head, pinched my arm, and kept myself present.

"Did she tell you about moving their wedding day?" I asked, trying to change the subject.

"Yes!" she exclaimed. "I am so happy they moved it up so we can be there. Those two have played important roles in my life. It will be so good to celebrate them and their love."

Weddings were rare in Toterrum. Typically, they occurred in secret, quiet places with only close friends and family. I knew people got married. I just didn't know the ceremonial aspect of a wedding.

"What do people wear to weddings?" I asked.

"I would show you, but Herita is better versed in this," she said. "Plus, I have a lot to get done today."

"She does love cultural clothing." I smiled, thinking about the Tubasas in Flaunte and how uncomfortably they fit.

As instructed, I went back to our house. Herita and Naso ran around gathering items in piles next to bags. Without being asked, I made my way to my room to gather my own belongings. I froze, Aurora's door wide open. Nothing stood out of place, like the room waited for her return.

Naso placed a hand on my shoulder and turned his head toward Herita. "What should we do about Aurora's things?" he asked.

"I know it sounds odd, but I'm taking them with me." Herita didn't stop moving. "I'm going to leave some of the clothes we gathered here but take some of the things she found important in Flaunte." She stopped one hand on her hip and the other pushing against her forehead. Her gray hair frizzled in the air. "I'm not ready to let her go, and keeping some of her things lets me hold a part of her with me." She bit her knuckle, a wave of tears trying to force their way out.

"We'll carry the bag," Naso said. "It'll be no problem. Right, Yaron?"

"Of course," I replied. "The Soothsayer said you would help me find some clothes for the wedding tonight?"

Herita's gaze jolted upward. "Wedding? What wedding?" She placed both hands on her hips.

"Zela and Lilah moved their wedding to tonight." I grinned, Herita mirroring my expression. "They wanted us all to be a part of it before we left."

Herita clapped so loud my ears tickled. "This is wonderful news! Something joyful within all the despair."

"A wedding?" Naso asked. "I don't think I've ever been to one before."

"I said the same thing," I added.

"I'll run to the market and buy some clothes for us all," Herita said. "You both finish packing."

Herita returned as fast as she left. She handed me a light blue jacket, dark pants, a white buttoned shirt, and a light blue bowtie. Faint sparkles covered the jacket, pants, and bowtie. Naso's clothing was similar but with a light gray jacket and pants with a dark blue buttoned shirt and light gray bowtie. Faint, light blue vertical lines covered the jacket, pants, and bowtie.

"You are looking handsome, Mr. Meek," Naso said with a light bow. His hair folded to the side with a slight sheen.

"You as well, Mr. Finn," I bowed back as we laughed.

Herita came out of her room in a navy dress with a white sheer covering the main part of the dress covered in large, white pieces of glitter. Her hair reached for the ceiling, tied up with sparkles covering her face. Her green eyes shined even brighter than normal. They reminded me of Aurora's.

"You look amazing!" Naso exclaimed.

"You look stunning," I added.

"I know," she replied as she stood in a pose. "You both clean up well."

Naso walked around the house, striking various poses with the most ridiculous expressions. Welcomed laughter found Herita and me.

Once the laughter died down, she took each of us by the hand. "We should all have fun tonight. We all have grief but are healing. This may be our last night of fun for quite some time. So, enjoy it. Promise me you will."

"I promise," Naso said.

My head ached thinking about Aurora. I tried not to think about my loss for the moment, but Herita squeezed my hand tighter, keeping me present.

"I promise." I sniffled. "For Aurora."

"For Aurora." They echoed.

***

At the lagoon, a group of unfamiliar people played a beautiful melody with stringed instruments. Large, round lanterns hung from the tree branches. Twilight took over as the lantern lights let off subdued lighting. The Luvalas appeared in a few twinkles before filling all the empty space between lanterns and the sky above with hundreds of yellow specks of light. White chairs faced the lagoon where a ten-foot stand stood with twenty White Grande Lilies covering it. For a moment, Aurora's green eyes appeared between the lilies before I realized that smaller, blue flowers actually filled the gaps in between the White Grande Lillies.

Ricochet walked up to me and rubbed his head against my leg, sensing my discomfort with those terrible, beautiful flowers. About fifteen to twenty chairs faced forward. For putting the ceremony together in one day, it looked like it had been planned and decorated for months.

"My friends all look amazing." The Soothsayer stepped up beside me in a dark blue dress with sleeves. Small blue ribbons hung from the back of her hair, tied into a bun. Snow white makeup lined her eyes and lips.

"Wow," I said. "You look beautiful."

She gave me a side hug. "Would you sit with me?"

"Of course." I looped my arm with hers.

As we walked to find seats, Ricochet followed. A couple of the angry Cerebrums, including Cerebrum Nicolai, glared as we passed. Ricochet growled in their direction, making them avert their gaze. We sat near the front.

People continued to fill the seats before the music shifted from a soft melody to a triumphant march. The religious leader from the services I attended walked toward the front in the same dark blue robe as the Soothsayer wore. After a second glance, a light blue heart with beams of yellow light coming off it with another darker blue heart in the center crested her chest. Zela walked in next in a similar jacket and pants lined with bright white stitching and a large, white bowtie drooping downward. Her blue hair shined bright, and stood tall in a wavelike style. She stopped next to the religious leader at the front.

Everyone then stood and turned in the same direction Zela did. Lilah walked in wearing a large, light blue gown, draping down to the ground and dragging across the ground as she walked. Glitter lined the dress shaped like White Grande Lilies. She held one of the flowers in her hand, her hair covered in the light blue flowers that lined the floral arrangement at the front. Luvalas surrounded her, trailing behind as if coordinated for the event.

Zela and Lilah shared teary, loving gazes and bright smiles. Once Lilah arrived up front, they faced each other and took each other's hands. The Luvalas outlined them in a halo of sparkling brilliance. Everyone sat.

"Friends and family." The religious leader held out her hands. "We are blessed to be together for such a wonderful union." She touched each of their shoulders. "Labyrintha has been especially blessed with two dynamic leaders in Petra and Zela. The Great Light shines and shows the truth behind all our intentions. These two have shown no signs of blemish or ill intent. They are truly followers of the Great Light and listeners of Mentality. People of Labyrintha, how do we know if these two are meant to be together forever?"

"Knowing only works if you listen," everyone replied.

"Then listen," the leader continued. "Listen to their proclamations to one another. I know neither of you had the proper time to write these, but I am sure the words will be beautiful and intentional, nonetheless. Zela, you may go first."

"Petra," she began. "My Lilah. When we first met as kids, I knew you were my best friend. We went through so many good things and so many bad things together. We have fought. We have had fun. We have cried. We have laughed. Every moment, I have loved my time with you. You know me more than anyone else does. More than anything, you respect me. You make me feel wanted and worthy of love. The Great Light has shined on your face and made it clear to me that you are my person."

Zela's lip quivered as Lilah pulled Zela's hands together, steadying a building shake. It was the most nervous I had seen Zela be. I giggled at the way my friend fumbled.

"Beautiful," the leader said. "Petra, you may now proceed."

"Zela," Lilah began, "my warrior. People look to me for leadership. They look to me for insight and making decisions. If I falter, I am judged. My anxiety runs deep day in and day out. You do not judge me. You hold me up when I fall. You bring me out of my darkness when I ignore the Light. You make me a better leader and a better lover. I do not know what I would do without you. The Great Light uses you to bring me back each time I fall. I know you are my person."

Exactly as expected, Lilah declared her love in such a proper, firm, and lasting way. The nervous warrior and the calm diplomat fitted together like destined, corresponding shapes. Something pulled at my chest and took the air from my lungs. Ricochet's Aura was right there to soothe me.

"Wonderful," the leader continued. "Beautiful, pure words. People of Labyrintha, you have heard that proclamation. What say you?"

"We have listened, and now we know," the crowd replied.

"Everyone can now take a moment and lift a prayer up to the Great Light for these two," the religious leader said. "Whether it be good fortune, happiness, or good health, present it to the Great Light for discernment."

A hush filled the space, the lagoon releasing small sounds from a bug or fish. The Luvalas pulsed their little lights as everyone bowed their heads and closed their eyes. I didn't close my eyes. I absorbed the surrounding environment. The growing night sky cleared with residual stars being revealed. A light wind blew through the trees. I took a deep breath and finally closed my eyes. I thought of Aurora. Praying felt odd to me, but it was for Lilah and Zela.

So, I lifted a prayer: *Great Light, don't let Zela or Lilah ever regret not telling one another how much they love one another.*

I opened my eyes and looked up at the sky again. My gaze drifted down to Zela and Lilah, who had their eyes open and were just smiling at one another. Zela whispered something to her. I love you. I read her lips. Lilah mouthed that she loved her back. Maybe my prayer came to fruition. Maybe they truly just loved one another that much. Everyone slowly started opening their eyes and looked back toward the front.

The leader pulled out a small vial filled with a shiny blue liquid. Zela and Lilah put their right pinkies together by the tip as the leader brushed the liquid from Zela to Lilah and then back.

"The blue dye shows that these two are part of the same stroke," the leader said. "Where one begins, the other ends. Where the other begins, the other ends. This is a marking of their union. Praise be to the Great Light!" She gripped their wrists and raised them in the air. "Now, join yourselves and the covenant between."

Zela and Lilah embraced for a passionate kiss as everyone cheered. They turned to us, and Zela said, "Now, let us celebrate!" She held Lilah's hand and raised both their hands to the Luvala-filled sky.

Servers carried out food and drinks from behind the crowd. The music transitioned from strings to upbeat, dancing melodies similar to those of the party at Lilah and Zela's house. Though the food within Labyrintha proved bland, the wedding food contained new spices I hadn't had before. Crispy bread smeared with tangy cheese and covered in pepper flakes became my favorite of the dishes. Sweet, bright red drinks warmed me the more I drank. And just like that, dancing consumed the crowd.

Zela and Lilah walked up to Naso, Herita, and me. We exchanged congratulatory pleasantries. Zela smiled brighter than ever.

I took Zela's hand, observing the blue dye. "Does this paint wash off?" I asked.

"It does not," Zela replied, pulling her hand away. "Next time, ask before you grab me." She patted my shoulder, hard. "The dye stains the nail and skin. If you look around, those who are married have their pinkie painted blue."

As instructed, I observed the surrounding citizens, observing blue streaks on some of their hands. "That's really cool," I said.

"We enjoy our traditions." Lilah wiggled her dyed pinkie before clenching her hand and lowering it to her side. "Not to bring up business, as I am sure the Soothsayer told you anyway but you will have a small team helping with your departure tomorrow." Lilah squeezed Zela's hand. "Zela will be a part of that team."

"I will make sure you get out of the city safely." Zela winked.

"You *just* got married," I said. "Someone else can make sure we get out safely. You should enjoy each other."

"Do not be foolish." Zela shook her head. "You are my friends, and I want to make sure you all get as far south as possible safely."

Lilah nodded. "We both feel the same way." She placed a hand on Zela's shoulder and smiled.

I didn't understand how they could be so reckless. They didn't need to risk anything for us.

"We couldn't be blessed by more capable hands," Herita said, poking me with her elbow. "And we truly appreciate it."

"Excuse us while we speak with the other guests," Lilah said.

Herita poked me harder, forcing me to smile. Lilah turned and pulled at Zela's hand while Zela cocked her head in my direction.

A loud gong from behind made my body vibrate even after the sound subsided. Loud whoops and hollers gave prelude to Lilah and Zela entering the center of a forming circle. Everyone made a dome over them with their hands, while the excess people, including me, formed a regular circle around the dome. Fast drums began a chaotic beat as each person hummed or sang an unfamiliar song. The group I was a part of shoved me to the right as we twirled in a circle while the dome in the center twirled opposite the outside pattern. Guitars joined the drums as people broke off from the circle, looping back in a pattern I didn't quite understand.

The Soothsayer ran over to Naso, Herita, and me and grabbed us, pulling us out to the dance floor as more groups broke off, forming their own smaller groups. Before we could decline the invitation, the Soothsayer Manipulated our Mentality Aura, making me know the steps of the dance. Before we knew it, we were doing the choreography, enjoying the entire affair. The dance eventually concluded with Zela and Lilah being hoisted in the air while being thrown up and down. At the end, everyone cheered as they lowered the married couple.

"What was *that*?" I asked the Soothsayer.

"Sorry, I should have warned you," she responded with a giggle. "This dance has been passed down since the beginning of Mentality—the Axiom. Many say the dance was taught by the Great Light itself. No matter if it was or was not, the tradition still brings everyone joy."

I pictured a blob of Light teaching choreography. Or maybe the Light put the choreography into their minds like the Soothsayer did to me?

"It was weird, but I loved it!" I replied.

"I'm still undecided," Naso added with his arms crossed and head cocked.

"Lighten up," Herita said as she elbowed Naso out of his abnormal serious attitude.

We spent the rest of the night dancing, laughing, and enjoying our last night in Labyrintha. The only thing missing was Aurora. She would have made the night perfect. When we went back to the house for the night, Herita pulled me aside. She embraced me for a hug.

"What's that for?" I asked.

"I needed it." She pulled away. "I think you did as well." She released a deep sigh. "How are you?"

I blinked away gathering tears, and looked up at the night sky. The musty mountain air gave me solace. "I miss her."

"Me, too." Herita hummed. "One thing I've thought about a lot since Aurora left for the Light has been haunting me. I think I'm supposed to tell you. The one thing I learned about love after all these years is it's messy. Love is full of chaos, stress, and makes you fall to your knees. It brings you to the highest points of our world to a breathtaking view while keeping you in the humblest spaces where you don't need anything else but love. Love changes you into your best self. Love gives life meaning. And last of all, love breaks your heart." She breathed in a deep, shaky breath. "But love still allows for the broken parts to heal and make room for new love."

I always appreciated Herita's wisdom. Did I love Aurora? Better yet, did I want new love? Though it was too late, I needed to move forward. The people I loved surrounded me and we would take the next steps of our journey as one.

14

NEW HORIZONS

Backpacks loaded and traveling clothes on, we met the Soothsayer, Zela, and two other Surprisants at the Cerebellum. Ricochet bounced around, excited to explore a new area. His Aura sparked around mine in jolted bursts of energy. Part of me felt his same energy, while the other part of me feared the Officers we could run into.

"Are we ready?" the Soothsayer asked, adjusting her straps.

"We are," I said, nodding to my friends.

"Cerebrum Brysen will be dropping some explosives off the east side of the mountain," Zela said. "Once we hear the booms, that will be our signal to exit the southern maze. This maze is only used for emergency situations. Very few know of this route, and I have honestly never been in it before. Consider yourselves lucky. The Cerebrums agreed this meets the standard very few have ever met. We should make our way there now."

Lilah emerged from the Cerebellum's doors. Bright-eyed, light-footed, and with a leap, she fell into Zela's arms, kissing each part of her face. "Be safe, my beautiful wife," Lilah said. She landed one last sensual kiss on her lips.

"Do not forget me," Zela kissed Lilah's forehead.

The prayer I lifted the day before came to total, beautiful fruition. Public displays of affection normally disgusted me, but theirs was something special. They had a love I wished I would find someday.

"Get a room," Naso said with a chuckle.

Zela shoved him, laughing. "Now, we depart!" she announced.

We followed her to the southern end of the city, where engravings covered a large stone. Zela ran her fingers in a certain sequence, and the stone shifted, revealing an underground path. A welcoming darkness displayed the same blue, glowing stones that illuminated the other parts of the maze.

"We must remain silent throughout this path," Zela said. "I do not want our position to be revealed. Keep an eye on me for visual signals. We will need to move quickly once we exit the maze. We have a two-day journey to our rendezvous point, if things go smoothly. And remember, knowing only works if we listen."

"Two-day journey to Hallow?" Naso asked.

"To our drop-off point—the Foglands," Zela replied. "From there, you still have more time to travel. The amount of time to get there is unknown since we really do not know where Hallow is exactly."

"We will have to listen to the Mentality Aura extra carefully at that point in order to find the lost city," the Soothsayer added.

"Exactly," Zela said.

Zela put one finger over her mouth as the group became silent. A rough path with occasional small boulders to navigate populated the old, poorly maintained maze. By the time we arrived at the other end, which for some reason I lost all recollection on how we made it through, we approached a small crack. Zela peeked through the crack and signaled with her hand to wait. Iri lit up off the Soothsayer's shoulder as the Soothsayer nudged at Iri to dim. A conversation came from the other side of the boulder. Based on Zela's reaction, I assumed they were Officers. Were Zela and the other Mentalists reading their minds? Would the Officers notice? Being a Mentalist would've been helpful in our situation.

Ricochet growled as his purple spots glowed. Zela glared in my direction as I quickly knelt and looked him in the eyes as I moved his Aura around. He immediately calmed down, bright purple spots fading. I continued to scratch his ears as we waited for Zela's command.

Each breath I exhaled, I took in less air in exchange. I worried my breathing would become too loud. It was a silly thought with the large boulders separating us from the Vigorists. After a few minutes, Ricochet yawned, a high-pitch whistle following. He panted his hot breath on my hand.

Naso kept moving his eyes from one Surprisant to the next. His leg bounced up and down. Only then did I notice my own leg doing the same. I needed to move.

Another few minutes passed, and Zela shifted, making me think it was time, but I didn't hear the explosion. She placed her hand on the cave wall and cracked her back. The moldy air made my head throb. I focused too much on my breathing again and my chest tightened.

Suddenly, a loud boom followed by shaking walls echoed through the maze. I jumped and threw my hand on my mouth to keep myself my letting out loud noises. Ricochet growled, but I held him tightly to my chest. Ten more booms followed, little pebbles falling off the walls. The Officers just on the other side of the wall began yelling, and quick footsteps shuffled outside. The steps became quieter and quieter until there was silence. Zela waited a moment before moving her hands over the boulder as it shifted, bright light filling the maze. Outside, a forest filled with high trees and an abandoned camp filled the area. Smoke still rose from a recently extinguished fire pit.

"We need to move quickly and quietly," Zela said.

Zela led us into the forest, which immediately became denser. Occasionally, she would turn while the group followed close, dodging branches, bushes, and rocks. I tripped on a rock and grabbed a branch, pulling myself upright. After further dizzying twists and turns, we exited the forest to an open field. Instantly, we crouched in nearby thick brush, Zela holding a finger to her lips.

Long, golden grass whistled in the air. Dusty air whipped across my face, making me blink. A very neutral, woody smell blew with the wind. Three Officers patrolled in the distance. Zela turned to Herita, who nodded and swirled her hands. Gripping onto each other's shirts, we traveled in an invisible line caused by Herita's Manipulation. Ricochet growled as I reached out my Aura to his, calming his distraught state. His anxiety transferred to me the closer we came to the unaware Officers.

One slip up and we would be caught.

One noise and we would have to fight them.

Heartbeat pounding in my ears, I held my breath as we passed them, distancing ourselves from their grasp.

Entering the next dense area of the forest, Herita dropped her illusion and Naso handed water to her. Then, Zela moved us forward.

***

An hour or so later, Zela stopped us for a break. Heavy breathing and messy, loud gulps of water echoed through the group. As fast as our break came, it ended. Zela led the same pattern, a slower pace once no Officers were in sight, until the sun set, and a makeshift camp was set up.

Sleep swept across the group, Zela on watch. Naso snored on one side of me while Herita mumbled on the other side in between soft whimpers. Unable to sleep, I watched the branch silhouettes dance in a soft breeze, soft moonlight gleaming behind it. Zela developed a walking pattern around the camp. Rather than lay in irritated restlessness, I joined Zela's walk.

"Couldn't sleep?" she asked without looking at me.

"No," I replied. "How could I with all of *this* going on?" I gestured at the world around me.

Zela ran her hands across the white leaves of a tree branch. "I love this forest," Zela said. "I have had to patrol here so many times, and this place is my personal favorite campsite."

"Is that why you know it so well?"

"Indeed," Zela said. She took a deep breath. "And the forest knows me well. I figured out my sexuality here, my love for Lilah here, and it has protected me from several attacks. I feel as if the trees provided me increased Mentality Aura when I need it most."

The tree branches rustled. The peaceful ambiance they created reminded me of the crystals in the mines.

"The mines were like that for me in Toterrum," I said. "Not the Aura part, but the whole idea of helping me figure myself out. I loved to go there and just be myself." I chuckled. "They also protected me several times from Officers."

"You and I are alike," she said. "You just get me."

"And you get me." I exchanged warm glances with Zela. "What are your plans once you get back to Labyrintha?"

"The Soothsayer said Lilah and I could take a small break at the cottage," she said. "I think we may just do that. We would probably travel to Flaunte or somewhere else if we weren't surrounded by Officers, but we will make do." She shrugged. "So much has happened recently that a break would be nice for both of us. Plus, we can celebrate our marriage with just the two of us."

"That sounds like a great idea," I replied.

We walked in silence, the forest floor shuffling beneath our feet. The wind whistled, cooling my skin. I crossed my arms to warm myself.

"We have started talking about having a family of our own," Zela said, breaking the silence.

"Really?" I asked. "This is going to sound stupid, but I'm going to ask it: How will that happen exactly?"

She let out a loud laugh, covering her mouth. Once she tightened her cheeks and adjusted her posture, she said, "It is not stupid at all. There are ways for one of us to get pregnant with a donor or possibly adopt one of the orphaned children." She paused, staring at the sky. "I think we may have one of each. We are ready to spread our legacy to the next generation. Teach them all we have learned."

I had never thought about a legacy. The idea amused me. Was I supposed to pass things on to the next generation? Immediately, I thought about Aurora. I shook my head, trying to get rid of the idea. Why would I think this? It didn't matter, she was gone.

The idea of adoption made me think. Had my parents adopted me? Was I supposed to spread their legacy? I had no idea who they really were or anything true about them. Hopefully, Hallow would teach me more about their Luckist heritage.

"When did you start thinking about a legacy?" I asked.

"When I fell in love with Lilah," she responded. "I saw our future together and started thinking about what that future would be. How it would be defined."

"I've never thought about that." I swallowed. "I'm hoping knowing my Aura will help define me."

"A long time ago, I was told that the Aura you Manipulate does not define you, it is your heart and mind that do," she said. "Any Aura can be used for bad just as much as it can for good. Are all Vigorists bad and all Perceptionists good?" She shook her head. "No. The Aura is the same between each of them, but the person is different. If you do not know yourself, how do you know the difference between good and bad?"

I didn't answer her question. My mind churned within her moralist dilemma. "Do you think I'll be having these same types of conversations with Luckists?"

She covered her mouth, chuckled, and shrugged. "How am I supposed to know?" She raised her brow. "But probably not. They are said to be a bit more...superficial."

"But I thought a person is *defined by their heart and not their Aura*?" I mocked her as she shoved my shoulder. "But seriously, couldn't the same be said for a culture and a person?"

She bowed. "Very true. Are you sure you are not a Mentalist?"

I swiped my hand in the air. "We aren't going through that again. But in all seriousness, I guarantee you that I'll spread your legacy." I placed a hand on her shoulder. "You've impacted my life in great ways, and I'll never forget it."

"I will do the same for you, Yaron," she said. "Well, since you are already awake and I think you are next watch anyway, I am off to bed. See you in the morning."

"Goodnight, Zela," I replied.

Once she departed, I sat on the hard ground and stared at the trees. I wondered what type of Mentality they would share with me. Instead, loud bustling came from the bushes. I jumped up, ready to attack. Ricochet popped out, and I let out a sigh of relief. Sitting back down, he curled up next to me.

"Are you the Mentality the forest is providing me?" I asked him as he licked my hand. "Well, I know you're my protector."

I thought about Zela, Lilah, and their relentless love for one another. Could Aurora and I have become that? I wasted so much valuable time chasing something that wasn't real. I grew angry with myself. Then, a wave of sadness made me hunch my back and rest my head on the tree I leaned against. My leg shook from my growing anxiety about the next day's march toward Hallow. Would Hallow help Herita? What if what I learned in Hallow caused more problems or more questions? Would my search ever end? My mind was exhausted, and my consciousness floated above my still body.

There were so many different feelings and thoughts. I had to stop dissociating, but alone, I didn't care.

"Stop it," I whispered to myself.

The Soothsayer said I needed to practice coming back to reality, even by myself. So, I tried staring at the trees again while pinching my skin. My consciousness returned to my restless mind, and an odd calm came over me. I started to relax and stare at the sky. Was it the tree's Mentality Aura?

I, for some reason, decided to write a letter to Aurora. It had only been a week, but I missed her so much. I knew it wouldn't go anywhere, but I needed to do it.

Aurora,

We all miss you so much. I miss you so much.
I'm sitting looking at the sky as we make our way to Hallow. We have a dangerous leg of our journey coming up, and hopefully, we make it to the Foglands safely.
I wanted to apologize for not listening to you more. I'm sorry for acting the way I did in Labyrintha. I'm sorry for who I became and am glad I made my way out in time to enjoy our lives together. I'm sorry it was cut so short, and I took so long to grow. Time is something I want back more than

anything else in the world.

There is so much going on, and losing you is starting to push at my heart. I'm afraid I'll become the same person I was when my mother passed. I can't let that happen again. My heart can only take so much, but I need to be strong and not push away the people I love.

Please, visit my dreams. I miss your meadow eyes.
Yaron

I folded the letter as a couple of tears fell onto the paper. I wrote her name and put it under some leaves. Just around that time, Fiona, one of the other Surprisants, came to take the next watch, allowing me to finally find some sleep.

By the next morning, we continued our alternating trek between forest and field. We approached a much larger field speckled with brightly colored flowers and five patrolling Officers. Despite Herita's invisibility illusion, traversing through the field covered with Officers proved difficult. We spent more time moving left and right than forward. One detour led to a patch of yellow flowers lining the ground, with one taller flower in the center with a bright orange center and drooping, translucent, yellow petals.

The group moved closer to the patch as Herita whispered from thin air, "Don't—"

The yellow flowers lining the ground crunched under invisible weight. The taller flower turned, like a human head, to face us. It leaned back.

"Run," Herita said as she dropped the illusion.

The flower expelled an orange poof of pollen that coated our group in orange hues. The Officers turned to face us. We were caught.

The Soothsayer charged at one of the Officers before Zela cut her off, ushering her away from the oncoming conflict.

"What are you doing?" the Soothsayer asked, Iri flying around her head.

"I'm keeping you safe," Zela responded.

The other two Surprisants fought two of the Officers while Herita knocked the first Officer out. Ricochet let out a beam of purple and green light, which stunned the Officers.

We used the opportunity to sprint toward the other end of the field. One more illusion from Herita, and the Officers ran in another direction. Charging through another forest, branches scratching and clawing at me, we stopped in the middle of the forest, no Officers coming from behind.

"We are close to the Foglands," Zela said, panting for air. She faced Herita. "Once there, your Manipulations will be easier. Get yourself hidden then."

"How much farther?" Naso said in between breaths.

Zela patted his back. "An open field remains," Zela said. "Just run."

So, we ran.

The number of trees decreased while our exposure increased. A dense fog appeared on the horizon—the Foglands. Just as hope ignited, a loud *kaw* doused it.

Emerging from the clouds came ten Darkened Elderkaws mounted with angry Officers. With dark-streaked nosedives and shrieks, they swooped at us. The Soothsayer, Zela, and the other Surprisants twirled their hands as the Elderkaws collided into one another, slamming to the ground.

The Officers forced their beasts hard to the ground, draining their Vigor Aura and leaping to the ground unscathed. Then, they stampeded toward us, closing in.

Zela turned and hugged the Soothsayer and me. "Thank you," she said. "Move swiftly." Her mouth hung open while facing me, but she smirked and ran off.

Herita, Naso, the Soothsayer, and I did as we planned and ran toward the Foglands. Herita threw up an illusion, causing thick mud to trail behind us, causing the Officers to think they were stuck. The screams of Surprisants caught my attention, with only three of the Officers fighting with them.

Another *kaw* from above and ten more Elderkaws rained down from the clouds. The Soothsayer twirled her hands. One Elderkaw flew straight up in the sky before nosediving into a turn. The beast crashed into the side of the Elderkaw formation, causing half of them to fall to the ground.

The other half nosedived in front of us, approaching straight on. Ricochet leaped into the air and stunned the Elderkaws with his flash. The beasts crashed into the ground but, like the others, the Officers stole the Vigor Aura and kept moving toward us.

Herita forced another Manipulation, faux dust surrounding us.

"Is everyone okay?" I yelled.

"I am," the Soothsayer said next to me.

"So are we," Naso yelled from the other side of the kicked-up dust.

A deafening roar from behind revealed an Officer swinging a weapon at us. He swung, but the Soothsayer moved her hands as he just missed my head. I kicked the Officer in the gut as hard as I could, causing him to keel over.

Another Officer popped out. Ricochet charged and bit his arm. I then took my Facts and hit the Officer in the throat. The Officer gripped my Facts, but I let go of it to run.

An explosion came from the other side of the dust as Herita and Naso emerged, running as fast as they could. Naso pulled out some kind of fruit and threw it into the dust, another explosion following.

Joining back together, we ran and ran. A fiery sensation burned across my legs. I heaved for more and more air, trying to muster any strength I had left. The Foglands quickly appeared. Once we entered the fog, Herita could free us from their sight. Just one last stretch.

Suddenly, three Waldabears stepped out of the fog. We stopped moving.

"Oh, crap," Naso said.

With loud roars and violent stampedes, the mounted Waldabears closed in on us. Splitting from their formation, one came straight on, another from the far left, and the third from the far right. Needing to split our attention, Herita and Naso took the one to the far left. The Soothsayer took the one on the far right. Ricochet and I took the one straight on.

Herita swung her hands, causing a forest to appear. The beast stopped. Naso shot the Officer with a smaller version of Cerebrum Brysen's launching device. The Officer fell off the beast. The Waldabear began to sniff around.

The Soothsayer moved her hands, which caused the Waldabear to turn its attention from her to the Officer riding on its back. Confused by the Officer, the beast thrashed at the rider. The beast clenched its jaw around the Officer and threw his limp body to the side.

Ricochet charged at our Waldabear and released another explosion of light, which stunned the Officer and the beast. I tried to bring my arms forward and punch the Officer's Aura away, but the Aura barely moved. What was happening? Why wasn't it working?

Instead, I moved my hands and accessed the Waldabear's Aura. A forest appeared with the sound of a waterfall in the background. The beast stopped in its tracks as I hopped onto its back and hit the Officer across the head with my fist as he fell off, unconscious. I didn't know what came over me, but I kicked the side of the beast as it started moving at my command. The beast eyed me but turned back forward, accepting my command.

"We need to move to the Foglands!" I yelled to the others as they watched me ride the beast.

"Not if we can stop you!" the Officer by the Soothsayer yelled.

He and the Officer near Herita and Naso twirled their hands toward their corresponding Waldabears. The beasts roared in pain as their legs gave out. A bright, translucent light veil covered each Officer. Their bodies remained the same size, but the bright veil extended from their arms and legs. Their extremities mimicked those of a giant. Limp Waldabears crashed to the ground, dead.

The Officer near Herita and Naso swung his extended arms, swiping them to the side. The one near the Soothsayer marched toward her. I guided my Waldabear to charge at the Officer. Just about to crush the Soothsayer with his giant leg, I met the Officer with the Waldabear's strength. The Officer turned to me instead and swung his arm, knocking me off the Waldabear.

My ragged body hit the ground like a toy, my body bruising, and little rocks dug into my skin. I hit my head on the ground, a dull ringing filled my ears.

Sitting up, I just watched as the Officer twirled his hands, draining the Waldabear's Vigor as it fell over, limp. The Officer's extremities grew even larger, roaring at the sky.

The ringing faded as I heard the Soothsayer ask, "Now what?" She helped me to my feet.

"We need to find the others," I replied. Pain radiated from my back because of all the rocks.

Herita and Naso ran toward the Foglands on our far right. The Soothsayer helped me as we ran to them. The smaller of the giant Officers came from our left, while the much larger Officer came from the right. We stopped running, surrounded.

Glancing over to Zela's area, I hoped they defeated them and were coming to our aid. In the distance, another giant Officer stood over the Surprisants. This Officer raised his arms into the air.

"No!" I screamed.

The giant Officer slammed his arms into the ground as a faint scream echoed across the field. Did he crush Zela? Was she okay? Everything went still. I struggled for air but needed to find my center. I couldn't give up. Zela gave us our moment.

However, my hope from seeing the Foglands only moments before fooled me. No hope remained. Everything that could have gone wrong went wrong.

"This might be our end," Naso said. He moved closer to me.

The Soothsayer placed a hand on his shoulder while she continued to support me with her other hand.

"At least we're together." Herita held Naso's hand. Ricochet growled next to my leg.

Observing the defeat on my friends' faces, pure anger washed over me. They didn't deserve this end. I could get them to safety. I would make sure it happened. I didn't want any more of my friends to die.

"Not yet," I said as I stepped forward, pulling from the Soothsayer's grasp. My worry about Zela, the pain from Aurora's death, and my fear for my friends' lives increased my anxiety. An odd mixture of adrenaline and terror made me drift out of my body, numbing all my pain. "Whatever happens, don't look back."

"Yaron—" the Soothsayer began.

Ignoring her, I clenched my hands, forming fists. All the aches across my body faded as I separated myself. I watched myself, as if out of my own body, punch at the Officers. I punched away the Aura surrounding the larger Officer first. He began to shrink.

"What are you doing?!" he yelled, watching his hands shrink.

Herita swirled her hands as dust kicked up. I ran away from the Foglands, which caused the Officers to chase after me. Ricochet followed, despite what I wanted. I turned and punched at each of the other Officers as they both shrank.

Not hesitating like the first Officer, the other Officer charged at me, swinging his arms. Ricochet jumped up and let off another stunning light. I used this opportunity to throw more punches and make a run for it. Herita, Naso, and the Soothsayer ran toward the Foglands ahead of me.

Looking back at the Officers, one of them made my legs give out as the other struck me across the head, already running at my side. I crashed into the ground, the ringing returning to my ears.

Ricochet stopped at my side. I pushed my Aura at him, begging him to leave me. I quietly said, "Run." He looked at me, then back to the Officers, and back to me again. Dissatisfied with my command, he grunted before licking my face and ran toward the Foglands.

"That's right!" one of the Officers yelled, placing a foot on my back. "We captured the fugitive!"

"But is that enough?" the larger Officer asked, standing at my side.

"We have orders to bring him back," the other Officer said.

The larger Officer shoved the other Officer and picked me up, staring into my eyes with his dark, colorless eyes. "But they only said they *prefer* him alive," he said. "Living wasn't a requirement." He lifted his large arm and threw me straight into the ground.

A new, sharp pain traveled up my spine, making my ribs vibrate.

"YARON!" Naso screamed from far ahead.

The Officer picked me up again and threw me. My limp body bounced off the ground, a sharper pain forming in my ribs. My legs and arms barely functioned, but I tried to punch at the Officer, making more of his Aura move away. I pushed through my pain and punched and punched until he was back to his normal size.

Trying to move my hand one last time, my arm fell to my side. I wheezed, trying to breathe. Every bit of my body had no energy left. The other Officer marched to me, reaching out to grab me again.

It was over. I was done.

Rather than fixate on my impending doom, I looked up at the cloudy sky. Bright, white blobs formed new shapes on the blue canvas from above. I saw my parents. They smiled at me. I saw Lady Sandra. I saw Zela. So much death.

My eyes drifted to the Foglands. Herita, Naso, and the Soothsayer came to the edge of the fog. My friends made it. I did something right.

Cold tears dripped down my bruised face as I looked at the sky above the Foglands. The dense fog reminded me of Aurora falling. I saw Aurora falling, meadow eyes emerging from a dense fog with bright flashes of yellow light. I would see her again soon. I would meet her at the Light.

An odd noise came from the Foglands. Another *kaw*. My heart sank. More Elderkaws would emerge any minute above my friends. They needed to run into the fog.

Just before I yelled at them, a brightly colored streak emerged from the fog. The Elderkaw that emerged from Foglands looked just like the one that killed Aurora. The beast flew straight toward us, faster than anything I had seen move before.

A furious gust invigorated my veins. Hard pulses throbbed across my body. All the blood rushed to my head. A newfound strength returned to my body, ready to kill the beast. If I could do one last thing, it would be to avenge Aurora.

I stood up and turned my body toward the beast. The other Officers turned their attention to the beast instead of me.

"YOU!" I screamed at the brightly colored beast. "I WILL END YOU!"

Just as I finished screaming, the rage echoing all around faded into pure focus. Aurora's face appeared. White Grande Lillies surrounded them. A sudden grief cut at my chest. It pierced me, pulled me down, and left me winded.

The closer the Elderkaw came, the more I realized it charged directly at me. Just before crashing into me, the beast turned its attention to the remaining giant Officer. Talons cut across the Officer's head, and the beast knocked the Officer to the ground.

Why was it attacking the Officers?

The beast turned back to the Officer on the ground and dug its talons into his chest.

The other Officer stepped in front of me and punched me across the face. "You little, weak *boy*," he said. "I'm going to end you." He kept punching me, each strike numbing my body even more.

The world blurred, and my sense of reality disappeared. I dissociated from my dying body, watching my life dissolve before me. An ocean formed around me. It reminded me of the ocean Aurora revealed when she rescued us in Toterrum. The Officer disappeared as I fell to the ground.

I was losing my mind.

Within a blurry fog, a girl covered in bright yellow light emerged. She approached me and reached out her arm. I reached back, gripping her hand as the world faded.

The Great Light took me forward and I heard, "Hello, Yaron."

15

THE RIDDLE

Shimmering stars and a striking moon created a dramatic canvas stretched above my view. The same star grew, transitioned to red, and transformed into a fist. I hadn't witnessed the charging star for so long, yet it seemed to move faster than before. Crashing into my body and plunging my motionless body underwater, I sank. Darkness surrounded me as I drifted from the moon above.

A bright light flashed to my side. I wanted to swim toward it, but my body didn't move. The light grew brighter, but I sank faster away from it. Suddenly, someone grabbed me from behind and swam upward toward the light. Familiar, soft hands gripped tightly to my arm. As we approached the light, it changed into a familiar shape. A flower. Not just a flower, but a White Grande Lily.

All the flowers only reminded me of Aurora's death. Had I entered the afterlife? Was this the Light taking me beyond?

My life served its purpose, and my motivation leaned toward accepting my end. Yet, I made it this far. Something brought me to the light. Finally able to move, I faced the darkened form that pulled me. Just a silhouette floated in the dark water, but green eyes glistened. Not just green, but meadow green.

The person opened their mouth and let out a loud *kaw*. I tilted my head, confused by the sound. Then, another *kaw*.

My eyes jolted open to find a brightly colored Elderkaw leaning over my head and staring at me. Red, blue, and green feathers covered its face as two black eyes with yellow dots reflected my face.

So many thoughts crossed my mind. My long-lost dream returned, bringing some familiarity back to my chaotic life. A sudden hatred for the beast staring at me festered. The Coral Elderkaw represented Aurora's death, and I wanted nothing to do with the beast, even if there was no way it could be the same beast that fell from the Black Stone Mountain with Aurora.

I jumped to my feet, ready to attack the bird, but it simply reached out and picked me up by my feet with its beak. Hanging upside down, I flailed and swung my arms, trying to strike the Elderkaw. Crusted bandages fell off me from my back, making me realize all the pain I should've been feeling from the attack wasn't present. I wondered what plants Herita used to heal me. I flailed again. After no success, I observed my foggy surroundings. Only fog, the ground, and the beast made up the space around.

"Put me down!" I yelled at the Coral Elderkaw. "Stop ruining my life!"

"Zen is only playing with you." A familiar voice spoke from behind me. It sounded like Aurora's, but it couldn't be. She was dead. My hanging body slowly rotated.

Twinkling, dim lights floated around in the fog, reminding me of the Luvalas. A figure stepped out of the fog, emerging from the nightmare that had haunted me since the day she left. Meadow green eyes blinked with sparks of yellow light. Brown hair glistened in the misty air. A pure, serene smile curled up her cheeks.

"Aurora?" I whispered, confused by what I saw.

The Elderkaw dropped me as I fell on my back. Ignoring the pain, I quickly stood and just stared at her. I stared into her wonderous, green meadow eyes, like a mirror showing the inner depths of my soul. Time stopped, and all the air in my lungs rushed out. My heart ached for this moment I never expected to happen.

"Aurora." My body floated in a bewildered stupor. "You're here." Time sped up, and I crashed into her embrace like a wave, finally finding the shore after years of searching. I had her. She was mine again.

"Hi, Yaron," she whispered in my ear, brushing her nose against my neck.

A rushing, tingling sensation started on my neck hairs before cascading across my entire body, my entire being. "I'm never letting go of you again," I said as I continued to hug her.

"I missed you too," she said so softly.

I backed away until our eyes locked into one another. Every detail of her meadow eyes pulled me in, the hints of yellow dazzling in a mesmerizing moment I could let myself slip into and never come back up for air.

Without hesitation, I leaned in and pressed my lips into hers. The delicacy of each smooth bump across her lips excited me like the moment I first met her. I pressed harder, her mouth hovering open and taking me in as I took her in. Then, I remembered so much had happened, and so much remained unspoken between us. So, I backed away. She still leaned toward me as her eyes fluttered open.

"Sorry," I said as blood rushed to my cheeks.

Maroon blotches reflected my own embarrassing joy. "Don't be," she said. "I wanted to kiss you as well." She opened her mouth but closed it, bringing her fingertips to her mouth.

"As much as I'm happy you're back," Naso interrupted, "let's simmer down on the romantic crap. The rest of us are still here."

I glanced over at my friends but quickly turned back to Aurora. If I only looked at her for the rest of my life, my life would be complete. Instead of voicing my infatuation, I blurted, "How are you alive?"

She giggled. "It's a long story."

The Coral Elderkaw let out a loud *kaw*.

Any infatuating, stolen glances I shared with Aurora transformed into sharp, menacing glares toward the beast. "Why is this...*thing* with you?"

"This is Zen, and we saved each other's life," she replied.

"You mean the thing that knocked you to your death?" I hated the Elderkaw. Aurora only stared back at me. I closed my eyes and tried to shield the bubbling storm growing from within. "Maybe you should start from the beginning. Catch me up."

Aurora reached out and scratched the beast's neck as it hummed.

"Well," Aurora said, "I was knocked down by Zen and began to fall off the cliff. His body fell with me as he injured his head during our original collision. I kept my eyes on you until you disappeared in the fog. After this, all I could see was Zen and me. I knew I needed to act fast and felt Zen's Aura pushing at me. I moved my hands and had no idea what happened. Some bright lights and Zen suddenly started to fly and nose-dived toward me. He caught me, and I held tightly to his back."

"Bright lights?" Herita asked.

Zen shifted, raising a wing and picking at something beneath it with his massive beak.

Aurora backed her hand away from the flailing beast. "We just missed hitting the ground as Zen soared right above it. We flew through a camp of Vigorists, who attacked us. While I tried to dodge their attacks, I hit my head on a branch and blacked out. When I woke up, Zen carried me by his claws as he flew. For some reason, Zen decided to save me."

She paused, placing her hand back on Zen, and he brought his wing back close to his body.

"Where'd he take you?" Herita asked.

Aurora shrugged. "I didn't know, and he kept on flying. I tried to tell him to stop, but he ignored me. I tried hitting his legs, but he would just screech at me. Not knowing his intentions scared me, but that disappeared as he continued to fly. We flew for two days straight. Sleeping while being dangled in the air is not an easy task. Luckily, it rained one of the days, so I drank water by holding my mouth open to the sky."

"My little improviser." Herita beamed.

Aurora blushed. "We eventually started flying over water until we arrived at an island. He landed by a pond and released me. I was so thirsty and hungry that I drank from the pond and ate some berries from a nearby bush. Then, a wave of dizziness came over me, and blood trickled down my head. The branch that smacked me in the head hurt me more than I thought."

Aurora moved her hair, revealing a little scabbed-over mark on the left side of her hairline. Zen reached out, grabbed her hair, and moved it back over the mark before letting out a little screech.

"I know, I know." Aurora patted his beak. "Then, I woke up on a bed of feathers and sticks. Zen was taking care of me. He even brought me berries to feed on as I rested until the ringing in my head finally stopped. Something came over me, and I tried reaching my Aura out to his as I did to Era's. He pushed back strongly. I know I already partnered, but something made me keep pushing. We partnered. I realized whatever I did when we were falling, I caused his Aura to give him energy to start flying again. He recognized that I saved him, and he decided to save me."

"*Another* partner beast?" Herita gaped. She observed the Elderkaw.

"I know, it doesn't make sense," Aurora said. "Still on the island, he showed no interest in taking me back, so I started exploring. There were many Coral Elderkaws inhabiting the island that was filled with trees. Not trees like Flaunte, but more like inland trees with needles instead of leaves."

"Were there other people on the island?" I asked while running my hand across my chin, the idea perplexing me.

"I think so," she replied, squinting. "I found some clothes hanging on a tree, but no people nearby. I started looking around in the area until I was attacked by another

Elderkaw. Zen swooped in and fought the other beast off. He then picked me up and brought me back to his nesting area."

Naso laughed and leaned forward. "It sounds like the Elderkaw that put you into a nest, Yaron."

I had forgotten about the one time I made myself look like a baby Elderkaw to save Naso from being taken away, back when I was thought to be a Perceptionist.

"It's kind of the same." Aurora giggled. "I eventually got fed up with sitting around and started trying to mount him. It had been days of not moving, and I needed to do something. If a Vigorist could do it, why couldn't I? After a few hours of trying, I finally mounted him, and he started flying. I struggled to get him to listen to me until an idea finally came to me. I reached my Aura out to his Aura and had him turn left. I realized I could steer him with my Aura as opposed to my physical strength."

I looked over at Ricochet, wondering if I could control him like that, but the other part of me didn't want to. "He didn't resist it?" I asked.

"No, he liked it," Aurora said. "He's so different from Era. We started flying south. After about half a day of all water, the Coral Forest and Tundra appeared. From there, we flew west back to Labyrintha. Tapping into Zen's Aura, we were able to hit an unthinkable speed." She patted her beast. "We stopped on a small hill one night to rest. While there, I received a letter from you, Yaron. You mentioned the Foglands, and we took off immediately. Luckily, we did otherwise, I don't know what would've happened to you."

"Wow," I said. That therapeutic letter I wrote actually helped and probably saved our lives.

"No one has ever had two partner beasts," the Soothsayer said. "This is unbelievable. And a Coral Elderkaw? No one has seen one of these beasts in years. They were thought to be extinct." Iri emerged from the Soothsayer's pocket and circled around the Soothsayer's head before settling on her shoulder.

"I'm as surprised as you are," Aurora responded. "What's that on your shoulder?"

The Soothsayer beamed. "Meet Iri, my partner beast."

Aurora gaped. "You're kidding? How?"

"Someone taught me what to look for, and Iri found me." The Soothsayer and Aurora exchanged bright smiles.

A hush came across our group. Such a long conversation perplexed me and seemed to perplex the rest. Zen picked at something under his other wing as Ricochet growled at his movement. Zen gave him a distasteful screech.

"How far into the Foglands are we?" I asked as I looked around.

"We traveled a couple of miles," Herita replied. "The Officers that first attacked us when the Surprisants took over nearly caught up before we entered the fog. They tried to follow us, but Perceptionists thrive in fogs." Herita twirled her hands in the mist.

"You didn't see Zela, did you?" I asked, gut aching at the thought.

"We do not know what happened to her and the others," the Soothsayer replied. "I hope she is okay, but..." She gave me a concerned glance. "It appears they were defeated."

The truth in her words made my heart sink. A reality I didn't want to face forced its presence upon me. My only remaining hope was they escaped or were possibly captured.

"From there, we wanted to make some progress before resting and allowing you to recuperate," Naso said, narrowing in on my distraught state. "And here we are."

I embraced Aurora for another hug, basking in every bit of joy her touch gave me. "I still can't believe you're alive."

Aurora chuckled. "I can't believe it either." She leaned back, looking at Herita. "Thank you for taking care of my aunt."

"She's family," Naso said. "Of course, we would. Let's be real; she took care of us."

"Can I talk to Aurora alone?" both Herita and I asked at the same time, ignoring Naso's jest.

"You can go first," I said.

"No, I think you should," Herita said as she lightly touched my arm and walked away.

I appreciated Herita waiting to share her bad news until after I had a chance to have my important conversation with Aurora. The Soothsayer and Naso left with her.

"Is this about the letter?" Aurora asked.

"It is," I replied with a smile. "You were right about Felicity. I ended things with her."

Aurora smiled a little but shifted her face back to a more serious look. "I'm sorry to hear that," she replied.

I chuckled at her attempted kindness. The Aurora I knew reveled in the moment, so I had to give it to her.

"Don't be ridiculous," I said. "You can gloat that you were right."

She smiled and said, "I was right." Her smile faded.

"I can't believe the letter found you." A tinge of worry made my head throb. Had she really read every word? I honestly never thought she would. What if she didn't think the same way I did?

"Well, I was alive, so it makes sense," she said.

"It does, but I can't believe it did." I looked at the ground and moved my foot across the ground. "I only wrote it to deal with the loss. If I hadn't, I would probably be dead now and the others captured."

"I'm glad you wrote it," she said. "It allowed for me to find you and tell me...other things." She smirked.

My spirits lifted and a wave of fresh energy ignited my chest and warmed my skin.

We both knew what she was talking about. "I like you, Aurora," I finally said, air rushing out my mouth from holding my breath. "I like you a lot."

"I like you, Yaron," she said. "I have liked you for quite some time."

She walked over and kissed me. Sweet floral scents wafted off her soft skin. All my anxiety and fear subsided whenever she was near. Every decision, every failure, and every success led to this very moment.

"So," she said as she slowly backed away, "Hallow? The lost city?" She eyed the Soothsayer from far away. "I take it she knows something?"

"She believes I'm a Luckist." I held my head high.

"Really?"

"Really." I took her hands into mine. "After I thought I lost you, something came over me as the Officers came down the mountain. I performed a new Manipulation I hadn't done before, which caused the Vigor Aura they stole from the Elderkaws to move back to their hosts."

The more I thought about the experience, the more I remembered punching the Aura away didn't work when I first tried. It only worked when I let myself dissociate from my stresses. Why did that work?

"What?" she asked. "You *punched* it away?"

"Yeah..." I clenched my jaw as Aurora furrowed her brow at me. "I did the same thing before you arrived outside the Foglands." I smiled. "The Soothsayer said these Manipulations weren't Mentality based."

"As always, I think she's right." She squeezed my hands. "Luck may be the answer. One minute, you perform a Manipulation like one Aura but then perform another that isn't." She pressed her lips together and shifted her stance. "You never settle for what someone tells you to be. You are Yaron of Toterrum, the Vigorist raised, Perception trained, Mentality rejected, Luckist bound."

Everything about this girl made me better. She gave me confidence, attention, and loyalty. How could I have ever neglected her like I did?

I blushed. "I'm an anomaly, I guess." I chuckled. My smile faded as I remembered what Zela told me the night before. "Zela said something to me that's been making me think. I'm trying so hard to figure out my Aura, hoping it will define me. She said it isn't our Aura that defines us, but what our heart is." My throat ached from sudden dryness. I swallowed hard, trying to push past it. Was Zela dead? "Our Aura is controlled by our hearts and defines whether we are good or bad. I'll always hold what she said to heart, so to speak." I blinked away tears forming.

Aurora pulled me close. "She could be fine." Her voice was unconvincing. She coughed as if recognizing her shakiness. "Anyway..." She fluttered her eyes and pulled back. "You seem different."

Then, the tears fell. "I thought I lost you." Seeing Aurora in front of me still didn't make sense. I could touch her, hold her. Yet, I still lost other important people. "I realized I have very important people in my life that I don't want to waste one more second being distant or angry." I took her hand into mine. "You, Naso, Herita, and the Soothsayer are my people now." My brain pulsed to the beat of my pounding heart. "I probably lost Zela." My voice cracked. "Asher is gone. Felicity and I aren't the same anymore." I took a deep breath, trying to steady my raging mind. "I've got to keep my eyes fixed on you all."

She kissed my forehead. "I'm glad you finally figured this out." To my surprise, she shoved my shoulder. "But can we not be this sentimental all the time? I've missed your sarcastic approach to life."

I looked past her to Zen. "I can do without your bird." I grinned.

"Yaron Meek, this bird saved both our lives," she said. "It isn't like it tried to kill me...oh, wait."

We laughed. I liked the way she said my full name. I hadn't heard it in so long. Hearing it reminded me of where I came from, which made me think about where Aurora came from.

"Herita better talk to you next." I sighed and squeezed her hand before releasing it. "Remember, I'm here for you."

The residual smile she held faded, softening into a solemn stare. She knew what was coming. A sudden, solitary tear fell down her cheek. I wiped it away with my right thumb before stepping away as Herita noticed and walked in my direction. She paused next to me as she passed. I put my hand on her shoulder.

"She's all yours," I said.

"I hope I find the right words," she replied.

"You always do." I released her shoulder and walked off.

I stepped next to Naso and turned to watch their tense bodies face one another.

"How do you think Aurora will react?" Naso asked.

"I think she knows," I replied. "But we have hope that Hallow can cure her." I turned to the Soothsayer. "Right?"

"Life has no guarantees," the Soothsayer said, staring at Aurora and Herita. Her gaze drifted to my scowl. "But the Luck Aura can hopefully improve the odds." She forced a smile. "I assume your conversation with her went well based on your smile."

And just like that, my scowl twisted back into a grin. "It went well." I shrugged, my smile growing even larger. "It went really well."

"So, you have two girls now while I have none?" Naso asked. "I apparently need to be moodier and *try to find my purpose.*"

His attempt at mocking my voice came off nasally and whiny. He grinned as I shook my head.

"Well, just one girl. Felicity and I are over." I forgot I hadn't updated him on my life decisions.

"What?" Naso exclaimed and covered his mouth. "Since when? Why?"

"You've said it the whole time, but she was using me," I said. "I was ignoring what all my friends said about her. The Soothsayer gave me the last push."

"You're telling me you've known me nearly our whole lives, yet you listen to a girl you just met?" Naso shook his head, hands raised.

"Are you able to reveal someone's past and let them revisit it while listening to peripheral conversations you did not know you heard at the moment?" the Soothsayer asked.

"You can do that?" he asked.

"I am the most knowing of Mentalists, Naso," the Soothsayer said. "I can do some pretty cool things." Iri twirled around her head as if echoing her partner's self-praise.

"Why have I never been offered these trips?" Naso asked.

"You never asked," the Soothsayer flatly said.

"Can I?" Naso requested.

"Sure," the Soothsayer replied as Naso jumped, moving toward her. She held up her hand, making him stop. Iri popped in front of Naso's face to reiterate that Naso should keep his distance. "Once we get to Hallow. I need to keep my wits and energy up in case of further ambushes. We still have a five-day journey left."

"Fine." He swatted Iri away and turned back to me. "But admit I was right this whole time about Felicity."

I shrugged. Ricochet moved past me, pacing around in a circle. His tail between his legs, he let off soft whimpers. Even after reaching out my Aura to soothe him, he ignored my advances and kept whining.

"Has he been like this the whole time?" I asked.

"He does not like being unable to see his surroundings," the Soothsayer said. "Those keen to the Perception Aura like to be privy to the dangers or opportunities around. Riddledogs favor their eyesight above all else. I think you can relate, but he is rather anxious."

I reached out and scratched his ear. He sat next to me, leaning all his weight against my leg while panting. Warm, moist breaths blew against my leg. The way his Aura fixated near the front of his skull reminded me of the way my Aura did the same when my anxiety flared.

"How did you figure that out?" Naso asked.

"His network," the Soothsayer and I replied at the same time.

"All of these insider tricks," Naso said before rolling his eyes and walking off. "We should probably start getting dinner ready."

***

We camped near a pond about the size of the one in Labyrintha. After catching a few fish, I gave some to Ricochet. Zen screeched in protest before Aurora caught a few more fish to feed her beast. Naso used some fruit from Herita's bag, and we had a little supper. Luckily, we had fruit to break up the taste of oily fish. Right at that moment, Herita and Aurora approached. Herita's arm wrapped around Aurora as both their eyes reddened into puffy messes.

"Thank you for coming up with a plan to combat my aunt's cancer," Aurora announced. "You really did take care of her." Aurora began to cry.

The Soothsayer stood and hugged her while Iri twirled around them in glowing light. "The Luckists will be able to help," she assured her. "We will get through this together." She reached out and grabbed Herita's hand.

Unified tranquility silenced us, but Naso broke the peace after a few moments. "We, uh, better eat this fish before your *bird* steals it." Zen crept toward the table while Naso used a blanket to shoo the beast away.

Aurora giggled. Then, she laughed. Her laughter intensified as it spread like an infectious disease among us.

"Thank you, Naso," Aurora said in between laughs. "I needed that."

"It's funny." Naso laughed softer, not as amused by what he said as the rest of us were. "But really, I wasn't joking. We should eat."

Zen snapped his large beak at the fish. He grabbed a piece and flew back by the pond.

***

Traveling through the Foglands consisted of a lot of the same—fog. This made knowing where to go difficult. We couldn't risk Zen flying above in fear of giving away our position if the Officers were following us. Naso came up with the clever idea to surround Zen in a cloud and surveil from there. Aurora used this opportunity to at least make sure we headed south.

The Fogland's landscape consisted of only black trees. The trunk and branches of the trees looked charred, with large, round, black leaves sprouting from the branches. The tree consistently appeared to look like wood after it burned and the fire was put out. Smoke rose from the burnt tree into the surrounding area. According to Herita, the tree was called a Torrefor and wasn't actually burnt. Taking on the darkest of all shades, the tree is able to absorb sunlight within the dense fog. The Torrefor produces its own smoky substance, making up the fog of the Foglands. In doing so, no other plants are able to grow in the space because of the lack of sunlight, making the tree the sole vegetation in the area.

"Burned and alone, the Torrefor is like my exes after I leave them high and dry," Herita joked.

Surrounded by a unique environment, we ran into curious beasts. The most interesting was the Phantari. The beast floated, not flew, across the fog in pulsating indigos and silvery tones, giving the appearance of what I imagined to be a ghost. In reality, the round body of the Phantari had little featherlike hairs fluttering on the rising and falling fog, the underside of the hair indigo and the top portion silvery. Dark purple eyes appeared and disappeared from under long eyelashes, mimicking the rest of its hair. The air felt colder around the beast, and the air fresher. I didn't know if the beast had anything to do with it, but a certain purity surrounded the beast.

Part of me toyed with the idea of just living in the Foglands for the rest of my life. The Officers couldn't find us, and I had Aurora and my friends. Yet, something pushed me forward. I needed to know my Aura.

One day during a Zen scouting fly, they came swooping down to the ground before Aurora quickly dismounted her beast. "We are on the edge of the Rolling Hills!" Aurora announced. "And I didn't see any Vigorists within view." Her excitement shifted; a serious expression turned to the Soothsayer. "Now what?"

"We play the Luckist's game," the Soothsayer responded.

I laughed, but the Soothsayer didn't flinch. "What game?" I asked.

"The riddle I found holds within it the keys into Hallow," the Soothsayer said. "*Look for the three of the leaf, but beware of the beef. Hold on tight, hold on fast, or you will never last. Steer into the ground or rely on what is found. Bend and sway and you are on your way. Do not believe all you see, instead, rely on being free. Crashing will be your end, and that is all I can recommend.*"

We all sat there silently until Naso asked, "Huh?"

"Hallow is a hidden city and protected by a particular way to enter," the Soothsayer said. "It is like the maze, but Luckists make it a game rather than knowledge being the only route. They are all about outcomes and possibilities."

Naso looked back and forth between us and the Soothsayer. "Again, huh?"

Herita let out a long, exhausted sigh. "Use your head." She tapped the back of his head.

"Is it truly clear out there?" I asked Aurora.

"We are safe," she replied.

"Based on the first part of the riddle, I think we need to find a plant," I said.

The Soothsayer pointed at me, grinning. "My exact thought."

Exiting the Foglands, the sun caught us by surprise, each of us holding up our hands to shield the bright light. Ricochet sprinted forward, running wide circles around and around in a bright green field. Large, rounded hills covered the ground further ahead like fluffy cushions on a large couch. The green grass shined so bright it almost looked golden in spots. Various flowers covered some of the hills in an array of colors. Reflected light caught my eye where the hills dipped down. The shimmer mimicked that of the ocean, yet much brighter like something radiant sat within its waters. Clean, crisp air blew across the grass, making the grass and flowers stretch far to their sides, wafting the flowers' sweet aroma in the air.

"Whatever plant we're supposed to find was mentioned to have three of something," I said, turning to Herita and Naso. "Can you think of a plant with three of something?"

"This is my first time in the Rolling Hills, and I don't know the environment," Herita admitted. "Which means it's time for...foraging!"

And just like that, Herita ran—no, skipped—into the field, observing each plant she passed. Some made it into her bag, while others were passed without consideration. Proving useless in our task, I observed the hills. Long, red beasts without legs leaped up and down through the grass in waves. Bright yellow Elderkaws, much smaller than the other kinds, traveled in flocks of twenty, swooping at much smaller black-winged beasts with fast-moving wings, zipping around in zigzag patterns.

"I think I found something!" Naso exclaimed.

We all rushed over to a patch of large plants with thick, light brown trunks and triangular leaves flapping in the wind in whips and snaps. As we approached Naso, he pulled on one of the leaves.

The ground quaked from booming, drum-like stomps. Naso turned to face whatever caused the shaking. Emerging up from the lower portion of a hill, a bulging, light blue beast stampeded forward. Long, tan horns and thick legs covered in light blue bushy fur stopped in front of us. Its large black eyes stared at us while it let out a dull, metallic-smelling roar, pounded its thick feet on the ground, and charged at Naso. His body flew into the air as the beast slammed into him. Zen shot up and caught him.

"Easy, Zen," Aurora said as Zen lowered Naso back to the ground before dropping him like a bag of sand.

His body thudded on the ground. "Ouch!" he yelled. "What is that thing?"

"A Bluffalo," the Soothsayer said. "I think we found our beef."

As soon as she said it, the answer snapped into my mind. "*Beware of the beef,*" I repeated the riddle. "This must be our plant."

"What now?" Naso asked, looking over at the plant. "I'm not grabbing that from that." He gestured at the plant and Bluffalo. "And even if I went back over there, I couldn't pull the leaf off. Its stalk is super thick."

"It's just one Bluffalo," Aurora said. As if provoked, the ground rumbled. Then, it shook. A herd of Bluffalos appeared as the ground quaked from the stampede. Aurora twirled her hands, making a chasm appear, stopping the herd from trampling us.

"Well, this is a problem..." Herita said, casual as ever.

The Bluffalo moaned while corralling back and forth along the illusion of a ridge. Aurora's arm shook as she held the illusion. We needed to come up with a plan. Zen, irritated by their moans, swept at the Bluffalo that completely ignored him. The Bluffalo shifted their heads back and forth, searching for what kept scratching them. Zen continued attacking yet they still didn't notice. Then, it hit me.

"They can't look up!" I declared. "Zen can lower us to get the leaves higher off the ground and bring us back over!"

"That may work," Herita said.

"Move fast!" Aurora screamed. "Zen!"

Zen turned his attention to Aurora, flew over the chasm, and landed in front of me. Ricochet growled at Zen as Zen reluctantly lowered his right wing. Even knowing what Zen did for Aurora, part of me still didn't trust the beast.

"Get on!" Aurora yelled through a clenched jaw.

I mounted Zen. His brightly colored feathers were much softer than I expected. He smelled of leaves and flowers. Launching off the ground, I wrapped my arms around his neck, eyes shut. The grumbling of the Bluffalos became louder as I opened my eyes, the large leaves next to my head. I reached out and grabbed the waxy leaf. I pulled, but it didn't budge. Zen brought his beak to the stalk, and in one snap, the leaf fell off. He continued this action until I held several leaves, all lighter than a feather.

Zen brought me back over and lowered me to the ground. Beads of sweat flooded off Aurora's face. She finally let go of the illusion, and the chasm disappeared. Ricochet launched forward and let out a flash of light, the Bluffalos scattering about in a fleeing rampage. I held out the leaves to the group.

"Now what?" I asked.

"*Hold on tight, hold on fast,*" the Soothsayer recited, taking one of the leaves and throwing it in the air, watching it glide back down to her hand. "They do not seem to be moving on their own. Yet, they are large enough to grab and hold onto. But for what?"

The Bluffalo stampede continued down the hill until I could only see their heads. Then, they turned to the left and kept charging. Walking forward, a large canyon revealed itself, the Bluffalo running along its edge.

"What about that canyon down there?" I asked, pointing.

We hiked down the hill until we came to the edge of the canyon. The bright green grass disappeared as reddish stones took over along the canyon's wall. The wind whistled as I looked down at the steep ledge, an uneasy dizziness overtaking my sense of balance. A river traversed the bottom of the canyon, traveling south. The wind picked up and ripped one of the leaves I held out of my hands. The leaf caught in the wind and glided across the river, no longer falling any lower. I shifted my gaze up to the group, pale and frowning.

"Are we supposed to...?" I couldn't finish the question, but they all knew what I was asking.

"Are you kidding?" Naso exclaimed.

The leaf disappeared around a bend.

"I think we're supposed to jump into the canyon with the leaf," I said.

"No." Naso shook his head so hard I worried it would rip off his neck. "Absolutely not."

The Soothsayer stepped right on the edge of the canyon, looking down as her throat bobbed. "I am afraid Yaron is correct." She sighed. *"Hold on tight, hold on fast, or you will never last."*

"Before we try this," Herita loudly said, making the Soothsayer jump as I grabbed onto her arm to keep her from falling, "we should think on the next part."

"Steer into the ground or rely on what is found," the Soothsayer announced. *"Bend and sway, and you are on your way. Do not believe all you see, instead rely on being free. Crashing will be your end, and that is all I can recommend."*

"I think we're just supposed to flow with the wind," Herita said.

"And crash," I said. "Crash at the end." I looked down at Ricochet, who backed a few steps away from me. "I'll go first, and you all follow along. Can someone help tie Ricochet to my chest?"

Ricochet flailed as Naso picked him up, Ricochet's back to Naso's chest. I reached out my Aura to calm my beast. Once strapped to me like a child to a mother, I stepped forward. The leaf flapped as I extended my arms. Without saying anything, Naso stepped forward and tied my hands to the leaf. Once everyone was ready, I paused on the edge of the canyon.

"If I end up falling into the river, don't follow along," I joked, taking a deep breath. "Wish me luck."

Then, I jumped. The floating sensation I first had when falling gave me such joy. Then, I fell faster and faster, breathing becoming difficult. The weightless feeling shifted into terrifying plummeting. My heart pounded against Ricochet's head, who wiggled at my chest.

Ricochet whined, trying to rub his nose into my face. Just before we hit the water, Ricochet started howling. I closed my eyes, waiting for my end. I held my breath and focused more on my violent heartbeat. All my efforts concluded because of a leaf.

Then, my body lifted into the air. I opened my eyes to the river rushing below and the leaves flapping in the wind, supporting our weight. Even tilting the leaf allowed for superior maneuverability. Up and down. Left and right. I looked over to the Soothsayer jumping next, followed by Naso and Herita. Aurora rode Zen down into the canyon and followed along.

Moving forward, the canyon twisted and turned. I moved along the river, pure happiness rushing across me like a child with a new toy. This was until giant stone towers appeared out of the water. Panic ensued, but I steadied my breathing and remembered part of the riddle: *Rely on being free*. So, I did just that. Rather than turn at each tower, I let the wind carry me.

Zipping back and forth between the rock towers, just avoiding the sides of the canyon, I dodged each obstacle. Every time I flew toward the towers, I somehow flew in between each without hitting them. I wanted to steer so badly, but I trusted the route. This continued for what seemed like hours. The towers became more frequent and much closer to one another. I swallowed down my fear.

Suddenly, a waterfall appeared, and I flew down into a deeper canyon area. The same sequence of towers appeared but at a much faster rate. My stomach moaned in sudden nausea, but I swallowed down the bile creeping up my throat, its sour taste remaining in my mouth. I moved faster and faster every minute until no towers remained, just the waterfall at the end of the route. The waterfall roared as if calling me to its presence. I was going to crash into it. As much as I wanted to stop the ride, I knew crashing was the answer, just as the riddle stated.

Closing in, droplets of water sprayed my face. Ricochet twisted and turned, howling louder and louder, yet it sounded like a whimper within the waterfall's roar. Right before we crashed into the waterfall, my leaf turned and flew along the waterfall before abruptly turning right in between the cliff and the waterfall. I flew straight up toward and cave ceiling, the waterfall pounding from behind, before I started to float down to the ground like a leaf falling from a tree.

My heart raced from all the excitement, terror, and relief to not be twisting and turning anymore. As I fell, the others zipped out from the waterfall and floated above me. Aurora and Zen just scooted in and crashed into the ground.

Something bright caught my eye. Looking over, glistening gold filled my sight. A bright golden city stood before me within a large cave. Beams of light shined through holes in the cave ceiling, lighting up each shimmering building. Great, golden bars separated us from the glamorous city.

As soon as I landed on the ground, shadows emerged from the cave's shadows and seized me, putting a bag over my head. Ricochet growled until he was muffled, and his flails subsided. His body lifted from mine.

Cool metal touched my wrists and bound my hands behind my back. Naso yelled something before his voice disappeared. Silhouettes moved but I could not see them because of the bag over my head.. The shadows forced me to my feet and made me walk. A loud *kaw* faded into muffled screams. Then, the sound of metal shifted like a gate was being opened to the city.

The bright, golden city became even brighter as we approached it, which I could faintly see through the bag. Guided through a doorway and forced to our knees, they ripped the bag from my head. A great golden throne stood before me where a man with bright green clothes and a golden crown around his head sat. His skin even looked gold as harsh green eyes observed our group.

"Welcome to Hallow," the man said. "Congratulations on defeating our game." He clapped a few times, the sound echoing around the cave, before abruptly stopping. "As for your reward, it will be death."

16

The City of Gold

Dark green clothing that hugged tightly to muscular bodies and arrogant expressions characterized each person surrounding us. Part of me expected it, and the other part of me was surprised at what a Luckist looked like. Not quite as burly as Vigorists, the Luckists had more athletic, sleek statures. Naso, Herita, Aurora, and the Soothsayer knelt bound next to me. Ricochet lay resting next to me, his chest heaving up and down. They had knocked him out somehow. Squeaking metal from far behind us ended in a loud bang, and the gate shut.

"Great Leader of Hallow," the Soothsayer began. "We mean no harm. We only—"

"Quiet, *Mentalist*," the leader interrupted with his palms faced forward as if quieting the Soothsayer by mere movement. "We will not fall to your persuasive words." He lowered his hands back down.

Iri popped out of the Soothsayer's pocket and was about to charge at the leader, but the Soothsayer whispered something to her partner beast before it dimmed and flew over to a nearby wall to perch. Bits of gold glistened in the distance.

"She's not just a Mentalist, she's the Soothsayer," I said, wanting to defend the Soothsayer like Iri wanted to. Iri brightened from her perch in response. "Treat her with respect."

The leader's dark green eyes pivoted to narrow in on me. "We trusted the Soothsayer in the past, never again." He leaned forward, resting his elbows on his knees. The tall, golden buildings spaced throughout the cave shined around him, giving him a bit of a heavenly glow. "Their kind gains your trust with wise words only to use them to trick you. They have always thought themselves greater than us." He leaned back, waving a hand in the air. "Find and capture opportunity."

"Find and capture opportunity," the rest of the Luckist echoed.

What was he talking about? Did a past Soothsayer do something bad? I glanced back at the Soothsayer to see her stern face. Then, her brow furrowed, and she looked down at the ground. Did she know something?

"Then listen to me," Herita said. "I come from Flaunte, and we seek something the Mentalists were unable to provide. I have cancer that the top doctors from Labyrintha couldn't heal. You hold much greater wisdom for what I need."

The Luckist leader cocked his head, smiling at Herita. He brought his right hand to his chin.

"She speaks truth," the Soothsayer said.

"Do not speak, *Mentalist*," the leader commanded.

The Soothsayer jolted her head back, lowering it again.

"This *Mentalist* is the one who said their very own Manipulators weren't good enough, which is why we're here," Herita said. "She stood before the Cerebrums and declared this. Whatever damage was done in the past, this is a different Soothsayer."

The leader rose from his throne, towering above most of the Luckists near him, and walked toward Herita. His V-shaped body had a thick white cloth draped across his broad shoulders, running from his collar to his cuffs. The green on his shirt slightly reflected light as he shimmered like the crown atop his head. After closer inspection of the shimmering crown, something was missing from the front center. A large divot was empty, appearing to have once held a large jewel. He leaned forward and looked Herita in the eyes. Herita didn't break eye contact.

"This one is fierce," the leader said. "You and this other girl come from Flaunte, do you not?"

"We do," Herita replied.

"Supporters of Mentalists then," the leader said. "Why would we help you when you did not help us? Take the Mentalist and Perceptionists off to the dungeon."

"Wait!" I yelled. Pivoting, the Luckist leader loomed his imposing stance over me. My heart raced, trying to reject whatever idea I had. I pushed past the doubt. "What...what story did you read? Luckists were the ones who abandoned Mentality and Perception."

"Yaron," Herita snapped.

Herita's sharp glare demanded that I refrain from talking. The Soothsayer had mentioned how prideful Luckists were and how to show them respect, but I didn't care. I didn't want him to take away my friends.

The leader's steps echoed across the suddenly silent crowd. He stopped in front of me and knelt, the dark green of his pupils making my skin crawl. He said, "You are a spitfire." He reached his hand forward and I braced for a strike. Instead, he patted my shoulder as he chuckled. "I like that. It is funny how the one who explained the history to you is the one who looks like the hero." He squinted. "Who are you?"

"Yaron from Toterrum," I replied. "Who are you?"

The leader smiled. "Excuse my manners." He grinned, nearly perfect white teeth except for one golden crown on his far-left tooth reflecting the light around. "King Resin is my name. I hold the record of leading Hallow the longest. I am the greatest King of Luck in history."

His voice echoed across the hollow cave. But that was it. A cave, hidden from the war outside, surrounded by a self-proclaimed great king.

"It is easy to remain great when you stay in hiding," I replied.

For the first time since arriving, the other Luckists murmured to one another. Harsh glares shot at me, but I didn't care.

"Easy there, spitfire," King Resin replied, a softer grin remaining. He lowered his voice, looking around at the other Luckists. "I said I liked you, and I am a patient man. But push me too far, and I will end your life."

"There is a war out there, and you're hiding," I said. My heart pounded with everything I said. "It seems to me the history Flaunte and Labyrintha taught me is correct. You did run and hide when things got bad."

King Resin scoffed. More specks of gold hid in his smile. "Why would someone from Toterrum be traveling with a Mentalist, two Perceptionists, and a..."

"I'm also from Toterrum," Naso responded with a squeak at the end. He coughed and lowered his voice. "My leader...King Resin."

"And another citizen of Toterrum be coming to Hallow?" King Resin finished his question. "This is most peculiar."

"Naso and I escaped Toterrum several months ago," I began. "We were rescued by Aurora of Flaunte, and she brought us back to her city. I can Manipulate Aura, but only recently learned Aura was a thing. Citizens of Toterrum are kept in the dark about Auras. I have no idea what I can Manipulate, so I was trained in Perception. I was found to not be a Perceptionist. We traveled to Labyrintha. I was trained under the Soothsayer and was discovered to not be a Mentalist. The Soothsayer believed I was a Luckist, and my dear friend Herita needed help with her cancer. We decided to travel to Hallow to seek your guidance."

"Even more curious," King Resin replied. "I received word of a grand escape from Toterrum. You two are the culprits. Impressive. Speaking of this, I have not heard any more word from our informants." He took a deep breath. "Either way, we will not help you. I appreciate your story, but I see no gain in this for me. Lock them away." He stood and turned around, walking back to his throne while the other Luckists grabbed us.

"I'm Rita and Thomlin Meek's adopted son!" I screamed, my voice carrying across the cave.

King Resin froze. "Stop," he said. Silence followed as he slowly turned around. His bold, green eyes softened as he relaxed his stance. "You are?"

"I am," I said as the Luckists released me. "I grew up in Toterrum with them. I recently learned from the Soothsayer they were informants for you."

King Resin's mouth hung open. "Have you heard from them?" His eyes drooped, anticipating my response.

I didn't know why but announcing what happened to them made me uncomfortable. What did it matter to him?

"They're dead," I said. My voice echoed through the hall. Within the silence, I looked up at the golden arch above his throne, painted green leaves across the structure.

King Resin fell onto his throne, resting his head on his hand. "Dead?" he asked with wide eyes and a delicate expression.

Did he know them? His reaction certainly made it seem so.

"I wrote to them in Flaunte, and the Officers eventually captured them, knowing they must know something about my whereabouts," I said. "They tortured them to reveal my location and killed my father after my mother revealed where I was. I was captured on my way to Labyrintha, where Gamma killed my mother as she gave her life to save mine."

"Rita..." King Resin blankly stared at the ground. "My sweet sister."

I observed his state, back arched to contain a soft whimper. His words didn't register, though they repeated in my mind.

"What did you say?" I quietly asked.

King Resin looked up at me, realizing what he had just said. "Rita was my sister." He gulped. "I am your uncle."

My head swam in confusion and questions. I didn't know what to say. I didn't know what to think. Had I just been given the clarity I had been searching for all this time?

"What?" I asked.

"I cannot believe this has been you the whole time," he said. "Rita never told me you were the one who escaped. You were the one who caused all this chaos. Cut his bindings."

King Resin stood from his throne and took a few steps toward me. The soldier cut my bindings. I stared at the burly man who held his arms open wide. His welcoming smile and the fact I still had family excited me. Striding forward, he wrapped me in a firm embrace. He smelled like fresh wood and citrus.

"You're my family?" I asked.

"Welcome home, Yaron," he said, pulling back while rubbing my shoulders. After one more firm pat on my arms, he gestured to the Luckists behind me. "Release the others. Anyone who is a friend of Yaron is welcome in Hallow."

And just like that, the soldiers released the others from their bindings. Ricochet ran straight to me, growling at King Resin before I comforted his Aura. Zen screeched and flew up to perch on the arch above the throne, spraying liquid out of his rear next to the throne. King Resin's scowl at the droppings reached the beast.

"Sorry about that," Aurora said.

"King Resin," the Soothsayer said, changing the topic. "I bring you a gift." She pulled out an emerald shaped like a triangle. The oddest flicker of light shimmered from within like it was on fire. She reached the gem out to him.

"The Trimerald of Luck." King Resin paused before touching the gem, a similar fiery light sparking in his eyes before fading. Removing his crown, he took the Trimerald and placed it in the similarly shaped indentation on the front. The Trimerald zipped into its long-lost position and set in like stone to a cliff.

"The return of the Trimerald was long overdue," the Soothsayer said. "Cerebrum Petra wanted me to hand deliver it to you." She watched him with such carefulness, obviously choosing each word with precision. "Our people want to mend our broken past."

"Thank you," King Resin replied with a smile. The surrounding citizens gaped at the interaction. "I am not sure if history will allow a true mending, but it is a step in the right direction." He turned his head, recognizing the Luckists' disdain for his reaction. "Prepare a feast for our visitors!"

The lack of movement worried me at first, but finally, one of the soldiers ran up to him. "King Resin, what about the celebration?"

King Resin furrowed his brow before relaxing his face. "Ah, yes," he said. "I forgot that was today." He faced us. "We have so many celebrations, you see. We will still hold the celebration but add seats for our friends at my table." His eyes darted around, searching for something or someone. "Trigger!"

A soldier with radiant, dark brown skin, a green shirt hugging tightly to his thin, muscular body, and dense, curly black hair ran up. Umber eyes outlined in bright white looked up to King Resin as he said, "Yes, my king?"

"Show our friends to the guestrooms," King Resin said. "Make sure they have proper attire for tonight's festivities." He placed his hand on his shoulder. "I am trusting you with this important task." He turned to us. "I must retire to my chambers. I will see you all tonight, and we will discuss your future then." He marched off with a group of twelve soldiers following close behind.

"Follow me," Trigger demanded, lacking introduction and common courtesies. "Your beasts may follow along."

Ricochet scoffed and stayed close to my side. Aurora nodded to Zen as he swooped down through a doorway and up to a hidden area. Stepping out of the Throne Room, the cave reached high. Buildings at least three to four stories radiated so much gold that the little amount of sunlight shining through small holes in the cave ceiling reflected light throughout the space. A damp, mossy scent filled the air. I was overwhelmed with all of the gold surrounding me. The other half of the cave appeared humble in stone walls and mossy rocks. Together, the golden city within a cave amused me.

"Your name is Trigger?" the Soothsayer asked.

"Yes, Leader Soothsayer," Trigger replied.

"Soothsayer will do just fine," the Soothsayer said. "I am no Leader." She smirked. "What type of duties do you have?"

"I am Squire to the King," Trigger replied.

"That sounds like a high honor," the Soothsayer said.

He straightened his back, smirking just a little before hardening his cheeks. "It really isn't," Trigger replied, his posture and tone relaxing. "I bring him drinks, wash his clothes, and scrub his crown." I laughed. Trigger glanced back at me and smiled. "So, you're a Luckist, Sir Yaron?" Trigger asked.

"I may just be," I replied, pondering at the idea of being called *Sir*.

After rounding a corner, I shielded my eyes from a burst of intense light. The polished gold lining every edge, corner, and artistic detail across each building reflected the small bits of sunlight shining from above. My eyes adjusted, taking in all the city's glory.

Everything was gold. The walls, the roofs, the pillars, the floor, and even the windows contained so much gold.

"Do you ever get overwhelmed by all the gold?" I asked.

A deep laugh bellowed from Trigger's defined chest. "We're a little extravagant if that's what you're getting at. It's nothing like the Hallow of the past, but we pride ourselves in our gold." He turned his body, walking backward while facing us.

"We have some gold lining our buildings in Flaunte, but not this much," Aurora said.

"Give me the name of your architect so they can add a little more humility to our buildings," Trigger said, somehow not running into anything while he continued walking backward. "Some see the gold as great, but others like me find it overbearing and irritating."

I found myself remembering the composure and careful words of Labyrintha. Just as I did, Trigger hacked and spat to the side. The Soothsayer gave him a disgusted look just as he did.

"Are all the Luckists this outspoken like you?" I asked. "The others we saw earlier seem more reserved."

"We are a free people," Trigger replied, leaping over a rock he didn't trip over, even without looking. "We speak what we want, and we do what we want. The king is the leader, but he can be overthrown by a challenger. Whoever wins a game of the king's choosing remains as king or becomes the new king."

"And King Resin has been the longest-standing king?" I asked.

"He's a very strong king," Trigger replied. "He has also kept us safe for many years." He tilted his head up and down before snickering. "I can't believe he is your uncle. You have strong blood running through you. I could only be so lucky." He pushed off a wall with his feet, did a little twirl, and landed, facing forward.

In Toterrum, everyone desired to be strong. As much as the idea enticed me, it didn't define me.

"We aren't related by blood," I responded. "I only benefited from being raised by his sister."

"It seems like she did a good job," Trigger replied. "You held your own with him. I think we'll be friends." He stopped in front of a hall with two open doors on the right. After gesturing with a little bow, he said, "Here are your rooms. The men will have the first room and the women the other. Clothing is in the closets. Don't be shy. All the clothes are yours to keep." He pointed down the hall where the top of a staircase began, bright trees looming. "Head out to the courtyard down the stairs when you are ready. I'll be waiting."

Shuffling into the first room, the others followed and shut the door behind. Iri popped out of the Soothsayer's pocket and buzzed around the room in freedom. Of course, the room popped with little accents of gold. Past the gold, the rest of the room held a simple layout. Two beds, a large cabinet, and a large window overlooking the city. Luckily, thick curtains hung on each side of the window, ready to cover the intense shimmer.

Herita shoved me. "I can't believe you spoke to King Resin like that." She huffed. "I thought you were digging us a shallow grave. Thank the Great Light he is your uncle. You need to be more careful."

"I shouldn't have risked you all like that," I admitted. "Something came over me. Speaking to him felt familiar, and I went with it."

"They were rather rude to us." The Soothsayer gave me an approving nod, and Iri bounced at the same speed as her nod. "And inviting us to a party right away? The whole thing is odd."

The part of me that trusted the Soothsayer clashed with what King Resin had said.

"What was the past Soothsayer comment about?" I asked.

The Soothsayer averted her gaze. "There is an area of the Soothsayer history that is blurry to me."

Why was she lying? The Soothsayer risked her life for me, told me important bits of Biome's history, and helped me find out more about myself, but why was she something now?

"You seemed to know what he was talking about," I said.

I had trusted my parents. I had trusted Ruth. My forehead tightened like the Soothsayer had taught me, preventing her from reading my mind.

The Soothsayer glanced up, aware of what I was doing. "The blurry area has always stood out to me," she said. "I have tried to discover its secrets, but I have failed each time. I plan to investigate this further, but the timing was not appropriate."

"You aren't lying to me, are you?" I asked.

"Yaron, I honestly do not know," the Soothsayer replied. "It seems like the more I explore the world, the less I know. I am learning. The nice thing about being a Mentalist is we desire to learn more." She shifted her stance, visible uneasiness rushing over her. Forcing a smile, she asked, "Did you see all those books on the way to our rooms? There were many foreign books to me, and I cannot wait to read them all."

"Right," I said, unsure of what else to say. The Soothsayer and I just stared at one another, a stiff silence growing in between us. I didn't know why I grew paranoid of her. Then again, I had been burned before. "The party is a bit sketchy." I nodded. "It kind of blurs my notions about the Luckists."

"Speaking of blurry parts of history," Naso said with a cough, trying to break the tension. "You now have an uncle who can hopefully clear it up." He patted my shoulder. "That has to be exciting."

"It is," I admitted, turning my attention away from the Soothsayer. "But I won't lie, it makes me a little nervous. I was hoping to find some answers about my Aura in Hallow, but my personal history is taking the forefront."

"Possibly more about your heart and less about your Aura?" Aurora asked, her words reminding me of my last conversation with Zela.

Zela. My heart ached from her memory and sacrifice. Was her sacrifice final? A steady drum beat in my head, making my ears throb.

"Possibly," I said. "Should we write to ask Lilah about Zela?"

"Yes," the Soothsayer replied. "I will write her. I need to update her on our arrival as well. I really hope she received positive word on Zela. I will see you all in the courtyard."

"I'll come with you," Herita said as they departed.

Aurora smiled at me, looking like she was about to follow them, but stopped as her eyes looked past me. "Yaron," she said, pointing to the bed behind me.

I turned to see a letter resting on the edge of the bed, glorious golden light reflecting my name in Felicity's handwriting. An irritated grunt forced me to turn away from the delivery.

"I can read that later," I said.

Aurora touched my arm. "I need to get ready anyway. Please, read it."

I nodded, though I didn't know if I was ready to read it. Aurora left the room before I could distract myself with further conversation.

"I'm going to shower," Naso said, taking Aurora's cue. "Are you nervous about it?"

"About you taking a shower? I think we could all benefit from you washing the stink away."

"Funny," he said. "The letter, thumb brain."

"I know," I said. "I'm not sure what I feel." I cocked my head. "And thumb brain?"

He put his hand on my arm and said, "Good luck, thumb brain."

I rolled my eyes, took a deep breath, and opened the letter.

Yaron,

I understand.

I do. I really do.

I would be lying to you if I said I was fine. My heart is broken. I'm broken not only because our relationship is over but also because you had a relationship with someone else the whole time. I know I lied to you, but you lied to me when you didn't tell me about this. We have both matured a lot, but I think some of the choices we both made damaged us beyond repair.

So much of me thinks it's best we stop talking, but the current situation says otherwise. So, let's keep this professional. For both our sakes.

The Officers camping near Labyrintha have moved (I did just learn the spelling). They believe you've moved, but they're unsure where. Asher was there at the Labyrintha camps. He told me. He wasn't there during the fight but later. He told me something happened that allowed someone to escape. The Officers are angry.

The leader of a place called Flaunte has been assassinated. They consider it a victory. A new person I've never met before has been added to the meetings. She's very pretty and blonde. Her name is Ruth. Her intel helped them assassinate the Flaunte leader.

She has also led a hunt in Toterrum for all spies from other lands. Most were executed. This was all a part of a mandated gathering. They lied and told the citizens these people had tried to escape, and this is why they were punished. I knew and told the others I trust that they were Manipulators like the Vigorists but for good.

The people of Toterrum are scared. We are losing the momentum we once had. Asher seems scared as well. He asked me if I have heard anything from you or Naso. I lied and said I hadn't. With everything going on, I'm not sure who I can trust.

Naso's mother isn't doing well. They have increased the disease in her. I did talk to her, and she didn't want to tell Naso. Please be careful when telling him this. I'm supporting their family as much as I can, but I'm afraid I'm risking too much already.

Sincerely,
Felicity

I crumpled the sides of the paper as I finished. How could she blame me? She was the one who took advantage of me. But did I have a relationship with Aurora before I ended things with Felicity? Was she right?

My pondering made my gut wrench. Then, my head pulsed in violent aches. Asher was so close to us. I couldn't believe it. I needed to tell Naso about his mother but when? I didn't want to spoil his mood before we went to the Hallow party. In a rare moment, my heart ached for Toterrum. Maybe Hallow had it right? Hiding kept them away from danger. Felicity deserved an update.

Felicity,

We have moved on to a secret place. We are trying our best to rally people together, but the other cities are worried of risking their own safety. We'll come up with something.
I hope you and Asher become friends. If I could write to him, that would help me mentally. I want to figure out if he has been corrupted.
I will tell Naso.

My best,
Yaron

I folded the letter and let it out the window. Naso opened the door to the bathroom, bits of steam rising above his shirtless torso. After taking my turn in the shower, I fell to the floor, beads of warm water ricocheting off my exhausted state. Maybe I could hide in the shower like the Luckists did in the mountains rather than give bad news to Naso.

The supplied clothing snapped to skin in the most revealing, tightly wound clothing I had ever worn. A form-fitted forest green shirt with golden accents and green pants hugged me so tightly that I stood straighter than I ever had before. Naso's golden accents of various triangles with smaller patterns lined his shirt, his muscles bulging the symbols into twisted messes. Mine had golden lines running from the front to the back vertically. Though tight, I moved as if I were naked. We met Trigger in the courtyard.

"Our clothing suits you both well," Trigger said, eyeing Naso's torso like a beast would a fresh meal.

"It's very comfortable," I said.

"I could do somersaults in it," Naso said as he stretched around.

Trigger crossed his arms as he bit his lip, watching Naso's body flex. "We are dressed for action, with a little flare."

Aurora, Herita, and the Soothsayer came next. Their clothing hugged snugly as well, but it was softer on the shoulders. Aurora's eyes glowed even greener with the matching shirt.

"You look beautiful," I said to Aurora as I embraced her for a kiss. Her lips tensed against mine but relaxed shortly after. I blinked at her and turned to the others. "You all do."

"Thank you, but please, don't kiss me," Herita said.

"If you say so," I joked.

"Let's make our way to the Golden Gala," Trigger announced. We followed him out of the courtyard to the city streets.

"What is this Gala for?" I asked. "Isn't it weird we're invited to something like this after only just arriving?"

"Another reason to have a party." Trigger shrugged. "We like parties." He paused. "But I guess they all have a purpose. This one is a celebration for the gold gatherers. We party for all their hard work. And it would be weird if these events weren't normal to our everyday living."

"You have a party for doing a job?" Naso asked. "Could you imagine if Toterrum did that?" He laughed. "We do jobs to avoid being punished, not for parties. Or maybe it's a different type of party…"

"The parties aren't always good, so they are sometimes a punishment," Trigger joked.

"Not the same," Naso replied, steadying his voice. "I don't think you quite understand what our punishments are in Toterrum."

"And I don't care," Trigger said.

Before Naso could counter, we arrived at a stone building painted gold. Very tall, narrow windows ran up the height of the building. Once inside, we entered a large room with lofted ceilings. Three gigantic golden chandeliers hung from the ceiling. There were large, square alcoves with various paintings highlighted by hanging lights. Mostly painted in abstract designs, the center design held a painting of the crown with the green triangle in the middle. The bright white stone floors were polished to a high gloss so that they reflected each person walking by. It looked as if each person was walking on water.

I couldn't believe I missed the next part when we walked in, but people flew in the air from ropes dangling from the ceiling. As they flew from the sky, they released the ropes and flipped so many times I became dizzy just watching. The way they moved defied reality. At times, one would fly in the air and grab onto the hands or feet of another.

On the ground, more people somersaulted at inhuman angles and speeds. They flew in the air and landed on top of other people doing flips. They formed towers or pyramids of people. One odd thing I noticed was that the people who did the acrobatics looked more like Trigger than my uncle. The people observing and drinking looked more like King Resin. I wanted to ask Trigger about it, but King Resin came into my view. He wore tight green clothing with flowing green fabric hanging from each arm. As soon as he saw us, he marched in our direction.

"Friends and family," King Resin proclaimed. "Welcome to the Golden Gala. You sit at the head table with me. Grab a drink and enjoy the company. I have others to greet. Please excuse me for now."

I wanted to talk to him, but he was gone before I could. I wanted to get to know my uncle as much as I could. Aurora walked up to me and held my hand. She could tell I was disappointed with his quick departure.

"The king must speak to all," Trigger said. "Don't let your hopes get too high. The most important person in the city will always be himself."

"Does he not have other family?" I asked.

"He was married, but she passed while giving birth to their child," Trigger responded.

"I'm sorry to hear that," Aurora said.

"Don't be," Trigger replied as he grabbed a drink from a nearby waiter and chugged it. "Keep an eye on yourself, and don't worry about others. Find and capture opportunity." He raised his glass before drinking it again.

"I can't say I agree with your statements," Aurora said.

"Good to hear," Trigger said. "Then let's drop the conversation."

Aurora tensed, glared at him, and stormed off. The Soothsayer smiled and followed her with Herita. Naso giggled. Trigger seemed unphased by her sudden departure.

"I feel like I should say you were a little rude," I said.

"Once again, good to hear," Trigger replied. "Do you always worry yourself with others?"

Yes. Yes, I did.

"Not always," I lied.

"Tell me, when you do, how does it benefit you?" Trigger asked.

"They care for me," I said, one of the acrobats nearly running into me as they flipped. I jumped to the side, closer to Trigger. "That's how it benefits me."

"Do you really think they would stop caring about you if you stopped worrying?" Trigger asked.

I didn't know how to respond. Music started playing and people began to dance. Fast feet moved while their bodies moved in perfect waves, almost sensually.

"What's going on?" Naso asked.

"Come with me, and I will find you a girl to dance with," Trigger said to Naso. "Or a guy," I swore I heard him whisper. Trigger turned to me. "Go grab your girl and put her in a better mood." He pulled Naso away.

I walked over to a disgruntled Aurora and asked, "Would you like to dance?"

"Did you hear the way he talked to me?!" Aurora exclaimed.

"Aurora," Herita said, "calm down and dance with Yaron."

I grabbed her hand and pulled her out to the dance floor. A younger man asked the Soothsayer to dance. King Resin leaned in and whispered something to Herita, causing her to blush. He then took Herita's hand and guided her forward. We tried to mimic the paired choreography happening around us. The dance proved simple. Left, left, forward, right, then back. Then, the movements repeated. Just as we had it down, the music sped up. The steps became more complicated as the rhythm sped up, so Aurora and I went at our own pace from there. Not a single surrounding Luckist fell out of step.

"This place is going to drive me crazy," Aurora said. "Trigger is especially condescending."

"I kind of like them," I admitted. "These people are where my family is from."

"There's always more to someone than they show you," Aurora said.

"Huh?" I asked.

She started to say something but stopped. "Nothing. Just be careful." Her body stiffened away from mine.

I chuckled. "Funny coming from the person that kept telling me to see the good in people back in Labyrintha."

"What?" She moved her hand away from my arm.

I reached out and grabbed her arm. "I didn't mean it like that. I mean there is good in them. I can tell. They are family."

"Not them..." She bit her lower lip and looked past me. Before I could question her, she said, "Maybe you're right. I'll try and be more open minded."

"So, can we have fun?" I asked.

Her teeth shined in a large smile, reflecting my face like the polished stone floors below. "Only if you can keep up with me." She started dancing faster as I kept up. Unburdened joy filled me with every interaction I had with her.

The music suddenly stopped, and King Resin separated from Herita. "Welcome to another gathering," he announced, the crowd silent. "People of Hallow, raise your glass as we cheer the gold gatherers. Find and capture opportunity!"

Everyone raised their glass and yelled, "Find and capture opportunity!"

"Enjoy this feast and hold the ones you love!" King Resin yelled as everyone broke off.

Tables lining the outside walls overflowed with plates of food. Once you gathered your food and drink, everyone made their way to a table near the back of the room, past an out of place indoor fountain. Of course, the fountain was made of gold.

After eating one round of food, anyone could get up to gather more. The idea frazzled me. Food didn't seem to be an issue. It made me think of the dried fruit my mother used to sneak to make a special breakfast bar. Instead, so many different types of meat sat before me. Most of the meat glistened red and juicy. The vegetables and fruit differed from the other areas we had been, much bulkier and less flavorful. One plate did more than fill me, but left a lasting desire for more flavor. The surrounding Luckists kept eating. For athletic bodies, they ate like their bodies would be larger.

"How is the party treating you all?" King Resin asked.

"It's very fun!" Naso exclaimed.

"The food is delicious," I said.

"Your people are very kind," the Soothsayer said.

"I am glad to hear it," King Resin said. "Tomorrow, we will have a meeting, Yaron. I would like to speak about your future here."

I sat up straight, my heart racing. "That sounds great!" I said. "I look forward to it."

"Good," King Resin said as a small belch escaped him. For being extravagant and regal, he acted so very human. "Excuse me. Now, I think my lady Herita should join me for another dance."

The way Herita's cheeks flushed made me happy. "Again?" she asked.

"A beautiful woman like yourself needs to be displayed," King Resin said. "Come! We shall dance."

She took his hand and ran out to the dance floor. Aurora just stared at Herita.

"What is it?" I asked.

"Nothing," Aurora said. "I've just never seen her smile like that."

"It looks like she has something for King Resin," Naso said as he elbowed Aurora.

"No..." Aurora drifted off, cocking her head toward her aunt.

"I think Naso may be correct," the Soothsayer added.

"Looks like you'll have to like these people after all," I said with a smile. I took her hand and pulled her out for more dancing. Other than the abrupt and rude welcoming, Hallow was proving to be a place I enjoyed.

17

King Resin's Time

I arrived at the throne room early the next morning. My uncle wasn't there. Trigger eventually found me and said he had to postpone. So, after finding the others, Trigger taught us some of their games. Most of Luck's culture centered around games. I preferred Luck and Slide, a card game with five different shapes that were supposed to represent each Aura. If you finished with one of each Aura at the end, you won. Naso preferred the physical games, which often involved throwing either a ball, disc, or some other kind of item at another person or at some kind of goal. No matter the game, Trigger typically won. He insisted he didn't use the Luck Aura, but the games were centered around Luck.

Another day passed, and the same thing happened. Trigger assured me King Resin was very busy. We learned how to play drums with some local street artists while they either danced at ridiculous speeds or played more complicated string instruments. Eventually, the drums were taken from us as we didn't keep the proper beat.

Each day, I grew more impatient with my uncle, especially when I learned he spent a lot of time with Herita. On the seventh day, I arrived again to an empty throne room.

"Here we go again," I mumbled to myself.

I wasn't surprised. Why did I matter to him? He was the king, after all.

Instead of leaving the throne room at that time, I explored the paintings on the wall. Bright colors covered each piece of art depicting past leaders. The interesting part was that they all looked like my uncle. Men with light skin and bright eyes. The pictures went back several kings. I assumed no pictures remained from the old Hallow before it was destroyed. The same crown topped each of the kings' heads, just like the one my uncle wore. The empty indentation where the Trimerald should've been was missing in a few portraits. Toward the back, one painting displayed another king, but the edges were burnt, and there was a rip in the canvas dissecting his face. I wondered if the painting came from the old Hallow.

The past mattered little to me, so I started walking back toward my uncle's picture. Something caught my eye as I stopped at the painting right before his. A brown-haired man with bright blue eyes and a thick brown beard stood burly with hair bursting from his chest. Larger than my uncle, based on what I could tell, his picture demanded my attention. He reminded me of a Waldabear. The great throne shined behind his body.

My attention returned to the actual throne. A crisp, green cushion covered the back of the chair. To the right of the throne sat a small garden. Trickling water lured me over to discover a small waterfall coming from the side of the cave and flowing into a pond. The smell of fresh water invigorated my spirit, while the sweet aroma of little yellow flowers gave me joy. The whole garden received a decent amount of sunlight, which allowed the plants to flourish. From around the corner, I heard a commanding voice say something I couldn't decipher. King Resin appeared with Herita, arms interlocking with one another. Herita pulled her arm away as soon as she saw me.

"I apologize for my tardiness, nephew," King Resin said.

"It's no problem," I replied with a forced smile, turning my attention to Herita. "What are you doing here?"

A childlike crimson flashed across Herita's cheeks. "King Resin requested my company for a walk this morning. I was already planning on going on one, so I accepted the offer."

"Herita is full of amazing stories and wisdom," King Resin said. "I have not laughed or enjoyed talking this much in some time."

"I'm a hot commodity for conversation," Herita said as they both laughed.

"Yeah..." I began but realized I had nothing further to say. Seeing Herita so happy after all her health issues didn't bother me whatsoever.

"King Resin has already arranged my meeting with the best Medical Luckists the city has to offer," Herita said.

Any irritation I had with my uncle vanished. My breathing steadied before it even riled up. He was just trying to help Herita the whole time.

"We like to call them Muckists, but the Medical Luckists do not like to be called that." King Resin scoffed. "Get it? We replace the L with the M in Medical—"

"We get it," Herita interrupted, patting his chest.

"I wonder why they dislike it," I replied in a sarcastic tone. "People normally love to be named after mud or gunk."

"Mud sounds like a wonderful name," King Resin said. We stared at him. "I am kidding. Luckists can be sarcastic as well."

The intimidating man we first met faded from view. Instead, a kind person who liked to joke stood before us.

"Yes, they can," Herita said. "Though not well." She nudged him. "I better head to my appointment. Enjoy your time together." And, in typical Herita fashion, she disappeared before we could say anything else.

King Resin stared at her as she walked away. "Uncle?" I started. "Do you like Herita?"

He shook his head as he drifted back into reality. "I was taught how vile Perceptionists are, but I really like this one. She is mesmerizing." He faced me, eyebrows rising and falling in rhythmic motion. "It seems that it runs in her family. I saw you with the girl."

"Aurora?" My chest warmed. "They're a very nice family."

"Nice..." King Resin watched me. "Anyway, I was going to tell you about your history."

"Yes, please." I nodded so hard I cracked my neck.

"What would you like to start with?"

I thought of my parents raising me when I was younger. How did they get into Toterrum at first? How weren't they caught? So many questions raced through my mind, but one stood out.

"What did you mean about trusting Mentalists in the past and being betrayed?" I asked.

He twisted his large head. "This is what you choose to start with?"

"Yes." The question haunted me since he first mentioned it, and I learned of the Soothsayer's inability to recall the past.

"I thought it would be about our family." He shrugged. "What do you know about the destruction of Rithbar?" He walked over to one of the banners hanging from a pillar and adjusted it.

"Something happened with Vigor and Empathy in Toterrum," I started. "Somehow, both leaders died. Empathy disappeared. The late leader of Vigor's daughter was angered and attacked Rithbar."

"Yes, yes." He flicked the banner as it snapped, and dust flew off it. The forest green brightened and made the depicted Trimerald in the banner's center stand out more. "I meant more of Hallow."

"During this siege, they sent a separate attack to the original Hallow and destroyed the city. This caused the leader of Luck to leave with other Luckists to save the survivors. After Luck left, Vigor sent a stronger siege against Rithbar with giants. Perception and

Mentality couldn't hold the capital. When they called on Luck, Luck didn't answer." I stopped, watching him shake his head. "They had abandoned the others. Perception and Mentality had to save their own people along with the non-Manipulators. They fled the city, and Rithbar was destroyed."

King Resin sighed and rubbed the bridge of his nose. "My poor boy, they tell you a warped truth."

I thought I trusted what the Mentalists and Perceptionists had told me, but I was intrigued by his disapproval. "Then, shed some light on the history," I said.

"Wise decision." He clapped his hands together, the sound echoing throughout the throne room. "You are right about something happening in Toterrum, but before that, there was something that happened in Rithbar and it involved every Aura. The leaders of Vigor, Empathy, Luck, Perception, and Mentality were all there. Empathy killed Vigor's leader, and Vigor's leader's daughter responded by killing Empathy's leader. Empathy fled the city after the debacle, attacked Toterrum, and disappeared. Perception, Mentality, and Luck remained in Rithbar." He crossed his arms and sat on his throne. "There was indeed an attack on Hallow, and Mentality agreed that Luck should leave to avenge their fallen city. Perception did not agree until they received a hefty financial gain from the situation." He rubbed his hands across the gold on his chair.

"Gold?" My question echoed across the room, and the gold within the room glistened as if in satisfaction.

A mischievous smirk curled up the king's face. "You know how the city is lined in gold? Where do you think the gold came from? That is Luck gold. The retreat from the city was decided as soon as the attack began. We were not going to win. Mentality devised a plan for Luck and Perception to leave before them. Luck left first, and Perception followed. Perception quickly spread a rumor, calling us cowards for leaving to save ourselves. While they coined us as cowards for fleeing, they looked less like cowards for fleeing later. As for Mentality, they remained, and the people of Toterrum *conveniently* forgot about Aura." He scrunched his nose as if catching the scent of something putrid. "The whole thing reeked of Mentality. A distorted reality by Perception, and a lost truth by Mentality." He leaned forward, sharp eyes drawing me in. "But *we* are the bad guys? Ha!"

More than anything, I was shocked by Perception taking a bribe to remain quiet. But his statements made sense. Gold riddled the city, and gold wasn't common in the area. I did question the fact that Toterrum forgot about Aura. Mentalists were the only ones capable of a Manipulation like that. My head pounded from thinking through all he said and also my trust being challenged yet again.

I bit my upper lip. "How do you know what is true and what isn't?"

"*That* is a brilliant question," King Resin replied. "Let me know when you know the true answer. But in all reality, you know the Mentalist involvement makes sense."

The excitement flooding his eyes as he gossiped further surprised me. There were hidden depths in my uncle.

"I do..." I sighed.

"And Perception and Mentality are very close." The gossip continued.

"They are..."

"Do you really think Luck abandoned the others?" he asked.

"Find and capture opportunity." Their Aura's saying rolled off my tongue so easily.

"My boy!" A single, loud laugh made the throne room shake. "Yet, foreign gold covers Flaunte. We *are* gold. We have always been ourselves. Proudly, I might say." He pressed his lips together before popping them. "I think you know the truth."

Part of me wondered if he could be part Mentalist, because he read my disbelief with Perception being at fault. My eyes drifted to the gold on the throne, the gold on the walls, and the gold on the pillar shining from the gold reflecting sunlight through the caved city. And what did Flaunte have lining its buildings?

"I don't discredit what you say, but I'm still struggling," I admitted, though I grew tired of the subject already. "What about my biological parents? What happened to them?"

He leaned back and rested his arms on the sides of the throne. "I am not sure what happened." He scratched at the throne's sides. "I do remember when Rita and Thomlin came back with you. During King Joel's reign, there was a large group of Luckists who were charged with treason and banished from the city. When they were banished, they were ambushed by patrolling Officers. Rita and Thomlin were a part of the team selected to search for survivors."

"Survivors?" My heart nearly leaped from my chest.

"They were specifically worried about their good friends April and Jash, who were a part of the exile. The search team was gone for over two weeks. During this time, King Joel's entire demeanor changed. Something about the situation made him go mad." King Resin's face went gray. "He became very hostile. I was planning to challenge his throne at some point, but not until he was much older." An audible gulp escaped my uncle. "He was my mentor."

The burly Waldabear king in the portrait next to my uncle's must've been King Joel. I glanced over at the painting. "Did you end up challenging him?" I asked.

"Patience, nephew," King Resin responded with a weary smile before continuing. "The search team came back and reported that over half of the banished people were killed. The other half were missing. April and Jash were among the dead. Rita and Thomlin were devastated. They had suffered a stillbirth not so long before they left." He scratched the sides of the throne with more aggression. "So many bad things were happening to Rita and Thomlin."

"I didn't know she had a stillbirth..." What I felt for the fake mother that made me feel unworthy shifted into something different as I saw her as the loving mother who wanted me. Like a consuming fire flickering down to a controlled candle, my mind found peace again.

"This was all until I saw Rita holding a baby." He chuckled. "It was you. She had no idea who your parents were." His hands stopped scratching the sides. "Happiness returned to her. King Joel demanded to know what your origin was. Rita kept telling him she did not know. King Joel was not satisfied with this answer and kept saying that Rita knew. He then demanded you be banished from the city. Rita started screaming. Thomlin was ready to fight King Joel, but I knew Thomlin was not strong enough to defeat him. This is when I knew it was my time to challenge him." He paused for a long time, staring at the wall. The scratching of the throne began again while his eyes shifted to King Joel's picture.

"Are you okay?" I asked.

"Yes, of course." For a moment, it looked as if he wiped a tear from his cheek, but only tenacity remained in his eyes. "We fought. My plan was to disarm him, but King Joel had no self-control. He came at me with everything he had. The battle lasted twelve hours. The throne room was left in ruins. I won. The cost was his life."

We sat in silence for a few moments. "I'm sorry you had to do that to your friend."

"It was to protect you," he answered. "I became King Resin and kept your unknown origin a secret. No one questioned it. It makes my heart happy to know you are a Luckist. You were the only exception I made as King, and it is good to know it really was not an exception. Hallow only allows Luckists to reside in its presence. We keep our kind pure."

A gripping pit rose from my stomach into my throat. My friends weren't Luckists.

"What of my friends?" I asked. "How long will they be able to stay?"

"I am still deciding what is appropriate," he replied. "It will certainly not be forever."

Though the answer didn't satisfy me, it would have to do.

"Why were the people banished?" I asked.

"Treason."

I expected him to say more, since he did like to talk, but the one word made up his answer.

"Do you know what the treason was?"

"I do not," he replied. "That is something I have yet to receive an answer about."

"If it would be acceptable, the Soothsayer may be able to help if—"

"That is not an option," he cut me off.

"She has the ability to read and retain all information," I said. "That seems like a great resource to use."

"We have a *Mentalist* living here. That is much more than I usually allow."

"But—"

"That is *enough*." He growled.

I sat there silently, looking away from him. I could see him trying to make eye contact with me, but I wasn't budging. If he didn't want to help, what was the purpose of our discussion?

"I think I'm done for today," I said.

He stood, letting out an exhaustive sigh. "I am sorry, Yaron. As much as you are my nephew, I am still the king. You may have had more freedom with your words in Labyrintha and Flaunte, but things are different here. People may freely speak their minds, but my decisions are final, and my voice is most important."

I snickered. "Understood, *King* Resin."

"Onto another matter, I also wanted to have a memorial for your parents soon," he said. "They deserve a Hallow departure."

"Whatever you say." I gave him one last glare and stormed off.

"There is so much of Rita in you." His words echoed as I walked off. "So much..."

Any bit of excitement I once held about having a living family evaporated through the holes in the cave's ceiling. I was just like my mother? She lied to me my entire life. I was nothing like her. My uncle was already keeping things from me. I wouldn't be tricked into trusting him like I did Ruth. Ricochet ran up to my side, growling. His Aura flared and ignited my own.

"Right?" I exclaimed to him as he barked in response.

The gold lining the buildings blinded me at times as we walked through the city. I took a few extra turns to allow myself to cool down. Ricochet enjoyed longer walks, so he didn't contest. The smiles from the citizens and the music flowing down each street lightened my heart. Street vendors steamed thick vegetables and their earthy scents filled the air. I did enjoy the culture of Hallow. It reminded me of Flaunte but with tasteless food. Eventually, Ricochet and I came to the garden just by my bedroom as Aurora and the Soothsayer walked down the staircase. Aurora narrowed her eyes.

"Back already?" Aurora cocked her head. "He didn't show up again?"

"He showed," I grunted. "We had a disagreement." My grunt turned into a growl.

"That sounds very characteristic of you when learning about an Aura the first time," the Soothsayer teased. "*Very* characteristic."

She joked, but I still remained unsure if I trusted her. Yet, I based any of my mistrust on my uncle, the king, whom I definitely didn't trust. All I wanted was some clarity.

"Very funny," I bantered back with a smile.

"What happened?" Aurora touched my shoulder, making shivers run up and down my arm.

I recounted what King Resin told me, finishing with when my parents found me with the banished Luckists.

"That's terrible," Aurora said. "How could they banish their own people?"

I shrugged, not knowing how to respond. Just like her, my head continued to swirl with questions and no answers. The Soothsayer narrowed in on me, causing me to keep my mind protected from any incoming Manipulations from her.

"You want to know about the treason crime," the Soothsayer stated.

Was she able to make it past my protection? She couldn't have.

"Exactly," I said. Why was I trying to not trust her? She understood me. "Two of their good friends were part of the banished group and died during the attacks."

"I can't believe King Resin did this," Aurora said.

"He actually wasn't king then," I replied. "King Joel banished the group. King Resin took over after."

Was my uncle actually a good person, and was I only trying to find reasons to mistrust him?

"What are the friends' names?" the Soothsayer asked.

"April and Jash," I replied, remembering the names well. "I think that's what he said."

The Soothsayer raised her brow. "I imagine you know what you heard. King Resin challenged King Joel to a duel for the throne?"

"He did," I replied. "He actually challenged it to protect me."

I questioned my doubt of him.

"Why would he have to protect you?" Aurora asked.

"Because it was unclear if I was a Luckist or not," I said.

"Why would that matter?" Aurora asked.

"To keep the city pure," the Soothsayer said, words crisp and clear. The starkness of her statement sank deep into my core.

"Only Luckists are permitted to live in the city," I said.

"We are a problem then." The Soothsayer touched her chin and nodded.

His vanity and exclusion irked me.

"That was another reason I left my discussion with him." I crossed my arms and kicked a small rock on the ground. It skipped across the dirt until landing in a flower bed.

"I cannot believe they are so fearful of differences they keep others out," the Soothsayer said.

I furiously nodded in agreement. I was glad to have friends who thought like me.

"Mentalists do the same," Aurora said, a sharp glare fixated on the Soothsayer. She clenched her fists at her side.

The Soothsayer and I snapped our heads in her direction. Apparently, I didn't have friends who thought just like me.

"We allow visitors," the Soothsayer responded. "Hallow does not."

"But you don't allow others to live with you," Aurora added and extended her hands. "Mentality and Luck have similar ideas about keeping things pure."

The Soothsayer sat quietly, chewing on her lip and staring ahead. Mentality and Luck had many differences, but their purist mindset couldn't be differentiated.

"We know you don't think like that," I said to the Soothsayer, trying to comfort her. She smiled in response.

"For how many differences there are between Hallow and Labyrintha, our core values are the same," the Soothsayer said. "It seems we both cannot escape the sins of our past."

Aurora shifted her stance and let out a deep breath. "I'm sorry I snapped." She scratched the back of her neck. "You both know how passionate I am about differences and inclusivity."

"I am sorry I had misplaced pride," the Soothsayer mused. "It is easier to point out other's flaws without addressing your own."

Little glances and shifting body positions created a somber silence between us. Our little conversation blossomed into a challenge to our identities and motives. Truthfully, the conversation exhausted me, and I just wanted to lie down.

"Where were you heading?" I asked.

"We were going to find a place to eat," Aurora said.

"I will go and grab Naso," I said, my stomach beginning to gnaw itself in hunger.

"He's actually with Trigger," Aurora said. "Trigger was going to teach him some new combat moves. Luckists move quicker than any other Manipulator."

With all my time learning another Aura, having Naso bond with someone else gave me peace of mind. He had Herita in Flaunte and Aurora in Labyrintha, but Trigger seemed different and didn't seem to mind that Naso wasn't a Luckist.

The walk through the garden, past the throne room, and up a main alley brought us to the city center. Rapid drum beats, deep horn notes, and strumming guitars riddled the street with so many melodies that somehow melded together into a disjointed but harmonious song. Each step I took matched the beat of the drums, nearly causing me to break into dancing. Children performed scripted choreography in some areas while others danced to random steps, both forms mesmerizing with their skill and tenacity.

The strong scent of spices burned from many food stands, making my nostrils flare from the warm scents. I coughed a few times, overwhelmed by what I imagined the food tasted like. The night before, some dishes were labeled as spicy. I avoided those and only ate the bland food. I almost tried a spicy option when I witnessed Naso gag from how hot the food was.

Other stands sold clothing and jewelry in bright tints of green with body-tight fits. Passionate bartering and discussions filled the space in between the stands. The people bartering over prices made it seem like they argued over the life of a child rather than their main objective— the price of bread. After the exchange of Hallow currency—gold coins, of course—and food was prepared, they acted as if no argument occurred.

Blatant glares and audible insults followed the Soothsayer's path. Her blue cape didn't hide her Mentality origin. Though she pretended not to notice, her cheeks tensed each time another person insulted her. My skin itched, and my head pounded, wanting to stand up for her, but we had to avoid exile.

"We should buy you some new clothes," I said.

"Why? Their glares do not bother me," she replied with a half-smile. "I see. You're anxious about it, though."

"Guilty," I said, paranoia spiking with another glare from a Luckist. "But we are still in their city and should respect them as much as we can, even if that includes disguising you a little."

"So be it," the Soothsayer responded, her face relaxing as if relieved. I requested that she change her clothes.

We searched through various stands for over an hour until we eventually found dark green, looser-fitting clothing. The Soothsayer beamed from not wearing another tight-fitting piece of clothing.

"I'm glad your uncle gave us some coins," Aurora said.

"Thank him for us," the Soothsayer added.

"Maybe if I talk to him again," I smirked as they both rolled their eyes in unison.

We found a small restaurant with an outdoor patio. Golden chairs on gray patios sat within vining plants hung from a pergola above. The food was hot and fragrant, a spice level they called mild, but I found spicy. We learned the food was primarily made with Purple Kernel, a starchy, filling grain. Each dish had a side of grains and beans.

"Even their food has personality," the Soothsayer said, coughing from a spicy bite.

Aurora and I laughed. "I don't think any of these people would fit well in Toterrum," I said. "Personality isn't welcome."

I thought of my parents and wondered if they used to be bold like the rest of Hallow. Had Toterrum beat it out of them?

The Soothsayer faced Aurora. "You should tell Yaron about what you told me earlier."

I drummed my fingers across the table, raising an eyebrow toward Aurora.

"It really isn't anything important." She pushed her hair back behind her ear, avoiding eye contact.

"Everything is important," the Soothsayer said, chin rising with her lofty attitude.

"Well..." Aurora adjusted her jaw. "I noticed something odd with Zen's Aura this morning. It was the same oddity I saw when I fell from the Black Stone Mountains. I pushed at it and Zen started flapping his wings very aggressively and knocked me over. The Soothsayer heard the commotion and brought Zen back to a relaxed state." She bit her lower lip. "It was really weird."

"He didn't attack you, did he?" I leaned forward.

"No." She shook her head. "I definitely did something."

"Oh," I said. "Like a Perception Manipulation?"

"I didn't," Aurora responded. "I swear." A loud caw came from above as if Zen heard her. "Whatever I did, it energized him."

"Energized him?" I asked.

"Yeah," Aurora replied. "I think it's the same thing I did during my fall. Something weird has been going on since then." A little yellow light twinkled in her green meadow eyes before fading. "My ability to see Aura is murky."

"The yellow light?" I asked.

Her forehead tensed. "What yellow light?"

"In your eyes," I said, a bit surprised at her question.

Aurora's face relaxed as she blinked, almost as if trying to look at her own eyes.

"One thing I will add is you are a very strong Perceptionist," the Soothsayer said, eyes shifting back and forth between us. "Your Manipulative abilities may be growing."

"Yeah," she said. "I haven't felt this much out of control since I first started Manipulating."

I couldn't help but watch her eyes. The little vibrations caused by looking up to where Zen sat above, back down at us, to her water, and everywhere else made me curious. The yellow light had been there since I first met her. I remembered when she first appeared and had put my mind to rest just outside Toterrum. Meadow eyes with flashes of yellow light stared down at me then. Suddenly, a concerned, present Aurora stared at me.

I blinked. "You'll practice and get better at it," I reached out my hand and held hers. "I don't doubt you for one second." I paused. "But why didn't you tell me about this earlier?"

"I...I don't know." She pulled her hand back.

I shook my head. "There it is again. Why are—"

"Watch out!" someone yelled as I looked up at a ball about to hit my face. Another person flipped in the air, caught the ball, and landed right in front of us.

"Look who it is," Trigger said with a cocky grin. "You're Lucky I was here. Your reflexes are quite slow and would be terrible at Fortunato."

Fortunato was a game nearly every Hallow citizen played. Over the past week, I played it a couple of times but didn't love it quite as much as Naso did. With everything going on in my life, I had no time to play it. Naso and Trigger, on the other hand, seemed to be playing the game whenever they weren't training. Part of me was envious of their free time. I missed playing games. On the other hand, the game involved a lot of physical contact and, of course, Luck. When one lost Fortunato, they were either penalized to pay in gold or by accepting a dare of the winner's choosing. The idea never deterred Naso, who continued to improve on the skill-based portions of the game. Just like that, Naso ran up behind Trigger.

"Sorry about the throw." Naso scratched the back of his head. "I didn't realize I threw it that hard."

Trigger slapped his chest. "That's because you're getting stronger."

"How was the training?" Aurora asked.

"Much more tiring than the Surprisants," Naso replied. "No offense." He glanced at the Soothsayer.

"None taken," the Soothsayer said.

Little glances were exchanged across our table. Trigger looked over at Naso. It made the interaction a bit awkward since no one said another word.

"May we sit with you?" Trigger asked.

"Pull up some chairs up," I replied, grateful for the silence to end. Our new group still needed to learn more about one another's characteristics.

While grabbing our leftover food and inhaling it, Trigger swallowed and said, "The three of you should join us next time."

"Oh, Great Light, no." The Soothsayer laughed. "I prefer books."

"Nerd," Trigger said with a snicker.

The Soothsayer crossed her arms. "We all have our gifts," she said.

"To gain and to know is the best gift to bestow," Trigger said. We all turned our heads toward him. He continued to eat as if nothing happened.

"You can be quite surprising," the Soothsayer said. "You train so much and, at times, are good at words. Do you hope to be king someday?"

Trigger stopped chewing and swallowed hard. He cleared his throat. "Why do you ask?"

"You seem to fit the mold." The Soothsayer smiled.

Trigger snickered. "To assume is to make an ass out of you and me."

A paleness swept across the Soothsayer's face. "Excuse me?"

"You and me." He grinned and turned away from her. "Yaron and Aurora, would you like to train with us?"

I looked at Aurora, and she shrugged. "We'd love to," I responded.

The Soothsayer gaped.

"Prepare to sweat." Naso pulled at his shirt which I hadn't noticed was hugging tightly to his body, dried sweat crunching as he pulled.

"Do you all swim?" Trigger asked.

"Yes," we all responded.

"Let's go," Trigger said as he rose, pulling his not as sweaty shirt off, and walked off, back muscles flexing in the gold enhanced sun. "Shine on me, golden light, and I seek your gaze until darkened night." His statement faded the further he walked.

"That was abrupt," Aurora said. "I think we need to grab swimsuits."

"But don't ask him questions like that." He glared at the Soothsayer. "You don't always have to analyze people."

"Excuse m—" the Soothsayer started.

"Meet us near the throne room's garden," Naso interrupted her and ran off.

On our way to grab our swimsuits, I reached out to hold Aurora's hand, but just as I grazed it, she crossed her arms in front of herself. My cheeks warmed, and my chest tightened. Something was off.

"What's going on with us?" I asked.

The Soothsayer glanced over and slowed down, allowing us to walk ahead. "What do you mean?"

"You're acting weird with me. I know I have anxiety, but I can't not notice it."

She stared ahead. I worried she didn't hear me. Finally, she turned to me. "I just have some things going on, and I don't understand them." She held my hand. "We're good." She smiled before looking forward again. I squeezed her hand tightly, but the tightness in my chest remained. Ricochet's Aura found me as the anxiety closed in. He popped out of a bush near me and rubbed his head against my leg.

After grabbing our swimsuits, we went to meet the others at the throne room garden, Ricochet following along. After heading to the northern part of the city, we approached a small, dense forest. Thick foliage with reddish leaves and soft bushes below held back the sound of running water.

"How does such a dense forest grow in a low-light environment?" Naso asked.

"Do I look like I know?" Trigger replied. "They just do."

"Insightful," the Soothsayer responded. "Their leaves are more of reddish tint allowing them to absorb lower levels of light."

"Blah blah," Trigger said. "You talk a lot."

"So, do you," the Soothsayer calmly responded. She looked irritated. If a Mentalist heard him talk to the Soothsayer like that, I imagine a fight would've broken out. "Know too much, and you'll miss lunch."

The Soothsayer let out a hissing sigh before rolling her eyes.

***

As we walked through the forest, soft leaves brushing across my skin, the sound of water increased. A waterfall appeared before us, falling from a tunnel near the top of a large cavern. It roared into a decent-sized lake below. We stood on a cliff about halfway between the top of the cavern and the lake's surface.

"Welcome to the Caved Lake," Trigger announced as he stretched his arms high, muscles flexing. Even his muscles had muscles. "Now, have some fun." He stepped back and jumped off the ledge, tucking his legs in while he flipped and screamed as he splashed into the water.

"Awesome," Naso yelled as he took his shirt off and followed.

We each took our turn jumping into the water. As I jumped, I expected chilly water to overwhelm me. Instead, warm water relaxed me. Ricochet looked down and let out a sigh before lying down. Iri zipped above his head before resting on the tip of his snout. Ricochet rested, unphased.

"Your beast won't jump in?" Trigger asked.

"He doesn't like the water," I replied.

I let my Aura brush against Ricochet's. Ricochet barked from above. The sound echoed all around.

"I think your beast can do more than you think it can," Trigger said. "Bring him to the training area sometime. Let's see what we can pull out of him. Maybe we can find out why he hates water so much."

"Yet, he used to live on an island," Naso said. "He should love water."

"Maybe that is why they never made it off the island," the Soothsayer said.

"*Maybe that is why they never made it off the island,*" Trigger mimicked the Soothsayer.

Expecting her to respond with a retort, the Soothsayer did something unexpected. She lunged forward and shoved his head underwater. "Maybe that will shut you up," she said. He rose out of the water and swam after her as she swam away. To my complete surprise, they laughed.

"They are so different," Aurora said.

"Yeah, but they have a thing in common—you would swim circles around them," I said as I shoved her head underwater.

She launched from the water and threw her whole body on top of mine. Water rushed down my throat as I pushed back, cracking through the surface. As I choked, she just laughed. Before I could retaliate, someone shoved me back under from behind. Turning while underwater, I immediately threw my body onto Naso's. He dodged my attack.

"You better watch your back," Naso said as he swam away.

"I'll destroy you," I yelled as I chased after him. He was much faster than I was, so I pushed my mind away from my body and then punched at his Aura to slow him down.

"Hey, that's unfair," Naso yelled as I caught up and shoved him under. I brought my fist back as the Aura returned to him.

"So is getting me from behind," I snapped back.

"Fair." Naso shrugged before splashing me.

A black silhouette from below caught my eye. Two more zipped by, circling around Naso. He followed my gaze before noticing them as well. They closed in on him before breaking the surface and flying over Naso's head and back into the water. About the size of Ricochet, I couldn't make out much more of their features. Ricochet barked from above while running along the ledge, following the beasts' silhouettes. His Aura slapped against mine, making my heart pound. Our heartbeats went in sync. His worry was my own worry.

"Did you see that?" I asked.

"Yeah, what was it?" Naso treaded in circles, watching the beasts leap again from the water in rapid arcs.

The beasts popped their heads out of the water. Two bald beasts without ears stared at Naso with large, round eyes speckled with green and blue spots. Wet, slicked, light blue fur lay so flat on their bodies that they looked bald. Two flat appendages extended from the water and splashed Naso as the hairs along their neck extended into a cone around their head. The cone vibrated as the beasts appeared to laugh, sending ripples across the water. My body rose just a little out of the water before falling back in as the cone recoiled. They then submerged and swam to Aurora, the Soothsayer, and Trigger to splash them, extend their hairy cones, and raise their bodies from the water just a little before dropping back in.

"Hey, now!" Aurora yelled as she splashed the beast back.

The beasts exchanged glances before humming and exchanging splashes with Aurora a few more times. They then submerged and swam to a shallow area where they laid their plump bodies across various rocks. At least twenty more beasts appeared next to them. The beasts lacked legs and arms. About six flat appendages stuck out from their sides, reminding me of the Rithbarian Riveroks. Faint spiral designs pulsed in red hues reflecting the sun's beams.

"Those are Caved Selos," Trigger said. "Very docile and playful creatures, but not when the sun sets. I suggest avoiding this area during the night."

"Those cute things?" I asked. I wondered what he meant. The only thing the beast threatened me with was the desire to cuddle it.

Trigger floated on his back in front of me. "Let's just say they are completely different beasts." Somehow, he made his body stand straight up on the water before he dove and swam away.

The Caved Selos rolled on the ground while playfully gnawing at each other's necks. I couldn't picture the beasts being something to avoid. One of the Caved Selos locked eyes with me. I thought I saw a little dot of red flash across its eyes, but it was gone before I could focus.

"Are you sure?" I asked, suddenly uneasy.

"Hey, watch this," Trigger yelled from afar.

I hadn't even realized he swam to the other side of the pond that quickly. He swirled his hands and shot out of the water onto the cliff. The superhuman way he moved reminded me of a Vigorist. He then leaped from ledge to ledge while swirling his hands until he was back on the ledge with Ricochet. A startled Ricochet growled. His Aura forced itself on Trigger's while Trigger's Aura just danced around Ricochet's, avoiding the contact.

"How did you do that?" Naso yelled.

"Luck," Trigger announced with a bow. He then jumped from the ledge, extending his body high into the air, did five flips, and finished with a perfect, crisp dive into the pond. Emerging just in front of us, a shiny water film encasing him before pooling into droplets, he wiped his eyes and blinked while breathing as if nothing even happened.

"That was amazing!" I proclaimed.

"When you lean into the Luck Aura, you can do amazing things." Trigger winked, droplets of water flicking off his long lashes. "I saw what you did with Naso. That was amazing as well. My favorite part of the Luck Aura is how it acts differently for each Manipulator."

"Why don't you leap up the cliff like Trigger did?" An arrogant grin curled up Naso's cheeks.

"I don't think I can," I replied.

"Don't think, just do," Trigger said. "Lean into the Luck Aura and let it guide you."

"Don't think?" The Soothsayer scoffed. "That is absurd."

"You're absurd." Trigger didn't even turn to face her. Before she could respond, he continued, "Have a goal in your mind and push on the Aura that glows most."

"Like now?" I asked.

Trigger nodded his head toward the cliff. Reluctantly, I swam up to the cliff, my gaze shifting up the steep stones to see Ricochet's small head sticking out from above. Closing my eyes, I envisioned myself on the cliff. My Aura moved above my head. I opened my eyes and leaned into the Aura, attempting to launch my body up.

Nothing happened. I pulled myself up onto a little ledge just as the water's surface. I nearly slipped but grabbed one of the stones hard, bruising my forearm. Envisioning rising higher, I pushed into my Aura. Nothing again. Sighing, I turned to face Trigger with a shrug.

"Stop overthinking it!" Trigger yelled. "Rid yourself of fear and do the action while leaning in. The rest will happen on its own. Find and capture opportunity!"

A cloudy image appeared in the corner of my eye. The view of the ledge I tried to jump toward appeared, but from a view above it. Ricochet grazed his Aura against mine. Confidence flooded my thoughts. Everything Trigger said sounded absurd, but I needed to learn more. So, I pictured myself accomplishing my goal. I pushed on the Aura, and I leaped up without hesitation.

For a moment, I felt myself moving upward, but then I stopped midair, and the sensation of falling sucked the air from my lungs. I bellyflopped a loud smack and stinging pain following. Ricochet's Aura zipped around my Aura until it latched on, pulling me upward. Rushing up to the surface, I gasped for air; the wind knocked out of me.

"Ouch!" Naso yelled.

"That looked like it hurt!" the Soothsayer added.

After regaining my breath, stinging pain still lingering on my reddened chest, I swam back over to them. "What did I do wrong?"

"The Luck Aura is different for each Luckist," Trigger replied. "There are certain Manipulations that are just not as good at as others. You seem to be limited in Physical

Luck. But what you did with Naso was very different. We will have to investigate this further."

"You could have said that before I jumped," I said as I looked down at my maroon chest.

"Now we know." Trigger slapped at my sensitive chest.

Though the slap didn't feel great, I couldn't help but admire the friends surrounding me. The goal of figuring out my Aura still seemed far away, but the number of people helping me grew. Nothing would stop me.

18

Family

Staring out the large window, a bright light shined across my face, nearly blinding me. The Luckists had a mechanism set up that as the sun rose in the morning, the reflective material placed around the cave bounced light throughout it like sunlight hit the land above the caves. I often had to remind myself that I was living in a cave. A shaking snore, followed by a few mumbles, erupted from Naso who was sleeping in the bed next to me. He often talked in his sleep—mostly nonsensible gibberish came from him.

A loud knock sounded on our door.

"Who is it?" Naso asked as he sat straight up, hair a mess, and eyes reddened and sleepy.

"Good morning, beautiful," I said as I walked by and petted his tangled head.

"That's what I'm here for," he replied as his head slammed back onto his pillow, and he went back to snoring.

I opened the door to Trigger. "Good morning, Yaron," Trigger said.

"Good morning," I replied.

He looked past me. "I see Naso is still asleep."

"He moves slowly in the mornings," I said. "I'll let him know you stopped by after he wakes up."

"I'm actually here for you. King Resin sent me to deliver a message." He handed over a sealed, textured envelope. I took it and turned it over to find a gold seal shaped like the Trimerald's triangle with small green dots etched into the gold. I broke the seal and opened the letter. Gray paper with golden text reflecting light covered the paper.

Nephew,

We will be holding your parents' memorial just past lunch. I would like to discuss some things with you before then. Please meet me.

King Resin

I crumpled the letter and pressed it on the table. Trigger leaned against the doorway, raising his eyebrows.

"What?" I raised my palms and gestured to my sides. "It's nothing."

Trigger slightly turned his head to the side. "Not my business." He leaned off the doorframe. "Did you want to train with Naso and me this morning?"

I nodded, grabbing onto any reason I could to distract or keep myself from seeing my uncle.

"We'll have to wait for sleeping beauty to wake up." Trigger nodded toward a snoring Naso.

I grabbed Naso's shoe by the door and chucked it at him.

"OW!" Naso exclaimed, jolting his body upright.

"There." I crossed my arms.

"That'll do it." Trigger chuckled, bright teeth shimmering in the morning sun. "I'll wait for you in the courtyard as one of you tries to make themselves a little more presentable." He walked off, the door shutting behind him.

"How long do you need?" I asked Naso.

"I need to figure out if I have a concussion first." Naso rubbed his head.

"So, ten minutes?" I asked, not waiting for a response and walking out to the girl's room. The Soothsayer answered with a bright smile. "Good morning," I said. "Is Aurora in there?"

"She is," the Soothsayer said. "Come in." I slowly leaned my head in with caution. "I would not welcome you in if any of us were indecent."

I nervously laughed. Aurora sat at a table near their window. "Good morning, beautiful." I leaned in over her shoulder and kissed her. I didn't know why, but I opened my eyes to find her kissing me with her eyes open. We pulled away from one another and averted our gaze.

"Hey there." Aurora coughed. "What did you want to do today?"

"That's why I'm here," I replied, that tightness back in my chest. "I'm going to train with Naso and Trigger this morning. Then, I'm getting lunch with my uncle and will probably sit with him during my parents' memorial."

"Should I meet you there?" Aurora asked.

"I think he's pretty serious about the family thing," I said. "I don't think you'll get to sit next to me."

"It is a Luck custom to have only family close during the memorial," the Soothsayer added. "No one else."

"Oh," Aurora said. "Will you be okay?"

"It'll be fine," I said. "Did you want to train with us?"

"I can't," Aurora said. "I told a certain *someone* I would help them find books and other documents in the Luck library."

"Why do you need help?" I asked the Soothsayer.

"I noticed that the door to the library explicitly says, 'Luckists only,' when I walked by yesterday," the Soothsayer said. "Though, I know the sign was only just created. I plan to get in there anyway, so a little Perception may help me accomplish this."

Mischievous grins bounced between them.

"I don't think I'll be able to talk you out of this," I said. "Just don't let anyone catch you."

"We've got this, Yaron," Aurora said. "Where is the memorial?"

"I'll make sure Trigger lets you know," I responded. "Make sure Herita knows, too."

"I'm supposed to grab lunch with her today," Aurora said. "I'll let her know." She grabbed my shirt and pulled me in for another kiss. "I'll see you this afternoon."

Blood rushing to my cheeks, I stumbled out of their room in a shaky haze. Naso stepped out our door as I walked up to it. He attempted to tame his hair, but it was still a bit of a mess.

"You ready to sweat?" Naso asked, slapping my chest.

***

We met Trigger in the courtyard, Ricochet at my side, and made our way to an open area on the east side of the city. A new perk bounced in Ricochet's step. His Aura kept grazing against my own. An uneven, rocky terrain covered the space, unlike the even, smooth training grounds of Labyrintha. Ricochet jumped onto a rock and sat, studying the space. I joined his survey to witness Luckists combating one another with brisk, swift motions. Each strike they made against one another just missed the target's face in what seemed like a coordinated dance. Yet, they grunted and pushed forward in frustration.

One girl launched herself at each opponent at an explosive, perfect speed. Each person she faced fell within a minute. She not only hit faster, but she dodged even faster. Even with the impressive flips and dodges from each opponent, she struck them as they landed, seeming to predict their next move. Each hit mesmerized me more and more, which explained why her foes appeared to be stunned every time.

"Who is that?" I asked Trigger.

"Mel," Trigger replied. "She's one of the best warriors in Hallow."

"She's amazing," I said, watching her take down another opponent.

"You have a good eye," Trigger said. "But that could be because she's your cousin."

All my attention centered on Trigger. "My *what*?" I asked.

"Your cousin," Trigger reiterated. "Your uncle's daughter."

"I have a cousin?" I asked. "Why am I just learning this? Why wouldn't my uncle tell me?"

"It's because they don't speak to one another," Trigger replied. "He doesn't acknowledge her, neither does she acknowledge him. It wasn't my place to tell you about her before, yet here we are now. It's rather awkward." He moved his gaze away, looking over at the training grounds. "Mel! Come over here!"

"What are you doing?" I exclaimed, heart racing.

Mel looked over to Trigger in the middle of a flip. Her foe took advantage of this and hit her in the chest. She fell to the ground hard and lay on her back. She then screamed and jumped to her feet from her back without using her hands. Throwing a flurry of barrages, her foe yielded. Reaching her hand out, she helped her opponent up and walked in our direction. Her dark brown hair was tied back, exposing her darker-toned skin, looking little like my uncle. Bold, copper eyes matched her swagger. Bits of dirt covered her face, but her skin still glowed bright even though dirty.

"Do not yell at me again, Trigger," Mel sternly said.

"Relax, stone face," Trigger said with a smile. Her expression didn't falter. Their juxtaposing demeanors made me chuckle. On one side, we had Trigger's confidence oozing with smiles and jokes. On the other side, we had Mel's hardened expression and fierce eyes also bursting with confidence. Different looks, but the same result.

Mel's stern expression shifted to Naso and me. "I saw you training yesterday," Mel said to Naso.

Naso looked over his shoulder and back forward, pointing to himself. "You noticed me?"

"I noticed how slow you moved," Mel broke his confidence with one statement. "You look like you were trained by a Mentalist."

Naso blushed and tried to muster a confident response. "I'm a trained Surprisant." As hard as he tried to stand up straight, his shoulders remained slouched.

Mel looked at him with disgust. She didn't even acknowledge his statement, which further stung Naso. After a long silence, she looked over to me and tilted her head forward toward me.

"What about you?" Mel asked. "Who are you?"

Ricochet barked at her harsh questioning of me. Mel shot a glare at Ricochet. He growled. Their Auras reached out, sparks zapping between them. Then, she nodded. Ricochet dipped his head, and they were good. She turned her attention back to me.

I cleared my throat. "Yaron Meek from Toterrum."

Her stern face softened for a second before returning stonelike. "You are my cousin," Mel said. "You are quite the talk of the city. The son of Rita and Thomlin has returned. King Resin's nephew makes his grand arrival." She patted my shoulder twice, hard, and pulled back.

"Have people been saying that?" I asked while rubbing my sore shoulder. "I didn't notice and honestly could care less what they think."

Mel snickered and nodded. "I am sorry about your mother and father," Mel said. "Rita wrote to me all the time. I miss her words." A glistening sheen appeared in her eyes before quickly evaporating when her fierce expression returned.

"Thank you," I said. "I miss them, but I'm happy I get to learn about the city they came from."

"I must continue my training," Mel stated as she twisted her arms side to side with a loud crack from her back. "It was nice to meet you, *cuz*. I will see you at their memorial this afternoon." She bowed slightly to Trigger. "And to you, future king." She smirked.

Trigger snarled as Mel walked away. It seemed like each day I was in Hallow I learned I had more family members. Was Hallow my home?

"She was different," Naso stated.

"How so?" I asked.

"Of the Luckists I have met, everyone seems laid back and happy," Naso replied. "She seems...much more serious."

"She keeps to herself for the most part," Trigger replied.

"I bet she and Aurora would get along," Naso said with a big grin. "They are both pretty and both a bit—"

I punched him in the arm before he could finish. "Watch it," I said.

"Ow!" Naso yelled. "You know I'm right."

I didn't agree or disagree; I only shrugged.

"Why did you she call you future king?" I asked.

"It's nothing." Trigger swiped his hand forward.

"You don't want to talk about it," I said. "I can respect that."

"How political," Trigger said. "Can we start training now?" We shook our heads. He pulled out a golden round object covered in little black spikes. "This is a Thettle. It's used in Thettle Shots, a game involving touching each individual spike until each retracts into the ball. Once no spikes remain, you win. However, you can only touch one spike at a time. Touch more than one at a time, and they won't retract."

He took the ball to his mouth and blew at it. Each spike extended even longer. Ricochet perked up his head and watched Trigger closely. The ball vibrated and shot away. Ricochet rushed after it.

"That's it?" I asked.

"Your beast will never catch it," Trigger said. "The purpose of the game is to work with your team, Ricochet in this case, and figure out how to trap the ball and accomplish the task."

"You underestimate Ricochet." Ricochet kicked off a rock, flew in the air, and smacked the ball with his paw. The ball slammed into the ground, vibrated, and shot off again with no spikes retracted.

"You underestimate the Thettle." Trigger slapped my back. "Your beast is very capable. But he can learn from you. Tap into his Aura and you'll be surprised what can happen."

Ricochet followed the ball, his Aura shivering in anticipation. I extended my iridescent Aura toward his Aura, but he ignored me. I pushed harder. He stopped and turned his attention to me. Unsure about what to do next, I watched his Aura, fixated near his eyes, as it pulsed toward the ball. He desired something. Of course, he did. But the way it collected near his eyes piqued my interest.

"What if..." I mumbled to myself.

I reached my Aura to his and intertwined them. Suddenly, a blurry image filled the center of my sight, like when you stare at the sun for too long, and it imprints within your field of vision. Just like during the siege on Labyrintha, I saw what he saw. The image took a moment to make sense, but I realized I saw the ball, but closer and in front of me. And from Ricochet's angle. Ricochet launched forward, and the dull image moved closer to me.

"What do you see?" Trigger asked.

"I...I think it's the ball," I said.

"Of course, you can see the ball," Naso said.

"No, it's closer." I glanced over at Ricochet lunging across the ground. "I think I'm seeing the ball from Ricochet's angle."

"It worked..." Trigger said under his breath.

I wanted to question his comment but instead leaned further into what Ricochet saw. Suddenly, the image of the ball no longer took the center of my sight. Ricochet looked beyond the ball. I saw where he tried to lead it. Without hesitation, I launched myself forward in the direction of where Ricochet tried to lead the ball. I planted myself and faced the charging spike ball whizzing in the air. In unison, Trigger jumped up, slapped the ball down, put my pointer finger forward, and touched one of the spikes. I jolted inward toward its center, one spike down.

"We did it!" I exclaimed. Ricochet barked in response. His Aura warmed against my own but with a cool after-effect. "You're happy." The temperature change his Aura went through represented happiness. I just knew it. For the first time, I understood his feelings.

"Nice work!" Trigger slapped my back.

"How'd you know that would work?" I asked.

"I read a book one time." He shrugged. Before Naso or I could say something, he continued, "Don't look at me like that. I read."

"You're full of surprises," Naso said.

"Now, keep this up," Trigger said. "Work together and finish off the Thettle."

Ricochet and I followed his order and accomplished the goal within fifteen minutes. As only a few spikes remained, it became easier to narrow in on the remaining spikes. At the end, Ricochet and I fell to the ground with heaving breaths.

"Nice work!" Mel yelled from the other side of the area.

I glanced over at her before she turned her attention back to her training.

"Thanks." I pushed out through my panting.

"Now, we will practice combat," Trigger said.

Heaving for air, I shot the meanest glare I could muster in his direction. The combat movements he taught us involved striking with the hands and feet while using the rest of the body as a counterbalance. Every movement worked toward an opportunity to strike. Nothing was left overlooked. After an hour of combat, I had no energy left in me.

"I have to head to lunch," I said, suddenly wanting to see my uncle so as to get away from Trigger's torturous training. "But I should probably shower."

"You smell like my butt," Naso said in between deep breaths.

"Hilarious," I replied. "See you later."

I made my way back to the room, but each staircase I climbed hurt my body. The shower's warm embrace washed sweat and dirt off my body. After putting on new clothes, I heard Aurora and the Soothsayer in the hall. Before I could open my door, they stopped just near mine.

"What did the letter say?" Aurora asked.

"She is dead," the Soothsayer said. "Zela and the other Surprisants were killed in the field."

Aurora's soft whimper cracked her voice. "Poor Lilah. They just got married."

A crushing pain hit my chest like a mountain crashing into my heart. Collapsing to my knees in a flurried landslide, the snowy caps on my glazed-over eyes melted into trickling streams down my cheeks. A sharp pain inflicted me and covered the rest of my body like a disease.

My good friend Zela died.

I could've let numbness wash over me like I had in Labyrintha. I could've gone cold and distant. Thinking about that made me remember that Zela pulled me out of my darkness. I whimpered.

Death continued to surround me. As much as I wanted to lie on the floor and weep, I had to make my way to lunch. I opened the door to Aurora and the Soothsayer glancing up at me, tears trickling down their cheeks.

"Yaron..." the Soothsayer began.

"I heard," I said.

"Yaron, I'm so..." Aurora's sentence faded as she reached out to me.

"I need to go." I pulled away and made my way down the stairs. Aurora didn't follow. Unsure of whether the Soothsayer stopped her or if Aurora knew I needed space, I walked as fast as I could. I stopped for a second in the courtyard and let out a gasp. My lungs tightened, and my ability to breathe slipped away. I knew Zela was dead all along. But with death becoming an all-present reality, my pent-up emotions finally exploded from me. The last bit of hope I had for Zela's life exploded.

The Soothsayer walked up behind me and stood quietly. We stood in silence for a moment before she said, "A good friend said to me one time, 'If we sink into the despair of losing someone, we do not uphold the legacy they displayed. Let the grief run its course, but remember all the person fought for and tell their story to others.' I have held these words close to my heart." She paused for a moment as she took a deep breath. "The good friend who said that was Zela."

I turned to the Soothsayer and fell into her embrace. Her cold tears dripped onto my neck. "She protected you," I said. "She fulfilled her duty and so much more."

"I know," the Soothsayer said. "A bit of me thinks if I would have not left, maybe she would still be alive."

"If I wouldn't have left, maybe she would," I said. "I struggled the same with my parents' death, but you assured me our destiny points us the way we're supposed to go."

"We are guided," she said. "May the Light watch over you."

"May it watch over us all," I said as I pulled away, nodded, and made my way to lunch.

Part of me wished I could stop forming relationships. People either died or betrayed me. But then I wouldn't have ever known Zela—her clever attitude and the direct way she asked tough questions. She was my friend and the Soothsayer was right, I would uphold her legacy and show the same loyalty to others.

My trip to the throne room became a blur. Emotionally charged and distracted, I stumbled into the room, where King Resin was sitting on the throne.

"Nephew," King Resin said. "I am glad you came." He observed me. "Are you okay?"

"I'm fine." I rubbed my eyes.

An uneasy expression darkened his face. "I want to apologize for yesterday."

I had forgotten about yesterday. Too many things swirled in my head. "It's no problem," I replied. "Where are we eating?" I clapped my hands together.

King Resin smiled. "Follow me."

He walked to the wall at the back of the room. There was a rectangular empty space for what looked to be a window, yet no window filled the space. On the sidewalls of the opening hung golden triangles. He reached up to the triangle on the right and spun it. The triangle spun so fast that it looked like a shiny circle. The wall shifted as a staircase appeared, spiraling upward. With a pat on my shoulder, he walked up as I followed along. The hidden door closed behind us.

"What is this?" I asked.

"A secret place only the king knows about."

We walked up a winding staircase. A hallway with small slits in the walls connected the top of the staircase to an unknown space on the other end. As we walked, I peeked through the holes to the city far below. Jagged rocks covered some of the view just outside the windows. After careful observation, the other end of the hallway stopped at the walls on the city's edge. As soon as we hit the wall, another winding staircase went upward until we came up to another triangle that he spun, and a door opened to the outside world.

The morning sun always made my eyes squint, but true sunlight after not seeing it in quite some time made me shut my eyes. I peeked through my closed eyes in spurts until my eyes adjusted to the sunlight. Sitting atop a large, grassy hill overlooking many other hills, I gazed at small lakes shining gold, spread across the area. Strong gusts of wind rustled the grass below and pushed my hair back. I had forgotten what fresh air smelled like. No longer did the smell of rocks dominate my sense of smell.

"Isn't it beautiful?" he asked, taking a deep breath.

"It is." I watched fluffy white clouds hover across the bright blue sky. Unlike my normal view of clouds, these clouds came straight at me rather than hovering above. Occasionally, the clouds collided with us, making it foggy for only a moment. Very cool, wet air made my skin tingle. Just as the clouds passed, the dew left on my skin evaporated in the warm sun.

King Resin pulled out a box hidden in a nearby bush. Fresh fruit and meat appeared from within the box when opened as we sat in the grass and ate. "I come here often to escape," he said.

Watching my regal uncle sit in the grass, with no throne and no gold surrounding him, the image made me chuckle. "I'm surprised."

"How so?"

"Everything is so extravagant and over the top down in the city." I gestured to the land surrounding us. "This is so…simple."

He tilted his head back and laughed. "Our—your mother and I—parents were gold gathers." He popped a little round fruit into his mouth and ate it in one bite. "We would often join them while they gathered and played in the fields. The grassy hills have always been a close to my heart." Tears shimmered in his eyes but he blinked them away. "And I thought I would get another chance to sit here with Rita."

"I wish she would've told me about this," I said. "She kept so many secrets from me, and I feel like I never really knew her."

A soft stillness came between us, only interrupted by the continuous wind.

"What was she like in Toterrum?" he asked.

"She was kind," I said. "She was kind to everyone, even the Officers. Naso's, Asher's, and our family were all close and looked out for one another."

"Asher? Herita's nephew?"

"Yes." A small, closed-mouth laugh escaped. Herita had been telling him a lot. "Mom always let me be freer than Asher's and Naso's parents let them. This makes more sense now that I know what Hallow is like. But it felt like something was always missing. I rarely saw her happy. I wanted her to be happy."

"She was always filled with joy." He ripped some grass from the ground and fiddled with it. "She loved to tell stories, make up worlds, and make me laugh until I cried. Thomlin brought out even more joy. He and her friends. But the week they left was rough. Between the miscarriage, her friends being banished, and her friends dying, something changed in her." He flicked the blades of grass from his fingers as they spun in the air, hovering just above him until falling in little tied-up triangles. "You were the only thing that brought her a bit of joy k. You and Thomlin. Nothing else seemed important to her. She despised Hallow and needed to escape. Thus, they volunteered to spy in Toterrum."

"Not the best move," I said.

"But a necessary one." His intense eyes found mine. "Something was broken inside of her. Losing friends and family does that to you."

His words continued to ring in my ears. I'd never empathized with words so much in my life. I lost my parents, Lady Sandra, Aurora for a moment, and now Zela. Everything became such a mess, and I hopelessly wandered, trying to find any semblance of meaning.

"I found out a very good friend of mine died," I said. "I just found out today."

Small specks of gold in his irises glistened in the sun. "I am sorry to hear this. Speak some words about your friend. I have learned this is an important exercise to do when death occurs."

I hesitated. "Her name was Zela," I said. "She was a Surprisant and my first true friend in Labyrintha. She pulled me out of a deep depression after my mother died. She taught me so much about myself. She died protecting my group." A soft tear trickled down my cheek as my head pounded, wanting to dissociate like it often did. "I feel like part of myself died with her, and every part of me wants to escape my reality. But the Soothsayer discourages this."

"How do you mean?"

"Well, I do this thing when my anxiety flares. I have an out-of-body experience where I detach from the emotions gripping me. She called it dissociation and encouraged me to remain present to deal with the feelings."

He flicked another grassy triangle into the air. "Did she know?" He laughed. "Dealing with emotions is great and all, but your body is only naturally doing what it's intended to do. If anything, that is a strength you have that others do not. Many people fold when the pressures of life close in on them. You." He pointed at me. "You can survive and function. Your dissociation is a gift. Do not ever think otherwise."

The brevity of his words invigorated me. He seemed to know exactly what I spoke of. "You really think this?" I asked.

"I *know* this. That being said, do not avoid your feelings altogether. Some may find that...deterring." He smiled. "But do not suppress that part of who you are."

He pulled out two cups from the bush and poured a golden liquid into it. He handed me a glass and raised his to the sky. I raised mine as well. "As for your friend, we shall toast her. To Zela. To an important friend who died for her friends. May her legacy continue to live on through our stories." He took a drink, and I did the same. The liquid was sweet, and created a warm feeling as it drifted down my throat. It made my head stop pounding as I took a deep breath in.

"Thank you."

"I am here for you." He held his fist to his chest.

I debated bringing the next subject up but decided I would. "I met Mel today."

His face went stern. "Mel, who?"

The connection forming between us frayed. How could he act like he didn't know who I was talking about?

"My cousin." I took another drink to keep myself from saying more.

He blankly stared at the ground and twirled his cup. Then, he cleared his throat. "Where at?"

"Trigger brought Naso and me training, and she was training at the same place," I said.

"Ah, of course." He smiled. "She is quite the warrior, isn't she?"

"She was phenomenal," I said. "Absolutely great. Do you watch her train?"

"I have seen her in passing, but Trigger tells me about her abilities." He picked more blades of grass and began weaving them into more triangles.

"She must get it from you."

"She must." He flicked two more grassy triangles into the air.

I leaned forward. "Why didn't you tell me about her?"

"I have my reasons." One of the triangles landed on his nose, and he blew it away.

"We should get dinner with her. I would love to see my family togeth—"

"No." His voice echoed around me. He pounded the ground.

I hesitated. "Why not?"

"For reasons you cannot understand." He ripped an even greater number of grass blades from the ground.

"I would if you told me." I tried to make eye contact, but he avoided my gaze.

He took a slow, deep breath. "Enough."

"But—"

"ENOUGH!" he yelled, little bugs zipping from the grass away from his booming voice. Part of me wanted to do the same. We sat in awkward silence, not even the wind breaking the stillness.

"Fine." I pulled a piece of grass and tied it together in one knot, flicking it forward.

"I may tell you sometime about our relationship, but please do not meddle with it. We are only just getting to know each other, and I do not think you have a right to this area of my life."

"Whatever you say." For every step I took forward with him, I took two steps back.

"Now," he said. "We should make our way back to my quarters so I can provide you with proper clothing for the memorial."

We stood as he drew a triangle into the ground. The door opened, and we made our way back to the throne room.

"Does anyone know about this route?" I asked.

"No," he said. "It is for the king only. The fewer people who know about it, the better. That reminds me. Do not tell your friends about this."

"I understand," I replied. "Thank you for showing me."

"You are family," he replied. "Let me know if you ever want to come up here with me again."

We arrived back at the throne room, walked through the garden to another staircase, and took it to his home. We went through a great hall with portraits of past kings in battle. It seemed funny to me that there were paintings of this. It wasn't like an artist could have painted the scene during the actual battle. My eyes drifted to other areas of the hallway. The ceiling arched with golden accents. The floor, lined with a continuous green carpet from the staircase to the end of the hall, brightened the space. Golden flowers decorated the carpet.

Several rooms lined the hallway, some with open doors and some with shut doors. Two gold squares with smaller golden details lined the dark green doors. A large fireplace with two large bookshelves filled one room. The floor creaked as I moved along. Old, musty carpet emitted a smell of antiquity.

Another room had a dining area featuring shiny gold plates and silverware placed across an empty table. An odd draft of cold wind blew out the door on my face. Little bumps covered my neck before warming and disappearing.

At the end of the hall, a rounded double door intrigued me because it was different than the square doors on each side. King Resin swung the doors sounding a low creak, and revealed a common area with large windows that reflected golden sunlight that blinded me.

Giant, stuffed green couches and chairs trimmed with gold sat in the center of the room, situated around a golden table. I ran my fingers across a rough, forest green wall crowned with gold trim that finished the green and gold-themed room. The faint scent of rich wood and cinnamon permeated the room. A rounded, closed door to the right and another to the left piqued my curiosity, and I imagined rooms with more green and gold.

"Excuse me as I go and grab the clothing," King Resin said as he entered the room on the right, shutting the door quickly behind him.

I surveyed the room and the artwork decorating the walls. My favorite painting was of the Caved Selos. The left side of the painting displayed a bright cave highlighting their adorable faces as they played in the water. As your eyes moved from the left to the right, the painting transitioned to pitch black. Only two sets of red eyes and sharp teeth appeared within the black. I wondered about Trigger's warning about the beasts at night. The red eyes drew my attention.

Suddenly, the door King Resin entered flew open, making me leap. King Resin emerged from the common area and handed me a long green robe with golden triangles lightly embroidered throughout. I held out the robe, unsure about what to do with it.

"This is passed down from generation to generation," King Resin said. "These robes are the clothing of our ancestors. We will be wearing them this afternoon."

A loud knock came from the rounded double doors. A guard entered. "King Resin," the man said, "I am here to pick up the clothing for Miss Mel."

"It is hanging in the closet by the door," King Resin said. The man opened the closet and grabbed a petite robe. "Thank you for taking this to her."

"It is my pleasure, King," the man said as he turned and walked out.

I wanted to bring the robe to her myself, but based on my uncle's earlier reaction, I decided against it. After putting on the heavy, velvety robe, we returned to the throne room. Since leaving the throne room only moments before, multiple chairs and vases of flowers covered the floor. Various people entered the space and sat down as slow music began playing in the background. In the center of the room, yellow flowers formed a circle on the ground. Only three chairs sat within the circle, along with two candles the size of me sitting in front of the chairs. The massive, pure white candles had to weigh more than I did. With all of the extravagant gold surrounding us, the candles looked dull.

"We will be sitting in the circle," King Resin said. "Only family is permitted within the healing ring."

"Healing ring?" I asked.

"The Luck Aura blesses those who it wants to bless." He twirled his hand as if bestowing the Luck Aura himself. "Those that Manipulate Luck are able to wrangle it only when they capture their moment. You must prove yourself worthy. Only during the loss of a loved one, a birth, and a wedding will Luck come to a person without pursuit. The area it enters must be pure to those who are within. Any imbalance and Luck will not bless the participants."

"How do you know Luck has entered?" I asked.

King Resin only laughed and didn't answer the question. His attention turned to Mel walking to her chair within the circle and sitting.

He huffed. "You should sit between us." He walked toward the circle.

Aurora, Naso, the Soothsayer, and Herita walked in and sat near the back. Aurora smiled at me and Naso waved. I waved and made my way to the circle, sitting in the middle chair.

I turned to Mel and said, "You look nice."

"We are wearing ancient carpets," Mel replied. "Do not stroke my ego with false statements."

"You're right." I tugged at the heavy material. "They're very itchy as well."

Mel smiled a little. "It is a shame we are the only family that remains," she said.

"Did my father have family?" I asked.

"He did, but they died a few years before they left the city," she said. "They never got a chance to meet you."

King Resin stood and lit the candles when the music stopped, and everyone went silent. As the wicks ignited, an image appeared on each candle as they burned. A draft of wind swirled at my feet and climbed up my body, a warming sensation following. As we sat there, my mother's and father's faces appeared in the candles' light. A weird tension formed in my throat in seeing them. They looked a lot younger than I remembered. Their faces appeared familiar, yet their eyes felt foreign.

"People of Hallow," King Resin said. "It warms my heart that so many of you are here to remember my sister Rita and brother-in-law Thomlin Meek. Many of you knew them before they dedicated their lives to relaying information from Toterrum. They were both very kind and very loyal Luckists." He raised his hands. "Today, we lift their Aura back to Luck. As Luck always does, their Auras will be taken and distributed to those they left behind. Their son, Yaron. Their niece, Mel. Their brother, King Resin."

Mel stood next and pulled out a bag. She reached in and took out golden sand that she threw over the flames. The sand sparkled in small bursts. She sat down next to me as the flames died and their faces faded. The golden ash trickled over our heads and fell onto King Resin, Mel, and me. The ash smelled of metal and glistened in the sun. The remaining sparks landed on the flowers surrounding us. The flowers burst into flames and quickly burned away, leaving black ash speckled with gold.

"Now..." King Resin began to say before pausing, a soft whimper escaping him. A singular tear fell down his cheek. He cleared his throat. "Now, their bodies are released, their souls free to travel to whatever end they desire to go. Let them find their family, their friends, and their stillborn child in the golden sun. Find and capture opportunity."

"Find and capture opportunity," everyone said.

And that was it. My parents' Luck covered us just like their love had once covered me.

19

THE RED STONE

In between my parents' memorial and Zela's death, my emotional energy hit empty, and I didn't want to deal with learning the Luck Aura. After a few weeks of quiet Hallow living, Trigger came up with the great idea for us to experience gold gathering. Originally, he was supposed to accompany Aurora, Naso, and me as we traveled with the gold gatherers, but King Resin requested he stay back for other matters. The Soothsayer decided to choose books over joining us. Herita needed to continue her cancer treatments, but I think she just wanted to spend more time with King Resin.

The terrain outside the city we chose to travel surprised me. Instead of soft, grassy fields, we took rocky, steep ledges. The route we used followed the base of the ledges that traveled up and down with boulders and crevices. The more the path kept its natural progression, the more any signs of life could be hidden to prevent anyone from finding Hallow. Our destination would be a one-day journey away. Ricochet came along, as did Zen, although Zen disappeared most of the time to hunt. Ricochet enjoyed the fresh air and sunlight, dashing up and down ledges, chasing little beasts he sometimes made into a snack.

"I'm disappointed with the lack of plant life," Naso said.

"Grass and wildflowers," Aaron answered.

As the head gold gatherer, Aaron led the group. Three other gatherers accompanied us. Bianca, Vee, and Guadalupe. Aaron was tall and mostly skinny—there was nothing bold about him. I expected leaders to always be burly and commanding. Aaron had a quieter voice and a warm smile. The only burly part of him was his slight belly.

"That is all the Rolling Hills need," he continued. "Grass and wildflowers."

"What do you forage for when you travel?" Naso asked.

"Grass and wildflowers," Aaron responded.

"You're kidding." Naso sighed.

Aaron chuckled, his thicker belly shaking. He didn't look like most Luckists. "Do they not joke in Toterrum?"

Naso's face lit up, always appreciating a joke. "We do, but I never know with a Luckist."

"We fish from the lakes and dig up Rooted Zarrups," Aaron said.

"Rooted Zarrups?" Naso asked.

Aaron pulled out a long yellow vegetable with a grassy top from his bag. Thin purple lines spiraled around the vegetable. "These are Rooted Zarrups."

"They come from the ground?" Naso reached over to observe the Zarrup. "Based on the shape, I would've expected it to be more of a bush vegetable."

"Not all living things have to be out in the open and flashy," Aaron said. "Some living things are more modest."

"You can't be referring to Luckists with your analogy?" Aurora scoffed.

"She perceives the connection but is ignorant of the facts," Guadalupe said with a grumpy scowl. Guadalupe didn't like Aurora from the moment she met her. I giggled a little but was quickly dismissed by Aurora's glaring look, as she tried to avoid my amusement at Guadalupe's continuous rejection of Aurora.

"You wear gold every chance you get," Aurora said. "I stand by my statement."

"You cover your city in gold that Hallow bribed you with to be quiet, yet you are still talking," Guadalupe snapped back.

Even though I told Aurora the same thing after my uncle told me, Aurora had a hard time believing the whole thing. The pulsing vein on the side of her head made me want to not believe it either.

"Easy on the Perceptionist, Guadalupe," Aaron calmly said.

Attempting to keep Aurora from erupting, I turned to Guadalupe and asked, "Guadalupe, how long have you been a gold gatherer?"

Just like that, the scowl meant for Aurora, and Aurora alone, morphed into a warm smile. "Since I was of age, young Yaron," she said. "I come from several generations of gold gathers. It was my calling."

"Did you know my parents?" I asked. The faint wrinkles on her face made me think she was around their age.

"I knew your mother only in passing," Guadalupe responded. "Your father and I were friends when we were much younger. He was a gold gatherer when he was younger. Before they were married."

"He was a gold gatherer?" The thought never crossed my mind. My uncle spent more time talking about my mother.

"Yes, but not a very good one." Guadalupe's rosy cheeks bounced as she laughed. "He was always very charming, though. You must have learned from him." She elbowed my arm.

"I'll show you charming," Aurora said under her breath.

"Here we are," Aaron proclaimed.

A large lake appeared just ahead. The crystal-clear water shimmered from the sun above and glistened from the gold below. Large greenish fish swam along the surface, nothing like the brightly colored fish in Flaunte.

"Should we set up camp here?" Vee asked, his broad shoulders stretched out, resting his massive arms on his hips.

"This looks like a prime spot," Aaron replied.

We helped set up the tents and a cooking area. Before I knew it, the area darkened as the sun disappeared behind a ledge. Naso helped Guadalupe gather Rooted Zarrups. Aurora and I helped Aaron fish while Vee gathered burning coals. The black rocks near the edge of the lake could be lit on fire and hold a controlled heat.

"You are very good at fishing," Aaron said to Aurora. "You make me look like a novice."

"Your fish are much slower compared to those in Flaunte," Aurora responded.

"I am not good at this," I said, gazing down at my empty basket.

"We all have strengths and weaknesses," Aurora said as she kissed my cheek. "At least you're cute."

An explosion of heat started at my cheek and rushed across my body. I let out a hum that I quickly snuffed under a fake cough.

"I think he kind of looks like the fish." Aaron held up a fish he caught with its face toward us. The fish's mouth slowly opened and closed. Aaron sniffed the fish. "He also smells like you."

I swirled my hands, moving the fish's pulsing Aura near its eyes. A stream started flowing from Aaron's hand back to the water. The fish became excited and flailed as its back fin hit Aaron across the face repeatedly until Aaron dropped it. Aurora and I laughed.

"That is less food for you tonight," Aaron said.

"It was worth it," I replied.

While we cooked the fish and ate it, the sun fully disappeared as the night sky cleared. There was not a cloud in the sky. Thousands of stars flickered above. The lake reflected the stars to look like dancing dots. A chill traveled up and down my spine, the view reminding me too much of my dream.

"We should go swimming," Naso said.

"Yes!" Aurora exclaimed. "If it's safe?"

"Only fish nibbling at your toes will threaten you," Aaron said.

They changed into swimsuits and ran toward the lake. "Are you coming?" Aurora asked me.

"Yeah, just a second," I responded, oddly nervous to willingly walk toward my dream, even if I wasn't.

I changed into my suit. Slapping water revealed they already swam far out. I jumped into the cool, refreshing water and tried to catch up. They were already in the middle of the lake.

"The water feels amazing!" Naso yelled.

I stopped swimming, intending to respond to him, but found myself breathless.

Something brushed at my feet.

Flailing in circles, I tried to search for whatever touched me. Then, it touched me again from behind. A large silhouette zipped by, much larger than the fish we saw earlier.

"What is it?" Aurora asked.

"Something touched my foot!" I yelled. My body went cold, and I tried to ignore my beating heart, but I couldn't.

"I bet it was a fish!" Naso exclaimed.

Not finding the silhouette again, I looked up from the water so as not to focus on what swam below and started swimming toward them.

Something touched my foot again, and my heart jolted into panic. I stopped swimming and searched for the silhouette.

"Do you see anything?" Aurora asked.

Just below, I noticed an unmoving shadow. Whatever it was just watched me. My beating heart pounded in my ears. Short, panicked breaths escaped me.

"It's probably nothing," I said to myself.

I took a deep breath and stuck my head underwater to get a clearer view since the waves I caused made the unclear. Six appendages stuck out of the black blob.

What was it?

Faint red swirls pulsed. Suddenly, two red eyes appeared as the silhouette charged at me.

I was right to panic.

I broke through the lake's surface and yelled, "Something is trying to get me!"

The beast bit my leg. A numbing sensation shot up my leg before my body went limp. My legs stopped moving. I floated to the surface on my back.

Struggling to breathe, I could only look up at the starry sky.

Just like my dream.

Laying still, I fixed on one star. Would it turn red? Would it transform into a fist? My heart pounded so hard that the water next to my ears bounced to the beat.

My nightmare was becoming a reality.

Several more of the dark beasts leaped out of the water over my still, floating body. The red swirls, rounded heads, and six appendages suddenly became recognizable—the Caved Selos. Except, the beasts had red eyes, like King Resin's painting, and were like what Trigger warned me about.

"Get out of there!" Aaron yelled.

Aurora swam up next to me, trying to push me upright, but my legs floated back up. "He can't move!" Aurora yelled.

She swirled her hands and created a bubble around us. Her Manipulation prevented the beasts from approaching us. Naso and Aurora started kicking and moving my body toward the shore.

One of the Selos leaped in the air and landed right on top of the bubble, falling straight through it. After the other beasts realized the illusion, they leaped like the other and fell on top of us.

Heavy bodies pushed me underwater. My friends pulled me back up, helping me alternate from drowning to gasping for air.

Aaron and Guadalupe swam to us. They swirled their hands, causing the Selos to stop swimming for a moment. Guadalupe held the Manipulation as Aaron took over, helping me swim to shore. He placed me on shore as I collapsed to my side, facing the lake.

Guadalupe screamed as a Selo bit her. Ricochet barked at the approaching Selos, ready to fight, but remained terrified to approach the water.

Vee ran up with a thorny plant and poked my tongue with it. As a dull sensation on my tongue, a cool liquid dripped into my mouth. Vee then ran over to Guadalupe and did the same thing. After several seconds, I could move my upper body and the rest of my body followed.

Ricochet barked at the retreating Selos, red eyes fading into the water.

"Why are Caved Selos out here?" I asked while gasping for air.

"I do not know why they are here," Aaron said. "They have never left the Caved Lake before."

"Thank you," Aurora said to Aaron and Guadalupe. "You saved us."

Guadalupe and Aurora exchanged smiles and quick nods.

"We are glad you did not get pulled under," Aaron said. "After they bite, their next step is submerging followed by drowning."

A wave of terror tightened my chest. I almost died. After several occasions of almost dying during battles, I should've been used to the idea, but such a relaxed moment that turned terrifying felt different. The beasts that I loved so much wanted me dead. Just like the Snobbler on the Blackstone Mountains

"Why do you think they left the cave?" I asked, trying to shake the feeling.

"I have no idea, but I think we should avoid swimming at night," Aaron replied.

"Yes, sir." Naso saluted.

***

The next morning, we ate leftover fish and Zarrups. Though the quiet night sky lulled us to sleep, an occasional splash woke me. The scabbed bitemarks on my leg still throbbed. Yet, we would be diving into the lake to gather gold when day came. Though I feared running into the Caved Selos again, at least the sun shone, which meant the beasts should be back to their docile state. At least I hoped so.

Aaron demonstrated how to use the cutting tool to gather the gold. They used a similar breathing apparatus to the one we used in Flaunte. We practiced trying to dive to the lake's bottom, but each time I tried, the pressure building in my ears became too much to handle, and the strength it took to swim downward was too much. Naso struggled as well, so we were chosen to help on the surface. Aurora, on the other hand, swam better than the Luckists. However, she struggled to handle the tool. So, she swam the gold to the surface and put it on the rafts that we swam to the shore.

To kill time, I recounted my experience with the Caved Selo to Naso. More importantly, I compared all the similarities to my dream. One of the times we swam the rafts back to shore, I stopped where the beast attacked me. Naso continued swimming as I lay on my back, looking up at the sunny sky. I had no idea why I felt the need to do it, but the similarities of the lake to my dream piqued my curiosity. The Soothsayer always encouraged me to lean into these inclinations.

"What are you doing?" Naso asked.

"I'm not sure," I said. "But I feel like I have to."

"Okay...weirdo." He splashed off.

I reviewed the instructions the Soothsayer gave me when meditating, which was kind of what I was doing. I tried to relax and open my mind, and took deep, slow breaths. The more I concentrated on my breathing, the more my mind calmed. Soft splashes moved at my side. Slowly opening my eyes, I looked over to the rounded eyes of a Caved Selo. Flailing my body back upright, the beast just splashed me, extending the cone around its neck. My body rose from the water before the beast lowered me down. The Caved Selo tilted its head down into the water like it was trying to tell me something. It dove underwater, twirled, and returned to the surface. The beast repeated its head movement and dove three more times, definitely trying to get me to follow it.

Against my better judgment, I put on my breathing apparatus, looked over at Naso close to the shore with his back to me, and followed the Selo down. Just as before, I had a hard time swimming down, so the beast swam back and swam under my arm, getting me to hold on. The Caved Selo vibrated its cone, and the pressure building in my ear dissipated, surrounded by continuous soft ringing.

Gigantic pillar-like stones appeared below and surrounded us as we submerged further and further down. Eventually, we came to a clear area where the Selo twirled in circles. Unsure of what the beast was doing, I noticed the beast flip its fins on the ground, kicking up dust. A red light appeared. The more the dust swirled, the brighter the light became. A glowing red rock appeared. My Aura shivered in response, a feeling I hadn't felt before.

I swam to the rock, hovered my hand over it, its red light flowing in between my fingers, and then I grabbed the rock. About the size of a small berry, a dull pulse pushed through my hand. The Selo twirled in circles, swimming upward. The pressure in my ears returned, so I swam up with the beast, staying within its vibrating pulse. Once I came close to the surface, the Caved Selo twirled one more time and swam off. Many other Selos swam from different areas, joining the beast that guided me. In a pack, the beasts swam to many little, dark, underwater caves on the edge of the lake, disappearing into the holes.

Breaking the surface, I immediately heard Ricochet obsessively barking from shore. Then, I noticed Naso searching for something underwater near me. He saw me, popped his head out, and exclaimed, "Where were you? I thought you were attacked again!"

Just before I told him all that happened, I hesitated. "I am fine," I said. "We should keep helping them."

"But..." Naso trailed off, furrowing his brow. He shook his head as I swam away.

The busy tasks allowed me to avoid conversation while letting me think about the Selo interaction and the red rock sitting in my pocket. When dusk returned and we sat around the fire, I avoided every conversation. The more I didn't interact, the more Aurora glared at me. It was only a matter of time before she pushed me to talk. So, I decided to tell everyone what happened.

"So, something happened today," I said, all their attention turning toward me. "I saw the Selos again today."

"What?" Aurora jolted forward, nearly falling.

"I was swimming the gold to the shore with Naso when I took a break near where I was attacked last night," I said. "A Selo bumped me, in its calmer state, and tried to get me to follow it underwater. So, I followed it." I sat on top of my hands.

"Are you kidding?" Aurora exclaimed. "They almost killed you."

"I know," I said, "but I felt something telling me I should." Aurora looked ready to yell at me, so I kept talking. "Well, I followed, and the beast guided me to an area on the bottom of the lake. There, I found a red rock." I pulled the glowing stone out of my pocket, its dim light pulsing.

"What is it?" Naso asked, an odd twinkle in his eyes.

"I'm not sure," I said. "I figured one of you might know since you're in the lakes frequently."

"May I see it?" Aaron asked.

"Of course," I said as I handed it over to him.

He looked at it very closely. "I do not recognize it," he said. "What about you two?" He handed it over to the other two. They shrugged, and returned the red rock to me.

"Could this be why the Caved Selos came out here?" Aaron asked, not looking at anyone but out at the lake. "It seems so." He answered himself. "But it's odd why they wanted you to find it. How did they even get here?"

"After I found the red rock, they all swam into small holes along the lake walls," I replied. "They then swam into small tunnels and disappeared."

"The water is all connected?" Guadalupe asked.

"Fascinating," Aaron said. "Thank you for sharing this information."

"Thank the Selos," I said.

"As for your rock, I do not know what to tell you," Aaron said. "It is not something we are familiar with, but I would not throw it out. It must have some significance."

"Great, more to uncover about you," Naso said with a deep sigh.

"Or, it could just be a cool rock," Aurora said.

Laughter swept across the group. I clenched the rock in my hand, watching it transform my skin into a reddish hue. My Aura trembled in delight.

We spent the next few days continuing our mission to gather gold. The concept still puzzled me. My mother spent all her time gathering grains for food, yet we gathered gold. By the end, Naso and I were able to swim to the lake's bottom and swim the gold back up with Aurora. When the Selo made my ear vibrate to help keep the pressure down, I tried making my own ears vibrate by squeezing my nose and blowing air out my ears. The trick worked, and the pressure decreased. However, they preferred us to swim the gold to shore since we were much slower than the rest.

On the last night, we spent time celebrating our success. We gathered the maximum amount of gold we could carry back. A bottle of the golden drink King Resin shared with me circled among the group. The bubbles tickled my throat, but after the third drink, I barely noticed them. Something caught my eye from above, like a dark cloud descending upon us. The cloud lit up in colors once it entered the fire's light. Zen landed hard on the ground next to Aurora, squawking. He nudged at Aurora's arm, his Aura spinning in chaotic circles. Ricochet stood alert, facing past Zen and growling at the sky.

"Easy, Zen," Aurora said. "What's going on?" Aurora stroked his side until Zen raised his wing. An arrow stuck out of Zen's leg.

"Everyone be very quiet," Aaron said as he put the fire out, the silhouette of dark smoke rising into the starry sky. He searched above as Guadalupe ran to the tent and grabbed a long, curved gold item. She handed one to each of the gatherers.

"What is it?" I whispered.

"Hirelings," Aurora whispered.

Aaron turned and nodded in agreement. "We need to hide in the rocks," he said.

We collapsed the tents and gathered up our supplies, shoving them behind the rocks. Aurora guided Zen behind them, but he was too big.

"Your beast needs to be away from us," Aaron said.

"Then I'm going with him," Aurora responded.

"You need to stay with us," I said.

"I'll be fine," Aurora said. "I need to make sure Zen is safe."

She moved Zen over to a larger rock close to the lake's edge.

"The Elderkaw flew down here," a woman's voice echoed from above. Silhouettes lined up around the ledge, looking down at us. "There it is." She pointed to the brightly colored, not-so-great-at-hiding Zen.

"Maybe if you didn't shoot it so quickly, it wouldn't have flown down there," a guy said.

"Have you ever seen an Elderkaw like that?" the woman asked. "I wasn't going to miss my opportunity."

They each mounted Blackened Elderkaws and flew down to the shore. Zen screeched at them. The other Elderkaws backed away as soon as they landed, nearly throwing their riders off.

"Stupid beasts," the woman said as she hit her Elderkaw on the side. "This is why I want this one." She pointed at Zen. "It's dominant over the others."

They dismounted their beasts and surrounded Zen, Aurora still hiding behind the rock. "What is the plan?" the guy asked. "We can't just attack it." Zen cawed loudly, almost as if in agreement.

"We will tie it down, and then I will work my Aura onto it," the woman said. "By the time I break its mind, it'll know I'm the boss."

She was a Mentalist. The idea of a Mentalist hired by Toterrum surprised me. The Mentalist pulled out some rope with balls tied to the end as she passed them to the others.

"When should we attack?" the guy asked.

"On my count," the Mentalist said, Aurora swirling her hands as they counted. "One, two, three!"

Zen moved toward the woman as the guy turned and swung his rope. I watched as Zen disappeared and appeared back by Aurora's rock. The rope flew at the Mentalist as the balls hit her in the face.

"Are you kidding me?" the woman yelled. "Get it together!" She chucked the rope at him as it hit him on the head.

"I swear I was aiming at the beast," he said. He picked up the rope, and Zen moved again toward the woman. He tossed the rope, Zen disappeared, and hit her in the face again.

"STOP IT!" the Mentalist yelled.

"You know I have good aim!" He stomped. "Something is messing with me."

The woman searched around, fixating on Zen, chattering his beak at her. "I think we have a Manipulator here," she said. "Start looking around!"

They moved straight for the rock Aurora hid behind, her panicked face looking over to me.

"We should attack," Naso whispered. "We can take them."

"This is a very dangerous group," Aaron whispered back. "We need to be patient. We have had many lose their lives to these specific hirelings. Plus, if we give this position away, we lose an area to gather gold."

I scratched myself, trying to contain my thudding heart. Aaron wasn't going to defend her, and I had to keep her safe. I couldn't lose her again. Extending my hands, I reached out to their Aura. All I could do was Manipulate Aura, but how without touching their Aura and alerting them to our presence? A sudden wave of Aura came from below. Though faint, it swirled in bits of rage, a familiar feeling. I pushed it forward as the Aura flared. The Aura flooded toward the lake. Ricochet's hairs prickled across his back, a deep growl beginning. I petted his head, trying to keep him quiet.

"We need to help," Naso started to rise.

"Just wait." I reached out, pulling Naso down.

A loud splash echoed from the lake. The hirelings turned toward the lake.

"What was that?" the guy asked.

Three more splashes and blobby silhouettes leaped across the water.

"Did you see that?" the Mentalist asked.

I made a motion to Aurora toward the water. She cocked her head, squinted, looked at water, and her eyes widened, and gave me a quick nod of understanding. She moved her hands as bits of gold floated up to the water's surface.

"Is that gold?" the man asked.

"You bet it is!" the woman replied. "Don't just stand there. We need to grab it before it sinks!"

Zen ran away from the hirelings in the opposite direction of Aurora.

"What about the Elderkaw?" the man asked.

"We can buy a new Elderkaw with this money!" the woman said.

They ran into the water, treading toward the gold.

"Gold does not float," Guadalupe whispered. I pointed over to Aurora, swirling her hands. "But why would she want them to get in the water?"

Suddenly, the blobby silhouettes jumped over the swimming hirelings.

"What was that?" the woman asked.

More jumps and glowing red swirls danced around the hirelings. Then, a whole bunch of small, rounded heads popped out of the water, surrounding their group. Bright red eyes dotted the surface.

"Swim away!" the man yelled.

I smiled and bounced up and down at my former predators, now preying on new victims.

"We can't! We're trapped!" another man yelled.

The precision with which the Caved Selos moved impressed me. Without one mistake, the beasts cornered the hirelings in an orchestrated dance.

"You idiots, Manipulate!" the Mentalist yelled. As soon as they swirled their hands, the beasts submerged underwater. The water went still. "We won."

Two of them in the water let out high-pitched grunts and flailed around in the water. They went limp, floating atop the surface.

"What's going on?" the woman asked.

I knew exactly what was going on as I touched the leg one of the beast bit.

"They are paralyzed," the man said. "Ow!" He then went limp and joined the motionless bodies.

The Mentalist swirled her hands as the Elderkaws took flight and flew over to them. She grabbed onto her beast's legs and just got out of the water as a Caved Selo jumped up and tried to bite her leg. She mounted her beast as she looked down on her group. She swirled her hands as she made the Elderkaws pick up two of the hirelings, the other two dragged underwater.

"You're not worth it, beast." She took off, flying into the night sky and disappearing.

"Brilliant!" Naso exclaimed as he came from behind the rocks. "That was wild!"

I ran over to Aurora and hugged her. "Are you okay?" I asked.

"That was close." Aurora rubbed her forehead and chuckled. "Great idea."

"I'm rethinking my stance on Caved Selos," I said.

"We should gather our things up and begin our journey back to Hallow now," Aaron said. "They will come back."

***

The next day, we finished our trip back. Aaron inducted us as official gold gatherers, some of the best he'd ever met. A newfound respect encircled our group, even in between Guadalupe and Aurora.

"You give me hope for Perceptionists," Guadalupe said, placing a hand on Aurora's shoulder. "I still do not like you, but I respect you."

Aurora chuckled, placing her hand on Guadalupe's. "And I you."

We made our way back to our rooms, seeking long-needed showers. A week of gold gathering made one very smelly. After my shower, I noticed a letter from Felicity sitting on my bed. Before I picked it up, a loud knock came from my door. I opened it to the Soothsayer, her body leaning forward, eyes baggy, and her hands raised.

"We need to talk."

20

Firesuns

Even though I opened the door to let the Soothsayer in, she didn't move. "We should talk somewhere private," she said.

Little winged beasts fluttered in my chest before their wingbeats slowed and made my gut twist. "Should we wait for Aurora and Naso?" I asked.

"We can talk to them later," the Soothsayer said. I wanted to question her further but grabbed the red rock, stuck it into my pocket, and followed her out.

"Where should we go?" I asked.

"That is the problem. Everything we say echoes across the whole city," she said.

I thought about the pounding waterfall at the Caved Lake.

"Near the Caved Lake?" I asked.

"That could work, but will it be loud enough?" the Soothsayer asked.

"Why are you being so secretive?" Suddenly, I noticed her strange behavior.

She looked back and forth, making sure no one was nearby. "Later." She held her finger to her lips.

"Welcome back!" Trigger appeared around the corner, a large smile on his face. "Where are you two off to?"

"For a walk," the Soothsayer said a little too quickly, shifting her eyes to me then back to Trigger.

Trigger raised an eyebrow. "Are you now?" he asked.

"We're going for a walk but want somewhere quiet," I said. "Any ideas on quiet locations?"

The Soothsayer glared at me.

"Relax, brain girl," he said. "You're looking for somewhere quiet and away from people? I get your drift." He nudged the Soothsayer. "The Caved Lake is a great location; just make sure you are near the waterfall, and it will drown out the noise."

The Soothsayer looked at him, a little shocked. "Thank you," she said.

"Enjoy your walk," he said as he nudged the Soothsayer again. "And work on your lying abilities, brain girl. A nervous face never upholds a case. Find the way to ply for the perfect lie."

We started on our way. "He is so arrogant," the Soothsayer said.

"But helpful," I added.

"I guess I can give you that."

Loud music thumped from an alley we passed. A small festival took up another few blocks. Many of the residents danced, played games, and enjoyed one another's company. Every time we entered the city, someone was celebrating something new. I envied their spirit of celebration.

Just as we entered the lake area, I noticed Ricochet following behind. He wagged his tail, his tongue hanging out of his mouth. Water splashed, the pounding falls drowning out all other sounds. We found an area to sit. The Soothsayer took a deep breath, eyes closed, finishing her little ritual with a smile. When she found information and shared it, nothing gave her more joy. I, on the other hand, worried about what information she was about to share.

"I did some digging on the exiled citizens during your discovery and had a hard time finding out why they were banished in the first place," she said. "This led me to read some information about the criminal activity during that time frame."

"How did you get that information?" I asked.

"Not important." She held up her finger. "I had some help. Anyway, on the specific day the exile occurred, there were three names listed under the word *treason*. From there, two pages were ripped out of the book. I believe these pages held the names."

"Two pages?" I asked.

"Yes." A curt nod and the Soothsayer's face darkened. "And based on the number of instances on previous pages, I estimate over a hundred people were exiled."

"Wow." The brutality of the situation took my breath away. "What about the treason?"

"It surprised me that whoever removed the pages left three names," she said. "From there, I started researching these names: April Flora, Jash Flora, and Benjamin Segrist. Each of them was born in Hallow, but as I followed the family tree, their grandparents were not born in Hallow. The origin is unknown, but it looks like Hallow took in a group of people from another area."

"But I thought Hallow only accepted Luckists to reside in the city?" I asked.

"That is why it is peculiar," she said. "Yaron, I think the people were *not* Luckists. I think they were Manipulators of *another* Aura."

I leaned back, water from the falls splashing my face. What Aura could it have been?

"Were they exiled because of this?" I asked.

"The facts are pointing toward this truth," the Soothsayer hummed.

If the information the Soothsayer found was true, so many new truths faced me. Would I find the answers to my questions about my origin?

"I've heard of April and Jash." I thought hard about where I heard the names and remembered. "My uncle mentioned their names when telling the story of my discovery. They were good friends of my parents."

The Soothsayer sighed and just stared at me. "I think King Resin may know more about this than he reveals."

Instantly, I thought through all the amazing things my uncle had done for me. He confided in me, and I witnessed his loyalty to our family.

I shook my head. "You're wrong. He cared for my mother and her friends so much that he challenged his mentor, King Joel, for the throne after their deaths were discovered. He said King Joel changed after the banishment and was unfit to lead."

"This could be true, but we may want to tread lightly with him."

As much as I wanted to trust my uncle, I couldn't deny what the Soothsayer said. The king could've easily lied to me. I had only just met him. But he was my mother's brother, and I trusted her. Except I didn't trust her. She lied to me my whole life.

"I am sorry I am causing you distress," the Soothsayer said. She hid her swirling hand behind her back.

I rolled my eyes. "Please, don't do that."

"I am sorry," she said. "Sometimes the Aura comes at me so strongly that I cannot control what I learn." Her cheeks flashed maroon.

She had so much power with the Mentality Aura that she couldn't always stop herself. "I know. I'm conflicted and perplexed by the situation. What about the third name?"

"Very little information is found," she replied. "He had ancestors that were not from Hallow as well."

A whole group of non-Luckists exiled from a city that sheltered them for an unknown period of time was odd.

"What should we do with this information?" I asked.

"Nothing. I am still searching for more."

The pounding waterfall filled the silence between us. Little fish jumped up near the waterfall's base, fell back into the water, and repeated their process.

"Where were they ambushed once out of the city?" I asked.

"Just north of the Rolling Hills, there is a forest further east still covered by the fog," she said. "The Dead Forest."

A shiver went up and down my back at the name.

"That seems like a fitting name," I replied. "Was it named after the...slaughter?"

I wondered if my word came off unsettling, but I couldn't think of another word other than *slaughter*.

"No. It just happens to be fitting. The name is indicative of the trees that appear dead but are actually alive."

The more I learned about living things outside Toterrum, the less I really understood living things.

"How does a tree appear dead but is actually alive?" I asked.

"I have not been there myself, so I cannot say. This is your decision, but I would ask your uncle if you were found near this forest."

She always understood what I wanted. "Then, I could look in that area for clues of my origin," I said.

"I hope this information was helpful to you," she said.

"Very, and I appreciate you doing this." I fiddled at my pocket, the red rock rubbing against my thigh. "I have another question for you. Have you ever seen a rock like this?" I pulled out the red rock and handed it over to her. The red glow illuminated her face.

"It glows." She twisted it around, the light flickering.

"It hasn't stopped glowing since I found it," I said.

She glanced up. "Where did you find it?"

"Well, when we were gathering gold, I had an encounter with a Caved Selo, which, by the way, attack at night. One Selo, the next day, guided me to the bottom of the lake. There, I found the rock."

"Curious." Her body twisted to face the lake, triggering my dream to enter my thoughts. "Does the lake remind you of something?"

"Are you reading my thoughts again?" I asked.

She blushed. "Sorry!"

"The night before I found the rock, I laid on the lake. It felt so...familiar."

"Like your dream," she added.

"Exactly." I let out a deep breath, relieved to talk about it. "The next day, right below the spot I laid, was the rock."

Her concentration returned to the rock. "I have never seen something like this before. However, a red fist from a star in the sky came slamming down on you. Right?"

"A red fist..." I trailed off. Red. The fist was red. "What if it was a red, glowing rock from the sky?"

She kept her eyes on the rock. A curious grin curled up her cheeks as little bits of red reflected in her intense eyes. "Possibly." She blinked, looking up as if awoken from a trance. "All of this is a theory, of course." She handed back the rock.

Though a theory, the entire idea held merit. Did the rock have to do with my dream? I stared at its captivating color. A small burst of energy flowed through me, tickling my Aura, just like the day I found it.

"Did you feel that?" I asked.

"Feel what?" She reached her hand forward, about to twirl her hand, but retracted.

"Nothing," I lied, appreciating her self-control. Though the Soothsayer provided such great insight for me, I wasn't ready to talk about the odd feeling the rock gave me. "I thought it was water."

She stared at me, sitting on her hands. "I will see what else I can find out about it," she said. "I have a theory—"

A rock clicked against the wall by us. Then, another. I popped my head around the corner, seeing Trigger standing far away.

"What are you doing?" I yelled.

"I was sent to find you!" he exclaimed. "I didn't want to interrupt or eavesdrop!"

The Soothsayer and I exchanged glances and walked over to him. "What's going on?" I asked.

"The king requests your audience," Trigger said.

"I just got back, and he already wants to see me?" I asked, rubbing the bridge of my nose. "How long until he wants me there?"

"Patience is not his strong suit," Trigger replied. "But take your time. He was spending time with Herita when I left, so you should be okay."

"Do you know what's going on with them?" I asked.

"I'm not sure, but I have never seen him this happy," Trigger replied. "For happiness comes once the heartbeat drums."

A snuff escaped the Soothsayer's nose. I expected to see her irritation over another one of his statements, but she smiled instead.

"Sometimes we get lucky, and sometimes we find what we are looking for, but sometimes love just makes things happen," the Soothsayer said.

"You think it's love?" I asked.

"I try not to learn people's thoughts, but when they are strong and pushing on me, I just learn things," she said.

"So, that's a yes?" Trigger asked. "Why can you not just answer clearly? Everything is so convoluted."

"I will be sure to speak at your speed next time," she spat back.

"Spicy!" he replied. "I like that. Ignite the fire of sass, and you're destined to be an—"

"Trigger!" the Soothsayer exclaimed.

The height at which Trigger's grin curled made him look more mischievous than normal. He swirled his hands, making his body levitate off the ground for a moment to turn and face us before lowering back down. "What? I was going to say, alas."

The Soothsayer squinted, shaking her head. "That does not even make sense."

"If you think about—"

"No, not your poetic sentiment," she said. "Your Manipulation. I have watched all the Luckists, and they do not move like you."

He crossed his arms, biceps bulging from his tight shirt. "I do *move* special."

"Gross." The Soothsayer scowled. "I have been reading and came across an ancient text talking about the Luck Aura's properties. How do the Manipulations look to you?"

His arrogant demeanor faded. "Like what the Aura does?" he asked. She nodded. "Well, it finds little blocks and moves them."

"Blocks?" I asked.

He nodded. "The blocks around us all."

The Soothsayer crossed one arm across her body and placed the other on her chin. "Blocks. Do they move?"

"Once I move the Luck Aura with them," he said.

"Curious." The Soothsayer looked at him as her eyes glazed over, deep in thought.

"Can you tell the king I'll be there soon?" I asked. "I have something I need to take care of in my room."

"He can just wait," he said. "I'm meeting Naso for lunch."

"Feeling disobedient today?" I asked.

"I have done my part already," he said. He faced the Soothsayer. "Care to join us for lunch?"

A brief stare-down occurred between them. The Soothsayer finally shrugged. "I have nothing better to do," she said. "I should go and get Aurora, though."

"Meet us at the Corner Deli," he said.

We parted ways. I made my way back to my room and saw Felicity's letter. It had been a while since I had received an update about Toterrum.

Yaron,

The number of 'sicknesses' has more than tripled. It is affecting so many people now. The last council meeting discussed a group that was nearly captured but escaped because of a brightly colored flying beast. This caused the council to become very angry and enforce much stricter curfews. Yaron, I think I need to stay away from these meetings. People are becoming more and more paranoid.

Have Naso check on his family. The Officers have been very harsh on them. I would like to tell you how, but the words are rough when written. It makes it even more real.

Asher is different. He is very different. He leaves the city for long periods of time and comes back more distant each time. He looks very tired and very alone other than Samson. Samson still seems cheerful. It has decreased, but whatever you did to him is still sticking.

On a less serious note, I know your birthday is coming up in the next month. So, early happy birthday just in case I don't get to say it or you read it on the day of.

Anyway, I hope your day and life treat you well.

Please send hope to us,
Felicity

A ball dropped down my throat and grew as it hit my stomach, and I leaned forward, wanting to vomit. The sickness and health of Naso's family worsened? I needed to talk to him.

What was happening to Asher? Had I been gone so long that he had changed that much? My throat tightened, my body detached from my mind. Dissociation to the rescue. My breathing steadied. Consciousness and reality collided back into one.

Then Felicity's mention of my birthday hit me. My birthday was *so* close. I had been away from Toterrum for nearly a year. The passage of time struck me. I barely remembered Toterrum. Yet, part of me was still tied to my home city. I needed to provide some hope for Felicity. An idea struck me. I could try and pull information from King Resin to help her. I quickly got my things together and made my way to the throne room.

King Resin and Herita sat in the garden just outside the throne room. Herita whispered something in his ear as she brushed her hand against his cheek. They erupted in giggles. My uncle's eyes widened and he turned in my direction.

"My boy!" He clapped his hands. "I was getting worried that Trigger's message was not making its way to you."

"I had a few things to take care of," I said. I looked past him. "Hello, *Herita*."

"Hello, *Yaron*," Herita replied. "How was the trip? I haven't seen Aurora yet."

"It was eventful." I moved my jaw from side to side.

She pressed her lips together, popped them, and opened her mouth before shutting it, wanting to ask more. I could tell. Instead, she said, "Look over here."

She pointed over at a bush. One half had yellow flowers, and the other half had orange flowers.

"What about them?" I asked.

"These are Firesuns," she said. "They come in one of two colors: yellow or orange. The bush dictates they are one of these colors, but not both."

"Okay." I replied, confused about what she was talking about.

"Look at this wonder," she said as she approached the bush and pointed at a large flower in the middle. One half was yellow, and the other half was orange. The petals layered one on top of another, radiating from the center. The flower had a beastlike appearance to it, ready to pounce off its host and attack. The most interesting part wasn't its beastlike appearance. The petals split exactly down the middle where the colors split, one half perfectly orange and the other perfectly yellow. "What I love about this flower is it was told you are either yellow or you are orange. This flower said, 'I don't think so' and decided to be both."

Something struck me about this flower. Herita's analogies often did. My parents were from Luck. My real parents were not. Yet, she didn't know the part about my real parents. This whole time, I was trying to decide if I was part of Luck or part of my real parents' origin. Maybe I could be both?

"I should look for Aurora and catch up," she said. "I'll see you both later."

King Resin kissed her on the cheek. She departed in a rosy-cheeked haze.

"Herita is quite the woman," King Resin said, still watching the space where she had been.

"She is," I replied, shifting my stance. "I have a question for you before we start today." He faced me. "Go on."

I steadied my breath, trying not to go in too hard. Yet, the words flooded my mouth. "Where were the exiled Luckists ambushed? My group is starting to talk about where to go once they leave Hallow. They want to know the safest routes and possibly where not to go."

I closed my eyes hard. So much for smooth.

Yet, he seemed to be fooled by my small lie. "I am glad you are being respectful of my wishes and help them figure out an exit plan," he said. "If I remember correctly, it was directly north of the Rolling Hills and the edge of the Foglands. The Dead Forest, I believe."

The Soothsayer was right. My distrust of my uncle consumed me again. He answered too quickly like the knowledge was readily available.

"Do you know if that is where I was found?" I asked.

My uncle's body stiffened, seemingly aware of my true motives. "My sister never said exactly where they found you, but I think she said somewhere near the ambush area." He placed his hands behind his back and stood even straighter. "You are planning to visit that area to find any hint of your origin, are you not?"

And that was it. King Resin knew.

"Yes," I admitted. "If there is even a small chance of me finding something about my birth parents, I want to find it."

He paced in front of the throne. "Find and capture opportunity." He chuckled. "I admire this. You are a true Luckist."

His reaction took me off guard.

"You aren't mad? I lied to you at first."

"There is something you want, and you are going for it," my uncle replied. "What is wrong with that?"

"Mentalists and Perceptionists are against this," I said. "I thought this was the way we are supposed to be living."

The thunder behind his unexpected laughter made my heart jolt. "Oh, my boy," King Resin said. "There is so much for you to learn. Each of us has our own theory of how the Auras were discovered. I am sure you were taught this, but Perception says the Perception Aura was given to them by the island. Mentality says the Mentality Aura was given to them by the Great Light. Luck found the Aura and took it for themselves."

"Took it for themselves?" I asked. "How does that even work?"

"Through sheer hard work and dedication, the original Luckists taught themselves how to see and move the Luck Aura." He twinkled his fingers in front of his face before clutching the air. "It was not given. It was not because we waited. We saw it and went for it. Too many people wait for things to be handed to them, but you need to know what you want and go for it. That is the secret to the Luck Aura. When you Manipulate, what is your goal or intent?"

I pivoted my head, the question perplexing me. Each time I Manipulated, my mind seemed to know what I wanted to happen and made it happen. Unsure of the validity of my answer, I questioned him further. "How do you mean?"

"When I Manipulate, I make a decision on what I want to happen to me or someone," he replied. "I picture it in my mind and push this onto the Aura. Perception teaches to move the Aura to the area they want. Mentality teaches people to read the Aura and rearrange it. They each let the Aura do the work for them. Luckists tell the Aura what to do. We are in charge of it. Think of Aura as the strongest beast you know. Now, do you simply talk the beast down and lightly guide it into your control? Of course, you do not. If you did this, the beast would destroy you. You must show the beast who is in charge. You are the powerful one who has dominion over it. You have control over your own destiny and what you want to happen."

I resonated with each word he said. After all the bad things that happened to me, after all the trust I put into others only to be disappointed, I needed to start thinking for myself.

"Do all Luckists do this?" I asked.

"No," King Resin replied. "This is why I am the strongest Luckist in the city. I learned this at an early age, and my abilities only increased from there."

This went against all that I had learned already about Aura. My ideas clashed with my values, but deep down, what King Resin said felt right. Each time I controlled Aura, I took control into my own hands. I discovered my abilities on my own. Back in Toterrum, that first push inside me to move the Aura caused amazing Manipulations to happen.

"This makes sense to me," I said.

"It should," he said. "You are a Luckist and know it deep down in your heart. This should also transfer to the rest of your life. So many spend their entire lives trying to please others—keep others happy. You have your own happiness to find. Anxiety and depression are very common outside of Hallow. Inside Hallow, we tell everyone to follow their own desires and let the natural aspects of anxiety and depression integrate into everyday life. Therefore, anxiety and depression are rare. Our people are genuinely happy and share their thoughts and feelings all the time."

My anxiety still took a toll on me. I continued to shove it down when it came at me. The Soothsayer had me talk about it more often, but it still often ran rampant. Maybe the Luckist lifestyle could finally remedy my situation.

"What if what you want interferes with someone else's desires?" I asked. "How do you determine who has the more important one?"

King Resin snickered. "The Mentalists really got to you. Stop thinking so much, and just go with your heart. If you keep waiting, opportunity will pass. Find and capture opportunity."

My head either pounded in admiration or terror. I couldn't tell which. My head only throbbed in pain. "It's hard for me to do this. Toterrum taught us to stay in line, and I find that still dictates my decisions."

My uncle paced the throne room in large circles, watching me like a predator watches prey. He said nothing, only watched me. After what seemed like an eternity, he stopped, his face lighting up.

"I want you to try and just do what you want to do this week," he said. "Do not think about it. Just do it."

Every ounce of my being shivered at the thought of doing whatever I wanted. Why did the idea seem so preposterous to me?

"I'll try." My chest warmed as soon as I said it, like my mind finally found the freedom it always wanted.

"Good," he said. "As for today, I want to teach you about Manipulating Luck and what it looks like. The first thing you need to understand is it looks different to each person.

We each have areas we feel the most comfortable with. Some of us focus on the physical aspect of the Luck Aura. This allows higher speeds, greater strength, easier climbing and jumping. This is an area that I have always felt comfortable in."

"Does that have to do with the Vigor Aura?" I asked.

"It does. We move the Luck Aura to interfere with the Vigor Aura. The thing about Luck is it is never quite as impactful as what a Vigorist can do. It is just enough, though, to change the odds." He punched at the air. "Another area is throwing off another's senses. This allows for sneak attacks and opportunities to flee or possibly steal something."

"Perception?" I asked.

"Perception," my uncle confirmed. "Once again, not as efficient as a true Perceptionist, but just enough to make a difference. We also can mess with Empathy and Mentality. They are not as common only because they are much more subtle and difficult to read or witness. Luck also has its very own area. This involves odds and outcomes. All Luckists see the Aura when something new or planned is about to happen. These are the odds and outcomes of what can happen. We can Manipulate this in our favor."

"How do you know the right way to move it in your favor?" I asked.

"Failure and practice," he said as he laughed. "A lot of it. Some are more naturally talented in this area, while others are less so. But we are all capable of it. And lastly, the best of Luckists gather Luck Aura from other things."

"What would gathering Luck Aura do?" I asked.

"It increases the sway a Luckist has with odds and outcomes," he replied. "The more they have, the greater their ability. They are imposing more Luck on themselves."

"Can they impose Luck on others?" I asked.

My uncle just laughed. "Yes, but have you met Luckists?"

"Fair point. When is a Luckist able to accomplish this?"

"Most never do," he replied. "Some accomplish it when they are younger."

I thought about Trigger describing the blocks when he moved the Luck Aura. Trigger's control of the Luck Aura became something I admired.

"Can Trigger?" I further questioned. "Move the blocks?"

"Yes," my uncle answered, furrowing his brow. "He has been able to for quite some time. I suggest you do not focus on this for a while. Focus more on balancing odds and outcomes." He cocked his head. "But I am not quite sure what you mean by blocks."

Instead of telling him about Trigger's blocks, I remembered how I always noticed the Aura when something was going to happen but was unsure if I was doing anything to change it. The next time I did something, I would try and focus on it.

"Do you have any recommendations to practice this?" I asked.

"A very simple practice is to take a ball and throw it in the air," King Resin said. "As the ball falls, watch how your Aura interacts with it. Then, move your Aura and see what happens. You will want to change what the ball will normally do to make it do something different. Once you get good at it, you can make the ball do what you wish. You will be controlling the Luck of it."

"That's simple enough," I replied.

"Light and easy," he said. "And you can just work your way up from there into more elaborate Manipulations. Which reminds me," he said as he departed the room without any further explanation. After a few minutes, he returned with a small, red ball. He handed it over to me. "This was your mother's. She used this to practice when she was younger, and I think you should have it."

I took the rough, red ball and stared at it. Something so small and so insignificant struck a chord in my heart, like I held part of her. "Thank you," I said as I quickly wiped a rogue tear I hadn't noticed form. "This means a lot."

"You are family," he said. "I will do anything for family."

A warm moment formed between us. I had family, and they cared for me. I had someone I could reminisce about my mother with. Did I ever have to leave Hallow? Was Toterrum ever really my home?

Toterrum. Felicity. I had to find some information for her.

"Did my parents find out anything useful against Toterrum when they were spies?" I asked.

"Curious topic change, boy." He crossed his arms. "They found out a lot of information."

"Like what?" I asked. "I still have people there who are important to me, and I want to help in any way I can."

"You are loyal like your mother," he said. "One bit of information I can tell you is about the walls of the city." He stared at a wall nearby with glazed over eyes.

I leaned forward, trying to get his attention but he just kept staring. "The walls of Toterrum?" I asked.

He rapidly blinked. "Yes." He cleared his throat. "I am sorry. Something crossed my mind. Nonetheless, the walls are strong. They are very strong. Too strong." He watched me. "The Officers take the Vigor from an unknown source and reinforce the wall with it. We do not know how, but if we can figure out the source and how they somehow transfer it to an inanimate object, we could use this information to enter the city if an attack ever occurred. But this would involve a full-on attack, and we do not have the numbers to achieve this."

The wall was fortified with Vigor Aura? I never knew that. The uneasy pull it had on me all my life suddenly made sense. Was the Aura encased within its bricks trying to siphon away my own Vigor Aura? A chill made my entire body quiver.

And just like that, I had helpful information for Felicity. "Thank you." I paused, pondering the latter part of his statement. "What if the other Auras joined together?"

He smirked. Then, he laughed. His laughter erupted into deep, guttural wheezes. "Oh, you sweet child," he said. "You are dreaming unrealistic dreams."

His laughter irked me. "I believe it can happen." I placed my hands on my hips. "I really do."

The shaky noises he made faded as he wiped his eyes. "If it happens, it will not be in my lifetime."

Time was so odd. I remembered my birthday coming up soon. I also remembered I needed to talk to Naso. I accomplished all I needed to with my uncle, who I grew more and more fond of as I spent time talking to him.

"Anything else today?" I asked. "I can practice with the ball for the remainder of the day."

"Go, play with the ball," he said with a smile. "Thank you for today. I found our conversation to be fruitful."

"As did I, uncle." I walked off, satisfied.

I veered straight for the city center, where my friends were most likely still eating. Just as suspected, they sat around a table, chatting away. Naso had just finished a joke that left Trigger in tears and the others politely laughing. Naso noticed me and smiled.

"Hey, Yaron," Naso said.

"Hey," I said, not wanting to change his mood. "Can we talk alone?"

The group's laughter ceased. Each of them gave me an unsettling stare.

"Sure." Naso cocked his head.

"You're full of private conversations today," Trigger said. "When do I get a private audience with the great Yaron?"

"You'll have to earn it," I joked. Naso and I walked away from the group.

"What's going on?" Naso asked.

I took a deep breath. "Felicity wrote me and said something really bad is happening to your family."

A flurry of shadows covered his face, eyes glossed over. "What's happening?"

"She didn't tell me but said to let you know," I replied. "Naso, they are inflicting the disease on many more people now. Felicity says tenfold the number from before." I hesitated. "I think they are even draining more Vigor from your family."

Naso shook his head. "I need to go." He stepped away as I reached out. He wiggled his arm out of my grasp and tried to walk off. "Please tell Trigger that I'm not feeling well."

"I will." I grabbed him again before he got too far away. He struggled, but I pulled him for a deep embrace. "I'm so sorry." His body shook within my grasp. "They're cruel people, and they'll pay for what they're doing. Once we learn more from Luck, we can—"

"They will pay." His body went still. "But you mean what *you* can learn." He pulled away, an icy glare looking deep into my eyes. "Everything we do is for you. You're wasting too much time, and our people are suffering because of it."

All the empathy I held toward him faded. "I understand you're mad, but we need people like me to do something about it."

He snicked, shaking his head. "Because *I'm* not strong enough?" he asked. "You're arrogant and pompous. Manipulators are the problem, and you're one of them." He poked his finger into my chest so hard, I stepped back. "Stop putting yourself on such a high pedestal."

I glared back him. He had the nerve to call me out. I wanted to scream at him.

Then, I recalled all the ways he helped me. From Toterrum to Flaunte to Labyrintha and finally to Hallow. I made him angry by trying to help him. As a friend, I should've talked it through with him, but he was right. Too much time had been wasted.

King Resin challenged me to do more things for myself. Rather than waste my time talking it through with Naso, Naso's Aura swirled in front of me, tempting me to move it. So, I pushed the Aura toward his heart. Naso's face softened, a deep, peaceful breath expelled from his mouth. Then, he shook his head, a fire returning to his eyes.

"Are you seriously trying to Manipulate my Aura right now?" he exclaimed.

I continued to watch his Aura pivot around. "You're emotional, and I'm trying to calm you down."

"Then talk to me!" he yelled. "Don't try and change our situation through a route that is easier for you." He pushed me. "You're so self-centered!" He stormed off.

"Be that way!" I screamed.

Why did I yell that?

I wanted to chase after him. I wanted to move his Aura and make him fall. I wanted to scream at him. But Naso's Aura slowed its normal speed, flickering in dim light. His Aura changed. Did he need me?

Trigger came from behind and said, "I take it we're not training today."

I leaned my head back, letting out a grunt. "Nope."

He placed a hand on my shoulder. "What happened?"

"The Officers are damaging his family even more."

"That sucks." He patted me one more time before removing his hand. "He should do something about it."

I turned to Trigger. "Are you kidding me? What can he do?"

Trigger twisted his expression. "That's a new one from you." He softened the arch of his brow and placed his hands on his waist. "We in Luck believe that all should find and capture opportunity, and that means *everyone* can. He and I have talked about this quite a bit, and he has been trying to come up with some type of plan."

Trigger told Naso the same things King Resin told me. I remembered the question I asked King Resin earlier—how do you decide who is right when desires do not line up with another's?

What was Naso planning?

21

Growth

Over the next few weeks, I grew in four distinct ways.

The first involved my friendship with Naso. Something I learned about fighting with your best friend was that the tension after the fight lingered for a long time. Naso and I avoided speaking to one another for so many days. Living in the same room with a person you weren't speaking to was awkward and uncomfortably quiet. I tried approaching him a few times, but the way he turned his body away from me completely deterred my desire to try again.

"Just let him have his space," Aurora often said.

"He'll come back around," Trigger reminded me every time with a slap to my shoulder. "He's your best friend, after all."

Their comments were kind but unrealistic.

I took to writing Felicity more often with shorter messages. I told her important information like the strength of Toterrum's walls being enhanced by the Vigor Aura. I expected her to give me better clarity to the Naso situation. Instead, she sided with him and wanted to find a quicker way to aid Toterrum, just like Naso wanted.

I wished my problems would just fix themselves, but the less I did, the more strained they became—even to the point that Naso would walk into our room, see me, and immediately leave.

A new hobby allowed me to find more time outside our room—the ball my uncle gave me. It was funny how a ball replaced the time I spent talking with one of my best friends. I spent a lot of my time practicing with the ball. At times, the ball's path changed, but part of me wondered if it was circumstantial rather than intentional.

When I came back to my room a few times, I found Naso holding my red rock, just staring at it. Before I could ask him what he was doing, he put the rock down and left the room without a word, a new paleness to his complexion and sluggishness to his Aura.

"Are you okay?" I asked as he passed.

"I'm fine." He slammed to door behind him as he stormed out.

I began to understand that friendships changed as you grew older and leaned toward different values. Naso wanted to protect his family at all cost. I wanted to unify Biome and liberate Toterrum.

The second way I grew involved my understanding of my family. King Resin spent more time teaching me about Luck. The more I learned, the more I felt like Luck was my Aura. I witnessed more and more of his leadership. Though a daunting presence to any citizen he conversed with, his true compassion and desire to help the city showed in private. He cared deeply for Hallow. Every minute he wasn't teaching me or swooning Herita, he worried about various aspects of the city.

On the rougher days of city politics, great bags formed under his eyes, and his irritability increased. I began to understand why he yelled. My uncle didn't take care of himself. Instead of growing angry with him when he lashed out at me, I waited until he cooled down and apologized. He apologized more often. I wondered if he did the same with Mel growing up.

Herita was a large reason for his apologetic attitude after tantrums. She showed great patience with him during these moments and made it clear when he acted rudely. His kingly attitude would narrow in on her, but her intensity never wavered. His expression would soften, and she would even get him to talk about what stressed him.

"We need a minute," Herita often said to me when our lessons ended earlier than normal.

I learned that no matter how rough family could be at times, they were vital to who I was. My uncle dedicated his life to Hallow and his family. I learned about all the stress involved with it and how to better support him.

The third way I grew centered on physical health and mental health. Herita's skin grew brighter. Her energy returned to the levels she held in Flaunte. But most importantly, she smiled constantly. Of course, she still gave each of us blunt words when necessary, but they often followed with laughter, arm touches, and compliments. She exuded pure, wonderful bliss. I believed she would fully heal.

Aurora continued to show affection to me, but often retreated when we talked about my Aura training or her time with the Soothsayer. I worried she didn't like me as much as I liked her. As my anxiety often did, it made me paranoid. Of course, Aurora liked me. Why would I ever think otherwise?

Trigger suggested poetry and taught me how to write it. Though it was an uncomfortable experience, Aurora found it cute and endearing. So, I avoided bringing up her studies with the Soothsayer, although I wanted to know what was going on. Relationships came with their joys, but they also came with their hard, secretive moments where communication became difficult.

The Soothsayer and I continued our investigation into my origin. Everyone newer to me took priority over the people who used to be important. Felicity and I faded. Naso and I drifted apart. I wondered if relational shifts were just normal with growing older.

I learned that I had to take care of myself and understand everyone grew and handled things differently. Sometimes approaches to situations clashed and needed to separate.

This led to the fourth way I grew—speaking hard truths. As Felicity and I wrote more frequently, the urge to truly share my mind overcame me. The casualness of our letters made it seem like nothing happened between us, that she never hurt me. So, I took it out on the letter.

Felicity,

I know these words may come harsh, but I need to speak my mind.
I used to think that you and I were all the world needed. I thought you and I were all I needed. After I found out how you first felt, I realized all I thought was a lie.
Toterrum crushed my soul and mind. I know it crushed you as well, but it wasn't the same. My life was harder. I thought you knew me. You understood what I was going through.
When I hit the worst part of my life, I thought you were there. I thought you stood with me. You may have kissed me in front of your friends, but it wasn't real. You weren't fighting for me. You were fighting for yourself.
Then, I realized I had someone who loved me. Loved me for everything I was. Someone who wouldn't give up on me and I wouldn't give up on her.
I said I was okay, but I lied. There was more to my life, to love.

I hope you find what you're looking for, but I know I found mine. Hopefully, this separate growth we went through brings joy to both of us. Truly, I mean it.

Past my candid attitude, I miss you. I miss what I thought you were and something I knew you never were. That's okay. I hope you're okay.

Sincerely,
Yaron

I folded the letter and released it out my window. A metallic taste sat on my tongue. I brought my fingers to my lips and found blood on my fingertips. I bit my cheek as I wrote the letter and now I was bleeding.

If I didn't speak my truths, I worried my mind would spin over and over until my anxiety took complete control of me.

Four ways I grew, and four lessons learned. I contemplated the past month and pushed myself from my bed ready for a new day, a new me.

Just outside my room, I ran into Aurora. Rays of light illuminated her cheeks and large smile. "Hi." She batted her eyelashes.

Instead of verbally greeting her, I leaned in and kissed her. Her soft lips tasted like berries. As we parted, eyes lost in one another, I said, "You look happy."

"I am," she said. "My aunt is beating her cancer. The doctors here figured out a treatment and feel like it may be defeated."

"That's great!" I exclaimed, wrapping my arms around her. My belief in proactive health continued its positive trek. "I'm so happy for all of our growth."

She squinted. "Growth? I guess so." Her fingers tickled my chest. "It feels unreal. I can't believe the Luckists would be better at treating her over the Mentalists."

"You and me both." I ran my hand across her back as her nails tickled my neck.

The Luckists knew how to heal Herita. The Luckists taught me to do more things for myself. I had spoken my mind over the past few weeks and never felt better. Hallow knew how to live life properly. Learning their lessons left so much more of my life to live the lifestyle out. To find and capture opportunity.

"I'm so happy our paths collided," she said. "If we wouldn't have, my aunt may be dead."

I laughed and had no idea why I did. "We are lucky." I coughed away any residual laughter.

"Precisely." She ran her thumb over my cheek, tickling it. "Luck is what we needed."

"I'm happy, we're all happy, and my uncle is happy." My uncle told me daily how happy he was.

"Speaking of that, he wanted to meet us all in the throne room. I forgot that was why I came over here." She kissed me. "You made me lose my train of thought."

We walked hand in hand until to the throne room that already held the Soothsayer, Naso, Herita, and my uncle. Herita stood close to my uncle's side. They whispered to one another, laughed, and she wrapped her arm around his arm while placing her other hand on his chest, patting it a few times. Trigger walked in, followed by an unexpected visitor—Mel. Why was she there? Then, it hit me. I looked over at my uncle and then to a beaming Herita.

I leaned close to Aurora and whispered, "I think—"

"Hello to all the people closest to Herita and I," King Resin began. "Or is it Herita and me?" He shook his head. "Whatever. We welcome you all here to share wonderful news." He clenched Herita's hand, smiled at her, and looked back forward. "I have asked for Herita's hand in marriage."

Aurora collapsed against me. I wrapped my arm around to support her as she stood back up. Engaged? The thought warmed me like the black sand beach back in Flaunte, one of my favorite memories. A flurry of fluttering beasts flickered in my chest. It made me hold even more tightly to Aurora. Her skin made my skin break out in little joyful bumps.

"And I said yes," Herita said as she smiled even more. She wiggled her hand in the air, one finger shining with a golden ring holding a triangular emerald.

Aurora covered her mouth, meadow eyes reflecting more and more of the surrounding light. She ran over to Herita, colliding with a hug. Trigger clapped, his singular noise echoing in the room before everyone joined in with the applause. As the cheering subsided, one slow clap continued. I glared at Trigger, thinking it was him, but his hands didn't move. Instead, Mel clapped at a mockingly slow speed.

"Priceless," Mel said. "Simply priceless."

"*Excuse* you," King Resin snapped.

"*Excuse* yourself, *King* Resin," Mel replied with an aggressive head shake. "You are so selfish. You act and decree that all Luckist must 'Find and capture opportunity' to give justification for your self-centered actions."

"I am finding happiness!" King Resin boomed. "You should be happy for me."

"You didn't talk to her?" Herita asked, sharp eyes thrown at my uncle.

"She will not speak to me," King Resin said.

"Maybe you should try a little harder!" Mel yelled, her voice echoing in awkward silence. "You certainly have enough time to spend with my cousin. Light *forgive* you try and speak to your *own* daughter." She raised a sharp, pointed finger at her father. "I *hope* you finally find the happiness you lacked with your own family." She stormed out of the room.

A horrible silence fell across the room only to be broken by a quiet snicker from Trigger, who looked over to Naso, expecting him to join, but was only met with an emotionless stare. Naso's face mimicked his dull, slow Aura.

"You need to speak with her," Herita immediately challenged.

"Not now," King Resin said.

"Yes, *now*." Herita pulled her hand away. "Besides, the Soothsayer has an adventure she wants us to all go on outside of Hallow. You can use this time to remedy your relationship with your daughter. Until then, I'm changing my answer from yes to a contingent yes depending on you putting an effort into your relationship with Mel." She held her chin up and turned away, walking to the Soothsayer's side.

The Herita we all knew so well came roaring back. It felt good to hear her speak so boldly again. Her energy had been depleted for quite some time.

"Fine," King Resin said. Trigger's snicker rolled into loud laughter. My uncle snapped, "Quiet, *child*."

"I only take orders from Herita now." Trigger continued his unrelenting laughter.

"Trigger, stop laughing now!" King Resin commanded, twirling his hand as Trigger stopped, choking on air. "Now, you will escort our friends on their journey outside Hallow and make sure they make it back safely." He turned to Herita, walked over to her, and held her hands within his own. "Please, be safe, and I will see you when you come back." He kissed her cheek and departed the throne room.

"What trip?" Naso asked.

"We are going to the Dead Forest," the Soothsayer announced. "It is just north of Hallow on the edge of the Foglands. We are going to try and find out about Yaron's real parents."

Naso huffed, shaking his head. "I'm not going."

"Naso, come with me," Herita said, walking up next to him and putting her arm around his shoulders. "We need to talk."

Naso reluctantly followed Herita out of the throne room.

"This is exciting!" Aurora exclaimed after their departure.

The idea of traveling excited me, but Naso's reaction hurt me more than I thought it would. No matter if I liked my newer friends more, Naso was someone I knew my whole life and the only person who understood what it was like being raised in Toterrum. Knowing Herita, he would end up coming. Yet, I worried about him. I shook my head, focusing on myself. Just like my uncle told me to.

"Naso put a damper on the excitement," Trigger nonchalantly stated, a softness to his voice. He momentarily glanced at the door Naso went through without moving his head.

"He's just in a mood," Aurora replied.

"No matter, I'm excited to leave Hallow for a trip!" Trigger stretched out his muscular arms and winked at the Soothsayer.

"When are we leaving?" Aurora asked.

"This afternoon," the Soothsayer replied, cheeks pink from being the recipient of Trigger's wink.

Trigger turned his attention to me. "Why haven't you said anything? I would think you would be excited about this trip."

I forced a smile. "I am. I'm just having mixed emotions about Naso."

"You care too much about others," Trigger said.

"And *you* do not care enough," Aurora defended me.

Trigger bowed. "Mr. Selfish at your service. Think of us, and life is a fuss. Think of just me and make life peachy."

The Soothsayer blinked, rolled her eyes, and turned her head to me. "The possibility of learning about your family of origin has to be nerve-wracking. Bittersweet, I think?"

Herita walked through the doorway without Naso. Her smile lacked conviction, but her face still glowed.

"How did that go?" Aurora asked.

"It went as well as it could." Herita shrugged. "His family isn't doing well. They responded to him this morning."

A weight fell within my heart, sinking toward my gut. The whole doing-things-for-yourself really conflicted with my ability to be a good friend. I had no idea he even wrote to his family.

"How is he doing?" I asked.

Herita pursed her lips. "Like a large tree during a windstorm." She stared at my confused face and leaned forward. "Strong, but shaky. He's writing them back before we leave. He'll be joining us."

"Good," I said, hoping to reconcile our relationship some. I decided to try and talk to him back in our room. It seemed like the proper opportunity.

Find and capture opportunity, after all.

"We had all better pack," the Soothsayer said. "We can meet in the courtyard. Herita and I will gather food to bring with us."

"Sounds like a plan," Aurora said.

Aurora walked with me back to our rooms. On the way, another festival was taking place near the city center. Based on the décor, it seemed to be a celebration of one of the local beasts. Many small beasts with four legs and puffy, bright green hair pranced around the city. Once again, everyone danced and enjoyed life.

***

When we were back at our rooms, I walked in to discover Naso, writing a letter on his bed. He didn't even look up to acknowledge me. I placed my red rock on a table near him to change my pants.

"My sister has been separated from my parents," Naso blurted out, making me jump. "They don't know where she is."

I faced him, watching his Aura try to flicker bright like it used to. Something cold curled around and grasped my chest.

"I'm so sorry," I said.

I wanted to reach out and hug my friend. I wanted to tell him we would figure it out. Then, the most harsh, invasive snarl curled up his face. A fire ignited in my core before he even spoke.

"But don't worry, we're going on a nice trip to find out *your* family's origin." He stood, running into my table and knocking the red rock to the ground.

Why did I even try? I took a deep breath and remembered he just received difficult news.

"I want your family to be safe," I said. "You know that. My parents were killed by the Officers. Do you really think I want to stay away while the rest of the people I care about suffer?" I huffed. "You're a fool if you think that's true. But we don't have the numbers to make a difference. I feel that I'm close to getting Luck to agree to help us. We have a good relationship with Mentality and Perception. We are gathering more and more hope, but we can't risk more just because we are impatient."

"I'm tired!" Naso screamed. He took in a deep, shaky breath as a tear rolled down his cheek. "I'm so tired of waiting and waiting." His voice quieted. "Talking and talking. I don't know how much more I can bear."

Harsh, dark bags hung under his eyes. The normal, peppy friend with crude remarks crumbled before me. He needed something from me.

"I read something that the Dead Forest has the ability to teach those who enter something useful," I said. "Maybe something helpful will come to you while we're there."

A little spark came to his eyes. "I don't know." He bent over to pick my rock up.

"It's worth a shot." I turned away to change my clothes.

"The Dead Forest," Naso whispered from behind.

I turned back to see why he said that again, but only found him staring at the red rock, close to his eyes. The red light illuminated his face in an ominous hue. His Aura flickered as his face looked to have more of the color sucked away from it. Suddenly, he blinked, focusing back on me and placing the rock back down on my table with a thud.

"I need to finish my letter." Naso turned his back to me and began writing.

I couldn't keep up with his waves of emotions. What I did know was I needed to support him. He had supported me.

"I'll let you have your space." I stood and paused near him. My hand moved forward but I stopped it before touching his shoulder. "I'm glad you're coming."

He didn't respond. As I exited the room with my backpack, rock in my pocket, he folded the letter and let it out the window. For a moment, it looked like the Aura carrying the letter was dark. I looked again, and the normal, brighter Aura glowed. Even though it had changed back, I had this strange feeling as I walked away.

***

Trigger led the group to the Caved Lake where we followed a path up the waterfall. He took a rock from the ground and drew a triangle on the side of the waterfall. He then ran up to the wall and kicked off it as he flipped in the air and landed on the other side. He drew another triangle. The waterfall stopped.

"Hurry," he said as he ran into the tunnel where the waterfall came out. We looked at each other and ran. The cave darkened the farther we ran into it before a green light flashed ahead. As we approached it, Trigger stepped off to a side tunnel and pointed down the tunnel, "Hurry, this way."

We each entered the tunnel and the Soothsayer came running up last. The cave rumbled as she ran faster. The Soothsayer just made it to the tunnel as the waterfall came gushing past us.

"Can you please give us instructions next time before you do something?" the Soothsayer asked in between deep breaths.

"I did," Trigger replied. "I told you to hurry."

The Soothsayer stood up straight and glared at him. He laughed and turned around. As he was turning, she twirled her hands as she said, "Hurry." He apparently forgot where he was going and ran straight into the tunnel wall.

"Hey!" Trigger yelled.

"Sorry," the Soothsayer responded. "I told you to hurry. Wiser is the jest until it hits your own chest."

They exchanged scowls before Trigger nodded in approval. I couldn't tell if they liked each other or despised each other. Either way, the rest of us always got a kick out of their interactions.

We followed Trigger who was holding a glowing green rock in his hand. The only other non-green light came from the filtered red rock in my pocket. The tunnel twisted in random directions, reminding me of the mines. We eventually came to a dead end.

"I assume you are going to make a doorway appear?" Aurora asked.

"That's the plan," Trigger said as he searched the space, patting the walls. "Only if I can find what I'm looking for. These tunnels are very old and not used much."

"I am sure you know how to get out," the Soothsayer said.

"Hopefully," Trigger replied. "This is my first time here, though."

"What?" Aurora exclaimed more than she questioned.

"Easy," Trigger said. "I have a general idea of what I'm looking for. Search with your eyes to only find lies. Look with your heart and find what it is smart."

"Can we help?" Naso asked.

"Yes, but I still don't know what it is." Trigger nervously chuckled.

"This is not funny," the Soothsayer said.

"I'm not trying to be funny," Trigger replied while feeling around and moving his head in a panicked search. "I really don't know what to look for. I know I draw a triangle…"

Herita walked up to the wall and pulled out a fluffy white flower that she crushed in her hand. The crushed flower glowed in luminescent light as she blew it on the wall. As the dust settled on the wall, a triangle appeared. She stared at it for a moment before she grabbed the glowing green rock from Trigger's hand.

"Hey!" Trigged yelled. "That's mine!"

Herita took the green stone and traced the triangle on the wall. The triangle glowed green like the stone. The wall shook, and a doorway opened to bright sunlight, blinding my senses. As my eyes adapted, fresh air and bright green grass took over my other senses.

"Next time, use your brain," Herita said as she threw the rock in the air and Trigger fumbled to catch it. "It can be helpful when you aren't lucky."

"Herita for the win!" Aurora exclaimed as she gave her aunt a high five.

"I would've figured it out," Trigger said.

"But you did not," the Soothsayer said as she walked by. "Herita did."

As the rest of the group walked past him, I put my hand on Trigger's shoulder. "Herita is the queen of figuring things out. Don't take it too personally."

"How far is it to the Dead Forest?" Aurora asked.

"About a day to a day and a half," Trigger replied. "We should be able to make it halfway before we camp and then finish the last leg of the trip."

"We should get it started," Herita announced.

Our journey began and we hiked straight north through green fields. The smaller Elderkaws soared above with melodic chirps. Little rodent beasts leaped up and down through the grass like fish at sea. The grass rustled with each jump. The most interesting beast I witnessed was a blobby, roundheaded beast with short fur the same color as the green grass. Faint blue lines glowed across its body. And the smell was terrible. An earthy, gassy stench wafted in the air as we came closer. Trigger called it the Field Selo, cousin to the Caved Selo. Unlike the Caved Selo, the Field Selo had no dark, evil nighttime version as part of its physiology. They just had the terrible smell.

Eventually, we arrived at narrow cliffs that cut between the hill's crevices. Though unlikely to see us, we had to stay out of view from patrolling hirelings. Trigger said our encounter with the hirelings was very rare. The hirelings didn't find much worth in wandering the vast Rolling Hills.

"What was it like growing up in Hallow?" the Soothsayer asked.

"Always looking for more information, aren't you?" Trigger inquired.

"Not this time," the Soothsayer relayed. "I genuinely just want to hear more about you."

Trigger laughed until he noticed the Soothsayer's genuine curiosity. "Well, it was a lot of time in a cave. The first twelve years of your life you aren't allowed to see the Rolling Hills that are just outside your home. This is only if you're lucky enough to display your Manipulating skills at a young age. I was lucky. I showed the physical side of Luck right away. My parents said I first showed it at six years old."

"Is that uncommon for Luck?" the Soothsayer asked.

"It's uncommon," Trigger replied. "It apparently made me a hard child to wrangle. My older siblings didn't appreciate their younger brother showing Luck earlier than they did. I was enrolled in combat training at age eight. When you get integrated into combat training, you only get to interact with others in combat training. None of my siblings were, so it was the only group I really knew. King Resin took me under his wings shortly after I began training. He said my abilities reminded him of himself."

"My uncle told me there are various forms of Luck Manipulators," I said. "Do they all get trained like you did as a combat trainer?"

"No, not at all," Trigger replied. "The emphasis is on physical Luck. This may be because the last two kings specialized in this area. Also, since the original Hallow was destroyed by Vigor, we wanted to make sure we could combat them if we ever crossed paths again."

"Other Luck Manipulators?" Aurora asked. "What do you mean?"

"Which Aura we can impact," Trigger replied.

"Ah," Aurora replied.

"What about the Luck-specific one?" I asked.

"What about it?" Trigger rebounded.

"When and how did you figure that one out?" I restructured my question.

"Pretty early on," Trigger replied. "It is the most natural area. The others we take control of and make happen the way we want. The Luck is seeing the odds and outcomes and moving them at the last second."

"What does it look like to you?" I asked.

"Balancing blocks," Trigger replied while moving his hands back and forth. "You see what way something is leaning toward or the direction it's favoring and the key is knowing the right amount of Luck needed to tip the balance in your favor. If you go too much, the outcome becomes too great the other way and fails. If you go too small, the original outcome still occurs. You need to find the right amount. The best Luckists naturally know the right amount. Why do you ask?"

"I'm still trying to understand it myself," I admitted.

"I saw what you did to Naso in the Caved Lake," Trigger said. "You naturally do what you want, and it happens. You'll understand the way to look at it properly in due time."

"The blocks," the Soothsayer stated.

"Yes, what about them?" Trigger asked.

"I briefly mentioned something about blocks to my uncle and he seemed confused by it," I said.

"I read something." The Soothsayer noticed Trigger rolling his eyes, about to respond in some kind of snarky way. "Yes, from reading. But I read about the blocks you see. It seems that early Luckists described the Aura as moving one's core around. Like a restructuring."

"Isn't that just what Manipulating is?" Trigger chuckled.

"Yes, but you are different." She paused. "Trigger, you move the Aura in a way that has not been talked about for centuries. You seem to understand the Luck Aura in a way that no one else does."

Trigger blinked, a grin curling up his cheeks. "You're making me blush with the compliment gush."

A flock of Elderkaws swept across the canyon, air whizzing past my ears. The group watched them fly off, conversation leaving with the beasts. The Soothsayer didn't let that last.

"What about your family?" the Soothsayer asked. "I have not heard you talk much about them."

"They tend the archives," Trigger said.

"Wait," the Soothsayer said. "Delmont and Raven?"

"Yes," Trigger said. "That's them."

"I love them!" the Soothsayer exclaimed. "They know so much and have taught me quite a bit about Hallow and the surrounding area."

"They lean toward Mentality with their Luck Manipulations," Trigger said. "Knowledge Luck. That makes sense why you like them. Though, they were only recently moved to this area since gold gathering became too much for their bodies."

"They are honestly the only Luckists who have shown kindness to me," the Soothsayer said. "They even know I am a Mentalist."

"They differ from many," Trigger said.

"What about your siblings?" I asked.

"They left Hallow a few years ago," Trigger said. "I'm not sure where they are or what happened to them."

"Were they captured during gold gathering?" I asked.

"No," Trigger said. "They left of their own accord."

I was about to ask more, but Aurora squeezed my hand. She widened her eyes toward me, pleading for me to stop talking. I wondered why she gave me that look, but I decided to ask a different question.

"I have another question, but I don't want to sound rude," I said.

"Not a great way to start, but shoot," Trigger replied.

"Why do all the kings look like my uncle and a lot of the gold gathers and service positions look like...?" I began but found finishing the question uncomfortable.

"Like me?" Trigger finished my question.

I opened my mouth but paused. Finally, I nodded. "Yes, like you."

"Very keen observation," Trigger said. "Not many people notice or even point this out. To put it simply, people want people who look like them to be in control when they hold all the money and control."

"But they gather the gold," I said.

"They are hired to do this," Trigger said. "It's their duty."

"That seems backward," I replied.

"I hear Toterrum is filled with mines." Trigger seemed to change topics.

"Lots of them," I replied. "We have crystals."

"Who mines the crystals?" Trigger asked.

I narrowed in on him, curious at his question. "The citizens..."

"Do they get to keep them?" Trigger asked.

"They don't..." I trailed off. What made Toterrum's mining different from Hallow's gold gathering? "I understand your point."

"But you're not enslaved," Naso said. "Why not take power?"

"We were in the past," Trigger said. "Believe me, a lot has changed. But these invisible barriers are in the way. I'm not sure if you noticed, but the physical Luckists primarily look like King Resin. Very few are selected, and they must display beyond excellent skill level. I'm better than most because I have to work significantly harder than anyone else. Otherwise, I'll be moved back to the position the rest of my family holds."

"My uncle does not seem to care about this," I defensively replied. "He seems to view you as equal."

"King Resin is kind to me and offered me the position I hold," Trigger admitted, "but he still does not see me as equal. Which is funny because his late wife looked just like me."

"I'm so sorry you have to deal with this," Herita said. "I don't understand what this is like, but I'll try to be more aware of it while in Hallow."

"It is what it is," Trigger said with a half-smile.

"What of my cousin?" I asked.

"What of her?" Trigger rebounded.

"She is..." I began but paused.

"Half-black?" Trigger asked. He laughed. "It's okay for you to say that. Your aunt was black."

I hesitated, unsure about what to say next.

"Yes, and very beautiful based on the portraits I've seen," Herita said, breaking my fumbling silence. "It was a big deal when King Resin married her." She hummed and looked up at the sky with twinkling eyes. "He broke boundaries."

"More or less," Trigger said.

"If you become the next king, that would be a big deal," Aurora said.

Trigger nervously laughed. "Yeah..." He kicked a rock off the ledge. "Just like King Resin expects..." He kicked another rock.

Once the sun began to set, we found an area to rest for the night, deep within a crevice. I was tasked with the first watch while the others rested. Herita couldn't sleep, so she sat with me. Time with her had become so rare, so I appreciated the company. She carried a bag of shelled nuts and plopped them down.

"So, the treatments are going well?" I asked.

"Very," she replied with a big smile. She pulled the nuts out one by one, cracked off the shell, and threw the inside portion back in the bag before discarding the shell on the ground. "They said I was lucky to get there when I did because the odds were against me. They were able to sway the balance back toward better health. They're saying a few more, and I should be clear."

"Fantastic!" I exclaimed. "I take it you're not traveling back to Flaunte then?"

"That's up in the air," she said. "Resin knows he will not be King forever, and he is starting to accept that. I think he's ready to rest some." She picked at her hand. "Oh, and the Flaunte council asked if I'd return and lead Perception."

"They what?" I exclaimed, the sleeping group shifting at my loud statement.

"Shh." She held up her finger to her mouth, a shelled nut held in her hand. "No one else knows. I'll probably say no." She threw the nut in her mouth and crunched it.

"You would be an amazing leader," I said. "You should think more about it."

She swallowed and began removing the shell of another nut. "You remember Great Captain Maurice?"

I snickered. "Do you really think I would forget Aurora's ex-boyfriend?"

She tossed a shell at me and laughed. "You never know." She jostled her head back and forth. "I think he would make a great leader. The council is unsure about this because he's so young. No matter what way things go, I think Flaunte will be in good hands. They need to be after Lady Sandra's assassination."

"How is the city recovering?" I picked up the shell she threw at me and began snapping it in half.

"It has riled them up," she said. "I think Flaunte will certainly support us when the idea of war is proposed."

"This is great news." I took the two broken parts of the shell and broke them in half again. "My uncle says Hallow may consider joining us if the others join in."

"I have already begun this conversation with him," she said. "Especially with our marriage, I think Luck is finally on our side."

"And I think Labyrintha should be as well."

Herita's face tightened as she loudly snapped a nut in half. "Don't assume this. Petra has not taken Zela's death well. She has shut down any entrances to or exits from the city."

I leaned forward and tilted my head. "Should we go back there?"

"No. I'm afraid they may not even let the Soothsayer back in right now, let alone you."

"We'll have to ask the Great Light for guidance." I nodded and looked up at the night sky.

"That we will." She looked up at the sky with me.

The crunch of three more nuts having their shells broken off echoed around me. I wondered about the purpose of the shell. Then again, our bodies protect things like our hearts. Was my skin just a shell protecting me, the nut within?

"Were you ever in love before?" I asked.

She shifted from a cross-legged position to wrapping her arms around her knees. "I was, or at least I thought I was. But it wasn't right. She wasn't kind to me and didn't see me as equal to her. King Resin sees me as an equal and treats me well. So, I may not have been in love before. Now that I think about it, I just didn't understand what love actually was."

Her thoughts on a shifting translation of love were new to me. At one point I thought I was in love with Felicity.

"Love is complicated," I said.

"You're more than correct with that statement," she laughed quietly.

***

At first light, we began our last leg of the journey. As we entered the edge of the Rolling Hills, the ground became more level, and we could see the fog from the Foglands form a high wall. The only thing I could make out were silhouettes of dark trees.

"These trees are the rarest and most peculiar of all trees," Herita said. "They actually take the moisture from the air as their water source and then emit small flakes that float high into the sky before returning to the tree. These flakes are the leaves of the trees that gather sunlight and bring it back. They call these trees Shadowleeks. The flakes make the fog even thicker than any other area."

"It's also said that breathing in the flakes makes you delirious," Trigger added. "We're going to want to pair up as we enter the Dead Forest to search for some answers. Make sure it's someone you trust a lot. My suggestion is to take whatever you can find and exit once you are able."

The Soothsayer stepped up next to me right away. Aurora chuckled at the Soothsayer's tenacity and paired up with Herita. Trigger paired up with Naso. At one time in my life,

Naso would've been my first choice. Instead, I found I didn't trust him, even after all we had been through together.

"And don't forget," Herita began, "keep your eyes on your partner. They will be your only glimpse of reality."

Though only a forest stood before me, its thick fog extended into my mind. My heartbeat quickened and my legs tensed. Was there a possibility I would lose my mind in this forest? I looked over at the Soothsayer. At least I had her to keep my mind grounded.

22

THE DEAD FOREST

Billowing layers of misty waves of fog fell and rose as a cascading, never-ending wall. A musty, muddy smell arose from the fog, which towered above until rounding off toward the Dead Forest that lay before us. Tiny sparkles of light floated along the alternating rise and fall of the fog. The pieces floating up looked duller. The pieces floating down were much brighter. At times, cool droplets from above and below tickled my skin.

Herita jumped up and down like the sparkles of light, offering up more facts about the Shadowleeks and the leaves transferring light. Though sunny, the fog wall instantly darkened the land before us, the lights drawing me into the ominous forest. They reminded me of Aura.

"Are you ready?" the Soothsayer asked me.

"Are you?" I eyed her without moving my head away from the fog wall.

We exchanged nods. The set pairs spaced out along the edge of the Dead Forest, each stepping in at the same time, Aurora and Herita on my left and Naso and Trigger on my right. And just like that, I could no longer see them. Only dense fog surrounded me.

Not too far from the forest's edge, the Soothsayer and I walked up to a large Shadowleek. The dark, tall tree with flaky bark and long, leafless branches loomed over us. Though it looked like every dead, rotting tree I'd seen in the past, the vibrant, invisible energy emanating from it made my skin buzz. Tiny lights—its leaves—from the branches while other leaves fell from the sky, landing back on the branches. Not a single leaf touched the ground as they fell. They all gravitated back toward their origin in a haunting, rhythmic pattern. Each time bright leaves touched the branch, the light transferred to the branch, disappearing almost instantly before a darkened leaf began floating back up, all the weight it once held released. My skin tingled after each glow. A curious sweetness in the air lingered on my lips.

"How are we supposed to look for something in such dense fog?" I asked.

"To my understanding, the Dead Forest will decide what it wants to show you," the Soothsayer replied.

"Is there a point of walking around then?"

"I gave you the only answer I have." The Soothsayer looked to her left, to her right, and up at the tree. "This is a very frustrating scenario for me. I do not know what to do."

I sighed. "Well, I guess we walk."

The Soothsayer moved forward. "Sounds good to me."

For a moment, we pointed in different directions on where to go as if it mattered. Eventually, we decided to turn right and walk away the large Shadowleek. More and more Shadowleeks appeared, but they were spaced far apart from one another, and none of the other trees came close to the size of the large one we first approached. Iri flew around in streaks of pulsing light. Her enjoyment of misty, foreboding fog contrasted with my own uneasiness.

"How have you been doing?" the Soothsayer asked.

"I've been doing well," I replied. "My drama with Naso isn't ideal, but all my other relationships are great. I'm glad to have family again. It makes me feel like my mother and father are still around and that our relationship is finally truthful."

"That is good to hear." She hummed as she looked at me, looked back, looked forward, and then cycled through the same motions again.

"Why are you asking?" I knew her well enough to know when she had an idea to share.

She let out a breath she had been holding in. "I know of a Mentality Manipulation that might be worth trying. It requires a lot of energy and requires us to be near the location of a memory." She took a deep breath. "It also requires you to be in a good state. I was hoping to try it and see if we can find any answers."

"Okay," I agreed without hesitation. "Same method as before?"

She smiled and gestured toward the ground. "Just lay down, and I will see what I can find."

"STOP!"

The intense scream made some small winged beasts fly up, their flaps echoing with the scream. Both noises slowly faded away.

"What was that?" I asked, exchanging glances with the Soothsayer, my voice echoing, unlike before.

"I have no idea," the Soothsayer replied, also with an echoing voice. "But it appears something is happening to our voices."

"Herita did say the forest can cause some weird things to happen."

"I certainly hope this does not last forever." Her voice mixed with my last statement in an irritating, endless cycle.

I laughed a little at the irony of forever and echoing. "Should we try this again?" I asked.

Loud bells rang all around us in deep, joyful melodies, forcing the echoing effect away. It was good to know the Soothsayer was hearing the same noises I was. Part of me worried I was losing my mind.

"We should just start," she said.

***

After finding a nice patch of grass to lie on, I rested my head back, the grass muffling the bells and their continued ringing. The blades of grass tickled me before packing down to form a nice blanket around my body. The Soothsayer touched my head, and she blew out over my face, a slight stench from dehydrated tainted her breath. The world started spinning, but this time, it spun much faster and for much longer, forcing me to shut my eyes. The bells continued their ringing until I opened my eyes, then they stopped. The same trees, same fog, but a silent atmosphere surrounded me, no Soothsayer in sight.

I stood up, searching for the Soothsayer, but forgot she never came with me in my visions. Yet, no other living person was near me either, an odd situation since past me needed to be around to access a memory. So, I walked. The chilly air made me shiver and the leaves from the trees didn't move up and down like they did in the present. Little puffs of fog came from my mouth. An uneasy sensation formed in my gut, making me worry. Then, a voice broke the silence.

"I can't believe we were exiled," a man said.

"He knew the whole time about who we were," a woman replied. "Why did it matter all of a sudden?"

"And treason?" the man exclaimed. "He thinks his throne of lies will protect him."

"Mommy and Daddy," a young girl's voice called out.

A man and a woman wearing large, blurry coats turned to a little girl in a smaller—but still large—coat. The little girl leaped into her father's arms. Though the coats appeared blurry, I swore they looked colorful. A small hood hid the little girl's head, but her small, innocent face peeked out.

"Hello, my little angel," the man said as he hugged her.

"I'm tired of walking," the girl complained.

"As am I," the woman said. "But we need to keep heading north. We aren't safe where we are."

"Why did we have to leave home?" the little girl asked.

The man and woman looked at each other, eyebrows furrowed. "Your daddy and I thought we needed to live closer to the ocean," the mother lied. "You'll love the ocean."

"Will there be fishies?" the little girl asked, her eyes big. A stuffed fish with red scales and a flowing tail hung from her grasp.

"The biggest fish," her father responded. "Bigger than your dad. It will be bright red."

He threw the girl in the air as she giggled, and he caught her. "My favorite color!" the girl exclaimed as they faded from view.

I spun around, searching for them, but no one could be seen. Loud drums pounded from behind as I turned to face a large camp. Hundreds of people sat by fires. Everyone performed various tasks. Some cooked. Some told stories and played games with children. Some lounged. Suddenly, their coats became fully visible, and I could see they were made with bright, multicolored fur covered in cascades of hair. Somber fear covered their expressions, but they still conversed and laughed with one another.

Someone sitting near the drums sang.

> *The sky looked for the sun all day long,*
> *Only to find him singing a song.*
> *The ground looked up and found the moon,*
> *She started dancing just past noon.*
> *From there they joined their song and dance,*
> *Light and dark would switch at every instance.*
> *This was until the earth yelled stop!*
> *She told them the beasts were about to drop.*
> *The beasts could not handle the constant change.*
> *They needed to respect their home and range.*
> *Since then, the moon and sun do not interact,*
> *Except when the earth forgets to distract.*

Only then does time become irrelevant,
Happiness becomes the only element.

The children danced to the drum's beat. Some held up stitchings of the sun. Others held up stitchings of the moon. Then they would twirl together, giggling.

The mother, father, and little girl from earlier sat by one of the fires with another couple. The little girl ran off with her stuffed fish to play with the other children.

"We'll make it north," the father said to the other couple. "We'll be safe."

"This is a scary time to have a child," the other man said as he touched his wife's stomach. "We want to make sure our child is safe."

"All we can do is hope," the mother assured them. "All of our children will be safe." The mother touched her own stomach as she looked at the father with tense, shaky eyes.

The father grabbed the mother's hand and rubbed her protruding belly.

"I hope we're as good of parents as you two are," the other woman said. "Everyone looks up to you both."

"Motifer will take us in," the father said.

"The lost city?" the other man asked. "How can you be certain?"

"I'll get us there," the father said. "Trust me."

"We have trusted you this far," the other woman said.

"Mommy, can you sing me a song?" the little girl with the red fish asked as she leaped into her mother's arms.

"Of course, my little fish." The mother winced and hoisted her daughter up. "What song tonight?"

"My favorite song," the little girl answered with big eyes.

The mother smiled and sang:

I hold you close; I hold you tight,
Nothing will break away our light.
Life gets hard and breaks you down,
But nothing will dim your smile crown.
I am with you, you're always told,
I love you, my dear, may you grow old.
If our lives take a different part,
Look for your fish and a fresh new start.

The little girl's eyes fluttered shut as the mother repeated the song. The beauty in the lyrics and her singing made my heart flutter and made me feel...at home.

Suddenly, a loud horn startled the camp. The peace resting over the camp burned away.

"OFFICERS!" a man screamed.

The echoing screams, the panicked movements, and the speed at which everyone grabbed all they could quickened my heartbeat faster than the drums that once brought joy to the space. The little girl's eyes jolted open as she looked around frantically.

"Mommy," the little girl said. "What's happening?"

"Quiet my little fish." The mother held her daughter's face close to her chest.

"Run!" the father yelled. "Run and hide far from here."

"But—" the mother began.

"I'll be okay," the father assured her, kissing the wife and the daughter's head as they went different ways.

The mother started running, an ambush appearing behind her before fading away. The faster she ran, the more the loud attack behind her faded into a dull roar.

"Mommy?" the little girl asked, soft cries lifting to her mother. "Where are we going? Where's daddy?"

"Hush, my little fish," she said as she ran. "We need to be very quiet."

"Are we playing hide and seek?" the little girl asked.

"Yes," the mother said. She found a bush and crouched behind it. "And we're going to hide here and make sure no one finds us. It's very important we don't make a single noise."

The dense fog surrounded them, the eerie silence only broken by their soft breaths. Ten Officers, decked out in their black and orange uniforms, stepped out of the fog,. Though I could see the mother and daughter hiding, the Officers couldn't.

"Sir," one of the Officers began, "I think we got them all."

"I saw two more run this way," one of the other Officers replied. "We need to keep looking."

The mother twirled her hands as the Officers' moods shifted. "I think we did great," the other Officer said, a happiness in his voice.

"I agree," the head Officer replied. "I'm so proud of us all." They turned and walked away, the mother and daughter's safety in sight.

Then, a crisp, heartbreaking sneeze broke the silence.

The Officers turned around and walked straight to the bush. Searching through the leaves, the mother leaped forward without the daughter as the daughter screamed. At the same time, the father launched out of the fog, attacking the Officers. Everything faded again.

Just as quickly as the scene faded, a new, terrifying scene appeared. I was surrounded by dead bodies. Hundreds of dead bodies covered with colorful fur coats. So many of the happy people lay dead. Next to one of the bodies was the stuffed red fish. I gasped and began to weep. I wanted to fall over.

Then, a familiar person appeared—my adoptive mother. Her brown hair and soft face made me want to run into her arms, but her arms were already filled with a baby. The baby's soft cries stood in stark contrast to the lifeless bodies that surrounded them.

"Take care of him..." I heard a woman's voice echo.

The view faded, and the Soothsayer appeared above me again. We wept and didn't say a word to one another. I sat up, wrapping my arms around my knees, and stared at the ground.

Something caught my eye, hidden in the ground below by dead branches. I moved the branches and found a faded red fish stuffed animal. The stuffed animal from my vision still lay where I last saw it. I picked it up and hugged it tightly to my body.

"AHHHHHHH!" a loud female voice screamed, breaking the silent moment I didn't want to end. It made my head pound into a raging headache. The scream lingered before fading away.

"What was that?" the Soothsayer asked.

Suddenly, my pocket glowed very brightly. I put the small, stuffed fish in my pocket. I reached into my other pocket and pulled out the red stone, glowing brighter than before. The Shadowleek next to us started to glow a faint blue. I hadn't realized it, but we were near the large Shadowleek we first saw when we entered the Dead Forest. Iri mimicked the blue tint of the Shadowleek.

"What's going on?" I asked.

"I am not sure," she responded.

"Why was I not in the flashback we accessed? I thought I had to be there."

"I...I...I have no idea." The Soothsayer leaned her head back, groaning. "My mind is going to explode. There are so many things that have no explanation. Who was that little girl?"

"I didn't recognize her," I responded. "Those people that were exiled were Manipulators."

"And they were not Luckists," she said. "They were also heading north to Motifer. That is the lost capital of Empathy. The man seemed to know where it was."

"So, they were Empathists?" I asked.

She took a deep breath. "It appears so."

"Why would they be concerned about being let in?" I asked.

"I imagine the city is very protective of who they allow in. A city can only remain hidden if people do not know about it."

"King Joel knew they weren't Luckists and exiled them. He lied." I clenched my teeth together. "This must be why his behavior changed. He sent them to a death sentence."

"And then your mother holding you," she said. "She had you when she came here."

"And what about the 'Take care of him'?" I asked. "Was that my real mother talking?"

"It is hard to say." She sighed. "I do not think we have enough information to make a conclusion, but we are heading in the right direction. They were not Luckists." She observed me opening and closing my mouth repeatedly. "Yaron, I do not believe you are a Luckist."

I stared at her for a few moments without saying a word. I didn't want to believe her, but what she said made sense. Why else would all of what I saw be shown to me? How would my uncle take this news? I grunted toward the bluish tree. Even after all I'd been through and all that I had learned, I felt like I had accomplished nothing.

"I think you're right." I groaned. "Now what?"

"Nothing," she said. "We will have to regroup and figure out our next step."

She reached out her hand and helped me stand.

"Can you please not tell anyone?" I asked. "I want the wedding to happen first before I tell my uncle. I'm afraid he will be very let down."

"I will not tell anyone until you are ready," she said. "Including Aurora."

A much-needed silence stretched between us. I wanted to talk about the little girl's death. I could tell the Soothsayer wanted to as well, but I wanted time to honor a girl I didn't even know—her death deserved our respect. I eyed my stone, still glowing, and fiddled with the fish in my pocket. The Soothsayer's gaze fixed on the glowing blue Shadowleek.

"Do you think this has to do with what we saw?" I asked, holding my stone up. "It did start glowing much brighter after."

"I think this stone is very important to who you are." She turned in the direction of the family we saw in my past vision. "Or important to who they are."

"Or both?" I asked.

"Or both..." she trailed off. She looked around, eyes widening.

"What?" I asked as she pointed, and I looked up. Black mountains surrounded us with great familiarity. We were in Labyrintha. A little girl laughed and ran by, not looking like the little girl in my vision. She wore the blue linens of Labyrintha and had curly brown hair, no more than five or six years old.

"Naomi, come over here," a woman's voice said.

The little girl stopped and ran over to an older woman, sat down cross-legged, and stared up at the older woman. "Do you have a present for me today?" the little girl asked.

"Now, now," the older woman responded. "Is that how we talk to people?"

"Sorry, grandmother," the little girl responded. "Hello, how are you today?"

"I am doing wonderful, sweet child," the grandmother responded. "How are you?"

"I ran around and had fun today," the little girl said with a big grin.

"You seem to be laughing a lot," the grandmother responded with a smile. "Now, I have a gift for you from my journey."

The little girl smiled and said, "What is it?"

"There are two things," the woman responded. "One is this." She held up a wooden toy that had a ball hanging on a string. She performed a movement, showing the toy was a type of game. "The other is this." She held up a blue toy shield with a blue flying beast on it. The little girl reached out to grab both. The grandmother pulled the toys away. "Easy now. You may only pick one."

"Why can't I have both?" the little girl asked with sad eyes.

"Sometimes life offers us choices," the grandmother responded. "We sometimes can only pick one."

The little girl frantically looked back and forth between her choices. "I don't know which one to pick."

"I *do not*," the grandmother corrected. "But you can only have one or none. Clear your mind and make your choice." The grandmother then looked over at the present-day Soothsayer and me as if she could see us.

The little girl took a deep breath and grabbed the wooden toy. Suddenly, the city lit up in flames behind them, screams echoing all around. The fire grew larger and larger, a golden hue encasing it. Though Labyrintha burned behind them, neither the grandma nor the little girl moved or reacted. The little girl only played with her new toy.

"Are you happy with your choice?" the grandmother asked. Her voice continued to echo as the burning city vanished.

Only the Soothsayer and I remained in the Dead Forest.

"What was that?" I asked. "I don't think we went back in time."

The Soothsayer blinked, still staring at where the grandmother and child sat. Glistening tears trickled down her cheeks. She quickly wiped them away. "That was my grandmother," she somberly replied.

My mouth fell open. "Then...was the little girl you?"

She nodded.

"Is your name...Naomi?" I asked.

"I have not heard that name in a long time," she replied. "My name was Naomi. Naomi Felm. You are the only living person to know this."

I knew the Soothsayer well. She had become one of my closest friends. But after hearing her real name and the secret it was, a new connection cemented itself between us.

"No one knew you when you were younger?" I asked.

"When you become the Soothsayer, you must make everyone forget your original identity," she replied. "You must fully become the Soothsayer." Tears trickled down again. "It feels good to hear my name. I had not realized I missed it, and no better person to hear it than my best friend." She blushed, tears still falling. "I miss my grandmother."

"I'm sorry she's gone," I replied, realizing she must have passed away.

The bluish Shadowleek caught my attention as it started to dim. My sight moved back to the Soothsayer, to her eyes. Glowing blue specks danced within her dark irises, like a stormy sea. "What's going on with your eyes?"

She touched her eyes. "What is wrong with them?"

"They have glowing blue specks in them."

"They do?" She paused. "They have never done that before." Her gaze drifted to my own eyes, her face lighting up as if discovering something. "Do you remember when you asked what Aura looked like to me?"

"I remember you didn't want to tell me." I smiled.

"We were both stubborn then." A little smirk curled her mouth. "Well, they are leaves. Little leaves swirling around, floating, then lifted back up as if the wind was carrying them." The blue specks shined again for a moment.

"That sounds beautiful."

The vulnerability between us gave me peace. All my fear from my vision, anxiety at what it meant, and heartbreak from the little girl's stuffed fish faded.

"I do not want to be alone," a voice said in the distance, breaking the ambiance.

"What was that?" I asked.

"I do not want to be alone," the voice said louder.

"Is that Trigger?" the Soothsayer asked.

"I do not want to be alone. I do not want to be alone. I do not want to be alone."

"I think he's in trouble," I said, realizing Naso was supposed to be with him. "We need to get out of here."

The Soothsayer twirled her hands and the blue specks in her eyes shined very brightly. The floating leaves above the Shadowleek stopped moving up and down. She looked surprised at her Manipulation, like she didn't mean to do it.

"Did you just do that?" I asked.

"I think so," she said. She continued to move her arms, Trigger's voice becoming clearer. A path cleared within the fog. We raced forward, the path continuing to lead us toward Trigger's voice. His cries echoed louder and louder. Two bodies suddenly appeared, and I collided with one. Aurora and I fell to the ground.

"Is Trigger in trouble?" Aurora asked right away as we jumped back up.

"I think so," I replied.

"What are you doing?" Herita asked the Soothsayer, eyes still glowing bright blue.

"No time," I said, racing forward.

The others followed as the Soothsayer formed a path. We ran, and we ran. Trigger's voice was so loud as the fog opened to the exit of the Dead Forest. Trigger sat curled up on the ground, weeping. As soon as he saw us, he jumped up and embraced me.

"I thought I lost you guys," Trigger said.

"Easy now," I said, patting his back. "We're okay." I looked around and didn't see Naso. "Where's Naso?"

"They took him," he blubbered and scratched at his face. His body vibrated both him and the grass surrounding him.

"Who took him?" I said as I pushed him away, staring into his watery eyes.

He looked up at me, reddened eyes begging for forgiveness. "The Officers," he said.

My body broke out in small, cold bumps. My chest pounded so hard that my skin itched at the vibrations, dying to shed from my body. They were near. They would take me back. Had they taken Naso back?

Trigger clasped his hands together. "They jumped out and took him." He rocked back and forth. "They disappeared. I tried to find him, but the forest did some crazy things to me. I couldn't find him."

Suddenly, Naso stepped out of the Dead Forest. "I'm right here," he said, calm as could be, which calmed my quaking heart.

Trigger ran up to him, looking him over, up, and down. He embraced him for a hug, trembling. "I saw them take you," Trigger said. "The Officers took you." He grabbed Naso's face and looked him over before releasing him and wrapping his arms around Naso again.

"It was the forest," Naso replied, seemingly unphased by the entire affair. "Something wild happened to me in there."

"I think something weird happened to us all in the forest," I said. "The moment we heard someone yell stop, things got out of hand."

"That was me," Naso said. "I yelled stop."

"You did?" the Soothsayer asked. "Why?"

"Trigger and I were walking and looking around," Naso began. "Suddenly, a group of Officers jumped out and grabbed me. I lost sight of Trigger. They took me to an area and threatened to hurt my family. I said I would do anything they wanted to keep them safe. They then disappeared. I wandered through the forest for a while. I heard some bells, a woman's voice saying to keep someone safe, a scream, someone asking if they were happy with a choice, and then Trigger asking to not be alone, bringing me here."

"Those are the same noises we heard," I said.

"Same for us," Aurora said.

The Soothsayer stared at Naso, distracted by something. "How many Officers?" she slowly asked, an oddly specific question for something we weren't there for.

"I think four," he said, his sight focused on the ground like trying to concentrate on something I couldn't see. "What were the sounds?" He raised his view to the group.

"The bells had to do with me," Herita said, quieter than normal. Her face nearly faded into the fog, a ghostly white.

"They did," Aurora agreed, giving her aunt a smile from the corner of her mouth.

"We were walking through the forest when we started hearing the bells," Herita started. "We thought it was odd, so we moved toward them. The bells became so loud once we entered an area with a tower and big bells clanging. At the base of the bell tower stood a bride and groom. They held each other's hands, entranced with one another. The sun then rose on the foggy horizon, quickly making its way to the other side of the forest, set, and then the moon repeated this pattern. Night and day flew by so fast in rapid flashes. The bells started chiming faster as the sun and moon rose and set. Suddenly, the sun and moon stopped, the bells' chiming slowed down. One last, deep chime let out as the bride and groom crumbled into skeletons, still holding onto each other's hands. Then everything disappeared."

As we silently stared at Herita, who was shaking, we no longer noticed Naso. Herita let out a single, long, shivering breath.

"Were they supposed to be...you and King Resin?" the Soothsayer asked.

"I...I couldn't tell," Herita quietly replied. "It was creepy, but it felt very real. The oddest part was that if it was meant to be me, was it saying that death was soon, or was it saying we would enjoy a long and happy life together?"

Aurora reached out and squeezed Herita's trembling hand. "Then we heard the woman's voice saying to please take care of him."

"That was me," I said, shifting attention away from Herita. "The Soothsayer tried to access my memories as far back as she could like we planned. A woman and a man appeared with their daughter, part of the exiled group from Hallow. They said it was because of King Joel. The exiled group weren't Luckists, but were most likely Empathists."

"On their way to Motifer," the Soothsayer added.

I nodded and continued, "King Joel knew they were Manipulators and made them leave for no reason. Then came the Vigorist ambush. The mother and daughter ran away. Eventually, the Officers found them, and we then saw the forest floor covered with dead bodies." I thought of the little girl's stuffed fish lying in front of us. I didn't want to bring it up, so I moved on. "Finally, my adoptive mother appeared, holding me as a baby in her arms as a voice said, 'Please, take care of him.' Then, my stone," I pulled it out to show the bright red stone, "hasn't stopped glowing since."

A chilly silence covered our group. Herita shifted.

"But aren't you supposed to be present in the vision for the Manipulation to work?" Herita asked.

"I am still trying to figure that part out," the Soothsayer said. "The leaves from the Shadowleeks are said to pull out great power from the Soothsayer. I may have tapped into a greater power that went well beyond memory."

"Curious," Herita said and turned to me. "What does this mean about your Aura?"

I shrugged, though I knew what it meant. I needed to be able to tell my uncle in my own time. "Inconclusive. Then, a scream threw us off."

Aurora raised her hand. "The scream was me." She blushed as the attention turned to her. "My aunt and I saw Flaunte. Era sat right in front of me, but she morphed into so many other kinds of beasts before changing into Zen. Zen sat before me and cawed very loudly. Many Vigorist ships appeared on the sea as they quickly approached Flaunte. Everyone in the city went about their days as if war wasn't coming for them. I screamed at them to run, but nothing came out of my mouth. The ships were going to destroy Flaunte. I felt a fire growing in my chest as I continued to try to scream." She stopped and let out a whimper. "I searched for my aunt and found her frozen, not moving. I felt helpless. Zen then flew up to me and flapped his wings at my chest, causing the fire to grow. The flames shined a vibrant yellow. I tried to fight it but looked into his eyes and relaxed as the flames grew."

Her green meadow eyes flickered in yellow flashes, like the meadow burned with the yellow flames she described.

"Your eyes..." I said.

She blinked, and the yellow flashes were gone like they had never been there.

"Suddenly," she continued, "I could scream. I screamed so loudly. The ships sank at my shrieks, and my aunt melted, able to move again. A safe Flaunte remained. Zen sat to my left, and Era sat to my right. Everything just felt...right. A burst of power erupted in my heart. Then, the world faded, and we heard a question floating in the air asking if we were happy with our choice."

"That brings the story to me," the Soothsayer said. "I saw my grandmother playing with me when I was a child. She offered me two toys and said I had to choose one. At first, I wanted both, but she said I could only choose one. I chose the wooden toy and saw a city burning while I played with the toy, and my grandmother sat there. She asked, 'Are you okay with your choice?' as the city burned around us. We then heard Trigger, and here we are."

Normally the biggest talker, the Soothsayer kept her description short and sweet. Piquing my curiosity, I shoved questions and insights away, respecting the privacy of her name.

"What happened to you?" I asked Trigger.

Trigger nervously laughed, trying to display his regular confidence. "Nothing much. I think we've heard enough."

"We all shared, it's your turn," Aurora said.

"I think we're good," Trigger said.

The Soothsayer walked up, looking like she might slap him, and instead collapsed into him with a great hug around his broad shoulders. "It is okay," she said. "We are here, and we will not leave you."

Trigger's chuckle morphed into a deep, exasperated sigh. "Okay," he said as she pulled away. "So, I started chasing after Naso. I couldn't find him. The forest then transformed into Hallow. I ran through the halls and couldn't find anyone. Something popped into my head." He moved his hands over his head and blankly stared at the ground without talking.

"Are you okay?" Herita asked.

Trigger shook his head and forced a weak smile. "I felt a crown that wouldn't come off. I was King, but there was no one there. I tried to find you all, but nothing. I then started to run out of the city, trying to rip the crown off my head to no avail. All the exits were sealed, and I was trapped in the city. I tried to Manipulate and felt more power than I had ever felt before, but nothing happened." He clenched his fists at his sides and stared ahead. His body vibrated as he clenched his teeth. "I felt so alone." A tear fell down his cheek as he met our eyes. "Then, the crown loosened, and I pulled it off my head and chucked it at a wall as it shattered. I screamed at the crown, and the walls started to fade." He stared at the ground, short, quick breaths making his chest quiver.

The Soothsayer rubbed her hand on his back, steadying his shivers. "It is okay," she said.

"Then, I was back in the forest." His shivering returned with heavy quakes. "But I still felt alone. I started running and kept saying, 'I don't want to be alone.' Over and over again." He formed fists and pushed them on the sides of his head. "I finally made it out of the forest but still couldn't see anyone. I broke down. I sat on the ground and kept screaming for what felt like hours." He looked at us, eyes shiny. "I then saw you. All the panic left my body. I wasn't alone." Another tear fell. "Fear of being alone ends when friends become known."

The Soothsayer wrapped her arms around him again. "You are *not* alone," she said.

Herita hugged him next. "You are not alone," she said.

Aurora and I followed and joined the group hug. "You are not alone," we said together.

I looked over at Naso standing there. The Soothsayer reached out her hand. "Are you going to join us, Naso?"

His face remained hardened. He eyed the ground before looking at Trigger. "Yeah," he said as if he only realized what we were doing. He stepped forward as Trigger grabbed him and pulled him in. "You are not alone," Naso said.

I noticed the Soothsayer eyeing Naso, brows furrowed.

"Okay, okay, okay," Trigger said. "I get it. Now get off."

Laughter and release parted us.

"Did we find what we were looking for?" Naso asked.

"I think we all learned something important," the Soothsayer responded.

"I think I did," I said.

"Good," Naso replied, stepping forward. "Let's head back to Hallow then."

23

Devoted

My dream came flooding back stronger than ever. The frigid water, flat and motionless, supported my still body. A crescent moon reflected on the glass-like water. Stars riddled the sky like paint spattered on a sheet of black paper. The same star began to shine brighter. It closed in on me as it changed to red. A glowing, familiar red drawing me in as much as I drew it in. Gaining speed, our collision was inevitable.

Right before it hit me, it stopped, hovering just before my eyes and no longer glowing red; it was just a large boulder floating in the air. Then it dropped, plunging into the water right next to me. The collision caused a giant wave that hurled my body underwater. I tried to swim to the surface as I saw the large boulder sinking into the dark water, barely lit by the moon's gleam. The rock stopped sinking, hovering like moments before but underwater. Except, I realized the rock still sank. I just sank with it. I tried to swim to the surface, but my movements only dragged me down faster.

Finally, I broke away from its pull and burst forward, up from my bed in a heavy sweat. The sun was just starting to peak through my window. Naso sat at my desk, staring at my red stone. After noticing me, he placed the rock down and went into the bathroom. Though I thought our relationship improved after our journey to the Dead Forest, I was wrong. I eyed my rock, still curious at his fascination with it, and flung my head back on my pillow, staring at the sunbeams reaching across the ceiling. The faint memory of the red star flickered each time I blinked, like residual bright light. I reached out to the red stone and held it above my head. I noticed that when I relaxed and stared at it, it would begin to glow a brighter red. The same red of the star.

***

The day's festivities took over my thoughts—Herita and King Resin's wedding day. I heard that Mel would be at the wedding, which was a big surprise for me. Herita found out she was coming but also said years of malice were often much more difficult to heal than a quick argument and talk. Only time would heal them, and attending the wedding was a step in the right direction. At least, Herita thought so.

Rather than sit in my room and wait for a Naso who wouldn't talk to me, I threw my clothes on and stepped out into the morning air. Just as I did, the Soothsayer and Aurora walked out of their room.

"Good morning," I said. "Up early, too?"

Aurora stepped forward, then back, then shifted side to side. "We have a lot to help my aunt with for the wedding," Aurora replied.

"So, no breakfast?" I asked, batting my eyelashes at her.

"Not today," Aurora said as she kissed me on the cheek and walked past.

As the Soothsayer walked past, I said, "I had my dream last night. It looks like the Dead Forest brought it back."

The Soothsayer stopped and crossed her arms while leaning closer to me. "That was quick. Anything new?"

"I know the red rock has the same glow as the red star," I said. "They definitely have something to do with one another."

Aurora stopped and turned to face us. The Soothsayer leaned in and whispered, "I am starting to think the red star has nothing to do with Toterrum."

"Can we please hurry?" Aurora exclaimed and stamped her foot.

The Soothsayer threw her hands in the air. "Yes, of course. On my way!" She turned to me. "We can talk about this later."

They ran off. I followed behind at a much slower pace. They veered for the throne room while I angled to the city center to find breakfast. Though the nights provided high energy and celebration, the mornings basked in glorious peace. I didn't get to walk in the city much early in the morning, but the morning sun shined differently on the reflected gold. Shimmering yellow specks danced across the ground, moving at the speed of the sun passing over the holes in the cave ceiling. As more sunlight entered, the specks faded into overwhelming daylight, lighting up every crevice throughout the city.

"Hey there, stranger," Trigger said as he stepped up next to me, staring at the ground as I did.

"Why are you up early?" I asked. "You don't strike me as an early morning person."

"I had to catch up on my duties after being gone," he replied. "Why are you?"

"Bad dream. And I couldn't get back to sleep."

"Want to join me for breakfast?"

"Absolutely," I said as we found a table.

"I couldn't sleep either." He poured a glass of water and took a quick drink. "The Dead Forest did a number on me."

"How exactly?" I jumped on his rare display of vulnerability.

"Find a pebble, know a little. Notice the boulder, life becomes brittle." He hummed, blinked, and narrowed his eyes on me. "I have spent so much time training in the Luck Aura that I don't have a lot of friends." He scoffed. "Actually, you all are the first real friends I have ever had."

His normal arrogance, his puffed-out chest, and his broad shoulders all faded into the simple human sitting before me. Frail. Broken. Approachable. Just like he was in the forest.

"Do you think people expect you to be the next king?" I asked.

"Sure." He straightened his posture as if expected to. "I think people would be disappointed if I wasn't. I'm the first hope for a king that looks different from previous kings. Of course, King Resin came from a gold-gathering family, but he still looks like all the others."

After Trigger's episode in the Dead Forest and his current humble posture, I wondered if Trigger didn't want what was expected of him.

"Would you?" I asked.

Head cocked and arms crossed, Trigger asked, "Would I what?"

"Would you be upset if you weren't?"

"Wow." He searched around, scratching his arms. Once he found no one around, he leaned in close. "I don't think I would be." His face darkened. "I think I would be more upset if I let other people down." With a glare, his Aura twirled toward his heart, glowing in bright colors.

"What do you want then?"

He laughed and leaned back, hands behind his head. His laughter faded as he observed my expression. "You're serious? Hm. You ask questions that I've never been asked before. You have a real gift." Hands still behind his head, he looked up at the cave ceiling, sunlight lighting up his face. "I want to see the world."

"How far away have you been?" I asked.

"The Dead Forest. And you were with me." He raised both hands and shrugged.

"I never left Toterrum until about a year ago." I smiled. "There are so many amazing things out there."

"I want to see it all so badly." He reached out toward the sky. "No more caves and no more gold."

We exchanged silent glances. His thirst for adventure matched my own. I grew thankful for the Dead Forest. It helped reveal bits of my past, strengthened the connection between the Soothsayer and me, and helped me form a new bond with Trigger.

"Hallow has been very different compared to Labyrintha and Flaunte," I said. "Hallow is much more about respecting yourself. The other cities are much more about pleasing others. It had to have been hard for you always being around people who only cared about themselves."

He threw his head back in loud laughter. "Very." He clapped. "That is why your questions are very surprising to me. They're genuinely not about yourself. I really appreciate it." His body curled up into himself again. "I've felt so alone most of my life."

"Well, you're not alone. You have me. You have Aurora. You have Naso. You have the Soothsayer. Also, my uncle and Herita, of course."

"Of course." He hummed. "No getting rid of them. The ones that latch on tight will never go out of sight."

Some of his rhymes were confusing, while others struck me in ways that made me contemplate my life.

"I think you and the Soothsayer would really get along," I said. "I know you both are very different, but she's very caring, and you both say astounding things at times."

"Maybe. I'm not going to lie. It's hard to look past her being a Mentalist. We were raised to dislike them."

"I get it." I shrugged. "Just give her another shot. I do have to tell you that your city has some correct ideas. I always looked out for other people and worried about what others thought of me. Hallow has taught me to value myself more. I feel more confident and at peace with who I am."

"You should be," he replied. "You truly are an amazing person. You're an excellent Manipulator, especially for how long you've been doing it. Plus, you're a really good friend."

"I'm glad you think so." I widened my eyes and took a bite of food.

"You and Naso will heal." He read my mind. "He's still trying to find his own confidence in who he is. He also really wants to find a quicker way to help his family."

"He just needs to be patient." I took another bite but chewed too hard in irritation. The sharp pain fueled my irritability. I ran my tongue against the small cut inside my mouth.

"But that doesn't mean he should stop looking for other ideas in case there is another way," he corrected.

I sucked on the cut inside my mouth and pondered his words. "I guess you're right. Ever since my family was killed, I haven't had to worry as much or look for ideas. I honestly feel less and less connected to Toterrum." I pressed my lips together and made sure no one was nearby. "I've become less motivated to help."

"The effects of Hallow in full force." He squinted. "You do know it isn't your responsibility to help them."

He was right. It wasn't my responsibility. I often worried about Toterrum but had never been told that it wasn't my problem to figure out. I owed nothing to Toterrum. Asher had changed. My parents were dead. Naso's parents edged closer and closer to death. Felicity used me. What was tying me to Toterrum?

Better yet, what was my Aura?

"Can you tell me a little more about the blocks you see when you Manipulate?"

He scrunched his face. "Abrupt." He looked around again, making sure no one was around. "Well, when I move my Aura around, it reflects off little invisible boxes. So, I know they are there though I don't fully see them. After some time playing around, I noticed I could Manipulate Aura to push the boxes around. From there, I realized the blocks cause me to do things." He poked at the air. "Like, use them as little steppingstones or launch pads to increase my Manipulations."

"Wow." I moved my Aura around and tried to see if I saw little blocks. Rainbow iridescence shimmered around, but no blocks. "Can I tell you something?"

"You've told me a lot."

"Funny." I shook my head. "You can't tell my uncle. I plan on telling him after the wedding. But I don't think I'm a Luckist."

"Whoa." He leaned forward with widened eyes. "You sure?"

I nodded. "Positive. My real parents weren't."

"Lights in the past reveal the truth fast. Your secret is safe with me, friend." He stood up. "Well, I better finish my errands before the wedding. It was good talking to you. I really enjoyed this."

"I did as well," I said. "I'm glad you're my friend." I hesitated. "One last question. Why poetry?"

"Do I not seem capable of it?" Before I could respond, he continued. "I know. I hide things, but words captivate me. I lean a bit more into the Mentality side of the Luck Aura." He put his index finger onto his lips. "Don't tell the Soothsayer." He winked.

"My lips are sealed." Trigger twisted his fingers like a key and threw the invisible key to the side.

I let out a single, closed mouth laugh. It took a while, but I began to understand his humor. Maybe it was because I began to understand him more.

He smiled, touched my shoulder, and we walked in opposite directions. I regretted underestimating Trigger the entire time I'd been in Hallow. Truly, Hallow contained quality humans.

As if on cue, Mel stepped out from an alleyway, walking ahead of me.

"Hello, cousin!" I blurted.

She turned around, and her face lit up. "Hey, cuz! Big day today."

"It is," I said. "How did the talk go with Resin?"

"King Resin," she corrected. "Curious that you know about that. Then again, your group seems to know everything about people." She shrugged. "But it went as well as it could. I can see some genuine change within him. It's like whenever he speaks about my mother. Still a bit pompous, self-centered, and flat-out rude, but I see hope. That's why I'm going to the wedding. I see hope with Herita. I actually just left breakfast with her. She's a good person."

"She really is."

She popped her head up as if figuring something out. After a slight chuckle, she gave me a weird look. "Doesn't this marriage kind of make you and Aurora related?"

I hadn't thought about that. "No." I coughed, and instantly, sweat trickled down my back. "She's the niece of Herita, and I'm an adopted son of his sister—"

"I am just kidding," she cut me off and clapped her hands together with a devious grin. "Lighten up. You are not being incestuous."

I choked and tried to slide into nervous laughter but only choked more. "Funny," I said. "Very dark."

"It runs in the family." She patted my back, helping settle my choking. "And it will not go away, I fear."

"We should grab dinner sometime." I coughed, and my throat finally cleared. "Get to know each other a little more."

"Sure. Why not?" She hit me on the arm hard. "See you at the wedding, cuz."

"You aren't heading to the throne room?"

She rolled her eyes. "No."

"I thought it was a family thing…" Suddenly, I felt like I said something I shouldn't have.

"For *male* family members only." She extended her hands, gesturing to her body. "Last time I checked, that's not me."

I blushed. "Sorry. I still don't understand all the Hallow customs."

"Something I wish to be seen differently someday." She glanced up at the light cascading from the cave ceiling. She patted my shoulder again and walked off as I walked in the opposite direction, toward the throne room.

A softer song played through the street where I walked. A Hallow citizen pounded on large drums at a methodical beat while humming something that reminded me of a slow heartbeat. I found my steps in sync with the beats and smiled as the song invigorated my already high spirits.

I carried that energy into the throne room. After finding an empty room, besides my uncle, I realized I was the only male family member he had. King Resin sat on the throne, crown glistening in the light. No one else surrounded him.

"Yaron, my nephew!" He rose from the throne, tight green clothes hugging his muscular frame, and embraced me in a hug.

My back cracked from his grasp.

"Very exciting day," I said.

"Very." He pulled back and guided me forward with his hand on my back. "Come. We must have a drink to start the day."

He walked to the secret doorway. Once the triangle began to move, the doorway opened. We made our way through the tunnel and up to the exit atop the cave. Pink clouds floated through the sky in painted globs. Long and fluffy, overlapping one another in a textured pattern, a light breeze blew them along at the same rate as the grass across the fields. King Resin pulled out cups and the drink from the same bush as before. After pouring and toasting, we had a long, deep drink.

"What is this drink?" I asked.

"Are you telling me you drank this last time without asking?" His booming laugh echoed across the field. "You are too polite. I never trust a drink someone gives me without knowing what it is. It is Hallow Spritz. Some call it liquid Luck. It makes you more confident."

"I like it." I took another drink.

"You should. This is the best one made in Hallow. To marriage!" We clicked our glasses together.

"I'm happy that you're happy."

He looked over the Rolling Hills and took a deep breath with his eyes closed. "I am more than happy. I had been despondent for quite some time until your group arrived. I know Luck is my Aura, but I have never experienced more Luck than the day we all met. I have my nephew. I have my bride. I am healing my relationship with my daughter." He hummed. "Luck is on both our sides. Life could not be better. Find and capture opportunity." He extended his glass again for another toast.

His genuine happiness made my stomach twist. He was so authentic while I festered with a lie. I wanted to tell him so badly I wasn't a Luckist.

"Uncle—"

"Yaron," he interrupted. "I must tell you something." His body collapsed upon itself, which made me nervous. "I...I knew the people exiled a long time ago." He swallowed. "They were not banished because of treason."

My mouth hung open. "What?"

"Herita told me what happened with you in the Dead Forest," he said. "I knew they were exiled because they were not Luckists. I had no power at that time. I tried so hard to change things. Your mother was very angry with me. It took her years to forgive me, though I do not believe she ever did." His voice cracked. He cleared his throat and blinked away tears. "This was why I eventually challenged King Joel. He was not fit to be King. He made a grave mistake that cost many lives."

For the first time since meeting him, my uncle lowered his head and kept his face hidden from my view. He had always been so confident and so kingly. A real, vulnerable person who made real mistakes sat in front of me. My chest warmed at the thought. I forgot that a powerful person could be vulnerable, and I respected that.

"I don't blame you," I replied, causing his gaze to rise just a little. "King Joel did this. You didn't. You welcomed a group of non-Luckists into your city. You fed us. You kept us safe. I know you think my mother didn't forgive you, but I forgive you. If that matters at all."

His head rose back to its regal height, though still with a soft gaze. "Thank you, Yaron. This means the world to me. But do not give me too much credit. The fact you are a Luckist made it easy to allow you all in." He took another large swig of the drink.

I had to tell him.

"Uncle..." I swallowed the pit in my stomach, trying to climb up my throat. I cleared my throat. "King Resin. I am not a Luckist."

He spat out the drink. His face went blank as he stared at me. "What? Of course, you are."

I held the hammer that was about to crush his heart.

"I didn't only learn what happened to the banished Manipulators, but I learned my mother found me there." My leg shook so hard I tried to hold it down. "My life was tied to those people who were exiled."

His face grew pale. "But..." He trailed off into a blank stare. "It cannot be. Did April give you to Rita?"

"April?" My leg vibrated so fast that it traveled up through my hand and up my arm. "What?"

"They were very good friends," he said. "April and Jash Flora. April was pregnant, but I assumed the child was killed when she was." His twinkling eyes fixated on me, his mouth hanging open. "Rita and April did everything together. Even had their pregnancies together. When Rita had the stillbirth, April was just as devastated."

A cacophony of shock, confusion, excitement, and nervousness drowned out the world around me. A strong ringing made my head throb. I needed to dissociate to escape what was going on. But I didn't want to.

"Did April and Jash have a...daughter?"

He furrowed his brow. "They did. How did you know that?"

The family the Dead Forest showed me was them. *My* family. Everything about the experience made sense. We witnessed the entire scene when the Soothsayer brought me there because I was the unborn baby in my mother's womb.

"I saw them in the Dead Forest," I said. "I saw their deaths."

"Yaron, I am so sorry." He placed a hand on my shoulder.

My heart ached at their loss, and my head pounded from the revelation. I wanted to know more about them. My soul rejoiced in finally knowing my truth. I had needed the truth all this time, and I finally had it.

Then, my hatred was fueled by Toterrum's brutality. An unrelenting fire burned in my gut and traveled up to my face before crashing into my mind. The Officers killed them.

"It wasn't your fault." I gritted my teeth. "It was Toterrum's. They killed my parents. Both sets of them." I squeezed my once shaky leg until my nails dug into my thigh. "They need to pay for what they did."

"And we will defeat them. We will avenge our families." He took my hand in his. "I promise. Hallow will support you."

A newfound passion coursed through my veins. The hope of an army I once thought to be impossible crept even closer into reality. Perception backed us. Mentality promised to join if Luck pledged their fealty. We had Luck.

"To revenge." I extended my glass.

"To revenge." He raised an eyebrow.

We clinked our glasses and finished the last of the drink. A somber silence hushed across us. He looked at the horizon.

"We are still family, Uncle," I said.

He turned back to me. "We are for certain. Now, it sounds like you need to find a lost city."

"I do?" Sudden laughter came across me. "We did find your lost city. It should be an easy task for pros like us."

"Very true, but I believe this one will be quite a bit more tough." He watched me. "Empathy? Wow."

My body warmed after the drink, but it burned at the idea of being an Empathist. I looked at my uncle, so happy we were bonded by fate—not by fate, but by Luck.

We made our way back to the throne room. We got dressed in traditional Luck wedding attire. King Resin wore a white suit lined with green and gold that hugged his body. My suit flashed in bright green and was lined in gold. It hugged tightly to every part of my body. Mel eventually joined us. She wore a green dress accented with gold. Her hair twisted in black swirls as speckled with gold sparkles. Green makeup lined her lips and eyes.

"You look beautiful, my daughter," King Resin announced.

"I suppose I do," she replied. "I hate wearing this. I look like a clown."

"Not a clown," I responded, "just a very unthreatening Caved Selo."

She swirled her hands as I slipped on the ground. "Watch your words, cuz."

"Easy now, children." King Resin chuckled. "Were you able to get everything I asked for?"

"I did," Mel replied. "This includes the human-sized ice sculptures, the dancing Caved Selos, the gold dust bomb, the party favor cups with your face on the side of them, and these." She held out two green triangles that he snatched.

"Do not give away all the surprises," King Resin said. He brought the green triangles and pressed them to his cheeks as they absorbed into his skin, and his wrinkles faded away.

So many things that Mel said shocked me, but the green triangles surprised me the most. The vulnerability he showed when we sat on the hills seemed so distant.

"What just happened to your cheeks?" I asked.

He didn't respond, so Mel did instead, "They are Crystalized Algal Collagen used to make a face appear younger. Someone wants to hide their wrinkles."

"I want to look my best," King Resin announced as he attached a sheer gold cape that flowed behind him. "How do I look?"

"Like a king," I replied, admiring his radiance.

"Like a king who is trying to hide wrinkles," Mel corrected. His smile disappeared. She noticed the confidence slipping away. "You look great."

"I know," he responded as he puffed his chest, and the confidence flooded back. "Now, we ride to the ceremony!" He marched forward, Mel striding to his side.

"Ride?" I asked as I followed them.

Outside stood a slender black-furred beast with long legs and a pointed snout. It had droopy ears and eyes hidden by fur. Among the black fur scattered gold hair. On the back of the beast sat an extended gold and green seat with a canopy big enough for multiple people. King Resin walked to the back of the beast, where he pulled on its tail a couple of times before the beast whipped him up to the seat. Mel followed, and then I walked up.

"Just pull and hold," King Resin said from the beast's back. "The Fuzlor is very gentle."

I followed his instructions and its tail whipped me up. The beast stood tall, which gave me a different view of the city. The Fuzlor prowled forward through the city. People would cheer as we walked by, and King Resin waved.

"Where is the ceremony?" I asked.

"The ceremony is in the Green Cathedral," Mel responded. "Believe it or not, Luckists used to be more religious like Mentalists. After the war, people no longer attended the services, but the Cathedral still stands for ceremonial parties. This is the oldest building in Hallow before the city became the second Capital of Luck."

"The old capital was different?" I asked.

"Well," she said, "it was Hallow as well. I think this town was called Gola before we moved the city here. No one knew about the small gold-gathering town of Gola, which made it a great choice. From there, it was built into this." She gestured to Hallow and all its gold and gloriousness.

Around the corner, a small cathedral, which I had not noticed before, came into view. Green stones stacked on one another and accented with gold art appeared much humbler than the rest of the city's grandiose gold. Nowhere as large as the Cortexes of Labyrintha, the cathedral still had a calming presence. As we came closer and closer to it, stringed music echoed from within the building. The scent of sweet flowers wafted in the air. We dismounted the Fuzlor the same way we boarded, via the tail. King Resin walked in first, and we followed behind.

Two open, green doors translucent with golden glass revealed many long wooden benches filled with hundreds of people. All the people cheered as we passed outside the cathedral. As we walked down a green carpet lining the aisle, Trigger, the Soothsayer, and Naso looked over at us from the front. Trigger and the Soothsayer waved while Naso turned away. At the front of the cathedral stood a large golden arch where King Resin already stood. We moved to the right of him and faced the large crowd. All the faces staring at me made me itch my arms.

The music transitioned to a soft, sweet song as Aurora emerged from the doors. She wore a beautiful yellow dress with green and gold accents. Her green makeup made her eyes illuminate in shades of green I'd never witnessed. Everything about her held my attention. She smiled, and I nearly fell to the ground, knees shaking. For a moment, I felt like we were getting married. The idea lit my heart in fiery flames.

"She looks very pretty," Mel whispered to me.

I didn't respond, so she elbowed me. "Yes, she really does," I finally whispered.

Aurora moved to the side as the music stopped. The musicians shifted before starting a grandiose song with trumpets. The whole crowd turned and faced the back door. Finally, my attention pulled away from Aurora.

A very bright light shined as a figure stepped forward, twirling her hands. The light faded, and Herita walked forward wearing a simple, sheer white dress. As she came closer, I noticed a very faint flower design with shimmering gold accenting the white. Pure white lipstick and makeup lined her face, and a large bouquet of various white flowers made her shine. The same flowers covered her hair with a single sheer white piece of fabric flowing behind her. I looked over at my uncle to witness a tear falling down his cheek. They exchanged joyous smiles that spread to everyone else.

The Soothsayer stepped in between them below the golden arch. She extended her hands. "Everyone may be seated." The smiles faded as loud mumbles flooded the room. The Soothsayer's left hand shook as she kept her right hand up and steady. "I am honored to help join this marriage between a Luckist and a Perceptionist. As many of you know, I am a Mentalist. This is the first time in a long time that three separate Aura Manipulators have peacefully been together. King Resin chose me to perform the ceremony because this marriage shall represent the union for the future among our three people groups. This is to be a long overdue peaceful reconciliation that will bear fruit."

The mumbles grew into grumbles and harsh scowls.

"All she says is true," King Resin announced, his commanding voice echoing throughout the cathedral and into the streets. "Today will be a celebration greater than our love."

And just like that, the grumbling stopped. King Resin smiled at the crowd, turned to the Soothsayer, and nodded.

"I have known Herita for most of my life," the Soothsayer began. "She is kindhearted and has an abundance of knowledge about the flora and fauna that flourishes throughout Biome. A knowledge that rivals my own. King Resin and I have only known each other for a short while. He is a wise king who has protected your city well. I am so happy these two found each other."

The Soothsayer turned around and lit a small candle. Its flame danced as she turned back around.

"It is customary to include our Great Light in Labyrinthian services. I will only say a couple of words on this," the Soothsayer said. "May the Great Light guide you, protect you, and cause good in our world until your lights are joined to the Great Light." She turned around and blew out the candle. Smoke rose through the golden archway until fading into the air. "I now turn to each of you for the vows you wrote to one another. King Resin, you may start."

The moment my uncle's eyes found Herita's, his strong stance buckled but he repositioned himself to make up for the slight. The quiver in his voice as he tried to say something but lost his words, blankly staring at her again caused the room to break out in mumbles. King Resin lost his confidence. Standing before Herita, he was just another man. Herita took his hands and held them up, the warmest smile curling up her cheeks and lifting his spirits back to their regular intensity.

"Herita." The perfect combination of bellowing firmness mixed with soft intimacy silenced the crowd. "You...you changed my life the moment you walked into it. I was a bitter man with a bitter life before you arrived. I never thought I could love again; I thought that ruling Hallow was my only purpose in life. This damaged my relationship with my daughter." He turned to look at Mel and gave her a curt nod before turning back to Herita. "I was very self-centered. You saw beyond this. You weathered my arrogance and stubbornness. You helped me grow and mature. You helped me start to mend my relationship with my daughter. I now know my life has much more meaning beyond being a king." He played with her fingertips, seemingly lost again in her presence. "Herita, please receive this vow and dedication to love you. To keep you safe. To see the world with you. To bring justice to Biome. I am beyond Lucky that you found me and helped me find the way to heal and become a better man. Until I die, I am yours."

He pulled out an emerald ring and placed it on her finger. Herita seemed to grow two inches taller as soon as the ring was on her finger.

"Beautiful," the Soothsayer said. "Simply beautiful. Herita, it is your turn."

Unlike my fumbling uncle, Herita recited her vows with conviction and tenacity. "Resin, the king of my heart. You were a jerk the moment we met." She paused, expecting a loud laugh from him, which he obliged. "Most would be deterred by this, but it made me laugh. I quickly realized my smile made you melt a little each time we spoke. You listened to me, but more importantly, you cared for me. I became a mother at a young age when I had no intention of being one. Aurora changed my life, and I put her first every moment since." Without looking, Herita reached her leg back and gently nudged Aurora with her foot. "Then, I met you, and suddenly, you put me first. I trust you. I know you. I love spending every moment with you. I know we are both older, but there is so much more life to live. Until I die, I am yours."

She took a golden ring dotted with emeralds and put it on his finger. Their Auras rushed toward one another and swirled in a myriad of bright colors and sparks. My heart raced as my eyes tried to keep up with the Aura's speed.

"It is with great joy," the Soothsayer began, "that I present to you for the first time, King Resin and Queen Herita of Hallow. You may now kiss your queen."

They embraced each other for a deep kiss while everyone cheered. Their Auras buzzed in delight. To my surprise, the next parts of the ceremony flew right by. They rushed down the center aisle and mounted the Fuzlor as it walked off. I stood there, watching the crowd leave their seats. Aurora stepped up next to me, facing the same direction I did. We witnessed true love, and yet part of me felt dissatisfied. Was it the speed of their relationship? Was it the fact that Hallow didn't hold my Aura? Sensing my discomfort, Aurora reached out and held my hand. Without hesitation, I pulled her in for a kiss. Our bodies intertwined at the same spot where Herita and my uncle had just wed.

Aurora helped clear my mind when I sank into anxiety. Aurora gave me happiness when I found life to be terribly sad. I viewed people in a better light, didn't give up on my beliefs when they wavered, and grew into a stronger person all because of Aurora. We fit together. We improved one another. We...

"I love you," I said. My heart curled around my lungs and forced all the air out. My eyes grew wide and my mouth hung open. The words came so naturally that I forgot I'd never said that to her before. I was shocked

She stepped one foot back, and my fear of rejection closed in. Then, she stepped back forward. "I love you too."

My Aura rushed to hers. The warmth covering my body made me impulsive. I moved in just a little too quickly to kiss her again. She didn't reject my advance.

"Get a room," Trigger said.

Aurora and I laughed as we pulled apart to face him. The sweet aroma of flowers still lingered on her skin.

"What happens now that the ceremony is over?" I asked.

"We make our way to the hall to celebrate!" Trigger exclaimed.

"This is only the second wedding I've been to," I said. "The other was in Labyrintha."

A short marriage that left a bitter taste in my mouth. A cold weight brought my head down and made my eyes heavy. I missed Zela.

Trigger patted my shoulders until I looked back up at him. "Then you haven't really had a party yet." He raised his eyebrows up and down.

His contagious excitement lifted me from my sudden sadness. He clapped his hands at a sporadic rhythm as we danced on our way to the celebration. One step forward, two to the side, and we learned a quick dance he had just made up.

When we arrived at the hall, two life-size ice sculptures of Herita and King Resin greeted us at the door, one on each side. The details on their icy faces made me shiver from their accuracy. I found myself turning away from their discomforting presence.

"Oh my," Aurora said. "I can't imagine my aunt loves this."

Herita and King Resin greeted people as we walked in. She pointed and laughed at the sculpture.

"Maybe she does…" I trailed off.

Naso stood in front of us as Herita embraced him for a hug. She whispered something to him and held his face with her hands. She said something else to him and kissed him on the forehead. His cheeks glistened from fresh tears he quickly wiped away before walking off. After the Soothsayer gave her congratulations, Aurora hugged Herita tightly and started to cry. This caused Herita to cry.

After they stepped back from their hug, Aurora said, "I'm so happy for you. I can't believe you finally found the love you weren't looking for."

"No one could contain me," Herita responded. "I guess I was wrong."

"I want you to know that I see you as a mother," Aurora said. "I always have. I'm sorry I never put you first."

"That wasn't your job, little minnow," Herita replied. "I was there to keep you safe. Hopefully, you found someone to keep you safe." Her gaze drifted to me, and she smiled. They hugged one more time before Aurora hugged King Resin.

Herita took my shoulders and looked me up and down. "I'm so happy you were here." She wrapped her arms around me in a tight hug, and the strong scent of flowers. "You have changed my life for the better. I left Flaunte, where I only had Aurora. I left Labyrintha, where I would have died from my cancer. Now, I'm in Hallow to found love and healing. Most importantly, you make my Aurora happy." She pulled back to look at me again. "I can't *wait* to see the day you join your hearts together. Thank you for everything, Yaron."

My chest tightened, and my eyes watered. "You're the one who changed my life. I was only along for the ride."

"Give yourself more credit," she said. "You're an *amazing* human who brings joy to us all."

The confidence Herita bestowed upon me made me feel like I could fly. I adored Herita with my entire being. She acted like a mother to me more than my own mother often did. We hugged each other one more time before I moved on to my uncle.

"My boy." King Resin patted my back and finished with a backbreaking hug. "Thank you for standing by my side. You are like a son I never had. We have so much life to live together. I know we are not related by blood, but you are and will always be family."

"I'm very happy for you, Uncle," I said as we parted. "I'm glad you have Herita to watch over your arrogance."

"A net can only contain a fire beast for so long," he replied. "Eventually, I will burn through the net. But I think this net will be able to more than handle the heat."

Our interaction ended as he turned his attention to the next person in line. This allowed me to take in the grand party before me. Dancing Caved Selos rolled across the ground. Luckists flipped in the air, golden clothes flapping behind them. The smell of sweet drinks and fresh food wafted through the air.

The rest of the night consisted of a seven-course dinner and a three-course dessert. The Caved Selos performed what I could only call a ballet until they were ushered away as the sun began to set. Dancing took center stage for the remainder of the night. A lot of Hallow Spritz was drunk.

Toward the end of the night, Aurora and I danced to a slower song. "I'm so happy to have our amazing friend group," I said.

"Me too," she replied while running her hand along my back.

My skin tingled but didn't push past a frequent fiery sensation building in my chest. "We all enjoy each other's company, but we also have a hatred for Vigorists," I said.

Her lingering touch on my back waned. Our bodies no longer close.

Deciding to push past the coldness she displayed, I leaned more into the passion. "I think we should start gathering the three Auras together and attack the city," I said.

"Maybe," she replied while her gaze drifted away from me.

I moved my head back into her view until she fixated on me again. "It can be my birthday present," I said.

She cocked her head. "Your birthday?"

"Yeah," I said. "It's tomorrow."

"We can talk more tomorrow about this plan." Her expression remained firm and unmoving. A pit dropped in my gut. "I have something I need to tell you."

I then remembered I hadn't told her explicitly about not being a Luckist. "I have something to tell you tomorrow as well," I added.

The night went perfectly, except for that distance growing between us. I didn't want the anxiety grappling in my mind to fester into the rest of the night. Our conversation would be addressed the next day. This night deserved celebration for my uncle and Herita.

"It's a date," she said.

24

THE CROWN

Still water, night sky. My anticipation grew. I searched the stars for the one star that always grew. I found its reddish hue and prepared my body for it to charge at me. I waited and waited. Yet, nothing happened. The sky remained clear, and the scene gave me…peace. Just a glowing red star, small amidst the thousands of other stars surrounding it.

I stretched out of bed with the sun shining through the window. For the first time since I had the dream, I didn't wake up screaming or in a deep sweat. I forgot dreams could be pleasant. My birthday began in an enjoyable way.

"Happy birthday," Naso mumbled.

"Thank you," I said, a bit surprised.

He did not say anything else as he closed the door to the bathroom, but it was progress.

A letter sat on my bed. Any pleasantness to my morning suddenly seemed close to ending. Felicity's letter would be the first time I had heard from her since I shared my thoughts. Rather than let it sit there and haunt me, I fumbled to unfold it.

Yaron,

Happy birthday!
I know this letter could come off awkwardly since the last one you sent, but we are still friends, and you deserve to get a birthday letter from me. My, much has changed since your last birthday. I laughed a little after I wrote that because, holy beast!
I know you don't want to talk business on a day like this, but I wanted to let you know that I found out one last bit of information before I go into

hiding. The council seems to think they are closing in on you. I know you've said you can't be found, but they seemed confident about it. Just keep an eye out.

I hope Naso and your new friends make you feel special today. You are an amazing person and only deserve the best.

Your friend,
Felicity

The weight sitting on my lungs, keeping me from breathing, lifted. I let out a deep sigh. Had my last letter made our relationship...better? She even made a joke about how much we changed. Maybe she grew like I had grown. I wrote her back right away.

Felicity,

I'm so happy to have a friend like you. I appreciate your kind words on my birthday.
Thank you for the warning, but the only way that someone could get to where I was is if they were told how to. I certainly can't see that happening. And please stay safe. I believe you will, but just make sure it happens.
I'll write to you with more business on another day.

Your friend,
Yaron

I folded the letter and released it out my window. Since Naso would most likely not talk to me, I made my way over to the others' room. The Soothsayer answered. "Happy birthday!" she exclaimed before hugging me. "I am so excited I get to be with you on your special day."

"Thank you!" I replied. "I'm glad you're a part of it."

Aurora ran over, pushed the Soothsayer to the side, and kissed me. "Happy birthday," she whispered. Her meadow eyes lifted my heart and melted my skin. "Are you ready to grab breakfast?"

"I am," I replied and put my arm out as she looped hers into it.

"Are we doing anything else today?" the Soothsayer asked. "Maybe dinner?"

"That sounds like a great plan," I said. "We'll find you later."

As we walked through the courtyard, Mel came around the corner. "Hello," she said. "I was wondering if I could steal my cuz for breakfast."

"We were actually going to get a birthday breakfast together," I said. "Can we do it later?"

"It's your birthday?" Mel asked. "Happy birthday!" She grabbed my shoulders and shook me.

"You can go get breakfast with her," Aurora said. "I can wait."

"Are you sure?" I asked.

Mel swiped her hand in the air. "We can wait."

"No," Aurora said, "go and have fun. I'll see you after." She kissed my cheek before walking back toward her room.

"Well, I am a jerk." Mel leaned on my shoulder and looked toward Aurora. "I did not even know it was my cousin's birthday." She patted my chest and turned to walk.

"Don't worry," I said. "We didn't even know each other existed before I came here. Where should we go?" I walked next to her.

"The Pastry Shop sounds great," she said. "Have you been?"

Not having been, I followed her into town. We entered the small shop filled with the wonderous smell of butter and warmth. Golden pastries filled the room. I picked four different ones and nearly choked as I gorged myself with them. A concoction of butter, flakey pastry crust, and sweet candies erupted in my mouth. The pastries ended up being the best thing I had in Hallow, even after being there so long.

"These are amazing," I said with my cheeks stuffed.

"They really are," Mel responded in the same manner. We laughed.

"I'm glad we can get to know each other a little more. Do you remember my parents well?"

"I do," Mel replied and leaned forward. "Though I was very young. Your mother was always kind to me. She was pretty good at combat, just like my dad. We always spent a lot of time playing, and she taught me some moves. I was destined to lean toward the Vigor side of Luck. Your father was quiet. He kept to himself most of the time. It had to have been hard to get any words in when he was always around your mother and my father."

"She wasn't very loud around me." I picked at the crumbs left on my plate. "I know we were in Toterrum, but it's still interesting to think about. Did my father lean toward the Vigor side of Luck?"

"If I remember correctly, he leaned more toward the Empathy side, which is very rare." She ate the last piece of her pastry. "He connected well with people on an emotional level, but this was always hard to detect." She grinned and nodded to herself.

"Was your father that different before the…?" I asked, not sure how to word my question appropriately.

"Before my mother passed?" Her grin faded, and she glanced at her plate.

"Yes." I expelled the breath I held in.

She crossed her arms and leaned back. "I would not know, but I heard he was much more family-oriented." Her fingernail picked something out of her tooth, and she flicked it to the side. "He became distant and very involved in his duties after my mother's death. His status as king was challenged often toward the beginning, but no one could ever beat him. I became very dedicated to my training. Trigger was always my biggest adversary. I interacted with Trigger the most. However, I did not talk to him. This was odd since he was the only person I might have considered to be my friend."

Their culture didn't foster friendship in the ways I expected.

"That had to have been tough."

A slap on the table made me jump before she started laughing. "You grew up in Toterrum. I think I had it better," she joked.

"Yeah…" I agreed but realized each place had its own disadvantages, something I had never thought about before. "Have you ever challenged him?"

She smirked and crossed her arm. "I have thought about it, but not to be a leader, just to put him in his place." Her arrogance matched her father's. "The other issue about me taking over is there has never been a queen. There are dumb rules in place that state a king can deny a challenge if the challenger is a woman. No woman has had an opportunity to even try."

"That's ridiculous."

"Maybe to you." She pointed at me. "But it is our culture. Our city was made this way, and I respect the tradition." After pounding her chest with her fist, she raised it up before bringing her hand back down.

For being such a strong woman, my cousin adhered to Luck's dumb tradition so easily. Maybe all the bold women I met in Flaunte and Labyrintha skewed my view, but Mel was more than worthy to hold power. I thought about my conversation with my uncle the other day. He spoke about stepping down.

"What happens if he steps down?"

She narrowed in on me. "That is an odd question. Do you know something I do not?"

"It's hypothetical." I shrugged.

"Fine." Her eyes rolled so hard that her body moved with the motion. "*He* gets to name the successor in that situation."

"Would you challenge the successor?"

Her head tilted far to the right, and she narrowed her gaze. "I am not sure."

"Do you want to be Queen?"

"It does not matter!" She snapped her teeth together. "Plus, we all know he expects Trigger to be the next king. I think many expect the same. Which, don't get me wrong, it would be a big thing for our city." Her finger found another bit of food in her teeth that she flicked to the side.

"So, you do?"

"Maybe."

"You do know becoming the next queen would be a big thing for your city as well?" I asked. "Really a huge thing. And his thing is your thing. You are a double package." I smiled.

She stared at the table and smirked. "Stop talking about me and what I want," she said, changing the conversation. "Enough about me. What do you want out of this life?"

I hesitated. "It keeps changing."

After shaking her head, she snapped in my direction. "What is it right now?"

I sat for a moment and looked up at the sky. "To just not worry."

"Worry?" She chuckled. "Of all things, that?"

"I worry about everything," I said. "What people think. What people say. About my looks. About my decisions. Over my identity and if I'm doing enough. Everything." My heartbeat pounded in my chest, begging to be let free. I took a steadying breath to calm it.

"That is deep, cuz," she said. "Do you think you can escape it all?"

"Maybe, but I'm not sure how."

"Let me know when you do," she said. "I think we could all use this special escape."

We spent the next hour talking about bits of our childhoods, including games and times we got in trouble. To no surprise, I learned she was a troublemaker. Eventually, we ended our time together and began our farewells.

"Thank you for breakfast," I said.

"Thank you for having breakfast with me," she replied.

"If you get the opportunity to challenge, I think you should do it." I patted her shoulder like she often did to me. "You would be a great leader."

"Thank you, cuz." The twinkle in her eye was undeniable. "I will think about it." Before I thought she wouldn't, she swung her hand forward and patted my shoulder harder than ever.

***

When I made my way back to my room, I found the Soothsayer and Aurora sitting in the garden. Ricochet lay next to Aurora as she petted him. Ricochet perked up, ran over, and leaped into my arms. I fell over from the impact. He enthusiastically licked my face. I learned that day that Riddledogs knew birthdays.

"Okay, okay," I said as I pried him off.

"How was breakfast?" Aurora asked.

"It was good." I wiped the slobber from my cheeks.

She grabbed at her other arm and shifted her jaw. "Can we talk now?"

So many important conversations on my birthday.

"Of course." We walked to the other end of the garden and sat on a bench near a bush of sweet-smelling pink flowers. "What do you want to tell me?"

"You go first." She shifted her seat several times.

"Okay." I closed for eyes for a moment and then focused on Aurora. "I was going to tell you this yesterday. Do you remember what I told you about my experience in the Dead Forest?"

"I do." She blinked without any other expression.

"Well, I'm not a Luckist." I let out a deep breath.

She chuckled, and then her face twisted into a more serious expression. "I thought that was obvious."

"It was?" I asked as she shrugged. "Well, the people I saw in my vision were my mother, father, and sister."

"What?" She gaped and provided me with the reaction I originally expected at my revelation. "That I didn't know."

I nodded and leaned closer. "I know. Their names were April, Jash, and Grace Flora."

Her face darkened as her eyes moved around before widening. "Yaron, I'm so sorry you had to witness their...deaths." She grabbed my hand.

As if pulling a lever, tears cascaded down my cheeks. I didn't have a chance to process the entire affair. We had been so busy.

That little girl was my sister. That stuffed red fish sat among dead bodies was hers. The terrible image consumed my thoughts, and refused to let go. It wasn't even my memory...except it was somehow. Nothing made sense.

"It's weird to know what they looked like," I said.

"I can't imagine." She rested her head on my shoulder, but her neck remained rigid before she raised it off and rolled her head in a circle before placing it back down, still rigid. "Then again, I get it. I've seen pictures of my parents. Herita feels more like my mother to me than ever before."

Her head bounced in time with my quivering breaths, though she didn't budge. She understood me. Both of us were raised by people who weren't our real parents. Yet, they were more like parents to us than we ever knew.

"I know you understand me." I rested my head on hers. My neck also didn't relax. "Just as I understand you."

Ricochet snored next to my feet, having drifted into a nap. Zen nested in a larger tree near the center of the garden. Aromatic flowers left the lingering scent of sweetness. I could sit in the garden with Aurora forever, but why didn't our bodies match how I felt?

"I can't believe you're an Empathist," she interrupted the silence and raised her head off my shoulder.

I smacked my hands on my knees, finally getting the response I wanted. "I *think* I'm an Empathist."

"Well, you're running out of options." She laughed. "Safe to say the conclusion is clear." She hesitated. "But no way to tell without an Empathist. Back to square one again."

I let out a long, deep, tired sigh. "Back to square one."

Then, we joined in on a collective sigh.

"How did King Resin take it?" she asked.

I appreciated her question about my uncle. He was kind of her uncle now. I shook my head and tried to get rid of that thought. If only Mel had never brought it up.

"Very well. He said I was still family, and that's all that mattered. He said it all made sense once I explained what I saw in the Dead Forest. He felt really guilty for what King Joel did."

Aurora shook her head. "But your uncle wasn't King. He shouldn't feel responsible. He didn't make the decision."

"That's what I told him." I shifted my position on the bench. "He said his sister was furious with him and blamed him. He never felt fully forgiven by her and said that could never happen now. I told him it may not matter much, but I forgave him, and I knew her."

"You're kind." She surprised me with a peck on the cheek. "I love that about you."

She made me feel better about the decisions I made. My cheeks hurt from the large smile curling up my cheeks. I tried to reel it in, but it just burst through. I found it impossible to hold back the ways Aurora made me feel. Then, her face scrunched in discomfort as she stared ahead.

"So," I continued, "I think we'll be leaving Hallow soon. For Motifer." I sighed. "Another hidden capital."

"How do we expect to find it?" She picked at her finger. "It's been hidden since the war. No Empathists have been seen since. Well, except for the secret ones found here."

"We'll have to talk with the group to figure that out." I seemed to always be thinking through things since leaving Toterrum. "Now, what did you want to tell me?"

She let out a deep breath like she'd been holding it in. She turned to face me, sitting cross-legged on the bench. "I've wanted to tell this to you for a while, but you've been so busy. You had been meeting with King Resin so much that the Soothsayer and I were doing a lot of reading and found out some interesting Manipulations with Luck." A little yellow twinkle floated in her meadow green eyes. "The thing about these Manipulations is some seemed very familiar to me, and others seemed very familiar to the Soothsayer. We quickly realized they were Mentality and Perception Manipulations...but done in tandem." Her body finally moved like the Aurora I remembered, free and wild.

"Two different Aura Manipulations done together?" I asked. "I didn't know that was possible."

"Nor did we. The Soothsayer read vague notes about them in the past but never instructions on how to do it. So, we tried it. We achieved some the other day. They are wild."

"You have to show me them." I stood up.

"Sit down." She pulled at my arm, forcing me back to my seat. "We will later."

I paused before putting my arm around her and gently nudged her. "This is big news! Maybe there are some things we can use to defeat Toterrum. Vigorists killed my parents, my real parents, captured your mother and brother, killed your father, and tortured us all. We can inflict pain on them."

Her eyes didn't ignite the way mine did. "You are fueled by hatred." She turned away from me.

I shifted a little away from her as the conversation shifted. "And you aren't? They've hurt us all so much. They deserve it."

"I don't think we get to decide what they deserve and what they don't." Aurora raised her chin and clicked her tongue in a condescending way.

The infatuation she had moments before was nonexistent. Instead of letting it be, I grew more irritated.

I raised my voice. "I know you want unity and cohesion between everyone, but not everyone will agree to this." I scoffed. "All Vigorists are already tainted by the current leadership. I say it is better to start with a clean slate."

She finally faced me with fire in her eyes, but that fire was directed right at me. "Do you hear yourself?"

I sat straight up and nodded emphatically. "My uncle agrees. This is why he agreed to join forces with Perception and Mentality. This is the start of a revolution."

Her face went pale. I worried she might vomit. A cool breath cooled the boiling blood in my veins and expelled a wave of sympathy. That fire I had dissipated.

I leaned close again. "Was there something else you wanted to tell me?" I softly asked.

"Yes." The yellow twinkle returned in her eyes. "While we were practicing the Manipulations and talking—"

The sound of yelling and racing footsteps sounded in the garden. Aurora and I ran to the streets, many people running in the same direction toward the city center. I grabbed someone running by.

"What's going on?" I asked.

"The king announced he's stepping down from the throne," the guy said. "He's announcing who will take the throne next." The man ran off.

Aurora and I exchanged quick glances and ran with the crowd.

"Did you know this was happening?" she asked.

"He only mentioned he wanted more than the throne, but never this," I said. "Did Herita say anything?"

"Nothing."

We came to the area just outside the throne room where King Resin stood on one of the short pillars on the sides of the doorway. The growing crowd became louder and louder. My uncle just watched them gather, not a care in the world. Then, he flinched.

"Silence!" King Resin screamed. The crowd obeyed him. "As many of you have heard, I have decided to step down from being your king!" An uproar echoed across the city. "As Hallow indicated many years ago, when a king steps down voluntarily, he may pick his next in line! I have thought about this and have decided to pick someone who has been by my side for many years!" Silence returned as my uncle gave a dramatic pause. "I choose Trigger Diad to take the throne in my stead."

The mix of emotions racing across the crowd was expected. Some began to clap. Others mumbled. Confusion plastered across others' faces. Eventually, a small area parted to reveal a bewildered Trigger. Every eye in the city looked upon my friend, waiting for some kind of reaction. Trigger straightened his back, but his eyebrows tensed.

"I don't think Trigger had any idea this was happening," I said.

"He looks confused," Aurora added.

"Trigger!" King Resin announced. "Make your way up to the front!"

Trigger hesitated before he slowly walked to the front and climbed up onto the other pillar opposite King Resin. My uncle grinned and raised his hands, Trigger mimicking his movement.

"Now," King Resin continued, "the normal rules still apply. If someone wishes to challenge Trigger for the throne, they may do so. Trigger must accept the time and place if this happens."

A wave of mumbles coursed through the crowd. Then, someone yelled, "I challenge Trigger to the throne!"

Another area parted and revealed Mel. Her intense glare shifted from King Resin to narrow in on Trigger. King Resin smiled more than he probably should before he turned to Trigger. "It appears there is a challenger," he said.

Someone from the crowd yelled, "But she's a woman!"

Another person yelled, "Women cannot challenge the throne!"

"It does say a woman can be denied a challenge by the current person holding the throne, but it never says they cannot take the throne," King Resin announced and turned to the opposite pillar. "Trigger, this is up to you."

Trigger somberly looked over the crowd. Then, his normal arrogant smile popped out. "I accept Mel's challenge," he said. "I propose we fight now in physical combat."

The crowd went wild. Cheers, screams, and shifts rushed across the city in waves of excitement.

"Silence!" King Resin shouted. The crowd continued to move but grew silent. "I am still King until this crown is given over! Until then, listen to what I say! Clear an area for this challenge to commence! No interfering, but all Luck Aura is game!" He gestured to Trigger and Mel. "Please take your sides."

Trigger leaped off his pillar and sauntered over to the far left of the crowd. Mel prowled over to the far right. Aurora and I were able to position ourselves in the front row of the circle forming around them. The arena was set.

"I think this is what my uncle wanted to happen," I said, watching my uncle's smile bounce back and forth between his protégé and his daughter.

"I think you're right," Aurora said.

"Trigger." King Resin looked over at him. "Mel." He looked over at her. "This is your first Hallow Challenge. Put everything you have into this fight. Luck is on each of your sides, but only one will command it more today. The battle ends when the other yields. Please begin."

An electric charge ignited my heart. I held my breath, unsure of what to expect. Who did I want to win? Who would I cheer for?

Both Mel and Trigger charged at one another. They swirled their hands as their speed increased. Just before they collided, Mel leaped in the air as she led with her right foot right at Trigger's head.

Trigger moved at the exact same time but led with his foot toward her ankle. Mel just flew over the top of Trigger as Trigger slid underneath Mel. The crowd gasped.

They quickly threw kicks and punches. Sometimes, they ducked and dodged. Other times, they struck their target.

Trigger veered toward a building, the crowd parting. He started to climb as fast as he ran. Mel followed. Trigger glanced back and twirled his hand. Mel's foot clipped the edge of a window. Shattered glass flying, she broke through the window into the building. He landed on top of the building and looked down.

Mel popped out of the other side of the building and snuck up behind Trigger. She pulled out two knives and threw them at Trigger. Trigger twirled his hands and turned as the knives changed direction and missed him.

Trigger off balance, Mel took advantage and kicked his gut with her left foot and kicked his head with the right. The force threw Trigger off the building.

While his body flailed in the air, he turned forward. Trigger grabbed at a pole sticking out of the building and twirled around it. Mel jumped from the top and flew feet first at Trigger.

Trigger released the pole right before impact and collided with her. They fell as one, punching each other while falling. Both landed on their feet on the ground.

The crowd cheered.

My attention turned to the Soothsayer and Naso, who broke to the front of the crowd, several people away from us. Aurora and I made our way over them.

"What is going on?" the Soothsayer asked.

"My uncle left the throne and named Trigger his successor before Mel challenged him," I replied. "Did you know about this?"

"I didn't," Naso replied. His pale skin and shaking arms made it look like he might collapse.

"What's wrong?" I asked.

"I'm just worried about the fight," Naso said, averting his gaze. The Soothsayer glared at him.

A cheer shifted our attention back to the fight. The simple punches and kicks ended. Front flips, back flips, cartwheels, and many other movements that were impossible for a normal person, especially at the speed they were going, followed one after the next. Mel landed on her feet as she twirled and made a dust storm kick up out of nowhere.

"Perception," Aurora said. "Wow."

I couldn't see them, but their punches echoed out of the cloud. Trigger's head emerged from the top of the dust cloud here and there. He then made a superhuman leap from the top and landed outside the dust. The dust settled to reveal Mel searching for Trigger. He launched up and landed on her shoulders before doing a front flip and hurling her body into the ground.

The crowd gasped.

She kip-upped while swirling her hands, and a hole appeared behind Trigger. Trigger leaped to avoid it, but it quickly vanished, another one of Mel's illusions. He landed off balance, and she grabbed his feet and twirled him around before slamming him into the ground.

He barrel-rolled into a launch before landing on his feet. A calm standoff fell between them. Blood and bruises covered their bodies, and they breathed heavily.

Trigger glanced over at me past Mel's shoulder. He gave me one little grin.

Trigger fell over.

The crowd erupted into chaotic screams and chants. People rushed toward Mel, King Resin leading the charge. He grabbed Mel's hand and lifted it into the air. "I present to you our winner!" he announced. "All hail Queen Mel!"

Some yelled, "We want a King!" Their ignorant chants drowned out by true cheers.

"All hail Queen Mel! All hail Queen Mel!"

"Find and capture opportunity!" Mel yelled.

"Find and capture opportunity!" The city's slogan echoed all around.

Instead of crowding around Mel like everyone else, we ran over to Trigger to help him up. He stood much easier than I expected him to. As if noticing my suspicion, he leaned into me, allowing me to help him up.

"Now, I can go see the world," he whispered to me with a wink.

Did he yield? Did Mel defeat him? I couldn't tell if he said that because of his relief or because he planned it. He didn't want to be king, and now he wasn't. I smiled at my friend, getting what he really wanted.

Mel parted the crowd and walked over to Trigger, took his hand, and embraced him for a half-hug. "Thank you for accepting my challenge," she said. Thank you for making me earn this."

As the crowd closed in on them again, I backed away. Just as I emerged into open space, I noticed Naso sneaking off. I wouldn't have thought much about it, but the Soothsayer followed him. Something was going on.

"Come with me." I pulled on Aurora.

"What's going on?" She stopped as I kept pulling.

My heartbeat sped up, and a weird sensation crawled across my skin. I turned to face her. "Naso's up to something."

We followed Naso toward the waterfall, where we first entered Hallow. He stopped and looked up and down at the entrance before turning to face us.

"Why did you follow me?" Naso asked.

"Whatever you are doing, please think about it," the Soothsayer said. "Is it worth it?" She swirled her hands as his face tensed. "Just let me in."

"Stop it." He whined, tears falling down his face. He formed fists and hit his head. "I can't take it anymore." He pointed at my glowing red pocket. "It's won. It's too late." He grabbed an axe sitting against the cave wall and swung it repeatedly. He chopped the rope used to open and shut the gate behind the waterfall. The gate flew open with a bang.

"What's going on?" I asked.

"Naso, what have you done?" the Soothsayer asked. "I resisted pushing past your barriers, respecting your privacy. But something felt off. You blocked my Manipulations, but your Mentality Aura moved oddly." She swirled her hands again, Naso no longer tense. Her face went pale. "Are you going to tell them?"

Naso gave each of us a quick glance. His face twisted and went so pale. After leaning forward, he heaved for air before letting out a deafening wail. "They were going to hurt my family. They were going to kill them." He wiped his nose. "And the voices." He hit his head. "The voices kept coming from the red rock."

"Just breathe," Aurora said. "We will help your family."

"I couldn't wait any longer," Naso said. "The rock wouldn't let me. Then, they wrote to me. We figured out to meet in the Dead Forest. They promised me they would help us if I helped them. The rock agreed."

Why did he keep talking about my rock like it spoke to him? Nothing made any sense, but a fire ignited from within. My throat twisted. My heart drummed. My brain throbbed. "Naso, what did you do?" I asked, not wanting to hear the answer.

"You have to run," he said. "Yaron, I'm so sorry. They're almost here." He looked at my rock, glowing brighter and brighter. "I don't want any of you to get hurt."

The Officers were about to enter Hallow. I hyperventilated. My mind tried to lift away from me and flee the situation.

"How could you?" I exclaimed.

"Who's almost here?" Aurora asked.

Naso swallowed. "The Officers."

25

Golden Flames

I wanted to punch him.

I wanted to push him down the waterfall, out of my life. My friend from the same city that persecuted our people betrayed me. He betrayed us. All the paranoia, all the anxiety stemming from my general distrust of people, was proven true. I'd been betrayed before and thought I wouldn't be again. Yet, Naso, shaking like an abandoned beast, cowered before me.

A blaze like never before erupted deep within me before consuming every part of me. My blood boiled, my skin sizzled, and my teeth pressed hard together, worried I may burn Naso with the flames. What if I just burned him away?

Before my anger lashed out, an overwhelming force pulled my burning Aura back. Normally a gentle feeling, Ricochet wrapped around my Aura, bright yellow lights illuminating my rainbow beams, and pulsated his presence to me like a massage on my back. He was on his way to me.

The floodgates of my mind flew open and tried to douse the flames but instead just clashed with the blaze. My anxiety poured into every inch of my body where the flames already existed. Dissociation would do nothing. What was true about my life?

Did my uncle actually care for me, or was it all a lie?

Were Trigger's recent confessions to me his way of trying to manipulate me?

Did Herita work with Naso the entire time to destroy me?

Did Aurora really love me?

My anxiety faded. For a moment, I believed everything might be okay. Then, my skin burned again, and my chest filled with hot air. Rage took over. Pure rage. My eyes locked on Naso. He hid his face like a coward.

"You betrayed us all!" I screamed. I punched his Aura repeatedly until he fell to his knees. "After everything we have been through, you did this?" I swirled his Aura to his eyes as his family appeared around him, healthy and happy. "Were they worth it? Were they worth endangering all of us?"

He wailed and finally looked up at me with his reddened, tear-filled eyes. "Just kill me," he said. "I know you want to, so just do it. I deserve it." He dropped his head. "I had no other choice. They were going to kill my family."

"And they killed my family!" I yelled. "I didn't betray us all! Not even for one moment!"

"Yaron..." Aurora said.

I shot a hateful glare at her. My heart burned. Her Aura pushed back without any Manipulation. A new terror drowned her normally bright meadow eyes.

Naso was right. I wanted to end him. I hated him so much.

But was I really someone who could just kill? I remembered the Officer I killed in Flaunte. His eyes faded away. The dread I felt afterward brought me down. Yet, I felt powerful.

The clipping of Ricochet's claws echoed from behind. Though electric, his Aura held my Aura back from doing anything I would regret. Ricochet stopped just in front of me, arched his back, growled at Naso, and then turned his attention to me. He barked, his eyes softened, and he whimpered. He showed no physical pain, but his Aura wavered. Naso didn't just betray me. He betrayed Ricochet. I looked around. He betrayed all of us.

I moved my hand back as the image of his family disappeared, and the tension in his body lifted. However, he chose not to stand. He knelt like a coward.

I stepped close to him, Aurora coming close to me. "You're not worth it," I whispered to Naso before turning and leaving him behind.

An odd noise began that counteracted the waterfall's pounding. I turned to face the waterfall. The noise grew louder and louder—the flapping of wings—so many wings. The cave walls vibrated. Naso rose to his feet. "Leave," he said. "NOW!"

Without hesitation, we rushed back to the city, to the throne room still surrounded by the joyous crowd. With each step closer, the cold grip of terror pulled at me. My legs weakened, and I was ready to fall over and give up. I couldn't handle another battle. Not again. Who would I lose this time?

The cheers and joy coming from the Luckist crowd intensified my worry. How many of them would die? I was in danger. They were in danger.

"What should we do?" I asked.

"We need to tell your uncle and cousin," the Soothsayer said. "We also need to gather what we can and figure a way out of the city."

"Shouldn't we help fight?" Aurora asked.

"I do not think the numbers will be on our side," the Soothsayer said. "We need to get as many as we can outside of Hallow."

I scanned the crowd for my uncle or Mel. The Trimerald from King Resin's crown caught my eye from the center of the crowd, Mel at his side. Trigger perked up and ran to us, his face twisting after seeing us.

"What's going on?" Trigger asked. His quick eyes analyzed each of us and the terror plastered across each of our faces. He looked past us. "Where's Naso?"

"We need to get to my uncle now," I said.

Without questioning, Trigger helped push through the crowd. We came to Herita first. "You need to get everyone out of the city," I said in between breaths. "Now."

"What are you talking about?" Herita asked with furrowed brows and her complete attention.

"They're here," Aurora said as she tapped Herita's arm. "Toterrum is coming through the waterfall as we speak."

"What?" Trigger exclaimed and looked back toward the waterfall gate. "But the gate."

Herita put her hand over her mouth and grabbed King Resin. She pulled him close and whispered into his ear. His face twisted, and he turned to face Herita with his entire focus.

"What did you say?" he yelled. He looked over to us as he pulled Mel over. He asked us, "How do you know this?"

"Where's Naso?" Herita asked as she searched around.

My fear collided with my fury at Naso. Right before I responded, the Soothsayer squeezed my hand and said, "Naso revealed Hallow's location in exchange for his family's safety. They are here. Naso broke the rope to the gate. It is wide open. We need to get as many people outside the city as we can."

Trigger stepped back with a blank gaze. "I knew I saw Officers in the Dead Forest," he said.

"This cannot be." King Resin stamped and pounded his chest. "We must fight."

"There's a time to fight, and there is a time to flee." Herita grasped her shoulders. "This time is to flee." She leaned close and placed her forehead against his intense expression. "Your army won't match theirs. Be wise, my husband."

King Resin gritted his teeth. "My decision is—"

"This is my decision," Mel interrupted and surveyed the Hallow citizens. "We shall flee."

King Resin stepped forward and stood over her. "That is not your decision to make."

Mel bumped her chest against his. "It is now." She grunted while holding intense eye contact with her father. "*Queen* Mel has spoken."

"What is the best way to get out of the city?" Aurora asked.

"The northern tunnels." Queen Mel pointed north.

"The ones like we took to the Dead Forest," Trigger said.

Queen Mel looked over to Trigger. "They still function?" she asked.

"They do," Trigger said. "So, the northern entrance should as well."

"Good," Queen Mel said. "I do not know where we should go from there."

"I do." Aurora stepped forward. "Enter the Dead Forest and then head west. The Forest will keep you hidden. From there, you will exit near the Lowlands and make your way to the ocean. From there, north to the entrance of Flaunte where the Rithbar River meets the sea." She placed her hands on my uncle and cousin's shoulders. "Perception will welcome our Luckist friends."

"You are sure?" Queen Mel asked.

"Certain," Aurora said. "I'll write them now when I go grab some things from my room."

"We can travel with you to the Dead Forest," I said.

"No, you will not." Resin shook his head and pointed at each of us. "You are their target. You must go a different way."

"But—" I began.

"He's right," Herita said. "We have to leave a separate way."

"Go and gather your things and meet back in the throne room." Resin clapped and pointed to the left. "Now!"

As we followed his command, Queen Mel announced to the crowd, "Friends of Hallow! Officers have entered the waterfall! Warriors, please defend the city! Keep the army confined to the waterfall's tunnel as long as you can! The rest of you gather what you can and make your way to the northern cave!"

The crowd's joyful noise transferred into screams and panic. "ENOUGH!" Resin yelled. "Listen to your queen if you want to live!"

Everyone went silent.

"Go!" Queen Mel exclaimed. "NOW!"

The stampede of the crowd roared behind us. We made it through the courtyard and to our rooms. As soon as I entered my room, I looked at Naso's things. I wouldn't see him again. The oddest mixture of pressure near my eyes and blood pounding and rushing to my head swirled within me, but I pushed it down and grabbed what I could. In a flurry of stuffing, some clothes, the red stone, and other small items were placed into my backpack. Just before I left, I grabbed the stuffed red fish. I remembered the dead bodies. I shoved the toy into my bag.

I ran over to the others' room. Herita stuffed a bag with what she could. The Soothsayer pondered over which books to take. She stared at one particular book longer than the others. Aurora finished her letter and released it out the window before grabbing her bag.

We ran back out through the courtyard and through the city. Black and orange uniforms riddled my view. The weight of my heart slowed the world around me. The Officers attacked Flaunte. They attacked Labyrintha. Now, they were in Hallow. The Officers outnumbered the Luck Warriors. Though the Warriors held their own, the number of Officers pouring in didn't stop. Ricochet ran up next to me as Zen swooped down to Aurora. Trigger closed in on us, away from the Warriors.

"Shouldn't you be fighting?" I asked.

"I was ordered to help you," Trigger replied.

Just then, my uncle and cousin were pushed into the throne room by a flurry of Officers, the doors swung shut. The remaining Officers filled the space by the throne room's entrance. The doors appeared to be locked as Officers pounded at them. My red stone glowed brighter than ever. I took it out and wrapped it in one of my socks, trying not to become a beacon for Officers. An odd gravity fell upon me, seemingly coming from the cave by the waterfall. A figure walked out, covered in a dark cloak, head completely hidden. Who was that person?

"We need to help them," Herita said.

"I know," Trigger said. "But the entrance is blocked."

I moved my attention away from the cloaked figure. "How do we get in?" I asked.

"Follow me," Trigger replied.

He led us through an alleyway before a group of Officers attacked us. I stepped forward and released the storm within me as I screamed and punched at the ten Officers. Their Auras diminished with each jab. Trigger charged at them and jumped in the air while kicking. I swore he flew like Zen for a moment as he knocked them out. After defeating the group, we approached a large drain. He climbed in through the large grates, and we followed. The scent of rotting water made me gag.

Holding my breath as we worked our way through the large drain, we finally came to the drain's grate on the bathroom floor. We ran through the interior courtyard into the throne room where Resin and Queen Mel stood. Before we could say anything to them, the front door to the throne room burst open as twenty Officers rushed in. We split up to fight the ones near us while Resin and Queen Mel attacked from the other end. I knocked out a few Officers, adrenaline forcing me forward, before turning my attention to the others closer to the door.

Then, I saw him. All the confidence I earned through training, all the Manipulations I learned from the three cities, and all the hatred I held toward Naso dissipated in the presence of this man.

"Yaron," the voice said. "What a pleasant surprise."

There he stood. Officer Grant. The man who beat me my entire childhood. The man I hated yet feared every minute of every day. I just stared at him. I remember when I attacked him a year before in Toterrum. It didn't matter that I defeated him then. I cowered like the small child still trapped behind my false confidence and the walls I built.

"Officer Grant..." My voice shook in response.

"I *owe* you this." He swung his fist and hit me in the gut. I flew back across the room, sliding on the stone floor. His amplified Vigor Aura punch left me reeling. Scrapes and bruises covered my back from sliding.

I gasped for air as I stood back on my feet. After steadying my breathing, I realized the fear no longer had a grip on me. He knocked it right out. I smirked.

"You're still weak," Officer Grant said as he calmly walked toward me.

"I was," I said, "but you haven't met the new me."

I swirled my hands and started punching at his Aura. His knees buckled. "What?" he exclaimed. "How can you Manipulate Vigor?"

I didn't have time to process his question. "I've learned some tricks." I continued to punch and close in on him.

Officer Grant crumbled before me, shriveling to protect himself from my pursuit. I would end him this time. He no longer had power over me. Just as I stopped right above him, a hand reached back to shatter the glass below his Aura, another person jumped over Officer Grant and struck me across the face. I fell on my back and faced my assailant, Samson.

"My old friend, Yaron," Samson said as he continued to pummel me, a large smile on his big, dumb face. I started to dodge the punches but felt my energy fade. Officer Grant was released from my Manipulation and swirled away my Vigor Aura.

Ricochet jumped in front of me and released a bright flash as I was able to move. Somehow, I just missed another one of Samson's hits. My body moved across the ground. Then, I noticed the Soothsayer dragged me back.

"Thank you," I said.

"Do not mention it," the Soothsayer responded. "You know them?"

I nodded before watching Ricochet get hit across the face as he yelped.

Any pain in my body evaporated in a heated rage. No one touched my partner beast. I swirled my hands to move Officer Grant's Aura to his face. The world shifted as everyone fell around us. Though it looked like our group had been defeated, Aura swirled and shifted the only way it did when people fought. Officer Grant admired his accomplishment, nonetheless.

"You lost." Officer Grant cackled. "You weak fool."

Iri popped in front of his face and swirled in glowing spirals. While Officer Grant remained distracted by the beast, the Soothsayer slipped behind him and touched the sides of his head. His body went limp, and his Aura went still. "Not quite," the Soothsayer said.

The world returned to the vicious fight. Samson looked at his father and exclaimed, "What did you do?" He swung his arms as the Soothsayer swirled hers. Samson struck two of his own Officers, knocking them out. "Stop it!" he exclaimed as he swung and hit two more.

With Samson preoccupied by the Soothsayer's Manipulation, my attention shifted to Herita. She swirled her hands toward the throne room doors, a faux wall appearing, which allowed her to shut the doors. She took a large brown fruit from her bag and cracked it open. The gray liquid inside of it dripped onto the cracks of the door and dried on impact. The pounding resumed on the door, yet the door remained sealed.

Queen Mel and Resin fought Officers near the throne, back-to-back. One of the Officers fighting with them caught my eye. I knew him. Or at least he was someone I used to know. He wore the black and orange of Toterrum.

It was Asher.

I gaped. I wanted to say something but couldn't. Then, Asher pulled a knife from his sleeve, threw it in the air, and punched it. The knife flew with great velocity and strength. It sliced forward and struck my uncle across his cheek. Blood sprayed as he fell back. The knife clunked against the throne and wiggled into a stillness on the top back of the chair. Asher pounded his hands toward the ground as Resin tensed his face in apparent attempts to stand but was unable to rise. Mel didn't notice as Asher stood above my uncle. He raised his hands in the air and swung down. An invisible boom went across the room. My heart stopped.

"ASHER, NO!" I yelled as Mel turned around to see her father on the ground.

Asher looked over at me. His rough face filled with dark shadows softened. "Yaron?"

Aurora echoed. "Asher?"

I charged at Asher and screamed. I punched and punched at his Aura, causing him to fall to his knees. A silent resignation was all Asher returned toward me. The innocent boy I knew looked up at me, bewildered and scared.

"What did you do?" I yelled at him.

Then, all the innocence went dark. A man weathered by war and death looked up at me. "My job," Asher flatly said. "Kill the king."

Who was this man? Where did the kid I used to play games with go? What happened to all the laughter we used to share? Only an enemy knelt before me.

Naso betrayed me. Asher betrayed me. My numb mind mixed with my fiery veins into an inferno of anxiety and rage. Tears streamed down my cheeks, trying to make their way to the inferno and put it out. I focused on the glass below Asher's Aura. All my fear and all my anger had one purpose. I sliced at the glass. His Aura fell to the ground, and Asher fell to his side unconscious.

My enemy fell.

I turned my attention to my uncle, where Mel held his head. I searched the area, and the only remaining Vigorist was Samson, who ran over to Asher. The Soothsayer followed closely behind him.

Finally free from battle, a dark wave washed over the inferno within me. My throat clenched, and the front part of my brain ached. New tears erupted from my tired eyes.

I knelt next to Mel. "Uncle?" I cracked out.

Trigger stood to the side and swirled his hands in circles toward my uncle. "Hurry," he cracked out. "This won't last long."

I looked to Trigger but Mel grasped my hand and moved my attention to Resin. My uncle was still breathing, but the breaths were short and wheezy. Herita ran up next to us as she pushed her head into his chest. She heaved for air, just like her husband below her.

"No, no, no." Each of Herita's words came off short, crisp, and quiet.

"The three people I love the most," Resin said in a weak yet stern voice. He tried to push out an arrogant smile, but all the blood across his face hid his bright teeth.

"Dad," Mel said. "I'm so sorry..."

He hushed her. "It's okay." He took a long, weak breath. "Mel, I love you. Please lead Luck into a new era, and do not forget to help the rest."

"I love you, Dad," Mel said. She formed a fist and beat it against her chest. Despite her regal response, glistening tears cascaded down her reddened face.

"Yaron," Resin said. "Take my crown." Another feeble breath quivered from him. "I don't want Mel to have a target on her head." He took my hand, and Mel's into his hands. "Your family has always loved you. Use my tunnel to get out."

He held an intense stare with me that I met no matter how much I wanted to cover my face and sink away. Another attempted grin shined from him. His nobility remained intact.

"I love you, Uncle," I said.

Resin looked past me as I turned to Trigger, looking down at his king. Trigger slowly nodded to my uncle and stopped swirling his hands before letting out a scream that transformed into a cry. My uncle pounded his chest and nodded back. Trigger screamed and twirled his hand again toward my uncle.

Resin took another short breath and shifted his attention to Herita. All his nobility faded. His lips shook as droplets of blood sprayed up.

"Herita," Resin began. "My sweet Herita." He placed a hand just above his heart and breathed in. His quivering lip calmed. "I said I would love you until my last breath. I wish we had more time. I will love..." His voice cracked as he touched her face. "I will love you..." He wheezed with sprays of blood and sweat. "Forever..." He cracked out before his hand went limp and his eyes blank.

"Resin..." Herita whispered. She squeezed his hand, but he didn't squeeze back. "Resin..." She shook him, but he didn't move. Her head dropped down. The pounding on the door continued, but the silence across the room deafened it. She took a deep breath and raised her head in a smile as she touched his face. "I'll love you forever."

Trigger collapsed forward. "I can't anymore!" he screamed.

Herita didn't even flinch at Trigger's scream. She kissed Resin's forehead and shut his eyes. Her head fell into his chest as she gripped his shirt. Then, she wailed. She wailed so loud my brain rattled in my head.

Each cheek sparkled in dazzling, cruel droplets. Our group gathered around us in a somber circle. Herita's body convulsed on top of Resin's chest. Mel covered her mouth to muffle her whimpers. Aurora and Trigger put a hand on one another's shoulder. My grief numbed me. Dissociation swept in and caused me to look anywhere but at my dead uncle.

Then, I stopped at Samson standing over Asher. My floating mind collided with my body and jolted me up. I marched straight for them. My skin crawled for vengeance.

Samson noticed my approach. He held up his arms as if to block me, but nothing was going to stop me.

"Stay away from him," Samson said with trembling arms.

"Get out of my way."

"You won't hurt him. I won't let you."

I stopped and threw my head back in aggressive laughter. "And he's yours to protect?" I pointed at my chest. "He was *my* friend, and you captured him. You have no reason to protect him." My attention lingered on the glass below Samson's Aura. With a flick of my wrist, the glass shattered, Samson toppling with it.

Asher's eyes fluttered open and transfixed on me. "Yaron?" That dumb innocence covered his face again. "Why are you so upset about a king dying?" His words ripped away his innocent ruse. His actions spoke volumes, but his callousness pierced me. Any semblance of the Asher I knew was gone at that moment.

"*That* king was my uncle, and you killed him!" I exclaimed.

Asher surveyed the area around him. He sighed when he realized that he was the only Officer remaining. "I did what I had to do." Asher looked up with his dark green eyes. "Do what you have to do."

I faltered. "What happened to you?"

"I became who I was meant to be," Asher replied. "Now, become who you were meant to be."

Who was I meant to be? Asher knew I had a storming rage inside me my whole life—anger fueled by my worry and anxiety. He knew me. I hated him, but he knew me. And for his actions, he would pay.

I let the anger flow into every inch of my body. I grabbed his Aura. I lifted it. The electric energy at my fingertips thrilled me.

I was just about to slam it down, but a bright yellow light blinded me. It reminded me of Ricochet, but it was so much brighter. I couldn't see anything except the light. Stumbling backward, I tripped and fell back. My red stone toppled out of my pocket, and its light pushed at the yellow light. Back and forth, the lights fought for dominance of the space. Then, the yellow light overtook the red light. The brightness faded, and my eyesight returned. The stone struggled to stay red, flickering in and out. I grasped the stone and tried to contain its brilliance. The red faded as the stone appeared to only be a stone.

I sat up. Blurriness and fatigue made my world foggy. As the world came back into focus, I stood back up and looked at Asher. I stumbled forward, watching his Aura, and tried to grab it. Nothing happened. I tried to punch it. Nothing happened.

The panic in my heart pounded in my ears, and the tightness in my chest made breathing harder. I didn't know what was happening. I searched the group for answers but only found furrowed brows, reddened eyes, and slouched postures.

Aurora ran over to me. "Yaron, we need to get out of here." Her green eyes contained large yellow sparks before they faded away. I had never seen them shine that bright a yellow before.

"My Manipulating..." I trailed off.

"Yaron," Aurora said again, "what tunnel was Resin talking about? We don't have a lot of time. The sealed doors won't last much longer."

I looked over at the Soothsayer who stood over Asher. She paused for a moment. I thought I heard her say, "We will meet again soon." She touched Asher's head, and he collapsed.

"I know the tunnel, but how do we get in?" Trigger asked.

The pounding on the door grew louder and louder. The sealed crevices began to crack.

"It's over here." I walked to the two pillars and spun the triangle. The door opened.

Trigger ran over to it. "We need to go now." He held the crown that once sat upon my uncle's head. The very crown Trigger only moments before didn't want.

The Soothsayer walked over to Aurora and whispered something to her. Aurora looked at the Soothsayer, and her face went pale. The Soothsayer handed Aurora a book. Aurora walked over to Zen. She whispered to Zen, and Zen took flight and dove into one of the throne room's windows as it shattered.

At the same time, Mel helped Herita to her feet and walked her to Trigger. Herita no longer wailed but looked defeated. "You all have to go," Queen Mel said. "I need to help my people escape."

I knew she had to. I walked over and hugged Mel. "Stay safe," I said.

"You as well, cuz," Queen Mel replied with a firm nod and one more smack against my already sore shoulder. "Until we meet again."

"Until we meet again," I said and patted her shoulder.

Trigger swirled his hands before pushing his hands toward Queen Mel. For a moment, the crown's Trimerald let out a little green blaze within Trigger's grasp. Queen Mel looked down and up, eyes widened. Trigger only smiled, the faintest spark of green light in his eyes. He entered the tunnel with Herita. Aurora ran over to me and kissed my cheek before going in. Her eyes still shined from residual tears, and fresh tears trickled down her cheeks. I followed her up into the hidden staircase. I stopped at the entrance as Ricochet rushed by. I watched the Soothsayer not step forward.

"Yaron," the Soothsayer began, "do not be mad. I must heal the damage Mentality has done to Luck. I pick the shield, not the wooden toy."

Iri rushed forward, letting off a blinding light that caused me to step back, and the Soothsayer slammed the door shut. A loud thud came from the other side, followed by the clinking of metal falling on the ground.

I put my hands on the wall and pounded at them. "Soothsayer! This isn't funny! Come with us!" No response came. I slammed my fist harder on the wall. I performed the triangular motion Resin used to open the door. Nothing happened. I slammed again while making the motion. Still nothing. A sharp pain came across my hands. Blood trickled down my wrists. "Come back! I can't do this without you."

A faint whisper came through the wall. "You have done so much without me already," the Soothsayer said. "I believe I figured out what the fog was trying to tell me. Please get out so I know what I am doing does not go to waste."

Aurora tugged at me from behind. "Yaron, we need to go."

Trigger yelled from further up the stairs. "What's taking so long? We need to get going."

I took my hands off the door as I followed Aurora. I welcomed the dissociation sweeping through me. Anything to keep my heart from dealing with any more heartbreak.

Trigger watched us walk up and looked past us. "Where's the Soothsayer?"

Aurora sniffled next to me. I had no tears left. "She isn't coming," I coldly replied. "She's going to help Luck escape."

He chuckled, but didn't falter. His face twisted. "What?" he exclaimed.

I pushed past him and ran up the staircase. We entered the portion with the holes in the walls that overlooked the city. I peeked through to watch Queen Mel and the Soothsayer fighting with the remaining Warriors. The Hallow citizens ran north through the alleyways. Just the day before, the people of Hallow danced to celebrate a marriage. Now, part of the city was covered in flames. Screams of terror echoed all around. No more joy. The gold on the buildings reflected the flames as an orange hue covered everything. It looked like the Toterrum orange ate away the green city speckled in gold.

I didn't know when, but the sun disappeared. Only darkness and orange flames remained.

Then, I saw him. Gamma. He commanded the Officers forward to destroy Hallow, the hidden city. My hatred for him brought my mind back to my body. The cloaked person I saw earlier walked next to him. The person kept leaning over to whisper something to him before turning away toward the waterfall entrance.

My rock pulsed for a moment, a spark of red coming from it. The cloaked figure turned and looked up, right at me. There was something...off about this person. My rock faded again, and the cloaked figure turned and disappeared into the waterfall cave's shadows.

Trigger nudged me as my attention drifted to where he pointed. The Soothsayer and Mel exchanged an embrace. Then, the Soothsayer looked up at our tunnel and nodded. Aurora took a deep breath next to me and waved her hands the exact same way as the Soothsayer. Out of nowhere, the glowing leaves from the Dead Forest floated around the Soothsayer and sparkled in blue hues. From far away, the Soothsayer's eyes began to glow blue.

"Great Light..." Herita whispered.

"What's going on?" I asked Aurora, who didn't respond. I looked over, and her meadow eyes glowed pure yellow. "What are your eyes doing?"

Aurora didn't even acknowledge me.

I looked back down at the Soothsayer. "Why isn't the Soothsayer going with the other Luckists? What are you doing?"

I stepped forward to grab Aurora, but Herita cut me off. "Let her do whatever she needs to," Herita said. I tried to step past her, but Herita wrapped her arms around me. I struggled in her embrace, but she hugged me tighter. "Shh." She rocked me back and forth. The sounds of Flaunte's beaches echoed all around. I knew it wasn't real, but the serenity still found me.

I glanced back out the hole to see the citizens start their way east instead of north. Queen Mel watched the group go and departed north, despite what her citizens did. The Officers followed the crowd. Everyone moved toward the Caved Lake. The Soothsayer walked behind them, but they didn't seem to notice her. The crowd turned toward the lake and walked straight into the water. They kept walking and walking until their heads submerged. Little red swirls brightened beneath the water. Further back, a larger blob with bright yellow swirls moved forward.

"What?" I whispered.

Aurora let out a breath, eyes fading back to normal, and fell over. Herita released me as I rushed over and caught her. Eagerly, she stood back up and looked out the holes. The Officers tried to follow them into the water while others noticed the Soothsayer next to them. The blue in her eyes flickered. Suddenly, the hooded figure I thought had left through the waterfall cave appeared right behind the Soothsayer. Iri shined brighter than ever and zipped around the hooded figure's head. Two bright red lights shot from the hooded figure's face and caused Iri's brilliance to completely fade away before she fell to the ground limp.

The Soothsayer's body went limp into the hooded figure's arms.

A high-pitched howl echoed across the cave, silencing all except the crackling flames. Then, many more howls came. One by one, little heads popped out of the water with little red eyes. The red swirls brightened as they surfaced. The larger yellow blob in the lake diminished into many smaller red swirls. Hundreds of Caved Selos surrounded the Officers in the lake. The beasts lunged forward and dragged the Officers under with screams riddled with gurgling water.

One by one, the Officers disappeared into the dark abyss. The other Officers on the edge of the lake ran away. They carried the Soothsayer back toward the city's heart. My gaze drifted to the far north end of the city, where Queen Mel stepped into the northern cave after the last of the group entered. She paused and looked over the burning city of Hallow one last time. She pulled a rock from above as a small rockslide buried the northern cave.

"What was that?" Trigger asked.

"Perception and Mentality together," Aurora said, her eyes glossing over. "Now, she's..." She burst into tears.

My brain ached as it searched for an explanation. My mouth gaped at what I witnessed. My heart sped up, and my skin went cold as I stepped back away from Aurora. My veins pounded at an uncontrollable beat that brought me back toward her. So many emotions ripped at my sanity. Aurora handed the Soothsayer over like it was nothing. No discussion. I wanted to yell at her. I wanted to scream. But what was the point?

"We need to keep moving," Herita said with a shaky, exhausted voice, breaking the silence.

We made our way through the remaining parts of the tunnel until we reached the hill where my uncle and I spent time together. The clear night sky shown above lent an odd serenity to a terrible situation. I glanced over at the spot where my uncle and I shared the celebratory drink. The spot no longer represented celebration. I missed him. Smoke billowed out of the various holes below, clouding the clear sky.

"Now what?" Trigger asked.

Various glances were exchanged, but no one had a plan. None of us knew what to do. None of us had much energy left.

"We can't sit here." Herita put her hands on her head and searched around. "We are too exposed."

"And we can't go by foot," I said. "They will see us." I looked at my frail, bloodied hands. "I can't fight right now. I can't even Manipulate."

"What do you mean?" Trigger stepped forward.

"Something happened when I fell over." I raised my hands up. "My red stone faded, and now nothing works."

Trigger cocked his head but looked around the Rolling Hills. "We really need to get going then. We can't defend ourselves with only three Manipulators."

Zen swooped down from above and landed next to Aurora. "Zen can take us east," she said. "We can figure out something from there."

"He can't carry us all," I said while pointing at Zen.

"He'll do two trips," Aurora said. "You and Herita can go first."

"But—" I started.

"You both had a lot just happen to you," Aurora cut me off and placed a hand on my arm. "You're in no shape to fight if a group finds us."

"She's right," Herita said.

"Fine," I said. Aurora grabbed me and hugged me. I pushed her away. "Why didn't you tell me about your plan?"

"There wasn't time to discuss." Aurora reached out and touched my arm again. "I'm sorry."

"Don't keep secrets from me." I wiggled my arm out of her grasp and stepped back.

"I know." Aurora's meadow eyes dropped, and her mouth kept moving. "There's one other thing." Why did it keep moving?

I hesitated. "What?"

"When I was falling off the cliff in Labyrintha, something happened with Zen," she began. "At first, I thought I was Manipulating Perception that allowed him to fly again, but the Soothsayer helped me find out it was something greater. Something I don't understand."

"Not Perception?" I asked. "What are you talking about?"

"It was...a light of some kind," she responded with a deep breath of relief. "Yaron, an odd power came over me." She stepped closer to me and gripped my shoulder. "I think I may have Manipulated something greater."

My jaw dropped as I just stared at her. "What do you mean something greater?"

"I don't know," Aurora responded.

I continued to gape at her. "I don't know what to say. So many things happened that I just don't understand." I pulled away from her. Was she trying to mock me? "I lost *my* Manipulating. What does this have to do with you?" I shook my head. "I don't know how Asher did it."

"He didn't," Aurora said. Her meadow eyes tried to pull me in. "I did."

The world slowed. I looked at the girl I thought I loved and stepped back. My heart gripped at my throat and pulled away my breath, but I still cracked out, "What?"

Tears trickled down Aurora's cheeks. "I Manipulated your Aura and made you fall over." She stepped toward me. "You were going to kill him."

I stepped back as fast as she came toward me. "How could you do that?" I remembered the yellow in her eyes. I searched her eyes for the yellow. Then, it hit me. "Were *you* the yellow light?"

Aurora held her hand to her chest. "I know he killed your uncle, but he's still my brother."

"How *dare* you." I stormed away from her. "You're the reason I can't Manipulate anymore."

My heart shattered. She betrayed me and chose Asher, of all people, someone she didn't even know.

"You need to understand—" she began.

"Leave me alone!" I marched over and mounted Zen, who wiggled his neck in irritation.

Herita touched Aurora's arm and walked over to Zen. She touched my arm and then mounted Zen behind me. The Luck Crown shimmered in her grasp.

"I'm sorry," Aurora said as she started to cry.

I wouldn't look at her. I *couldn't* look at her. So much rage pulsed through me, but it moved its attention to her. Asher was a Vigorist. He killed my uncle. She saved him and took away my abilities. Zen flapped his wings and grabbed Ricochet with his claws. He flew off, and I watched Aurora and Trigger shrink in the distance.

"We both lost someone important to us today," Herita said from behind me. "I would've probably tried to kill Asher as well, but Aurora was trying to keep you from doing something you would regret."

"She needs to stop making all these decisions by herself. It isn't fair." My eyes recharged and released another round of sorrowful tears. "Asher killed my uncle."

"And he killed my husband." Her words came off sharp. "Is death meant to be repaid with death?"

I didn't respond. My heart hurt too much. Herita was right. I knew Aurora and she wasn't trying to hurt me. She wanted to help me. I remembered her falling with the White Grande Lillies and my promise never to lose her again.

***

After about an hour of flying, the ocean appeared below. Zen flew down, and we dismounted. Ricochet ran around, happy to be released. Zen screeched at us and then took off to get Aurora and Trigger.

I blindly walked over to the ocean's edge. I needed to wash my face. Tears crusted my eyes and face. I scooped up seawater and rubbed my face with it. The salt stung my eyes. I tried to wipe the salt away with my sleeve. Herita cried behind me. She stared at my uncle's crown and then wrapped her arms around it. The full moon shone from above, leaving a whitish glow across the land, just light enough to see her.

"Resin..." she whispered in her sobs.

My eyes went blurry again, so I washed them with water. When I regained my sight, something caught my eye from the ocean's horizon. The moon tricked me with its bright reflection. I rubbed my eyes again to rid myself of my delusion, but there it was again. A small boat came straight toward me. A woman with white hair and a multicolored coat sat on the boat's edge. She sang a familiar song.

"Herita?" I asked. "Do you see this?"

Herita stepped up next to me, looking at exactly where I was. Ricochet started growling on my other side with his purple and green spots glowing.

"Keep back!" Herita exclaimed. She started twirling her arms to make a wave charge at the boat.

The woman in the boat stopped singing. "We mean no harm," she said from the boat as the boat went straight through the wave.

"Who are you?" I asked. A familiarity struck me about her appearance. Though it was an odd thing to think, she looked like Supreme Leader Sagiterra. Was she still alive? I cracked out, "Sagiterra?"

The boat hit the shore as the white-haired woman stepped out of the boat. Smooth skin and a stark youthfulness covered her face. A man I hadn't noticed looked over at us from the boat.

"I'm unsure who Sagiterra is, but my name is Xenia," the much younger woman than I thought I saw said. "The Soothsayer wrote me, and I'm here to help."

"She did what?" I asked. "Where...where are you from?"

"Motifer," Xenia responded with a warm smile. She slowly swirled her fingers, and an odd sensation pulsed across my body. Winged beasts fluttered in my chest and lightened the weight that pulled me down. I looked over at Herita, and we both had big smiles on our faces. All the death and agony we witnessed seemed lighter.

"What?" I asked.

Xenia simply answered, "Empathy has decided to answer your call."

Epilogue

"**N**aomi..."

"I am here," I responded to the black void.

What wonder such a desolate place could hold when nothing sat before me, behind me, or anywhere near me. One may call it serenity.

"Naomi..."

In wonderful pirouettes, I spun my body around. At first, I searched for the speaker. Then, the myriad of sparks and swirling lights devoured my attention. I reached out to bask in their glory for only a moment before they faded away.

"I know you," I whispered to the wonder.

"Naomi..."

The wonder before me gathered into curious clouds and transformed...no, transfigured into a blob. No, a shape. I always enjoyed unusual objects.

Wait, why did I?

A wave of recollections of a person enveloped my mind. A person who adored knowing everything. Her simple brown hair, petite stature, and questioning umber eyes reminded me of a mirror. No, a reflection.

"I know you..." I touched my head. "Knowing only works when you listen."

In an intense collision of terribly wonderous thoughts, I remembered everything. Labyrintha and its glorious Blackstone Mountains protecting it from the world around. The Foglands and a dreadful loss met with a surprising return. A thunderous waterfall opening to a golden city engulfed in furious flames. The death of a King. The sacrifice of a Mentalist. The lost boy from a walled city that completely changed my life.

And lastly, red eyes.

"Yaron..." A singular tear chilled my cheek as it toppled down, down into the black abyss surrounding me.

"Naomi," the glowing shape demanded. An old woman with glowing wrinkles and shining hair turned her head to the side and smiled. "My granddaughter."

"Grandmother," I cracked out, my heart bleeding out and down like the tears falling from my tired face.

"You must wake, child." She touched my arm and left a wet chill lingering on my skin. "You have much to accomplish."

"I did everything I could," I said. "I made the proper decision and saved all I could."

"And for that." My radiant grandmother paused. "I am so, so proud of you."

My heart lurched at the sudden influx of loving affirmation she gave me. I did make the correct decision. All the validation I longed for finally found me.

"But there is more to do," she said. "Remember what I taught you, sweet child. Let wisdom guide a foolish heart."

"And guide a wise heart to a joyful fool," I finished with a satisfied hum.

I had not heard those words in many years. My chest buzzed with a fluttering fever. The warmth invigorated my bones.

My grandmother touched her cheek and extended another smile. "You will do wonderous things, Naomi, my sweet child." In twinkling blinks, her body began to fade. "My Soothsayer..." Starting from the outer edges, the Aura flickered away until one last glimpse of her face remained. "I love you..." And as quickly as she came, she was gone.

"I love you..." I clenched my chest. Not a bit of sorrow sat there, but the continued buzzing of her lasting love.

After one last, peaceful breath, I gasped for air and opened my eyes to a foreign space. Great stones lined the walls with a barred window across from me. I sat up and surveyed my surroundings. A desk filled with blank paper and pencils, a small, simple bed with dull orange coverings, and a table with two chairs filled the cold space.

I rose from the bed and found myself untied. The cloaked figure with the red eyes cleared my mind and captured me. The rounded door to my left drew me in. I grabbed the handle and pulled so hard, but the door did not budge.

"Hello!" I knocked hard on its metal frame. "Is anyone there?"

No response.

The window beckoned me next. I gripped the freezing metal bars and searched across a gray, clouded sky. Below my prison, endless cobblestone streets lined with townhouses covered my entire view. All until my eyes found a terrible, powerful structure—the wall.

"Toterrum," I whispered to myself.

A buzzing noise drew my attention from behind. I turned and found a little, glowing beast. How did I miss it?

"Iri?" I cover my mouth. My partner beast tried to fly but fell back to the pillow. "Oh, my brave friend." I ran over and sat next to my beast, stroking her furry head.

Iri fought the cloaked figured, trying to save me. Though it was a foolish endeavor, I admired my partner beast's valor. She must have fallen into my pocket or embedded herself into my clothing.

Echoing footsteps came from the other side of the door. Closer and closer, whatever approached would enter soon. A panicked beat found my tired heart and made my skin crawl like it was covered in crawling bugs.

"You must hide," I whispered to Iri and covered her with my blanket. "Do not move, my friend."

A click came at the door. An eerie creak echoed around the room. My chance came to escape, and I had to take it. Just as the figure stepped forward, I grabbed their rigid Aura and forced it to the person's head. The briefest images appeared. A tree covered in blue leaves flashed across my mind. One leaf brighter than the rest glowed like a blue sun. A gust of wind came and the leaves fluttered away. Something caught my eye from above. A bright red light appeared and materialized into a misshaped mass. A star but cracked.

Like a plant being ripped from the ground, my mind jolted back into existence. The being's eyes pulsed in a surge of crimson power. Their Aura became fixed and unmovable. I tried again, yet nothing.

"That...will do nothing, oh, wise Soothsayer," the being said. A mixture of high-pitch notes and a baritone buzz masked the voice. Their stature stood firm, not too burly and not very busty.

"Who are you?" I demanded. "Why did you take me?" A curious thought hit me. "Why am I not dead?"

The hooded being sauntered over to the chair, pushed it out in a sharp creak, and sat. They crossed their right leg over their left in wave of moving cloak. In the dark shadows of their hood, two dim red dots fixated on me. My spine nearly folded in on itself in a sudden frigid shake.

"Hm," the being said while folding their hands over one another. "I could never kill you, Soothsayer. It goes against my inner self."

Each word made my skin pop into little, cold mountains lining a barren wasteland.

"Who are you?" I forced out.

"I am the one who seeks a missing piece," the being leaned forward. "I am the one who seeks the stone." They leaned even closer. "I am the one who will break your mind."

Their eyes erupted into an overwhelming bright scarlet. Both of their hands raised, my Aura was forced toward me and clashed against me like a punch to the face. I gritted my teeth and pushed back, but their power overwhelmed me.

So, I did the next best thing—my eyes found the desk and I focused on the wooden legs. I cleared my mind and only thought about the desk. Nothing else.

"I will not fold," I said.

I believed my words with my entire existence.

And so began the worst era of my life.

***

Shades of Aura will continue in *The Hopes of Toterrum*, the final installment of the Toterrum Trilogy.

THE AURAS

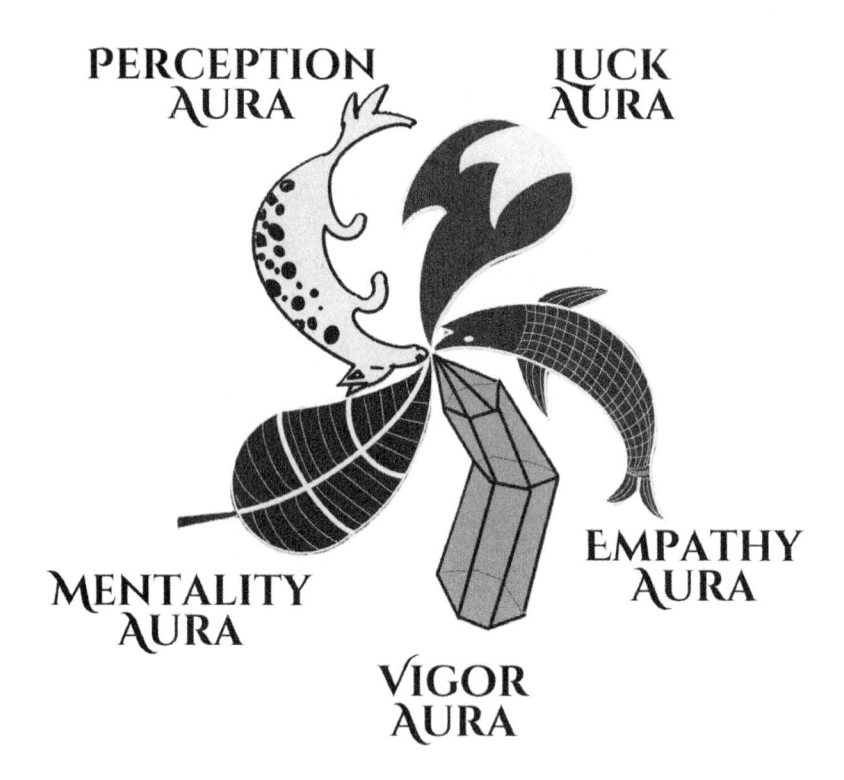

PERCEPTION AURA

LUCK AURA

MENTALITY AURA

EMPATHY AURA

VIGOR AURA

PERCEPTION AURA
Aura of the Illusions
Manipulate the Senses

CAPITAL - FLAUNTE
SIGIL - BEASTS
COLOR - YELLOW
SAYING - "WE SEE WHAT WE SEE."

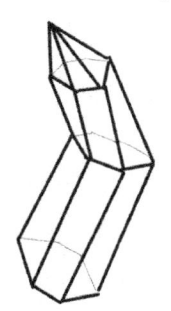

VIGOR AURA
Aura of Power
Manipulate Strength

CAPITAL - TOTERRUM
SIGIL - CRYSTAL
COLOR - ORANGE

MENTALITY AURA
Aura of Knowledge
Manipulate Thoughts, Ideas, and Memories

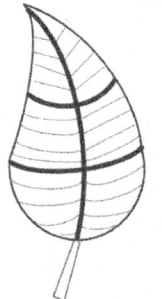

CAPITAL - LABYRINTHA
SIGIL - LEAF
COLOR - BLUE
SAYING - "KNOWING ONLY WORKS IF YOU LISTEN."

LUCK AURA
Aura of Opportunity
Manipulate Outcomes and Probability

Capital - Hallow (Lost)
Sigil - Flame
Color - Green
Saying - "Find and Capture Opportunity."

EMPATHY AURA
Aura of Emotions
Manipulate Emotions

Capital - Motifer (Lost)
Sigil - Fish
Color - Purple

City Hierarchies

Flaunte Council

Lady Sandra
(Country Leader)

Etty Shoreline

Allen Sand

Brian Nemone

Vacant (formerly Ruth Char)

LABYRINTHA CEREBERUMS

THE SOOTHSAYER
(WISDOM)

CEREBRUM PETRA
(DIPLOMACY)

CEREBRUM BRYSEN
(STRATEGY)

CEREBRUM GRACE
(PATIENCE)

CEREBRUM ALEX
(VALIDATION)

CEREBRUM FABEL
(ARTS)

CEREBRUM NICOLAI
(HISTORY)

CEREBRUM CALLUM
(INNOVATION)

CEREBRUM LEONIDAS
(BIOLOGY)

CEREBRUM TELUM
(DIALECT)

Hallow Court

King Resin
(Country Leader)

Mel
(Daughter)

Trigger
(Squire)

Toterrum

Grand Baron Gamma
(Country Leader)

BEASTS OF BIOME

RIDDLEDOG

Habitat: Forests near lagoons on the Island of Flaunte
Abilities: Glowing bright spots, expel blinding light, minor Perception Aura manipulations

Height: 2'3" Weight: 50 lbs

WALDEBEAR

Habitat: Forests across Biome
Abilities: Extreme power, able to track items/people from far distances

Height: 8'1" Weight: 600 lbs

RITHBARIAN RIVEROK

Habitat: Open seas surrounding Biome
Abilities: Sense danger before it comes, water manipulation

Height: 10'3" Weight: 350 lbs

SILVERBACK RIVEROK

Habitat: Rivers and lakes across Biome
Abilities: Invisibility in water and speed

Height: 6'2" Weight: 250 lbs

DARKENED ELDERKAW

Habitat: Tall trees in open fields across central Biome
Abilities: Power and manipulates wind

Height: 7'3" Weight: 150 lbs

CORAL ELDERKAW

Habitat: Rock cliffs on little islands off Biome
Abilities: Extreme speed and maneuverability

Height: 6'8" Weight: 140 lbs

CRYSTAL ELDERKAW

Habitat: Lagoons of Flaunte (very rare)
Abilities: Produces drowsy dust and photographic memory

Height: 2'8" Weight: 40 lbs

TUNDRA ELDERKAW

Habitat: Dry, snowy fields in northern Biome
Abilities: Extreme durability and crushing claws

Height: 6'4" Weight: 135 lbs

GOLDEN ELDERKAW

Habitat: Grassy fields in southern Biome
Abilities: Ear piercing screeches

Height: 1'7" Weight: 15 lbs

LUVALA

Habitat: Bushes near the Blackstone Mountains
Abilities: Produces own light, soothes emotions, clears minds

Height: 7" Weight: 1 lb

REFLA

Habitat: Open fields in central Biome
Abilities: Temporary mind control, glowing mane

Height: 8'7" Weight: 285 lbs

CAVED SELO

Habitat: Lakes within the Rolling Hills' caves
Abilities: During day: fast and kind, during night: cruel and powerful

Height: 3'7" Weight: 195 lbs

FIELD SELO

Habitat: Fields in the Rolling Hills
Abilities: Able to move blades of grass into gusts of wind and minor camouflage

Height: 3'6" Weight: 180 lbs

CRAGGLE

Habitat: Forests on Flaunte Island
Abilities: Iridescent fur, super speed, long distance eyesight

Height: 11'5" Weight: 385 lbs

KANTERFLUFF

Habitat: Mountain terrain near Blackstone Mountains
Abilities: Able to climb vertical structures, rock crushing claws, able to jump extreme heights

Height: 8'8" Weight: 168 lbs

SNOBBLER

Habitat: Snowy peaks of mountains
Abilities: Able to survive without oxygen for long periods, extreme digestive system

Height: 6" Weight: 2 lbs

TUNDRILLA

Habitat: Forests in northern Biome
Abilities: Able to climb any surface, extreme strength, camouflage fur

Height: 11'4" Weight: 425 lbs

GRUFFLING

Habitat: Rocky cliffs on Blackstone Mountains
Abilities: Able to jump long distances, extremely durable fur

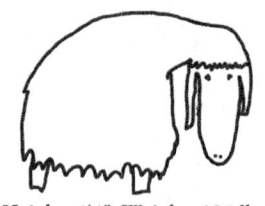

Height: 4'4" Weight: 105 lbs

PHANTARI

Habitat: The Foglands
Abilities: Able to gather and move light, control and change temperature

Height: 3" Weight: 1 lb

BONDU

Habitat: Fields within the Rolling Hills
Abilities: Manipulate ground into hills, enhance plant growth

Height: 6'7" Weight: 15 lbs

BLUFFALO

Habitat: Northern Rolling Hills
Abilities: Able to move the ground, while running, produces electricity in horns

Height: 7'5" Weight: 750 lbs

FUZLOR

Habitat: The Rolling Hills
Abilities: Able to soothe via singing, elastic limbs, moveable body parts

Height: 18'7" Weight: 650 lbs

MOUNTIFF

Habitat: Across central Biome
Abilities: Able to slow down time for brief moments, can go long distances without nourishment

Height: 6'6" Weight: 295 lbs

CORALA

Habitat: The Coral Forest
Abilities: Temporary invisibility, mimic other sounds perfectly, extreme speed

Height: 5" Weight: 1 lb

GREAT PHERREL

Habitat: Great Plain
Abilities: Can move stripes across its body, create static shocks by rubbing stripes together

Height: 4'7" Weight: 175 lbs

COBRA EEL

Habitat: Reefs of Biome
Abilities: Able to survive on land and water, can fly and swim, can manipulate body length and size

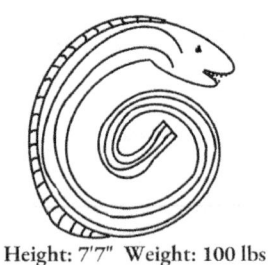

Height: 7'7" Weight: 100 lbs

FESELING

Habitat: Fields in the Great Plain
Abilities: Expels a mucus able to melt most items and defecates an antidote to burns

Height: 7" Weight: 1 lb

FUNNELFACE GUPPLE

Habitat: Reefs across Biome
Abilities: Can swallow light, shoot out spikes, camouflage

Height: 4'2" Weight: 85 lbs

PRISMFISH

Habitat: Reefs across Biome
Abilities: Teleport short distances, can create underwater cyclones

Height: 1'1" Weight: 25 lbs

Printed in Great Britain
by Amazon